I0527734

Pawns:

Stalemate

PAWNS:

STALEMATE

BY
DON KESTERSON

Pawns: Stalemate. Copyright Don Kesterson, 2020. All rights reserved. No portion of this book may be reproduced in any form whatsoever, except for brief quotations in reviews, without the prior written permission of the author.

ISBN-13: 978-0-9984707-5-7 (Amber Publishers Company)

Library of Congress Control Number: 2020915270

http://www.donkesterson.com

Cover design and typesetting - Eric Fritzius

While historical timelines, persons, and events are depicted, the main characters of this work are fictitious. They interact with historical figures as a way to show a view of the depicted historical events.

Other Books by Don Kesterson

The President's Gold

Gold of the Spirits

Pawns: Magic Bullet

Pawns: Kings in Check

Ring of Freedom

PRELUDE ONE

MARCH 30, 1965
US EMBASSY SAIGON

Major Steven Hebert trudged the hallways of the US Embassy. Despite the air conditioner running full blast, it was muggy in the building, and his mind was not in Vietnam. It had been almost three months since he'd dropped off his mother and his brother Jeremiah at his uncle's home deep in the Louisiana bayou. Being 8000 miles away, his mother's monthly letters were important to his psyche. Yes, he was a big tough guy, but those letters always brightened his day, just as much now as when he first enlisted over a decade ago.

Steven rounded the corner. Peer de Silva headed into his office, right on time for their ten a.m. appointment. De Silva waited for him, and as soon as Steven cleared the doorway, de Silva motioned for him to shut the door. De Silva walked to his credenza and sorted through a stack of papers, then spun around. Steven remained standing in front of his desk. "Sit down, Major," de Silva said.

A knock sounded on the door. "Come in," de Silva ordered.

CIA Analyst George Allen stepped through the door. "Morning." He took a seat next to Steven.

De Silva went back to sorting through his papers. "Can I call down and get Barbara to bring up some coffee?"

Both Steven and Allen shook their heads.

De Silva straightened his suit coat, eased into his desk chair, and looked directly at Steven. "We are aware of your ties to Lansdale and developments around Indochina." He returned to sifting through his stack. Finally, he pulled out a single page and placed it on his desk. "Major Hebert, you were with me last year. You saw my program. I think it will work." He raised his eyes and looked at Steven. "Don't you?"

"Yes, sir." Steven nodded.

"It needs expanded, which is exactly what I have proposed." De Silva leaned back in his chair. "I want to add another five thousand South Vietnamese. Take them up to my property, have CIA officers and military advisors train them for three months, then turn them loose. My plan is actually a little bigger than what Lansdale proposed."

Steven stroked his mouth with his left hand. "I really think you're onto something." He wanted to say more. *Had de Silva identified why the northern teams had failed early on? Had their issues been solved?* However, he was reluctant to ask.

Allen rubbed his jaw. "I just returned from an intelligence gathering mission around South Vietnam, and I can tell you this conflict is going much worse than the MACV believe—or maybe *wish* to believe."

De Silva pounded his fist on the desk. "You can't believe the pushback I'm getting from the military—and the White House. Last winter, I asked Lucien Conein to get me an assessment of the VC camps surrounding Saigon. They're in a much stronger position than I anticipated, and they're growing."

Allen shook his head. "There seems to be a concerted effort around here to give the White House only good reports. Why?" He waved his hand. "This is dangerous. Plus, you know the military asked me to do an analysis several years ago, which they were to keep updated. They have never updated it. I would like to see the South Vietnamese government begin a political campaign against Communism, plus show how it will impact their people if the communists take over. They have got to start winning the hearts and minds of the Vietnamese people. They must have a cause to fight for. As of now, the people are uncommitted."

De Silva placed both hands on the table and stood up. "My boss in D.C. said they believe my plan would turn this from 'McNamara's War' into 'McCone's War.' This is just an example of the political optics of the situation here. For goodness sakes, they're worrying about all the wrong things."

Allen looked at Steven, then back to de Silva. "Right after Johnson and Westmoreland put Marines in the theater, I've documented an increase in VC activity—not to mention the attack on our base at Pleiku."

Steven rubbed his forehead. Everything he and Nguyen Tao had discussed was playing out. Established military bases would create a fixed target for the VC to attack. "US troops have been trained to fight the Soviets in a conventional war." He gestured with his hand. "Only a few companies have been trained for guerilla warfare."

De Silva put his finger down on the piece of paper he'd pulled out of his credenza. "George, the attack on Pleiku resulted in nine soldier deaths, 128 wounded, and 122 aircraft destroyed. In my program, now operational for around a half year, they have only lost six men while killing 167 VC. Why?" Before either Allen or Steven could respond, de Silva continued, "They are a moving target. We don't stay in villages for more than a couple of days."

Allen drummed his fingers on the arm of the chair. "I don't think the bombing campaign will work in the long run. The North Vietnamese and their pawns, the VC, are willing to stay engaged and wait us out."

Steven wondered if Allen had a solution for stopping the movement of men and supplies on the Ho Chi Minh trail.

De Silva leaned over and stared out the window, then stood up and looked down at the street below. "What's going on down there?" He refocused on Steven and Allen. "It's my opinion the VC now have two tactics." He held up two fingers, then grabbed his first finger with his other hand. "One, ambush our military; and," he said and grabbed the second finger, "continue to terrorize the rural people and their civil leaders." He paced away from the window. "The night belongs to the VC, through torture and murder. They scare people into feeding and hiding them."

Steven nodded. It sounded like de Silva was tuned into the real situation, like Lansdale, who also wanted to change reveille to night time for the military. *These two men really see this fight against the Viet Cong the correct way. Not worried about growing poppies.*

"We have better weapons, but they have better spies," Allen said. "Not all of them are willing, but the VC intimidate South Vietnamese into giving them information. We don't have—and likely will never have—spies like theirs."

De Silva walked back to the window. He tilted his head one way, then the other, as though focusing on something. "My program is supposed to protect the villagers from the VC coming in the night. It's far more advanced than the failed Strategic Hamlet Program."

Allen patted the arm of the leather chair. "What do you think we can do about the terrorization in Saigon?"

The phone on de Silva's desk rang.

After de Silva picked up the phone and listened for a couple of seconds, he held his hand up to his lips and covered his other ear with his hand. He mouthed, "agent, bad connection."

George Allen leaned over and whispered something to Major Steven Hebert, then got up and waved goodbye to de Silva. Steven followed him out of the room.

De Silva listened intently to the agent's report while looking out his second floor window at the street below. A Vietnamese man pushed an old gray Peugeot up the street. As he continued to listen, his secretary stepped in the office and waved.

De Silva cupped his hand over the receiver. "Barbara, can you get me a new notepad?"

Barbara Robbins scurried over to the cabinet, grabbed a white legal pad, then slipped back over to de Silva. He nodded as he took it and begin writing notes. De Silva drew a deep breath, then leaned back over to again look out his office window. Within a few seconds, a South Vietnamese policeman pulled up behind the man pushing the car. The Vietnamese man ignored the policeman as he continued pushing the car. Finally, he stopped directly under de Silva's window. The police gestured while poking the old man in the chest with his finger and pointing at the car. The old man looked at the car, then took off running as fast as his old legs would carry him in the opposite directions. The policeman pulled his gun and pointed it in direction of the old man. Another car pulled up alongside the policeman. Gunshots rang out toward the officer, who returned fire.

De Silva glanced around the old Peugeot. A detonator was burning. "Barbara, get down!" he yelled and attempted to dive under his desk.

An enormous explosion sent glass and shards of metal flying all around.

The meeting had recharged Steven, who ran down the steps two at a time. He was in a hurry to resume his duties. He hadn't been in a very good mood for several days after learning about the marches at Selma, Alabama. One thing he could glean from the absence of letters or other information—his mother and brother were safely out of the reach of either Carlos Marcello or the French Corsican Brotherhood's thugs.

Just as he reached the ground floor, a tremendous explosion bounced Steven off the wall to the ground. He lay there, stunned for a moment. He gathered himself, sprung back to his feet, and ran out the front door. Steven glanced around. People lay on the street, bloodied. A car bomb had exploded next to the Embassy Building, directly under de Silva's office. Smoke was still smoldering from the car. Steven sprinted back up the stairs toward de Silva's office.

When he got to the second floor, George Allen sat on the floor, leaning against the wall, examining his multiple cuts.

Steven ran over and leaned down. "Are you okay?"

Allen looked up at Steven and nodded, his glassy eyes blinking. He wrapped his arms around himself, then put his head back down and pointed toward de Silva's office.

Seeing how bad Allen was injured, Steven pulled his head back up slowly. "Are you sure?"

Allen's head dropped back down again and pointed repeatedly toward de Silva's office.

Steven ran through de Silva secretary's office door. Glass crunched under his shoes as he hurried to the secretary, who lay lifeless on the floor. Steven grabbed her wrist. No pulse. He proceeded through the door to de Silva's office, glass continuing to crunch as he walked. De Silva lay in a pool of his own blood. There was so much blood on his head, Steven couldn't determine where it all was coming from. De Silva was still alive, but he was bleeding from his eyes, ears, and throat. "Mr. de Silva, it's Steven. I'm going to help you." He looked around for something to press to his neck to stop the bleeding. Glass and metal shards were embedded in his face. Steven rifled through the doors on his desk, finally finding a handkerchief. He leaned back over and pushed it into de Silva's hand, then brought it up to his neck. "Hold this on your neck. I'm going to try to get you up. Is that okay?"

De Silva didn't respond.

"I'm going to get you some help."

"Who else?" De Silva whispered.

Steven got up and picked up de Silva's phone. *No dial tone.* He ran toward the door. "Continue to hold that on your neck."

Steven picked up the secretary's phone. It was dead, too. He sprinted out her office door. As he ran past George Allen, Allen asked, "De Silva?"

Steven continued running. "He's bad, but I think he'll make it."

"Secretary?"

"I don't think she made it," Steven shouted back as he reached the stairway.

Steven skipped steps to the ground floor, then ran into the closest office. Paper was strewn about the floor, tiles were hanging from the ceiling, glass was everywhere, some of the lights hung, still swinging. He picked up the closest phone. *Dial tone.* He dialed the South Vietnamese police to report the bombing plus request ambulances, then he sprinted down the hallway toward the diplomatic wing of the Embassy, running past injured and dazed personnel gathering in the hallway.

The wailing sound of sirens filled the air. Toward the end of the hallway, he was met by fellow Marine guards running in his direction. "*Report, report!*" Steven commanded.

The on-duty sergeant replied, "All secure, Major. We have major damage everywhere, lots of people hurt in this wing. Deputy Ambassador Johnson is among the wounded. He's in his office."

Steven raced off in that direction.

PRELUDE TWO

APRIL 16, 1965

REGISTER–GUARD, WASHINGTON BUREAU - WASHINGTON DC

Rita Sullivan sat at the teleprinter, sending her notes from yesterday's interview with the leader of the Students for a Democratic Society—more commonly known as the SDS—in Washington for the big march occurring later today. The spokesman she interviewed over the phone identified himself only as Clark. He was a little more radical than expected.

A knock sounded on the locked front door.

Rita had started locking it out of concern for her own safety. At any minute, she feared Cadillac man storm through the front door and assault her. She spun around in her chair to face the door.

A woman waved at her through the glass window.

Rita pushed her pencil behind her ear as she walked over. "Can I help you?"

The woman pushed a card and a badge of some kind against the glass.

Rita looked at the FBI badge closely. It identified the woman as Agent Stephanie Keeton. "What do you want?"

Agent Keeton put the badge back in her purse. "I have important information for you. It may have to do with your safety."

Rita raised her eyebrows and turned the lock. She pointed to the chair on the other side of her desk, then returned to her seat. She folded her hands on top of the desk. "Well, I'm betting the FBI is not here to help me, but to find out what I know about the big SDS protest today."

Agent Keeton laid the card on the desk as she sat down. "No, I'm a desk jockey at the FBI. I actually shouldn't be here. I do research for agents out in the field. That's all I do. But again, that's not why I'm here."

"Okay. I'm all ears. How do you even know who I am?"

Agent Keeton bit her lower lip. "First off, you must agree this meeting is strictly off the record. Nothing I'm about to tell you is to be written down. Agreed?"

Rita's stomach turned. "Okay. No notes."

Keeton leaned toward her. "As I said, I do research for agents in the field. Last year, several of us in the local office took an interest in the murder of Mary Meyer. During my research, I discovered your name in the police investigation notes of the Meyer case."

"Why was the FBI watching Mary Meyer?"

Keeton brushed her blond hair back with her hand. "There are some things I *just can't* tell you." She paused for a minute. "So I read your statement. And something caused my jaw to drop. That's why I am here. Your statement claimed you were in a hit and run on your way to the Meyer residence."

Rita swiveled in her chair. *Do I talk about this?* Her fear heightened. "Yeah, so?" *I got to be cool here.*

Keeton leaned forward. "I believe you didn't tell the detective the whole story. For whatever reason, they never followed up with you—at least not officially."

"No, I was never interviewed again."

Keeton stared at Rita for a minute. "I'll tell you more, but you have to open up to me, if I'm going to help you."

Rita drew a deep breath and nodded slightly.

"One of our top agents was tailing Mary Meyer. In the fall of 1963, I was asked to do some undercover work for a lead agent. It was just me and another female agent. It sounded like easy work. Go to a bar and make notes. We were to try to arrange a meeting with a, uh, congressman with some power. That was all."

Rita ran her hand over her tightly bunned hair and leaned forward. "What bar? No, let me guess. The Quorum Club?"

Keeton nodded. "Of course. Anyway, somehow we got made. Still to this day, I don't know how. But I won't bore you with the details. We decided it was best to leave before our meeting. We just walked out. But we were chased throughout the night by a black Cadillac. It took me half the night to lose him, and I'm a professionally trained driver."

A chill ran down Rita's spine.

Keeton raised her eyebrows and nodded. "That's what I thought. That got your attention. Your hit and run was with the black Cadillac."

Rita slowly nodded.

"In the morning, our lead agent came and got us. When he saw the black Cadillac, he bound out of his car to confront the driver, who took off."

"Did you get a look at the driver?"

"Of course. We learned he's a henchman for Bobby Baker. We never identified him because we never heard from him again. The lead agent wanted to protect us from Director Hoover, so it was swept under the rug." Keeton paused. "Until we started studying the murder."

"So you think he was Mary's killer?"

Keeton frowned. "Her murder appears to be a professional hit." She leaned closer to Rita. "Isn't that what you think?"

Rita sipped her coffee and pointed toward the coffee pot.

Keeton shook her head. "What do you think?"

"It seemed like a professional hit to me. The local detectives wanted to buy a quick story and bury this. The man they have in custody, Raymond Crump, Jr., doesn't fit the profile of a murderer, let alone a professional killer."

Keeton looked out the front door. "As for the man in the black Cadillac, I don't know whether he's a killer or just someone hired to intimidate. From what I know about Baker, it doesn't seem like he's involved in murdering people. But Baker is connected to the mob." She lowered her head. "There's one other fact I want to tell you from our lead agent's investigation. One day he observed CIA Agent James Jesus Angleton going into Mary Meyer's home right after she'd left. We knew he was a family friend, but we believe the CIA was investigating or watching Meyer, too."

"You think the CIA killed Meyer? Or had her killed? But why?" Rita decided not to mention the journal Meyer wanted to give her. *Let's see if the FBI knew about it?*

Keeton shook her head as she got up from the chair. "I don't know." She frowned. "You have my card. I can't say any more. I just wanted to come and tell you what happened to me. I always thought it was one of Baker's men following me. I assumed it was similar to what you went through. You can call me if you learn anything. I'll help you if I can, but I can't give you information from our investigation." Agent Keeton headed to the door. "Remember, I wasn't here."

Rita stood. "Thank you very much. I do appreciate it."

Rita had learned a lot, but Keeton still hadn't answered all her questions. *Why was Mary Meyer murdered? What was so important in her journal that was never found—as far as I know? Did the CIA kill her for her journal? Why?*

Rita pulled out her notes from her investigation. She had no record of CIA Agent James Jesus Angleton. His name didn't appear in the official police investigation, either. Also, no note of him being a friend of the family. *This was a new lead.* Rita dug further into her personal file on the murder. *There it was.* The old asshole, her former boss, Petit said his brother-in-law was Ben Bradlee and he was former CIA. *Whoever killed Meyer had the driver of the black Cadillac keeping me from meeting Meyer. But either Baker or the CIA would have the connections to contract a professional hit on Meyer. Do the threatening phone calls about articles on*

Johnson fit with the CIA? Not likely. Still nothing tied together. But Stephanie Keeton did give her a tip—Bobby Baker was tied to the mob. How did she draw that opinion? Keeton must know more. As for me, should I risk contacting Mary Meyer's sister?

Rita went back to the teleprinter. She had to put the identity of the man driving the black Cadillac on the back burner for now. He hadn't harassed her since Johnson was elected President. *Do I need to start digging into this again with this new information?* She continued working on her article for tomorrow's paper. *Keeton had known about this for some time, and the day after I do an interview with the SDS she decides to come by and tell me about it? Is that a coincidence?*

CHAPTER ONE

SEPTEMBER 15, 1965

TAN SON NHUT AIR BASE - SAIGON

The CIA charter jet slowly dropped out of the midnight sky toward the runway at Tan Son Nhut Air Base. General Edward Lansdale turned around and gave a thumbs up to the members of his team. His captains, Colonel Charles T. R. (Bo) Bohannan and Nguyen Tao, nodded in return. Lansdale turned back around and stared at the landing lights as the jet touched down on the runway. It had been almost ten years since he had last been in Vietnam.

As the group deplaned, Lansdale announced, "We meet at my villa at 0600. We start to work first thing in the morning."

Lansdale sat in his villa, sipping a whiskey on the rocks, hoping to get sleepy. The meeting was four hours away, but he was excited. He pulled out his legal pad and jotted some notes. *I want to operate just like we did with Nenita Force in the Philippines and earlier here.* He took a sip of brown

1

liquid, then picked up his pen and wrote: *Train enough men until we have four officers with as many as fifty soldiers.*

He nodded. Bohannan should be able to train these men in less than ninety days. We should be able to get them in the field as soon as they're ready. Then he wrote: *Will not have the backup army forces like we had in the Philippines!*

Lansdale left the pad laying on the desk and walked around his small living room trying to stretch. He wondered what to do with Tao. *Do I keep him in Saigon or do I send him to work with Vang Pao? No, let's see how this plays out. I can send him where I need him. Now for Hebert, what do I do with him? Leave him at the Embassy? He's going to hate that, but I don't need him in the training mission. I need him when bullets are flying.*

Exhaustion crept over him. Lansdale walked into his small bedroom and lay down in his clothes.

Lieutenant Colonel Lucien Conein stared at his phone. *He needed to call his old boss, General Atonine Guerini.* If someone else made the call before he did, it could hurt the trust he'd spent two decades gaining. The call would undoubtedly start a firestorm he'd need to handle shortly after the word *hello* was spoken. Finally, Guerini should be in his office. Conein picked up the receiver and asked for an international operator.

"Person to Person call for Atonine Guerini, from Lucien Conein. Will you accept the call?"

"*Oui.*"

Conein played with the telephone cord. "*Bonjour,* General Guerini. *Êtes-vous bien?*"

"Lucien, something must be up for you to call me."

"*Oui.* Lansdale arrived in Saigon last night, late."

There was a long pause. Had the connection been lost? Finally, Guerini said, "Can you find someone to whack him *this* time? Or, do I have to send Sarti from South America to handle the situation *this* time?"

Conein rubbed his left temple with his hand. "Let me handle this, General."

"Let me remind you about 1953, when Lansdale went to the Plaines de Jarres. We just now got our airplanes back up to full operations. Are you still one of us? He needs to disappear. Do you hear me?"

Conein gritted his teeth. "Let me handle the Lansdale situation. You have my word. My word is still my code."

"*Like last time?* You were in charge. I trusted you." There was another long pause. "Did you meet with Ky?"

"Everything is good with Premier Ky. He's on board." Conein cleared his throat for emphasis. "His monthly fee has been agreed to."

"I expect a full report from you soon. And handle the Lansdale situation," Guerini said. "Don't take too long, or I will handle it myself."

"Yes, General."

The pounding on the door awakened Lansdale. He looked at the clock on the bed stand. 0500. *Three hours sleep, maybe.* He opened the door to Bohannan. Lansdale grumbled as he walked into the kitchen to make a pot of coffee. Just because someone couldn't sleep was no reason to show up this early.

Bohannan sat down at the kitchen table. "I want to set up twenty-four-men teams responsible for advanced scouting, special missions in and out, and quick strikes." He paused for a moment. "I believe I can train team leaders with some military background within sixty days. Therefore, these teams could be operational within ninety days—sixty days, best case. Finally, once in the field, they would work hand-in-glove with civilian irregulars, maybe some of the ARVN special forces."

Lansdale got up from the kitchen table and pulled down three coffee cups. He filled one for himself and one for Bo. *I wish Napoleon Valeriano would have joined us.* "I thought we needed larger forces. Maybe fifty men with four officers? I had a conversation with de Silva before I left Langley, and he detailed his South Vietnamese operation. It's closer to what you have proposed than my plan." Lansdale took a large drink from his coffee cup.

Another knock sounded at the front door.

Lansdale answered the door, then walked back into the kitchen, followed by Nguyen Tao. Once they were seated in the kitchen, full cups in hand, they listened intently as Lansdale walked them through his plan for the Pacification Program. "We wanted to try to implement this program using a similar set up when we were here in the fifties. Unfortunately, we won't be able to do the raids into North Vietnam, at least not in the beginning." Lansdale cracked half a smile.

The men looked at one another. Tao started to speak, but Lansdale held up his hand. "When we restart our operations, one of the things we must follow and understand is Mao's definition of guerilla warfare: the enemy advances, we retreat; the enemy camps, we harass; the enemy tires, we attack; the enemy retreats, we pursue. This is how we will operate, and this is definitely how the VC operate."

"Is this supported at Langley? D.C.?" Tao asked.

Lansdale drew a deep breath and rubbed his chin with his left hand. "Yes, at least with the powers that be. Helms is on board with us, de Silva's teams will continue their operations while he remains in D.C. healing up. That man is lucky to be alive." He got up from the table and poured more coffee, then folded his arms over his chest. "Anyway, continuing with the D.C. side, John McNaughton is completely on board, and Roger Hilsman has finally come around. I think he gets it. You know he was a guerilla leader in the CBI theater?" Lansdale raised his coffee cup to his lips. "Also, I've been told George Ball wrote a memo to Johnson about the US underestimating the resolve of the NVA and VC, thinking our superior fire power isn't effective in guerilla warfare. I won't even go into his comments about the instability of the South Vietnamese government. Finally, Daniel Ellsberg has been assigned to work with the media and to keep his hands on the D.C. pulse. He's due any time. I'm going to get him hooked up with the press people here. Basically, all we have to do is avoid Maxwell Taylor and Westmoreland, who can't stand me or my plan."

Tao raised his eyebrows as Lansdale spoke. "What about Shackley? Do you plan to meet with Conein?"

Lansdale raised his head, looking at the ceiling. "As you know, there are at least two, maybe three divisions within the CIA. It's always been that way." He tapped the table. "Shackley and I have worked together for several years without any problems." Then he curled his lips. "Conein. Conein needs me. He told Hebert he wanted me here to fight the VC—my way."

Bohannan started laughing. Lansdale turned and glared at him, but it didn't make any difference.

Lansdale pursed his lips and nodded. "You know, I didn't get enough sleep to appreciate your sense of humor." He pointed at both men, then allowed himself to crack half a smile. "The damn Corsicans have been trying to kill me for years. I'm still here, aren't I?" Lansdale gritted his teeth. "I'm still not sure these new trainees can carry out the surgical strikes like we did in the fifties. We'll just have to see."

Bohannon slurped some coffee, then said, "I'm headed up to base camp in the morning. I should be ready to start receiving trainees in a week."

Lansdale nodded and looked over to Tao. "You, I don't have an assignment yet. First off, you got to get back to your moped shop. Be high profile. We will need you on missions when we're trained."

Lansdale escorted his team members out the front door. After he closed the door, he sat down to plot his next moves. *President Johnson acted as though it were his decision to bring me here to run the counter-insurgency operation, commonly called the "Pacification Program." I know better.*

Henry Cabot Lodge, who is returning here as ambassador. He requested my services shortly after he presented credentials on August 25.

He needed to make contact with his old friend, Pham Xuan An, to get a good read on the situation in South Vietnam. With An now at *Time Magazine*, he should have the best information. *The man knows everything going on around here. Always has.*

Lucien Conein sat in his jeep in a secluded spot and watched both men walk out of Lansdale's villa. He worried he'd been seen. He sat for a few minutes to make sure they all drove off. Once he was sure no one was looping back, Conein pulled in front of the villa, then went up to the front door.

Lansdale opened the door and stared at Conein.

"Are you just going to leave me out here?" Conein asked.

Lansdale stepped aside, and, with an exaggerated motion, waved him through the door. "Come on in." His head moved as he scanned Conein from the top of his head to his toes and back up.

Conein went straight to the kitchen, grabbed one of the half-filled coffee cups off the table, dumped it into the sink, and filled it with fresh coffee. "I assume you know why I'm here?"

Lansdale refilled his cup with the last of the pot and leaned against the counter. "Well, either to ask to join our team or kill me. Which is it?"

Conein took a sip. "I'm glad you brought some American coffee. I've missed it." He turned and slid into one of the kitchen table chairs. "To answer your question, neither. But I will tell you the Corsicans have already called me to sanction the hit."

Lansdale frowned. "Figures."

"I'm not interested in rejoining your team either. As you know, I told your *tizzun*—"

"I told you not to use that word around me. If you can't be respectful—"

Conein wiped his hand through the air. "I need you over here to help fight the VC. So I came to negotiate. I need you alive."

"What do you want to negotiate about? I just got here."

Conein tipped up the cup and finished the brew. "The Corsicans want to maintain the business relationship with Vang Pao. I believe I can get them to agree not to sanction the hit, if you promise you won't interfere in that business relationship."

Lansdale walked over to the table. "Look, I'm here to fight the VC. I have a very complex plan I wish to implement, and it will require my full attention. I can assure you, I'm not going to interfere in the Corsican's *business*. Now, call off the damn hit."

Conein nodded. "I'll sell it. You won't have any worries. If you need help, I'll help you."

Lansdale reached out his hand. "So we have a deal? I don't want to be looking over my shoulder every minute or have body doubles for them to take potshots at."

Conein grabbed his hand. "I better go and make some calls. I'll handle it. You'll probably have to meet with one of their representatives. They won't trust me telling them anything without one of theirs as a witness."

Lansdale shook his head. "Okay. Whatever it takes, so I can focus on my mission."

Conein stared into the empty coffee cup. "You should be aware that last December, de Silva wanted me to survey the areas around Saigon for VC camps. I can tell you that more than half of South Vietnam is now controlled by the VC, including just about every area outside of Saigon. You have an uphill battle."

Lansdale dropped his head. "I have plans to take out the VC, but the amount of time wasted has made my plan a great task."

Lansdale and Conein walked to the door. Lansdale stopped. "Do you remember when I first met Colonel Gambiez?"

Conein nodded and started laughing.

Lansdale continued. "That son-of-a-bitch had me sit down at the small table he always sat at with that big old Alsatian dog under it growling at me the whole time, thinking it would intimidate me. Dumb bastard even told me the dog was a trained killer."

"I would have loved to have seen Gambiez' eyes when you told him your hands were in your pocket because you had a small automatic pointed at his stomach that would kill him." Conein laughed. "The colonel was a damn boy scout."

Lansdale half smiled. "Yeah. As Bogart said, 'It was the beginning of a wonderful friendship'."

As Lansdale reached for the front door, Conein looked him directly in the eye. "This place has changed a bunch since 1957. The damn Viet Cong have been pouring in over the border for the last three years, and the South Vietnamese have been waiting for the US Marines to bail their asses out. I know you've seen George Allen's report. Well, no one has taken the time to update it, to speak of. That's why I need to find a way to keep Vang Pao's army funded. He's the only one trying to fight the VC and the NVA. Your little plan better go into Laos and Cambodia, if you really want to make an impact. The ARVN—the South Vietnamese Army— and the US are playing by rules."

"The only thing ARVN has been doing is playing a waiting game. Do the Corsicans still control Vang Pao?"

Conein pointed his finger at his chest in an exaggerated fashion. "Vang Pao is controlled by whomever I say controls him."

Lansdale folded his arms across his chest. "So you're working with both the Corsicans and Shackley?"

Conein looked at Lansdale for a minute. "I need to go. Stay in touch."

Conein strode from the villa. *Now everything is in place. I'll transfer the first payment over to Premier Ky, and we're off and running. I have resolved all the problems and paid off the right leaders.*

Major Steven Hebert walked the hallways of the Embassy. It was almost time to go off duty. *I'm glad I'm in Vietnam. The Civil Rights Movement in the United States has gotten heated.* While race issues existed in the military, they certainly weren't as pronounced. Moreover, he wondered if he could be as benevolent as Dr. King. Steven always believed his rank and shooting skills buffered his personal treatment. As he approached the ambassador's office, he ran into Captain Jefferson, who was about to go on duty. After he briefed him of developments, Steven walked into Meredith's office for his meeting with Ambassador Henry Cabot Lodge. He was aware that Sergeant Tim Mitchell was in the ambassador's office getting a communique to send out. Meredith was beaming. Obviously, she was happy to be back working for Lodge again, and he shared her enthusiasm. He even noticed Tim was stuttering less around Lodge. *Maybe Tim is finally growing up.* When Tim walked out of the ambassador's office, Lodge called for Steven to step in.

As soon as he'd settled into his chair, the Ambassador asked, "Major, I have reviewed your updated security plans for this facility that you revised after the last bombing. Are you confident we are as safe as possible?"

Steven fidgeted in the chair. "Well, nothing is fail safe. I have real concerns about the Department of State hiring South Vietnamese. In the beginning, it wasn't an issue, but the Viet Cong are now operating in and around the city, so how do we know who is VC?"

Lodge looked at Steven over his glasses. "You know we have our orders. Now, I want you to go back and review all the plans from security to evacuation. We're stuck in this building until the new Embassy is built."

"Yes, sir." Steven started to get up.

Lodge cleared his throat. "Major, I'm not done. Tell me, have you had any further contact with Thich Tri Quang other than the two meetings Taylor detailed to me?"

Steven was taken back by the abruptness of his question. "Of course not, Ambassador."

Lodge reached behind him on the credenza, picked up several sheets of paper, and waved them around. "What I am about to tell you is in the strictest of confidence. This is a letter from the Thich Tri Quang, written in May of this year."

Steven raised his eyebrows but remained silent.

Lodge continued, "His position hasn't changed. He says he still believes in the US efforts and fighting. But he believes the Catholics in the country are not strong enough anticommunists *and* that the Americans are still favoring the Catholics over the Buddhists." He folded up the letter. "Where does he get this stuff?"

Steven remained silent. Lodge was using his old tactic of sitting silently to see if he would talk.

Lodge turned around and placed the letter back on the credenza. "Temporarily, I think the latest regime change has cooled everything down here."

Steven remained quiet. He knew a little bit more about President Nguyen Van Thieu and Premier Nguyen Cao Ky. Particularly Ky. He could be bought. Lansdale and Tao had told him stories. Steven wondered why Lodge's old buddy Conein hadn't filled him in on Ky. Steven could never figure out how an Air Force general could be so powerful in a country with almost no air force.

Lodge pouted his lips. "Tri Quang is very complex. I've got to figure him out. It's critical to South Vietnam."

Steven nodded. "In one of my visits, Tri Quang said he would talk to you. I think you're about the only one he really trusts."

CHAPTER TWO

SEPTEMBER 26, 1965
AP BAU BANG, VIETNAM

Tao hadn't seen Steven in over half a year. He'd enjoyed his time back in the United States visiting with his son, Luc. While in the States, the CIA put him behind a desk at Langley. For the first time in his life, he enjoyed advising operatives rather than leading missions. It gave him more time with his son, his last living family member. Tao imagined that soon Luc would settle down and start a family. *Someday, I want to be a grandfather.* Luc was his only hope of rebuilding the Tao family.

Tao's employees had his Vespa moped store running with great efficiency, but he still had to follow Lansdale's advice to keep a high profile. Tao looked at the clock on the wall. It was time to meet Steven. He walked out to his old Peugeot and drove off.

Tao drove out to the old shack outside of Saigon, the place he'd first met Steven merely a year and a half ago. Their mission to keep ground

14

troops out of Vietnam had failed. Kennedy was dead, MacArthur was dead, and troops were now beginning to stream into Vietnam. Frankly, Tao didn't know if he and Steven would work on another mission together.

Steven walked into the shack singing. Within a few seconds, he was seated across from Tao. Steven rubbed his chin. "So we haven't met in a long time, and you decided to meet way out here?"

Tao shook his head, smiling. "Still singing '*Dream a little Dream of Me*'? Anyway, lots to cover. Too many ears and eyes in Saigon at the moment."

Steven laughed. "You lose the backroom at your shop?"

Tao smiled. "This is a secure place to meet. Word is the Army secured the southern part of the Binh Duong Province. I have much to tell you."

Steven placed his hands on his hips, drew a deep breath, and nodded.

Tao looked down at the old rickety table. "This is complicated. I'm contemplating returning to the States, *permanently*. I don't want to retire—not that I'm allowed to retire from the CIA—but I spent about six months back in Langley as an analyst and adviser. It allowed me to be around my son. Lansdale wants me to hang around and work with our old team, but my time doing missions—"

Steven frowned. "Thought you wanted to find your family's golden chalice. And get the people who burned your family bible."

Tao looked away. *The golden chalice does hold secrets, but I'm so tired.*

"What's Lansdale got to say about you retiring?"

"He doesn't know yet. We had an operation meeting yesterday, and it just didn't feel right. However, I wanted to sleep on it."

15

Steven furrowed his brow as he pursed his lips. "I assumed I was going to be left out of his new operation."

Tao got up from the table. He contemplated telling Steven everything he'd learned when back in the States, but decided he couldn't compromise his source. Lansdale was disappointed with the appointment of former Vice Admiral Raborn to replace his old adversary, McCone, because it was now obvious Johnson was appointing people to continue his philosophy of building troops in Vietnam. The military—or the Military Industrial Complex—was in several congressmen's hip pockets, as well as the White House. They were against Lansdale's proposal for Vietnam, so the ground war was going to escalate. Lansdale and anyone associated with him were going to become insignificant. Tao had lost his drive because of what he'd learned, but he couldn't do that to Steven. Steven still had his drive. "Lansdale may have known the best way to execute this fight for the freedom of the South Vietnamese. But he's going to be rendered irrelevant. The CIA is too splintered to support him. And the Army—"

"Is going to run over him. They refuse to listen to anybody but other Army generals. I have seen de Silva's program. It works. Guerilla warfare must be met with guerilla warfare."

Tao put his hands on his hips as he turned around. "American youth are turning against this conflict. When I was back in the States, I saw it firsthand. We're approaching a tipping point. You're too young to remember, but almost all of the country was behind the military and the politicians during World War II. This conflict is different."

Steven frowned. "We're here fighting for your country. Your country has to get behind our effort with effort of their own."

Tao walked back over and leaned over the table. "The people have to be led. Since Diem was removed, they haven't had leadership. Without a strong leader, the people and the military are rudderless. And in the countryside, the Viet Cong are intimidating the people to collaborate with them."

Bullets rained down on the small shack from every direction.

Tao and Steven hit the floor simultaneously as Tao looked at Steven. Tao reached under his shirt and pulled his Colt M1911. "All I got is my nine millimeter."

Steven shook his head as he unholstered his 1911, then whispered, "Me, too. We're outgunned and likely outmanned."

Tao glanced around, observing the bullets coming through the old shack. "It looks like they have us surrounded."

Steven crawled over to Tao's position. "How many magazines you got?

"Two, plus a full one in the gun."

"Me, too." Steven thought for a minute. "Any ideas?"

Tao stared. "You first."

"Custer's Last Stand. Back to back, facing the door and that window." Steven raised a hand off the floor as he pointed at the window opposite the door. "We try to kill enough of them to get to our cars."

Tao bit his lip. "Or either car."

"When there are fewer bullets flying, they are moving toward us. I'll try to get to the window and get off some shots. Don't waste a round. We'll need them all. They likely know there are only two of us."

Tao nodded. "Maybe they'll get sloppy and think we're dead since we haven't returned fire."

Steven looked up at the ceiling. After a few minutes, everything got quiet. No enemy fire. He crawled to the window on his belly. He drew a deep breath, got into a crouched position, then peeked out the window. No one. No one was there in any direction that he could see from the window. He crawled back over to Tao. "Surely, they haven't left. Would they try to make a frontal assault without support from behind?"

Tao shrugged. "We gotta get out of here."

Steven looked around. "I'm going to the front door. They could be getting ready to burn us out or bomb us out."

Tao nodded. "Okay, check out front. We gotta go."

Both men took deep breaths, then moved toward the door. Steven held his 1911 down at the ground, ready to step out first as Tao opened the door. He peeked around, but, again, he couldn't see any sign of the enemy. "I'll cover your move, then I'm going out the back window and circle around." Steven looked back at Tao and pointed for him to exit toward his Peugeot.

The moment Tao exited the shanty, bullets rained down on him. Steven fired off seven rounds from his handgun in the direction of three of the shooters. Tao was hit in the shoulder but signaled he was okay.

The shooting stopped. Steven signaled he was moving as he put in a new magazine. Tao gave him the thumbs up. Gunshots sounded from behind the shack. He needed to make a move.

Tao moved carefully, staying below his Peugeot to open the driver's side door. The minute the door opened, more bullets rained on him. The gunfire behind the shack picked up again as well. Tao peeked up just in time to see four VC running at him. He wiggled the car door again while staying low, then moved back to the front of the Peugeot and fired, shooting all four of the charging enemy. A burning pain shot through his left arm, while another bullet grazed his left ear, but there was no more gunfire in front.

Tao carefully walked along the side of the shack to provide support for Steven. He dropped his empty magazine and inserted a new one.

When Tao got to the side of the broken-down structure, there was no sign of Steven. The jungle was silent.

When Steven heard the gunfire in front of the shack, he jumped out the window, firing his handgun in the direction of the three identified shooters. Miraculously, he covered the ten feet to the first jungle foliage to provide him some cover. He heard movement off to his left. He figured their cover was coming from his right, behind him. However many VC there were, they were likely charging him. He changed out his magazine. Seven rounds left to get out of this mess. Again, he heard gunfire out from the front, but for the first time, he heard handgun fire. Tao must have gotten in the position to get off some shots. He thought he counted seven rounds, but he couldn't be sure. Now, it was silent around front. Steven crawled off to the right toward the anticipated position of the enemy. He had to get into the jungle to get more cover, to equal up the odds for his survival. As he crawled, he made certain not to shake anything that would tip off his position.

Off to his left, gunfire rained down on his position. Then handgun fire sounded. Tao must have engaged the VC attacking his position. Just then gunfire came over his head, very close to the shack. Two automatic weapons fired. When they stopped and he heard magazines drop, he made his move. He jumped up and fired four at their last positions. He hit both men. He only had three rounds left. He pulled his knife from his boot and moved toward the enemy, handgun in one hand, knife in the other. He found one man dead—a boy about thirteen. Steven moved toward the other position and found only a trail of blood. He heard rustling through the jungle away from his position. Steven ran a few steps, then thought he might be running into a trap. He turned and ran back to the edge of the jungle near the shack. He shouted to Tao, "Coming out! Don't shoot me."

Tao sat on the ground, trying to stop the bleeding from his arm and shoulder. Steven looked at him. Blood streamed down the side of his face from the grazing shot to his ear. Tao was bleeding pretty good. They went to his Peugeot and quickly pulled out some rags to make bandages. Steven looked off in several directions. "We're lucky these were a bunch of young kids. We better get out of here—one got away. He's wounded, but I don't know how bad, and he could be bringing back help or mortars."

Tao nodded. "Let's go. I think I can drive."

Steven helped him to his car. "Tao, I got a bad feeling about this. Get in your car and go. I'm doing the same, while I can."

Tao started his Peugeot. "I guess this area wasn't as secure as I'd been told?" He pulled away as Steven started his jeep.

Steven spun the tires as he pulled in behind Tao. Neither car was more than fifty feet from the old shack before two mortar rounds blew the shack to bits.

CHAPTER THREE

SEPTEMBER 28, 1965

TRAFFICANTE RESTAURANT - TAMPA, FL

Santos Trafficante looked over his banking statements. A man sat before him who had stopped by to get a real estate loan to start up his business in Mississippi. Trafficante was only half-listening to the man's request. What he wanted the money for didn't matter as much as his ability to repay the loan—which would come at premium interest. Once the man had finished his proposal, Trafficante folded his hands on his desk top and looked him in the eye. "How do you intend to repay this loan? You know I'm going to hold the title to the house."

The man shifted in his seat then glanced at the two bodyguards standing on either side of Trafficante's desk. "I was hoping to keep the title, but I understand. What is my interest rate going to be?"

Trafficante held up both hands, extending his fingers, as he spoke. "You obviously couldn't get a deal at the bank, which is why you came to me. Take it or leave it."

The man lowered his head. "Prepare the papers."

Trafficante waved his hand for him to leave. As the man stood, the bodyguards walked him to the door. "I'll get the papers drawn up." He nodded. "One of my attorneys will call you."

When the man was out of the room, one of the bodyguards said, "Frank Furci is here for his appointment."

Trafficante nodded and returned to looking over his bank statements. He restacked several of them on his desk. Then he turned around to the safe behind his desk and spun through the combination. He pulled up on the handle. *Clunk.* The door opened. He pulled out several bundles of cash, then slipped them into the center desk drawer. He closed the safe, then looked at the bodyguards over his glasses as he waved to one of the bodyguards to send in Furci.

Furci strutted into the office, a toothpick in his mouth, and sat down opposite Trafficante.

Trafficante continued going over his bank statements. He pulled one out of the stack and wrote notes on the page. Finally, he looked at Furci and snarled. "Get that damn toothpick out of your mouth."

"Yes, sir, Mr. Trafficante."

Trafficante waited until the man got up and placed the toothpick in the wastebasket. The two bodyguards moved closer to Furci as he leaned toward the wastebasket, then returned to the chair. Trafficante reached in the side drawer, pulled out a cigar, patiently trimmed the end, and lit it. "I have an

23

assignment for you." He took a couple of hard draws off his cigar. "I'm sending you to Asia. I want you to go to Hong Kong, Taiwan and Saigon. I want to establish a network for product disbursement in all those cities. Got it?"

Furci pursed his lips as he nodded.

"In Saigon, I want you to find me some military personnel—you know, mess custodians and club managers. No, better yet, find soldiers who are in charge of officers clubs." Trafficante looked at the two bodyguards. "Maybe some USO clubs, know what I mean?"

Furci rubbed his chin, then held both arms out, palms up. "How am I supposed to do all this? I mean, how am I to afford all this travel? You know I may need to grease some palms along the way, too."

Trafficante reached in the center drawer of his desk, pulled out several bundles of cash, and waved them in Furci's face. "I want to know where every dollar is spent, including whoever you grease. *Capisce?*"

"Do I tell everyone I'm representing you?"

"Of course, you dumbass. Maybe you aren't smart enough to handle this assignment?"

"Mr. Trafficante, I am the right man for the job, I swear."

Trafficante handed him the bundles and waved him out the door with a nod to his bodyguards.

Once Furci was out of the room, Trafficante reached over, picked up the phone and dialed. "Carlos, this is Santos. My man is leaving in the morning."

Carlos Marcello replied, "The Blonde Ghost has everything in place. Let me know when your man is back."

Trafficante took a big draw off from his cigar, then blew out the smoke. "We're going to make some real green."

SEPTEMBER 30, 1965

SAIGON

US EMBASSY

Ambassador Lodge stared out the Embassy window. His one year absence from Vietnam weighed on him. Vietnam had changed dramatically; now, US troops were directly engaged in the fighting. According to CIA Analyst George Allen, the Viet Cong were in control of large portions of the countryside because the South Vietnamese had done nothing. Plus, the VC had infiltrated many of the cities. As soon as US began moving troops into the country, the Viet Cong began efforts to take down the South Vietnamese regime with an offensive in the Southern Highlands and the Central Coast. Lodge believed in the South Vietnamese people, but he also believed they lacked the proper leadership. This had greatly hindered their ability to resist the ever-growing Viet Cong presence. He had a plan to change this environment. He had been focused on Vietnam since he'd lost his bid to be a Republican presidential candidate. The only reason he returned to his old assignment was because he believed in Pacification. He wanted to oversee its implementation, and he wanted to make a difference. Many of the US Army and Marines now encamped in the country hadn't been trained for guerilla warfare. It was critical they make a concerted effort not to injure non-combatants if they were going to win the hearts and the minds of the South Vietnamese people. Once the military cleared an area, they should immediately start building small local governments. Lodge believed in building the country from the bottom up, as reflected in his own "Ten Point Program for Success."

He buzzed Meredith to come into his office with her steno pad to dictate his plan. He wanted to distribute it to Lansdale, plus send a copy back to the State Department and the White House.

As soon as Meredith was ready, Lodge spoke as he picked up his glasses. "Ms. Brown, I want my plan distributed to the President, Politico-Military, and Lansdale."

Lodge proceeded to dictate his ten point plan. When finished, he took off his glasses and looked at Meredith. "Type this up, then bring the first draft in for me to correct. Now, I wish to dictate a cable to go to the President."

Meredith flipped the page over, then nodded at the Ambassador.

Lodge began:

"I appointed Edward Lansdale, with his complete approval,
to be chairman of the US Mission Liaison Group . . . ."

When Lodge finished dictating his cable, he nodded. "Get that to Mitchell to transmit."

Meredith smiled as she got up and returned to her office.

Lodge sat patiently. He'd put himself in a difficult position requesting Lansdale to come back with him to run this program. He believed the rewards could outweigh the risks. Lansdale had knowledge, and it was knowledge Lodge needed. *Can I control Lansdale? Yes. Yes, I can. Lansdale must implement my Pacification plan my way. Surely, he knows that it was because of me he's here, where he wanted to be. Two presidents, two years, but it was me who brought him here.*

OCTOBER 4, 1965

SAIGON

The helicopter slowly descended to the small landing pad in the middle of the jungle. General Edward Lansdale hung out the open door, ready to jump as soon as the bird was on the ground.

With a jolt, it landed harder than normal. Lansdale jumped off and jogged underneath the swishing blades.

Bo Bohannan held his beret on his head. "Welcome, General Lansdale. Can't wait for you to meet our men."

Bohannan and Lansdale walked into a small block building with only a table in the middle and ten metal chairs randomly placed around it. The two old friends sat at opposite ends of the table. Bohannan spoke first. "These men will make good team leaders, maybe even a couple of them instructors after a year in the field."

Lansdale held a hand over his mouth as leaned toward Bo. "How do they compare to our old team in the art of counter-subversion and counter-terrorism?"

Bohannan smiled a toothy grin. "Nobody can replace our old team, but these men aren't too bad. I want to take them out tonight on their first real mission test. We're going to fly up to Da Nang, drop in on a simple mission—just some recon—Ho Chi Minh trail and one of the VC's bigger camps."

Lansdale rubbed his chin. "So, if they are successful, when can you get the next bunch ready?"

Bohannan took a deep breath. "Maybe two months, ten weeks tops."

Lansdale jumped up from the table. "Take me out to meet them."

Bohannan stepped in stride with Lansdale. They were off to the small barracks about a quarter mile from their present location.

Lansdale paused for a minute, turned and looked around. He wanted to get special teams back into North Vietnam to terrorize the Viet Cong while they were training men. But he now knew that might not be possible. *The politics of war.*

NEXT DAY

Edward Lansdale sat in his favorite chair in his villa in Saigon sipping on a glass of Crown Royal with his notepad and pen. Ambassador Lodge had faith in him for the mission he'd wanted to implement two years ago. *Lodge is the only one who saw my potential to fix South Vietnam.* The objective was to strengthen the political structures in these areas so the Viet Cong would no longer have influence over the people. The South Vietnamese needed to learn to believe in themselves, which was what the Pacification program would do. With the US troops now encamped in South Vietnam and more due at any time, the Viet Cong had increased intimidation and terrorism tactics.

He needed to update Ambassador Lodge and the CIA about the Pacification program team, appropriately named US Mission Liaison Group:

> "Past week devoted to getting GVN into sound start again on Pacification program . . . US Mission Liaison Group shaping up into realistic instrument for working level teamwork on Pacification by all US Missions...."

CHAPTER FOUR

OCTOBER 21, 1965

WHITE HOUSE - WASHINGTON DC

President Johnson sat on the couch opposite Secretary of Defense Robert McNamara and Secretary of State Dean Rusk discussing the latest developments in South Vietnam. Rusk brought up Lodge's cable from the day before. "Mr. President, what is your opinion on this update on the Pacification program? He seems concerned about the long term presence of US troops."

The President ran his hand over the top of his head. "Lansdale's really in Lodge's head." He picked up a cable from Ambassador Lodge and waved the piece of paper around. "Lodge believes in the Pacification program."

He turned to McNamara. "Any new engagement between US troops and the Viet Cong? We sure could use some more success like Operation Starlite."

"The forty thousand new troops granted to Westmoreland have yet to engage."

McNamara took off his glasses and cleaned them with his tie. "I bet it won't be long until Westmoreland asks for more troops."

Rusk pounded the arm of the couch. "Lodge has always wanted to be in charge. He and Lansdale make a good team. It will only be a matter of time before they're at each other's throats."

President Johnson dropped the cable on the coffee table. "I don't have any faith in this Pacification program—whether it's run by us or the South Vietnamese. Until we can push out the Viet Cong, I don't see any way for this program to work. Westmoreland and I believe this is all about what our troops can accomplish. Lodge, more or less, says that in this damn cable."

McNamara picked up the cable and glanced at it. "Clearly, Lodge doesn't believe the communists will ever be willing to negotiate. He may be right. We sure haven't seen any evidence of that."

Rusk leaned over the table and spun the cable around to read. "At least he defined 'satisfactory outcome' for peace in Vietnam." They all laughed.

Johnson sucked air through his teeth. "I still want to see Westmoreland get going. This cable has no value to me. Look at it." He picked it back up and read the cable out loud.

When he finished reading, he shook his head emphatically. "How does he think we're going to get there?"

McNamara fidgeted on the couch. "Lodge's program will only work if our troops can take back some territory."

Johnson rubbed his mouth. "Look, Lodge knows the troops will enhance this program." He paused as he ran his hand over the top of his head. "I can't emphasize this enough. Westmoreland has to engage. We have bombed the shit out of North Vietnam and received absolutely nothing to show for our effort."

"I believe Lodge will make better headway with President Thieu and Premier Ky than Maxwell Taylor." Rusk raised his hands. "He's much more diplomatic."

"Maxwell just couldn't connect with those young South Vietnamese leaders," Johnson replied. "Their egos just wouldn't let them see the leadership he was offering."

Rusk looked back at the Lodge cable. "I think the South Vietnamese would be better at running the Pacification program than Lansdale."

Johnson nodded. "Lodge is looking for someone to run a similar program by the South Vietnamese. As to Lansdale, we'll see how he does. This is his big chance to do what he says he can do. We let Lodge and Lansdale sink or swim with this program."

NOVEMBER 12, 1965

REGISTER–GUARD, WASHINGTON BUREAU

WASHINGTON DC

Rita Sullivan sipped the last of her morning coffee. She pondered the two job offers—one from *Life Magazine* and one from WFAN TV Station Channel 14. She worried she was getting pigeon-holed as an anti-war reporter focused on the protests around the Washington DC area. Recently, she'd decided not to cover the twenty-five thousand person march that had included five Medal of Honor recipients. Not because she was against the march, but because she'd underestimated the turnout and the impact. It was a huge miscalculation on her part.

Rita tried to line up an interview with each of the five Medal of Honor recipients. She wanted to discover why they believed in the Conflict so she could get a different prospective. However, each had politely turned her down.

Earlier this month, she'd been called to the Pentagon to witness a protest. However, traffic had prevented her from getting there in time to witness Norman Morrison, father of three, a Quaker and a pacifist, stand below Robert McNamara's third floor office, pour kerosene on himself, and then set himself on fire to protest the Vietnam Conflict. When Rita finally arrived at the scene, she was repulsed and gotten physically ill from the stench of burning flesh. She thought she could write an article comparing Morrison to Vietnamese Mahayana Buddhist monk Thích Quang Duc. Most of America remembered the monk setting himself on fire in the streets of Saigon in June 1963. But as she sat and contemplated the article, she couldn't bring herself to write about a man who left his three children fatherless. Since she'd been raised by a single mother, she knew first-hand of the struggles. The editor of the *Register-Guard* even told her she could write the article from that prospective, but she didn't want to dignify his act. She saw the meaning of the Vietnamese monk's act, a single, religious man, making that call for himself, but Morrison had more than himself to consider. Witnessing the aftermath of Morrison's suicide-protest had caused her to question her career path. Yes, she wanted to be a reporter of the news, yet she was being pushed toward the anti-war side. She had to come to grips with that before she could make any decisions about her career.

She'd even questioned herself regarding the surprise visit in the spring of this year by FBI Agent Stephanie Keeton. She'd realized that the Baker-thug intimidation ended when Johnson got elected President. *It was all about bad press.* While she didn't have the real name for the thug other than his alias, Jack Armstrong, it just didn't seem important now. The one thing that still was troubling was the Baker thug's role in stopping her from getting to Mary Meyer's home. It was clear phone taps came into play. *Was she being watched by the CIA? Maybe even the FBI? Is that why Agent Keeton came by to see me? To check me out or plant a bug?*

Rita reached in the center drawer of her desk and pulled out Stephanie Keeton's business card. Perhaps it was time to take her up on her offer to talk again. *Time for more questions—and maybe this time she would have more answers.* She dialed the number, and they agreed to meet for lunch at her desk this afternoon. Rita had enough time to make a quick trip to the library to research newspaper articles on Baker.

Rita Sullivan walked out of the newspaper archives room at the library. Her decision to open her eyes to the world caused her to laugh at herself. She'd discovered two articles, one in the *New York Times*, the other in the *Washington Post*, that showed connections between a corrupt businessman and President Johnson. The common thread was Bobby Baker, who was the go-between for payoff and material bribery. One of the file pictures showed Bobby Baker with an employee at the Quorum Club. The name "Jack Armstrong" was written under the employee. As Rita walked to her car, another light bulb went on for her. *Do some research on corporations Baker was involved with.* This man was as dirty as the character "Pigpen" in the cartoon strip *Peanuts*. She looked at her watch. She barely had enough time to get back to her office to meet Stephanie.

Rita pulled up to the local deli at 11:45AM. Stephanie should be at her office any moment. She ran into the deli and picked up salads. As she walked to her office, she had an eerie feeling she was being watched. She put the salads on her desk. *I should lock the door.* As she was about to put the key in the lock, she discreetly looked up and down the street to see if anyone was watching her. *Nothing suspicious.*

At a quarter past twelve, someone pounded on the door. It was Stephanie.

Stephanie almost knocked her down. She closed the door behind her and turned the lock, then looked at Rita. "I'm sure I was followed here."

Rita's heart raced. "When I walked out to pick up lunch, I felt like I was being watched. Are we just paranoid?"

Stephanie shook her head. "No. I haven't had that feeling in more than a year." She sighed. "I'm not a super sleuth, but I know I was followed." She walked toward the table. "But it wasn't a black Cadillac this time. It was a white Chevy Impala."

Rita handed Stephanie a salad, and both sat quietly for a minute. "That may be why I didn't identify anyone watching me—it was a different car." She jabbed her fork into her salad. "I wanted to see if there was any more information from the FBI on the Meyer murder."

Stephanie took a bite of salad. "There has been no interest at all since the lead agent left. Weird, isn't it? For half a year, there was a lead agent assigned to watch her—then nothing, no follow up. No interest, even after she was murdered."

Rita considered for a moment, then jumped up and ran to her bottom file cabinet drawer. She opened her purse and pulled out her private note pad— her personal notes on the Meyer investigation. She flipped back and forth over a couple of pages. "So the FBI views this as a state police matter only?"

Stephanie shrugged. "So it seems."

Rita licked her lips. She knew the name of the driver of the black Cadillac. *Does Stephanie know? Should I tell her? Or does she know and won't tell me?* "Well, let me give you some background that you probably don't have. Meyer died in October 1964, then in May of this year, Bobby Baker's secretary died in a plane crash. I did a little homework on this woman, Nancy Carol Tyler. She was up to her eyeballs in Baker's illegal activity, plus was having an affair with him. When she started making a scene about him leaving his wife, she had an accident."

Stephanie squirmed in her chair. "I'm sorry, I don't mean to be rude, but what does that have to do with us being followed? I don't see the connection between Meyer and Tyler."

Rita bit her lower lip. "When Tyler was first called before the Senate Rules Committee about Baker's business, she took the Fifth Amendment. Supposedly, and I have this from a good source, she left town and went back to Tennessee. Then she decided to come back and make a play for Baker again. When she was told *no* this time, she started making public scenes." She leaned toward her friend. "And here is the zinger. She wanted to testify before the Senate again, only this time, *not* taking the Fifth."

Stephanie took another bite of salad, then a sip of her Coca Cola. "While that's compelling and very sad, how is that relevant to us being followed? Baker is up to his eyeballs in too many things to be concerned with us, don't you think?"

"Do you know why the agent was assigned to watch Meyer?"

Stephanie fidgeted in her seat. "No clue. Top Secret. The agent only reported to the director."

Rita decided it was time to push. "Can you give me the name and the phone number of the special agent watching Mary Meyer?"

Stephanie sat up straight. "No *way*. *Absolutely* not. I came here to help you in the beginning, to give you information to keep you safe."

Rita ignored the comment. "When was your agent taken off the Meyer case?"

Stephanie looked up at the ceiling and closed her eyes. After a long pause, she said, "I don't recall completely, but it was maybe a week before Kennedy was assassinated. He was sent to San Francisco."

Rita picked up her pencil and made a note. Then she flipped back and forth between some other pages. "Okay. So up until today, you have not had the feeling of being followed. Then I call you, and you believe you're followed here." She made another note.

Stephanie took a sip of her drink. "That's right. So that means they must be listening in on your phone. You know, if it's the government, they have to have a warrant to do that. I'll check that discreetly, but I'm betting there isn't one."

Rita took a drink of tea, keeping a piece of ice, which she chewed on. "When the Meyer murder trial started, this past summer, I went every day. On the day the verdict was pronounced and Crump was declared innocent, her husband was there. Naturally, her sister Antoinette Bradlee and her husband Ben were there. Cicely and James Jesus Angleton were there. Bradlee acknowledged me as he left the courtroom after the verdict. How did he know me? The next day, he called me and offered me a job at *Newsweek*. Needless to say, I turned him down. Now, I know Ben Bradlee, Cord Meyer, and James Jesus Angleton are all CIA. So they could easily wiretap my phone both here and at home."

Stephanie nodded. "If Bradlee read the detective's notes from the police investigation, he could have put two and two together and figured out who you were. You think that is why he offered you the job?" She paused for a second then frowned. "So now you think the CIA is after you? Not Bobby Baker?"

Rita drew a deep breath and contemplated long and hard before speaking. "I don't know." She ran her hand over her pulled back hair. *Should I tell her all I know?* "Let's think about something. You told me that CIA Agent James Jesus Angleton went into Meyer's house one day after she left home. Why? Was he after something? Or, did he tap her phone?"

Stephanie looked at the clock on the wall. "I don't have a clue. What's your point? How does that relate to you?"

"I'll tell you something I've never told anyone else. Please keep my secret."

Stephanie nodded.

"The day I was going to see Mary Meyer, we were to go for a walk. She was very worried about her own safety. I remember the conversation like it was yesterday. She was desperate for me to come by, I said, 'Miss Meyer, I shouldn't tell you this, but I'm waiting on word that Khrushchev might be ousted. Potentially huge breaking news. My staff wants me in place to take this call.' Then Mary said something I will never forget. 'I have something for you that might be just as revolutionary. Maybe more so. I'm scared, and I have to give someone a copy of my journal for my own protection. You're a journalist. You're my someone.'"

Stephanie's eyes grew large.

Rita continued. "I remember thinking, what could be more revolutionary than Khrushchev being ousted? I asked her for a clue." She paused. "Mary snapped at me. 'Not on the phone. It's too dangerous. They might be listening.'"

"I told her I couldn't lose my job over missing the call on Khrushchev." Rita looked down at her half-eaten salad. "Get this, the last thing she said to me was, 'If something should happen to me, I just want to make sure my— that this gets out.'"

Stephanie's face grew very white. "*Damn.* She knew. But why then did she go on that walk? That doesn't make sense." She paused. "So neither the journal nor the copy were ever found?"

Rita raised both hands. "I don't know. *I don't know.* Was Meyer tied up with Baker or the CIA? Or both? One thing was for sure—Meyer was tied to somebody that was spoken of in that journal, and they didn't want it out."

Stephanie bit her lower lip as she looked down at the ground for a second. Like she knew more. She got up from her chair and walked to the door. "I want out of this. I'll check some things for you, but I won't call you. I'll send you a letter to your home address."

Rita reached in her purse and pulled out a card, quickly jotting down her address. "Here's my address."

Stephanie walked back over, snatched the card, then shot out the door. Rita strongly believed the FBI knew more, and Stephanie either could not or would not tell her. When her mind cleared, she realized if they were followed by a white Chevy Impala, they were trying to blend in, not stand out. The black Cadillac stood out—it was meant to intimidate. Now that wasn't the case. *Had she been followed all this time and just not known?*

40

Baker is probably connected to the black Cadillac, intimidation. But the white Chevy Impala? I believe the CIA or the FBI. Rita flipped through her private notes. *Stephanie has never made any comments about Baker's connections to Senate's investigation into Don Reynolds, or to the Miami Mob, or to their operation in the Caribbean. Surely, the FBI knows this? For God's sakes, Baker is connected to Meyer Lansky, Sam Giancana, Santos Trafficante and maybe Carlos Marcello. Will Antoinette Bradlee talk to me?*

A chill ran down her spine. She'd considered Stephanie a confidant. If the FBI were after her, she'd just given her too much information.

CHAPTER FIVE

NOVEMBER 18, 1965

WHITE HOUSE - WASHINGTON DC

President Johnson waited for Robert McNamara and Dean Rusk to show up. They were bringing the latest analysis of the Battle of Ia Drang Valley. Johnson had requested and received another one point seven billion dollars from Congress for the Vietnam Conflict in early August. Since then, the Viet Cong had blown up fuel storage tanks near Da Nang in retaliation for the Air Force bombing of their fuel tanks in North Vietnam. The air strikes hadn't slowed the VC. Johnson was anxious. He desperately needed some good news, something that General Westmoreland had been promising but had failed to deliver. The anti-war movement had gathered more momentum several weeks ago with forty protests around the United States, plus London and Rome. Johnson flipped his pencil over and over, alternately tapping it on his desk.

Finally, his personal secretary, Geraldine "Gerri" Whittington, buzzed to advise that McNamara and Rusk had arrived.

42

Johnson bolted from behind his desk to meet the two men as they stepped into the oval office. Both carried briefcases and sat down on one of the couches.

McNamara took his seat and pushed his glasses back up on his face. "I just received the after-action reports from the Pentagon on the Battle of Ia Drang Valley."

Johnson nodded. "This administration needs some good news. Robert, what do you have for me?"

Rusk looked at McNamara. "Go ahead, Robert."

McNamara opened his briefcase, pulled out several sheets of paper, then laid a large folder on the table. He handed a sheet of paper to each.

Johnson grabbed the pages. "Robert, just tell me what this says as I read it."

McNamara laughed. "Mr. President, this was a two-day fight against the North Vietnamese Army in which two thousand enemy were killed. At the end, remember, NVA retreated into the jungle and disappeared. We lost seventy-nine soldiers, while one hundred twenty-one were wounded." McNamara picked up his copy and pointed. "Here is an important fact. This was the first battle that our ground troops were supported by B-52 air strikes."

Johnson sat back and smiled. "So that's a great military victory, wouldn't you say?"

Rusk pointed at one of the paragraphs. "We must improve our introduction of troops to the battlefield. We could only land eight helicopters carrying six men at a time in the LZ. It took us way too long to get our men into the battle. Otherwise, we might have inflicted greater losses on the NVA." He picked up the full report, then flipped through it.

Johnson frowned as he picked up his copy and adjusted his glasses. "Looks like our intel on the number of enemy troops were off quite a bit. So we won the battle despite bad intel and bad execution." He threw his glasses on the coffee table.

Rusk leaned back in his chair. "It says here that the battle intel was obtained on October 19 when the NVA attacked our US Special Forces camp at Plei Me."

Johnson glanced at both men. "What do you mean?"

McNamara nodded. "Information gained from the dead bodies."

Johnson pursed his lips. "Westmoreland wants to continue our 'search and destroy' missions. It looks like this is good military strategy. What do you think?"

McNamara nodded. "We must remain on the offensive. We have increased the troops by an additional twenty-eight combat battalions, with support that will total 125,000 new soldiers. Are we fulling engaging?"

"Westmoreland has to keep pushing," Johnson said. "He says if he can put the enemy on their heels, we can win in just over a year."

McNamara said, "Any more updates from Lodge on the Pacification program? How is he getting along with Lansdale?" He looked at Rusk.

Johnson waved his right arm around with the summary report in hand. "I don't pay a whole lot of attention to those reports. These are the kind of reports I'm interested in."

Rusk cleared his throat. "Well, Lodge maintains that Lansdale's first teams will be in the field within a couple of weeks. Each of those teams consist of about twenty men. As the program grows, he's expecting the teams to grow in size. The first groups will focus around the larger cities in South Vietnam. Lodge will advise me of any update."

Johnson shook his head in disgust. "See what I mean? Westmoreland and the military. This is where we're going to get results."

NOVEMBER 23, 1965
US EMBASSY
SAIGON

Steven Hebert walked back to his quarters after he finished his duty about the same time as Tim Mitchell walked out of the communication area. When Tim saw Steven, he waved a piece of paper. "I just printed this out and was going to bring it to you."

Steven waved at Tim to bring it over. "What is it?"

"Recap of the heavyweight fight between Muhammad Ali and Floyd Patterson. Guess it got pretty ugly." Tim handed the paper to Steven.

Steven read the article that came from a newspaper he'd never heard of:

"On November 22, 1965, Floyd Patterson became the
next victim of heavyweight champion Muhammad Ali.

Patterson had taunted Ali before the fight with statements like 'The image of a Black Muslim as the world heavyweight champion disgraces the sport and the nation,' plus he continued to call him Cassius Clay.

"This only infuriate Ali who had responded, 'Patterson says he's gonna bring the title back to America. If you don't believe the title is already in America, just see who I pay taxes to,' he said. 'This will be a mismatch. Floyd Patterson will be no match. He's too short, he's too slow, he don't have the reach, he can't take a punch, he don't hit hard and he don't have the footwork. This will be a mismatch. I'll hit him about six times to every miss that he throws.'

"It turned out to be a one sided fight, as Patterson could not land any affective punches. The fight resulted in a brutal beating of Patterson, whom Ali toyed with after a sixth round knockdown. Patterson's corner desperately massaged his back between rounds, and tried to persuade him to quit. But Patterson stubbornly, and unsteadily, fought on, after the knockdown before the referee halted the slaughter in the 12th."

The article included a quote from former heavyweight champion Joe Lewis, one of his dad's favorite boxers:

Lewis was quoted as saying. 'He could have knocked Patterson out whenever he wanted, but let's face it, Clay is selfish and cruel,'

"After the fight Ali admitted, 'Yes, I carried him for six rounds, I am showing you good boxing. You'd be the first to condemn me for killing him cruelly. He has got beautiful children and I wouldn't want to hurt him just for the pleasure of the audience. I beat him with my creative and scientific ability and not by punching him too hard.'"

Steven was speechless. He liked Ali as a fighter, but he also liked Floyd Patterson. Ali's position on Vietnam had made it difficult for Steven to like him out of the ring, despite his bringing up some causes for Negro people.

CHAPTER SIX

DECEMBER 1, 1965

SAIGON

Steven Hebert sat in a little restaurant waiting for Ethan Graham, who was on leave, to show up for dinner. It was unlike Ethan to be late.

Steven glanced again at his watch. This was one of his last meetings before taking his own leave. It had been almost a year since he'd heard from his mother and brother, which, he hoped, meant they were doing okay. But he was going home to check on them. Maybe the Warren Commission report had pacified the American public. No one wanted to search for the truth.

Finally, Ethan flopped down at the table. Before speaking, he pulled out a polaroid of himself in a new uniform. It was obvious why he was late— he'd already been at a bar for some time.

Ethan smiled, but before he could say anything, a waitress stepped up to the table to get their orders.

As soon as the waitress left, Steven asked out about Ethan's new assignment. He could barely contain himself with excitement to find out. Steven wanted to hear stories. He missed combat duty. It was strange. The more he was around the diplomats, the more he wanted out. All the time he'd spent spying on the diplomats for Lansdale had only opened his eyes to how the political system worked, and it wasn't anything he cared about. Right now, Steven was living vicariously through Ethan's war stories.

After Steven and Ethan ordered their meals, Ethan glanced to make sure no one was listening, then quietly stated, "I was transferred to the Third Battalion of the Third Marines." He looked around again. "I have been assigned as part of the security team for the Seals training the South Vietnamese at Da Nang."

Steven folded his hands on top of the small table. "Nobody seems to be doing anything?"

Ethan half smiled. "Heard of Operation Starlite?"

Steven nodded.

"You're not going to believe this," Ethan continued. "A Viet Cong deserter informed General Thi of a major build-up of enemy marine units in the Van Tuong village complex, twelve miles southeast of Chu Lai along the coast. So the big chiefs rapidly put together a battle plan. Next thing you known, we got amphibious landings, helicopter assaults, coupled with artillery and air strikes hitting the village of Van Tuong. We kicked their ass, Steven."

Steven stared at him. "Seriously?"

Ethan nodded. "We had to move fast with that information." He leaned back in the chair.

"So how did you get leave?"

Ethan glanced around to make sure no one was listening. "They're moving us to the Que Son Valley for another operation."

The waitress returned with drinks. Ethan reached over and grabbed the young Vietnamese girl's butt. Steven lowered his head and shook it. *Damn, E still acts like he's seventeen.*

After the waitress left, Ethan continued, "Last month, we participated in a little operation called Blue Marlin. They loaded a bunch of us on boats, and the Navy boys took us up to Hoi An. We kicked the *shit* out of some VC, who didn't want anything at all to do with us. They disappeared pretty fast. We couldn't follow them, as our Navy boys were coming back to pick us up at a designated time."

Ethan continued, "We killed almost six hundred Viet Cong." He paused. "Yet, we lost forty-six of our own. Shouldn't have lost that many. The fighting was vicious."

"E, that's just about the biggest fighting we've heard of here. Did any South Vietnamese units participate?"

The waitress sat down another round of drinks at their table, Steven got a coffee and Ethan some kind of Irish Whiskey. "We caught the VC, attacked them from the sea so they didn't have their usual escape route."

This brought a smile to Steven's face. He'd been waiting for some engagement, any engagement of the Viet Cong. A US Marine victory was music to his ears. While Ethan enjoyed his whiskey, Steven enjoyed the story of the Marine battle victory. HUH RAH.

SAIGON
US EMBASSY

Edward Lansdale sat in the outside office visiting with Meredith. Lansdale leaned toward his secretary and asked, "Meredith, where are you from?"

She beamed. "My family is all from Boston. We're part of the Browns in the Brown Brothers Harriman."

Lansdale was surprised to learn her father was a member of *the* Brown family. They were obviously well-connected politically and socially. Which meant he had to watch his words, because the Brown, Harriman, and Lodge families were all tight. Lansdale smiled. Steven was supposed to tell him about things going on at the Embassy, but he'd have no way of knowing about those family connections. *I'm the only one who could understand how these elites of the world think. Hebert wouldn't have a clue how they all tie together.*

Meredith's intercom on her phone buzzed. She picked up the receiver. "Yes, Ambassador Lodge." She nodded and smiled at Lansdale. "The Ambassador will see you in his office.

Lansdale strolled in and sat down opposite the ambassador.

Lodge took off his glasses, placed them on his desk, and leaned back in his high-back leather chair. "How is everything going with our Pacification program? I need to keep developments in front of the President."

Lansdale couldn't believe it was already *their* program, no longer just *his* program—but maybe that was a good thing. Finally, someone in a higher position than him believed. "It's going well. Premier Ky is making pretty good progress. He says he has someone in mind, but until he has accepted the assignment, he won't divulge his name."

Lodge looked around the room. "What role will Minister Thang have?"

Lansdale smiled. "Figurehead, the man out in front. This new guy will be doing all the dirty work. Anyway, I have some bad news. You may already know it, but I didn't. Prime Minister Ky told me that according to his figures, the South Vietnamese government only controls twenty-five percent of the population today."

Lodge jumped forward, pounded his hand on the desk. "We know things have deteriorated here. Now, what can we do to overcome this?"

Lansdale bit his lower lip. "It gets worse. Ky says Thang told him it could take up to two years before their government can have control of fifty percent of their country. The people of the countryside don't believe in the government of generals, and the people don't feel like the government can keep them secure." Lansdale knew Lodge wanted results faster. "I'll have this under control soon. My men are working now. If the South Vietnamese see my teams having success, it will cause them to push harder, accomplish more."

Lodge shook his head. "I'm going to have a meeting with Colonel John Paul Vann. He has made several requests to be a part of our Pacification program. He has some ideas he wants to share about how we implement our program. As you know, he came back here in March as an official with the Agency for International Development. They sent him to the III Corps area."

Lansdale bristled. *Another individual who wants to run everything.* "I have read his reports. He has the same positions as we do on the ground troops, but he doesn't have a very good opinion of the preparedness of the South Vietnamese Army." *Lansdale hoped his assessment of Colonel Vann would impact Lodge's decision on bringing him on board.*

Lodge rubbed his chin.

"Vann wanted to help train the South Vietnamese Army, but got sidelined for some reason."

Lodge leaned forward. "I must continue to have positive news to send to Rusk. As you know, Washington is filled with officials seeking a military solution here."

Lansdale nodded. "Yes, Ambassador, I have experienced it for the past two years. You're the only one to really understand this program."

"When Westmoreland came over here, he told Johnson and McNamara he could win in just over a year." Lodge shook his head as he spoke.

Lansdale rubbed his chin. "But now he knows better. I heard he now says it will take him three and a half years, which will include a lot more troops than he has over here now."

Lodge sat quietly, and then finally replied, "Funny, the only two who understand the program are the two people who have lived among the South Vietnamese. Our time is short to succeed."

Lansdale relaxed a little. "Ambassador, we're going to succeed."

Vang Pao's Headquarters
Long Tieng, Laos

The helicopter swooped below the last set of jungle trees in the clearing that would make most men ill, but the pilot and Lieutenant Colonel Lucien Conein enjoyed the thrill of it. *I haven't had this much fun in a long time.* However, the same could not be said about Julian Romano. They buzzed over several of the soldiers standing guard on the runway at General Vang Pao's headquarters at Long Tieng, Laos, before landing. Before the blades stopped turning, Conein reached up to hold his Aussie Bush hat on top of his head, ducked down and jogged toward Vang Pao standing at the end of the runway. Conein nudged Vang Pao and whispered into his ear, "I don't think Romano had such a good flight. He may need to find a bathroom."

Julian Romano stood in the doorway of the helicopter. He grabbed hold of the safety rail and eased to the ground. He doubled-over, one hand holding his stomach and the other his mouth.

Vang Pao pointed toward the camp's latrine.

Romano walked barely a straight line past the two men, then started jogging, finally almost sprinting toward the tiny building.

Conein took off his hat and banged it on his leg, laughing so hard tears ran down his face. While Romano was in the latrine, Conein straightened up. "Guerini sent Romano to talk to you because you want to raise your prices. You do whatever you can to benefit you and your men. If you raise your prices, my cut goes up, so I don't care. I can tell you Shackley will be back here before too long to negotiate more for the CIA." Conein paused as he looked around. *I can't tell Vang Pao the CIA and the US Government shut down Shackley's drug network in Miami. I got to keep Vang Pao propped up until Shackley and Trafficante get their operation re-established.* Conein continued. "We'll just get Buell to help you all grow more."

Vang Pao nodded slightly.

Romano stumbled out of the bathroom with a little more color in his face.

Conein whispered, "We haven't talked. *Got it?*"

Vang Pao stood completely still.

Romano walked up to Vang Pao. "Atonine Guerini sent me to talk to you about some of your latest demands."

Vang Pao nodded. "Let's go to my office." He walked in front of the two larger white men.

Conein put his arm around Romano. "Glad you're feeling better. Now, let's go get some business done for General Guerini."

Romano almost stumbled, scuffing up his Bruno Magli's as they hurried to Vang Pao's headquarters.

The three men entered the office. CIA Agent Pop Buell was already seated around the large table with his feet up on the table. Conein strolled over and looked down at a Laotian map spread across the top. Vang Pao stepped around to the other side and reached for the map, but Conein slapped his big hand down, pushing it back to the table. "Tell me about your most recent battles with communist Pathot Lao and the North Vietnamese Army."

Vang Pao pointed at a spot on the map. "We must retake the Plaines des Jarres. *It's the only way* to have a platform to attack the Ho Chi Minh trail."

Romano interrupted Vang Pao. "If you can re-take the Plaines des Jarres, we can get our planes in there to pick up our poppies easier. Guerini doesn't like having to drop drums of poppies into the Gulf of Siam. We need better, safer access. Frankly, Guerini wanted me to come and find out why you want to increase your cut of the profits. With the fighting getting ready to increase in Vietnam, our ability to get these poppies out are going to become even more difficult. The Corsicans are in a turf war back in Italy. We don't—"

Vang Pao raised his right hand. "Romano, your family's problems are in Europe. There is no fighting going on around your homes. Please don't bore me with your small turf war stories. We need food and weapons. My soldiers are dying, and their families have needs. My costs are going up, my risks are going way up. Feel free to not buy—seek other sources. I'm confident I can find buyers at *my* prices. Now," Vang Pao paused and jutted his jaw, "I'm prepared to offer you more so you can make more."

Pop Buell spoke for the first time. "Romano, we're working with the general to increase crop production. We've been able to increase production each year for the last several years. I think we can continue that trend. You're still getting your product and making your heroin and opium. What the hell is your problem? You're raising your prices—your users will pay more. You and I both know that." Buell pulled a revolver from his belt and spun it around like an Old West cowboy.

Romano looked at Conein. "Lucien, whose side are you on?"

Conein took a step toward him and got in his face. "I brought you here to resolve a business dispute. I heard a solution in what Vang Pao said. You must not have been listening?" He pointed toward Buell. "You heard him tell you what his capabilities are and will be. Now, I got nothing in this, but I'm a good listener. Perhaps you should take this back to Guerini. I know you don't want to go home and tell him you couldn't resolve anything. Do you?"

Romano tried to step out of Conein's space, then looked at Buell and frowned at Vang Pao. "Okay, *okay*. I'll recommend this deal." He stuck out his hand. "The sooner you can produce more product to help us offset our costs, the better."

Vang Pao stepped forward and took his hand. "We're going to request the US government try to get us some support to retake the Plaines des Jarres, but it's going to take some time."

Conein nodded. "Atonine Guerini will be satisfied with this deal. You did good, Julian." He put his arm around Romano.

Romano squinted. "Let's go so I can get back to Hong Kong."

Conein looked back at Vang Pao. "I will carry your message for more aid and military support back to my boss. Do you have any other requests?"

Vang Pao shook his head.

Conein took his arm off Romano and pointed out the door. "Let's go. I'll try to calm down our helicopter pilot this time. You know these cowboys are hard to control."

As Conein walked, he realized the loss of the Plaines des Jarres was also going to impact the CIA's 118A Strategic Intelligence Network. He would have to brief Shackley, who would have to pass on this information to

Marcello and Trafficante. Since they were trying to build their network and had cheaper avenues for supplies, they would easily absorb these price increases. *Ah, it's been a very profitable day.* As he breathed a sigh of relief, Conein knew a day of reckoning was coming. His time in the middle of the heroin business was running short.

CHAPTER SEVEN

DECEMBER 6, 1965
US EMBASSY - SAIGON

Major Hebert sat in Meredith's office waiting to see the ambassador. Meredith looked up from her typing and asked, "I understand you're getting some leave time and going home for Christmas?"

Steven was very excited to go home and see his family, but before he could even open his mouth to answer, Meredith continued her own one-sided conversation. "I'm going home this Christmas, too. Our family has a big traditional Boston Christmas. I missed it so much last year. All the Brown families and their friends gather and walk to Christmas Eve Mass, then return home for a big party."

As Meredith continued to talk, Steven drifted into thoughts of his own family. He was startled by Meredith slamming her hand down hard on the table. "You haven't heard a single word I've said, have you?"

Just then, Ambassador Lodge buzzed Meredith to send in the Major. Steven marched into the ambassador's office, who motioned for him to be seated.

Henry Cabot Lodge wrote something on a yellow pad. Finally, he looked up. "I have a security assignment for you. You will go to the Tan Son Nhut and pick up Congressman David S. King and bring him back here. Part of his trip will be high profile—the other will be top secret. He may want to do a little press conference. Then, very early in the morning, you will escort the Congressman to the Metropole Hotel for a 'meet and greet' with some enlisted men at breakfast. Afterward, escort him on to Tan Son Nhut for his flight back to the States. Is that clear, Major?"

Steven acknowledged his orders and left.

Steven drove across town to pick up the Utah Congressman. He wondered how Tao was recovering. The CIA had wanted to send him back to the States, but he refused to go. Steven had stopped by the hospital to visit with him, but since he'd been discharged from the hospital, Lansdale had kept Steven too busy with menial assignments to catch up with Tao. Steven was beginning to lose his patience with Lansdale and his own lack of quality assignments.

When he arrived at the airport, the plane was scheduled to land at any minute from Honolulu. The last thing that Steven needed was time to think.

Within a few minutes, the plane carrying the congressman parked on the tarmac. Steven looked around before walking up to him to show his military

ID. The congressman followed Steven back to the vehicle. No presser. The ride back to the Embassy was quiet.

As they walked down the hallway to the ambassador's office, Congressman King still didn't say a word. Steven wondered if he was just that quiet. When they walked into Meredith's office, she advised the congressman to go on in to see the ambassador. Steven heard Lansdale's voice. He remembered Lodge telling him the congressman had come for a top secret meeting, but he didn't know Lansdale was going to be a part of it.

Steven dismissed himself from Meredith's office. He desperately wanted to listen through the door but resisted the temptation.

Edward Lansdale glanced at Ambassador Lodge as Utah Congressman David S. King detailed the plan of the US Government's new agency, the Joint United States Public Affairs Office (JUSPAO), a combination of several different agencies. King had been sent by President Johnson to advise the Embassy and Lansdale of this change. The idea was to combine military, US Information Agency, and several departments within the Department of State. Lansdale leaned back in his chair and dropped back his head. Before he could even kick off his mission, Johnson was meddling into his affairs. This new agency was to service public affairs, public diplomacy, and psychological operations—Lansdale's mission. When Lodge questioned the President's goals and objectives, King reiterated that he believed this agency would help the South Vietnamese people.

Lansdale liked what he heard, but he was certain that if the politicians were trying to get involved in the psy-ops, they would only screw it up. *What do politicians know about this? They're just usurping the authority of those who know. Typical politicians. Damn Johnson, McNamara, and Rusk are meddlers.* Lansdale was hoping Lodge would step into this mess and try to set some ground rules. When King got done with his presentation to Lodge and Lansdale, he said, "In conclusion, 'The real war, however, is being fought not for the bodies but the minds of the Viet Cong. The work of JUSPAO is no less significant because it receives so little recognition. In my opinion, it's our ultimate weapon.'"

Lansdale couldn't believe his ears. *Our government wants to rehabilitate the Viet Cong. This is just crazy thinking. They are communists.*

Lodge looked over at Lansdale. "How did you, or should I say, our government, come up with the idea to take over the psychological operation?" He pointed back and forth between himself and Lansdale. "We're much better prepared and briefed on running this. General Lansdale is the preeminent expert in this field, and I would be a close second."

Lansdale was flattered by the compliment. *I wondered when Lodge made the list.*

Congressman King squirmed in his chair and cleared his throat. "In March of this year, Carl Rowan, from the US Information Agency, and General Harold Johnson, Army Chief of Staff, came over here and prepared a study. They concluded there were many difficulties and inefficiencies of uncoordinated psychological operation."

Lodge looked at Lansdale again and frowned. "Okay, but neither the General—" He pointed at Lansdale. "Nor myself were here at that time. We're here now. With all due respect, this is our operation."

King leaned forward. "I have my orders. Now you and the General have yours. The President sent me over here to deliver the message. Now, you all can work with us to make this better, or—"

Lansdale got up from his chair before the congressman could finish his statement. "Ambassador, Congressman, I have an appointment I can't miss. Thank you for including me."

Lansdale glanced at Meredith as he walked past her desk and straight out the door. In the hallway, he watched Major Hebert walking away. *That son-of-a-bitch was listening into our conversation. I'll remember that.*

Major Steven Hebert was called into the ambassador's office and stood at attention upon entering.

Ambassador Lodge looked up at the Major with a disgusted look on his face. "Major Hebert, you're to take Congressman King over to the Metropole Hotel early in the morning." Lodge looked at the Congressman. "Please give the Major a time you wish to be there."

Congressman King turned around and smiled briefly at Steven. "I assume the men will be down to breakfast at six. I would like to be there at five-thirty."

"Yes, sir. We should leave at zero-four-forty-five, Congressman."

Ambassador Lodge looked at the Congressman and nodded. "That will be all, Major."

Steven exited back into Meredith's office. Lansdale had barely spoken with him since he'd returned to Vietnam. Steven wanted to get out of the Embassy, but it was going to take some cooperation between the military, Ambassador Lodge, and Lansdale in order to make it happen. Nothing was going to be easy, even if everyone was on board.

CHAPTER EIGHT

DECEMBER 7, 1965
WASHINGTON DC - WHITE HOUSE

President Johnson sat at his desk in the oval office. Dean Rusk and Robert McNamara sat quietly on the couch. Johnson couldn't believe the developments of the day at the U.N. The Soviet representative had made a speech on the general assembly floor blasting the US over their bombing of North Vietnam. In his speech, he reiterated the Soviets position that they had no interest in requesting nor convening a new Geneva Convention on Vietnam. To make matters worse, the Soviet representative continually referred to the North Vietnamese as patriots, while calling the Americans the aggressors. Johnson was livid.

The Soviets were playing the U.N. to its fullest. All the while, they had increased their support with more funds and the newest weapons for North Vietnam.

Johnson steamed for a minute. "I can't believe those lying sons-a-bitches get up there, lie through their teeth, and everybody in the general assembly stands there and accepts it as gospel. We need the U.N. on our side. Damn."

Johnson had hopes that a trip by a British diplomat to Moscow would get the North Vietnamese to come to the negotiating table regarding peace talks, but this too failed miserably. Moreover, after his plane landed in London, the British diplomat told a gathering of the press he didn't believe North Vietnam would come to the table even if the US stopped bombing. Johnson felt like he'd no business making that statement to the press.

Johnson wanted to get a settlement and get out of Vietnam. But he wanted to do it his way. There were mid-term elections coming up next year, and he wanted to continue to pursue his domestic agenda to end poverty in the United States. He even had a name for it—the Great Society.

Just last week, McNamara had briefed the President that recent troop increases would result in an increase of the US casualty rate to as much as one thousand deaths per month. It was a fact that hadn't slipped by Johnson. These numbers would likely impact the elections.

McNamara opened his briefcase and pulled out a piece of paper. "According to military intelligence, the North Vietnamese have been moving more and more supplies and men along the Ho Chi Minh trail into the South, particularly since we introduced ground troops to the theater."

Johnson pounded his hand on the desk. "Tell me something I don't know."

McNamara opened both arms palms up. "I know for a fact General Westmoreland is going to ask you for permission to go into Laos and Cambodia with ground troops."

The President's face flushed bright red. He stood up and walked around his desk. He had a meeting coming up with Westmoreland, but the constant request for more troops was wearing on him.

Rusk finally spoke up. "Mr. President, we know the Chinese control northern Laos. We can't go into Northern North Vietnam or into Laos, as it might be misinterpreted."

Johnson had placed himself between a rock and hard place, believing he had to tiptoe around the Communist Chinese. They were sending limited financial support but a large number of supplies. He was afraid if he became too aggressive against the North, it would bring the Chinese Red Army into the Conflict. Just like Korea.

0445

DECEMBER 7, 1965

US EMBASSY

SAIGON

Steven walked to the motor pool and got into the diplomatic vehicle. He was to meet Congressman King in front of the Embassy. Steven's revised security plans called for him to load diplomats behind the building. Once the Congressman was in the vehicle, they drove off toward the Metropole Hotel.

On the drive, the Congressman was silent, watching as the streets and the buildings passed by.

As they pulled up to the hotel, Steven took a moment to observe the hustle and bustle of the early morning before he exited the vehicle. *Check my watch. 0530.* He walked to the billet in front of the hotel, presented his military identification to the military policeman on duty. The MP carefully examined them, handed them back, and saluted the major. Steven opened the door and escorted the congressman into the hotel. He walked with Congressman King to the large dining area now armed with several additional MPs who were going to take over security. The congressman ordered Steven to return at eleven o'clock.

Steven returned to his vehicle. He drove off to Tao's Honda Moped Shop. A huge explosion sounded behind him. From the direction of the hotel. Steven spun the vehicle around in the middle of the street and sped back to the hotel. As he approached, he heard gunfire. When the hotel came into view, the front two stories of the structure were ravaged.

He focused on a gun fight between an MP and several VC as he continued his approach. He stopped and pulled out his handgun.

One of the MPs threw down his shotgun and pulled out his nine-millimeter hand gun and started firing. Steven got a fix on the spot and sprinted toward it as the VC fired machine guns at the MP. When Steven was close enough, he fired at the two VC. They turned their machine guns toward him and fired just as he ducked into a doorway.

What sounded like a hand grenade went off a couple of blocks away. Machine gunfire struck up and down the doorway where Steven was trying to get some cover from the gunfire. Several Marines emerged with guns firing. The VC jumped into a car on the street and drove off as gunfire rained down on them.

Steven ran to assess the situation at the hotel. As he approached, he noticed an MP lying outside the billet with blood coming from his arm. Several of the other soldiers came over and, with Steven's assistance, they got him up. "Get some men out here to secure this place," Steven shouted. "They may be back with more friends."

Steven sprinted through what used-to-be the front door. He climbed over chunks of concrete and rebar in the direction he'd last seen Congressman King. People ran helter-skelter and wounded lay on the floor. In less than a minute, he stood next to the congressman, who was unharmed, though a little dazed. Steven relieved the two MPs guarding him. "Come on," Steven said to the congressman, "let's get you out of here to safety."

A couple of the other diplomats and a few ranking officers joined Steven.

"You must leave," one said.

King stood with his hands squarely on his hips. "You will provide me with security. I am staying to help with the recovery operation."

Steven glanced around at the others who had gathered. "We need to leave, and leave now."

King looked at Steven for a brief moment, then walked away.

Steven followed close by, then slipped in front of the congressman. "If I am responsible for your security, you must go get checked out to make sure you're okay. If you are, then we can return and you can help with the recovery."

King reluctantly agreed. They crossed the street to the Navy hospital to get a quick examination. Steven told the congressman he was going to check in with Ambassador Lodge.

As they walked, Steven scanned the surroundings area. He wasn't convinced the VC attack was over. Snipers could be on the rooftops or cars with shooters were still real possibilities. In the middle of the street, Steven looked down and thrust his arm out, stopping the Congressman There was a claymore mine in the street. "Clear the area," Steven shouted. "Secure the street." He froze as he pointed down. "*Mine, mine.*"

Several other soldiers ran over to where he stood. When the first soldier arrived, he accessed the situation and shouted, "Get an explosive expert over here immediately!"

Steven grabbed the congressman under his arm. "Come on. Let's get you into the Navy hospital." As soon as Steven got the attention of a Naval physician, he went to a desk phone and called Meredith's desk. Immediately, she put him through to Ambassador Lodge. When the Ambassador came on the phone, Steven said. "As I am sure you've heard, there was a VC attack at the Metropole Hotel, but Congressman King is okay. I have him at the Navy hospital getting checked out."

"Get him out of there as soon as he is done there and back over here."

Steven looked down at the ground, as he knew what he was about to say would set Lodge off. "King wants to stay here and help with the recovery process."

There was a long pause. Finally, Ambassador spoke. "Okay, then get the congressman out of there as soon as possible. There are more bomb threats throughout Saigon. Let him get his photo ops," he said. "Then he'll be ready to go."

Steven walked back into the emergency room. The nurse pointed him toward the waiting room. Within a few minutes, Congressman King emerged with the doctor, "Hey, Major Hebert, come over here while this nurse takes a picture of me and the doctor." Congressman King pointed at a nurse holding a camera. Steven shook his head. Before they exited, Steven went outside first and again made sure the streets, roofs, and windows were secure before they walked across the street.

The congressman seemed genuinely concerned about people as he moved among the soldiers and officials to makes sure all was well. His standard question was "where were you when all hell broke loose?" The congressman had no problem maneuvering over the rubble that once made up the front of the hotel.

CHAPTER NINE

DECEMBER 7, 1965

US EMBASSY - SAIGON

Edward Lansdale had to take time away from his management of the US Mission Liaison Group, commonly referred to as the Pacification program. Today, Lansdale was meeting Conein and the Corsican representative at one of Conein's favorite hangouts, the Continental Hotel bar. Lansdale wasn't to bring any security with him, as Conein had promised to provide him with all the security he would need so as not to make the Corsican representative nervous. Lansdale had thought of having either Tao or Hebert join him, but at the last minute, decided it wasn't a good idea to cross his old friend.

He parked directly in front of the hotel to make his entrance as much in the open as possible so there would be plenty of people around. Lansdale strolled into the bar and looked around. Wherever the commotion was, that was where he would find Conein. At a table in the far corner, he heard that laugh. He was seated with two men and a woman. Undoubtedly, Conein was telling stories to keep them "entertained." He gestured for Lansdale to come over. As Lansdale walked over, he saw two more of Conein's men leaning on the bar watching him.

When Lansdale walked up to the table, Conein waved the two men sitting with him to leave. The woman remained. Conein pointed to a chair opposite the woman. Lansdale sat.

"Edward Lansdale," Conein said under his breath, "I want to introduce you to Helene. She would like to speak to you."

Lansdale reached his hand out to Helene, but the attractive French-Vietnamese wearing a low-cut blouse that exposed the tops of her large breasts made no move to accept his offer. He pulled back his hand. "So you wanted to meet me to discuss what, exactly?"

Helene leaned forward, her breasts resting on the table. "Atonine Guerini wanted me to look you in the eye and get your word that you would no longer try to undermine our operations here in the mountains," she said in a low voice. "Well?"

Lansdale jutted his jaw, glanced at Conein, then nodded. "You have my word. I have my hands full with the mess in Vietnam that I have to straighten out. Your operations are not why my government sent me here." Lansdale pointed at Conein. "I can't believe Guerini would not take Lucien's word, but if that's how you want to do business, I have said it to your face. Now, I expect you to tell Guerini to call off the contract on me, so that I can get my job done." Lansdale poked his finger at the table repeatedly. "You tell him that for me."

Helene looked over at Conein, who nodded in agreement. "Guerini, has authorized me to agree to those terms, Mr. Lansdale. You don't screw us, we won't kill you."

Lansdale put both hands on the table top. "We're done here."

Helene looked over at Conein, who nodded in agreement. Without another word, Helene got up and left.

Lansdale pushed up from the table.

Conein raised his hand. "I got something we need to discuss. Sit back down."

Lansdale pressed his lips tightly together. "Now, what?" He sat down.

Conein looked around to make sure no one was within ear shot. "We have a little problem with your friend, Daniel Ellsberg."

Lansdale leaned forward. "What the hell? The man hasn't been here very long. How could he have pissed off anybody already?"

Conein drew a deep breath. "Daniel is messing around with one of the Corsican's mistresses, and he doesn't like it. We don't need any more trouble. These men get real up tight when someone is messing with their women. Even their mistresses."

Lansdale looked at Conein. "He's your friend, too. If you want to deliver that message, I suggest you deliver it yourself. And if the Corsican were a real man, he could deliver it himself rather than ask you to be his messenger."

Conein said, "I'm just trying to protect Ellsberg. This could get a little messy. I had to threaten to kill the man if he went after Ellsberg."

Lansdale laughed as he got up from the table. "I got to go meet Ambassador Lodge. I don't have time for this Corsican mistress shit." He got up and walked out of the bar.

Lansdale strolled into the ambassador's office and sat down opposite Henry Cabot Lodge.

Lodge took off his glasses, placed them on his desk, and leaned back in his high-back leather chair. "How is everything going with our Pacification program? I still need to keep developments in front of the President, particularly with them trying to...." His voice tailed off without finishing his sentence.

Lansdale was concerned about the President's micro-management style, which was already showing with his stepping into the Psy-Ops program. "Premier Ky has selected his man to take over the program for the South. I haven't met him yet. I sent my top analyst, Daniel Ellsberg, out to do some surveys. The VC have set ambushes outside the capital along the eastern border of the Hau Nghia, which is only thirty miles west of Saigon. They have made that road almost impassable. The Long An Province Chief told Ellsberg that out of the 220,000 residents, as many as 200,000 are controlled by the VC."

Lodge nodded. "Unbelievable." He thought for a minute. "Isn't Cu Chi in that area?"

"Yes, sir. Cu Chi is a VC hub in that province. I have it from a good source that there are a series of tunnels going into Cambodia, which I'm sure ties into the Ho Chi Minh trail."

Lansdale relaxed a little. "Ambassador, we're going to succeed. I have put one of my top intelligence men covering the area along the Cambodian border."

Lodge wrote on his notepad.

Lansdale fidgeted in the chair. *Why am I sitting here while he's writing? I got more important things to do.*

Finally, Lodge put down his pen, picked up the phone and buzzed Meredith. "Please get Major Hebert and have him step in here."

Lansdale rubbed his chin. "Do you need me here any longer?"

"Yes."

Within a few moments, Major Hebert entered the Ambassador's office, then took a seat next to Lansdale.

Lodge spoke, "In light of the attacks throughout Saigon, I want to discuss security for our Embassy and for our personnel."

Lansdale glanced at Hebert and Lodge. *Why am I here for this? It has nothing to do with me.*

Steven drew a deep breath. "Ambassador Lodge, permission to speak freely, sir?"

Lodge sat up in his chair, folded his hands on his desk. "Go ahead, Major."

Steven looked at Lansdale, then began. "Ambassador, we have too many South Vietnamese working at the Embassy. Some of them are drivers, workers, and so forth. I can't help but believe that some of these individuals are spies for or could be Viet Cong. At the moment, I believe that's the biggest issue here regarding security."

Lodge glanced at Lansdale then frowned at Steven. "Our Department of State absolutely demands that we do it. I have no control. It's a public relations' item. You'd think I'd have control over the Embassy, but I don't.

Frankly, Major, I have brought this up, and it has been shot down on a number of occasions."

Steven's jaw twitched.

Lansdale nudged Steven, sending him the silent message, *Don't say any more.*

The Ambassador said, "Ed, I wanted the Major in here, so that both of you would hear this. If you need any extra security while you're moving around, you get your soldier here—" The ambassador pointed at Hebert. "—to provide it for you. Your role is too critical, and I expect the Viet Cong to make attempts on your life."

Lansdale looked at the ambassador. "Thank you, sir. I may need to take you up on that. The more successful we are, the larger the target on my back grows. But for right now, I'm fine."

DECEMBER 7, 1965
WASHINGTON DC

President Johnson sat on the couch opposite Robert McNamara. They were discussing the mounting resistance of the youth in America. On November 27 an estimated 35,000 participants started at the White House, marching and chanting anti-war slogans before heading to a rally at the base of the Washington Monument. At the moment, the youth were at odds with the general public, but the situation could change.

McNamara looked him in the eye. "Mr. President, the North Vietnamese believe the war will be a long one, that time is their ally, and that their staying power is superior to ours. What if they manage to drag out this war? The youth are turning against this pretty quickly."

The President stood and paced behind the couch, back and forth. "Are our new, tougher laws regarding burning draft cards having any impact?"

"It's still a big deal at these protests," McNamara said. "I can only hope the new thousand dollar fine and up to five-year prison sentence will prevent the act from becoming a fad. But that law has only been in place since August."

Johnson continued to pace. "Have you and the Joint Chiefs come up with a list of North Vietnamese bombing targets?"

McNamara reached into his briefcase. "Yes, Mr. President, General McConnell and I have agreed to our targets in North Vietnam. Naturally, McConnell wanted to hit more than I would approve. I don't believe the press would have given you good reviews had we gone with all his targets. And he feels like the press was unfair with him in his target selection in Operation Rolling Thunder."

Johnson leaned over the couch. "Hand me the list."

"Yes, Mr. President." McNamara passed it over his shoulder.

Johnson snatched the list out of McNamara's hand, then headed for his desk. Johnson put his glasses on and intently studied it. He nodded. "I approve Operation Tiger Hound. I really like the idea of including more branches of the military. Hopefully, even the Vietnamese and Laotians can contribute some. Let's get started, ASAP. I really want to ramp up the bombing with the B-52s on the Ho Chi Minh trail. Let's send a message to North Vietnam. We've got mid-terms coming up. Vietnam can't be the central issue."

DECEMBER 9, 1965
WASHINGTON DC

Rita Sullivan couldn't stop shivering on the walk to her apartment from the closest bus stop. Her raincoat kept the miserable drizzle out, but the cold penetrated. *What a dreary night. I'm so cold.*

A car pulled up beside her and slowed down. Rita glanced out of the corner of her eye. A white Chevy Impala. Despite being in high heels, she ran. Luckily, she was just a couple of steps away from the stairs leading up to her apartment. She got inside her apartment and locked the door. Her heart pounded in her ears. *Was she just being paranoid, or was that the white Chevy Impala that had followed Keeton? Or was it just a white car?*

Anxiety had plagued Rita. She had to reply to both *Life Magazine* and the WFAN TV station by Monday morning about whether she was accepting their job offers. Her last major column covered the protest in

Washington DC by the Students for a Democratic Society, commonly known as the SDS. It included quotes from their president, Carl Oglesby. Plus, she'd been able to interview Oglesby. While other news agencies covered the protest, her column had drawn the most national attention and triggered the new job offers.

The WFAN interview had gone very well. The owner had big plans. While it was currently a radio station only, the station manager said their owner was buying a local TV station that was not yet on the air. The owner was going to put the TV station up, and Rita was offered their investigative reporter role with a chance to work her way into an anchor position.

The *Life Magazine* interview had gone well also. The executive editor had promised her a column at least every other issue, which amounted to once a month. She would be allowed to present her idea for a column. If approved, she would be responsible for her own research for the column. *Life* was one of the top magazines in the country with a large circulation.

Finally, Rita calmed down. The glass of wine from her refrigerator had done wonders. She let her hair out of its bun and ran her fingers through her hair to detangle.

The phone rang. *Was it her stalker? Were they starting to call her again? She had just seen the white car, so they knew she was home.* Slowly, she picked up the phone. "Hello."

"Hey, blondie, this is Ed Boland."

She relaxed. Ed was her old friend from the *Washington Star News.* "Ed, how are you?"

"I'm well. Heard through the grapevine you're looking for a career move."

"Who told you that?"

There was a slight pause, then Ed replied. "I got a call today—checking your job history."

Rita drew in a breath. Word sure did get around fast. *Wonder if my employer back in Eugene, Oregon, knows I'm job hunting?*

Boland continued, "I know you're talking to *Life* and WFAN."

What was done was done. She may as well tap into his expertise. "I'm torn between the two opportunities." She gave him the details of each.

Boland listened, then said, "Both are good opportunities to grow, but the TV station is a little risky."

Rita had thought the same thing about the risk, but the exposure might be better for her career. She tipped up the glass for the last drops of wine. "I turned down an uninspiring offer from *Newsweek* last summer."

"Yes, but that was just because you were going to the Crump trial. It probably was a good idea to turn it down."

A chill went down Rita's spine. *How did Ed Boland know she attended the Crump trial? She hadn't noticed a reporter from their paper in the courtroom.*

"Petit wanted me to ask you if you'd be interested in coming back to the *Star*," Boland continued. "He said he'd work with you. Bring you back and put you with your old cohorts, Miriam Ottenberg and John Sherwood. You can continue to cover anti-war protests or Vietnam. Your choice."

"If Petit was serious, why didn't he call me? I'm sure he's still a jackass. I left because of him and his attitude toward me. He's just fishing, and you can tell him I said so."

"No, blondie," Boland replied. "When he told me, I asked if he would let me make the call. I told him you and I had been close at one time."

"Goodbye, Ed. This isn't real, and if it *were* real, it wouldn't be good."
Rita hung up the phone.

Rita fumed. Johnathon Petit was a plain jackass. He was just fishing. As she sat trying to cool off again, she grabbed a second glass of wine—just like the old days at the University of South Carolina with her friend Meredith Brown. She put her feet on the couch. *We used to have so much fun finding a couple of frat boys and going dancing.* Her friend had gone to work for the state department with the idea of saving the world. She was a pioneer woman climbing the ladder to new heights in Saigon. *I wonder what Meredith does now to relax? Is she safe? I don't believe this is what she signed up for—explosions going off all around her.* Rita had lost count how many had occurred in Saigon. She'd been so wrapped up in her own job hunting, she'd forgotten the peril her best friend was in. As she finished her last sip of wine, she decided to write a letter to Meredith.

CHAPTER TEN

DECEMBER 20, 1965

NEW ORLEANS AIRPORT - NEW ORLEANS, LOUISIANA

Steven Hebert walked through the airport toward baggage claim. He saw the sports section of an old newspaper. The headline caught his attention—"Sayers Runs Wild." He picked it up and read as he walked. Gale Sayers had scored six touchdowns for the Chicago Bears in a 61-20 win over the San Francisco 49ers. The game had been played on December 12. Talk about old news. Steven had started following the Bears after they drafted both Sayers and Dick Butkus in the same year. He paused for a moment to finish reading the article. He had plenty of time to kill while waiting on his duffle bag to get to baggage claim. When he finished, he walked over to the large waste container and stuffed the newspaper. It was good to be back on US soil. It had been almost a year since he'd heard from his mother and brother.

Steven watched those hustling through the airport. It was decorated for Christmas, people carried large packages, and families greeted one another.

He walked up to the baggage claim to pick up his duffle bag—it was easy to spot his bag mixed in with the hard suitcases of the other passengers. He'd decided to take a commercial flight once he got to Hawaii. He could've taken a military flight, but it was faster to get State-side going commercial. As he waited, several of the other passengers either exchanged a nod, smiled, or even wished him a Merry Christmas.

Once he had his duffle bag in hand, he hopped into a cab. His initial idea was to go to a hotel on the south side of New Orleans. On the cab ride, Steven decided he would be ahead to go to the Naval Air Station at Bell Chasse, Louisiana, outside New Orleans. It would give him a head start for his morning drive down to Labadieville. Steven needed to make sure his mom's place was safe before bringing her and brother Jeremiah home.

He grabbed some food at the PX, then went and bedded down at the base. Steven tossed and turned all night in bed, he struggled to get any sleep.

The next morning before daylight, Steven picked up a jeep from the motor pool then off to his mother's home. As morning broke, intermittent fog interrupted the low and gray sky. He passed few houses, but almost all of them had some sort of Christmas decoration out in front or on the roof. Despite the weather, the drive was relaxing. As he neared his mother's house, rain started to fall. He parked in front of his old home.

He walked around outside. No evidence anyone had been around, obviously including the return of Jeremiah's kidnappers. It looked safe to bring his family home. So, he continued on to the bay to rent a fan boat. As he drove, he turned on the radio. This far out of New Orleans, all he could pick up was powerful AM stations. It was either Top 40 or country music. He listened to the Top 40 for a while. He bounced around on his seat to "Wooly Bully" by Sam the Sham and The Pharaohs, then "Crying in the Chapel" by Elvis, and "Ticket to Ride" by the Beatles. Just as he was about to flip the dial, "Help Me, Rhonda" by the Beach Boys came on. Tim would be cranking that up if he were here. Steven let out a big belly laugh as he thought of his friend back in Vietnam. When the song was over, he turned the dial trying to find some New Orleans blues, but he was too far out in the country, so he turned it off.

Steven pulled into the parking lot above the dock. An elderly black gentleman sat in a tiny, three-sided building with a fifty-five gallon drum in front with a fire. He stood and talked to the old man for a few minutes about the hunting and fishing this time of year in the bayou. How many people had come this way over the last year? With the old man's answers to these questions, Steven knew his family was still safe.

He boarded his fan boat and was off into Terrebonne Bay toward Uncle Jake's home. As he pulled away from the dock in the thick fog, he immediately broke into his father's favorite song—and now his favorite song—"Dream a little Dream of Me."

The conversation with the old man on the dock took him back to the days of his youth when his father would take him out on one of the trips that would turn into a life lesson. Steven didn't appreciate them as much then as he appreciated those stories and memories now. They had prepared him for life. His father had wisdom and knowledge he'd gained from his days as an IRS investigative agent and later as a New Orleans police detective. The biggest lesson Steven learned from his father was that everybody makes mistakes, but cheaters are usually lazy and make bigger mistakes looking for short cuts.

Steven piloted the fan boat up to the dock at Uncle Jake's shack. He was met immediately by his uncle—carrying a shotgun. Steven put up his arms as he shouted out, "Uncle Jake, it's Steven! Put on your glasses so you can shoot straighter, old man."

His uncle lowered the shotgun. He laughed and cussed almost at the same time. He gave Steven and arm up to the dock and then put his arm around Steven's shoulder. Jeremiah and his mother LaBelle came out of the shack to greet him.

Steven ran over and hugged his mother, then his brother. "Are you all ready to go home?"

Tears filled LaBelle's eyes. "Oh, Steven," she said, over and over.

Jeremiah thrusted his fist in the air.

"Hey, big brother, I'm glad you came now. I want to go back to college," Jeremiah said. "I think I want to go to Howard University in Washington DC."

Steven was smiling. They all walked toward the old shack. Steven told them to get their stuff gathered up, and they could leave soon. In the hour it took for them to get everything ready, Steven visited with his uncle.

Within two hours, Steven was on his fan boat with his mother and brother, plus their belongings. He ran the fan boat a little slower on their trip back across the bayou with little conversation. He wanted to make sure his elderly mother had a safe ride to the mainland.

When Steven docked the fan boat, the old black man was gone. *That's very strange. As long as I've been coming here, that old man has sat in the three-walled structure in front of the fifty-five gallon drum. Or he was always around.*

Steven glanced around as he carried all the baggage to the jeep. He was concerned, but he didn't want to let on to his mother or brother. As soon as they were driving, the chatter in the jeep became almost too much to handle.

"Are you sure we're safe at home now?" his mother asked.

Steven glanced away from the road to look at his mother. "I've checked it out. Everything is fine. Otherwise, I wouldn't have come to get you."

"I can't wait to get the house decorated," his mother said. "Steven, will you take me to the store to get some food?"

Jeremiah pounded the backseat of the Jeep. "While y'all are doing that, I'm going to call my friends around Labadieville—plus call Howard University to find out about enrolling this coming spring."

The sun was about to set when Steven pulled into the driveway. Jeremiah sprung from the jeep quickly. Steven went around to the back of the Jeep, pulled out his mother's stuff, and carried it into the house. He took one more trip around, not only was he concerned about Jeremiah's kidnappers, Carlos Marcello's boys, but in the back of his mind, he was concerned about his own problem with the Corsicans.

Steven's mother walked into the house and immediately went to the broom closet to start cleaning. "Just put my things on the bed," she called.

"This place needs tidied up a bit. And then we need to go find a Christmas tree."

AFTERNOON

DECEMBER 21, 1965

CABINET ROOM IN THE WHITE HOUSE

Secretary of Defense Robert McNamara glanced up at President Johnson, seated at the head of the large table in the cabinet room of the White House. The President read over his report from his most recent trip to South Vietnam. This was McNamara's second meeting of the day with the President. While the President read, McNamara huddled quietly at the other end of the table talking with Secretary of State Dean Rusk and Jack Valenti, who had the unofficial responsibility of "handling" the Republican leadership in Congress. Earlier, the President had requested the second meeting to brainstorm what to do about Vietnam. McNamara believed he knew what was coming in this meeting. *Discuss General Westmoreland's strategy for victory in Vietnam and why he'd lost his patience with the turmoil on the Pacification program in South Vietnam. At the moment, there was a lot of confusion over which version to support—the US or the South Vietnamese.*

President Johnson laid down the report, as he looked at McNamara. "I assume from this report you're unsatisfied with the current Pacification program's progress in South Vietnam?" He took off his glasses and tossed them on the pile of papers. "I don't have any faith in the counterinsurgency or Pacification program, whatever the hell they call it."

Rusk closed the report he'd just glanced over. "I don't think there's been any change in the last two years. Even with all our commitment to more troops, more civilian services, more CIA operations. Nothing."

The President shook his head. "I had high hopes we could resolve some issues with all the confusion over there regarding this Pacification program. It's not working. Lansdale and Lodge aren't getting the job done. I think I'm going to have to put my people in charge. That's what I should have done in the beginning."

Rusk leaned back in his chair. "I got the impression that Westmoreland believed in Lodge and Lansdale's Pacification program. Remember, even he said back in September that this was a political war as well as a military war."

"Westmoreland does, but where do you start?" McNamara asked. "The people of the countryside are being terrorized by the Viet Cong. Nobody is safe. These intelligence reports show the VC are in control of over half of South Vietnam and they have added an estimated 35,000 more troops along the Ho Chi Minh trail." He chuckled. "Westmoreland has a funny way of looking at it. He calls their North army regiment the 'bully boys with crowbars trying to tear down the house'—wherein South Vietnam—he calls the guerillas and the political fighters the 'termites.' He believes he has to drive out the conventional forces first."

Valenti looked at each of the three men, then asked, "Do you have any feedback from the Vietnam Coordinating Committee? Weren't they doing a study on this program?"

Rusk nodded. "Harvard Professor Henry Kissinger prepared a report after he returned from Saigon. He believes there has been little integration of the US programs—US AID is ensnarled in this web. The entire system must be overhauled with a central power overseeing it. Kissinger thinks the program should be run out of the Embassy to get the cooperation of Ambassador Lodge."

McNamara nodded. "The South Vietnamese leadership is paying little attention to Lansdale. He doesn't seem to have the influence over the new leadership like he did over the old guard. I would've thought if Lansdale still had any clout, they would all be seeking his advice. I'll tell you this, these new leaders seem to be gravitating toward US organizations that have money—and Lansdale has no money to offer. Therefore, they see him as having no power."

President Johnson rubbed his mouth as he sat there slowly nodding. "I think we replace Lansdale with Assistant Ambassador William Porter. This will keep Lodge on board. We move Lansdale to a position where he liaisons between the Embassy, President Nguyen Van Thieu and Premier Nguyen Cao Ky. That will give him something to do."

"I like it," Rusk said. "Everybody should have to answer to Porter. Lodge will think he's still in control, but we'll know every minute what's going on."

Johnson looked at McNamara. "Well, any opinions on my proposal to stop the bombing of the North on Christmas Day? Should get me some good press."

McNamara bit his lower lip and drew a deep breath. "I don't know. What will we gain?"

Rusk replied, "The press should view this favorably. There can't be many valued targets left in the designated areas."

McNamara leaned back in his chair. *The sooner Westmoreland's Operation Game Warden gets started the better.* "We have to be very careful of our troop numbers. Westmoreland wants more troops."

"You can be sure that Red China is watching our troop numbers, too. We don't want to have them pouring their army into Indochina," Rusk replied.

McNamara ran his hand over the top of this head. "Westmoreland has his hands full. Not only does he have to fight the enemy, but he has to train the South Vietnamese Army and get some areas opened up so pacification can begin." He paused as he looked around. "I believe Westmoreland is going to ask for more troops. He wants to go into Laos and Cambodia to take away the North and the Viet Cong's safe haven. They can fight, then slip over the border without concern of pursuit."

Johnson steadied his gaze on McNamara. "How many troops are in there already?"

McNamara reached in his briefcase and pulled out a file. "One hundred eighty-four thousand, three hundred troops in Vietnam right now. But I can tell you why he wants more. The CIA believes that ninety thousand South Vietnamese soldiers have deserted this year alone."

Johnson slammed his fist down on the conference table and stared at Valenti. "Do you see what we're battling here? This situation is appalling."

The room went silent. Johnson got up from the table and started pacing. "Okay. I say we pause the bombing on Christmas Day and see if we can get the North to the negotiating table."

McNamara looked at Rusk and Valenti as he shook his head. "The North Vietnamese still believe they can outlast us."

Johnson's face turned red. "I'll go back to why I called this meeting. Can any of you give me a reason not to stop the bombing of the North? To try to get them to the negotiating table?"

No one said a word.

Johnson got up from the table. "I got the answer I was looking for. I'll get a draft of the announcement drawn for our review." He looked at his watch. "Got to get ready to go to Texas for Christmas."

CHAPTER ELEVEN

CHRISTMAS EVE
MARIETTA, GEORGIA

Rita Sullivan sat in her mother's home in Marietta, Georgia. "Are you going to get ready for midnight mass?"

Her mother leaned back in her recliner.

Rita wanted to just stay home and visit with her mother, but she would undoubtedly want to visit her aunts in Atlanta. She stood and walked toward her small bedroom. "Can we just go to church, then come home?"

Her mother mumbled something as Rita left the room. Rita changed her clothes, then returned to the living room. She was as dressed up as she cared to get. "Come on, Mother. Let's go and get this over with."

Just as they were going out the door, the telephone rang. Rita's mother shuffled over and picked up, over Rita's objection.

"Who is this?" her mother repeated several times into the phone. Finally, she held it out to Rita. "It's for you." Her mother made a face.

93

Rita frowned as she walked over and picked up the black receiver. "Hello?"

"Miss Sullivan, this is Senator Morse. I'm so sorry to call you on Christmas Eve, but I have to ask you a question."

Rita slowly shook her head at her mother as she wrapped her finger in the phone cord. "Can't this wait?"

Senator Morse replied, "I'm afraid not. I can't take the chance that your phone in Washington might be bugged. You have a contact in the FBI that's a confidant. I need to know what the FBI has on me."

Rita ran her fingers through her hair. "What? How do you know about me talking to someone at the FBI? And what are you asking me to do? You must be out of your mind."

"Johnson turned Hoover loose on me. Since June, when I was in the anti-war protest with Benjamin Spock and Coretta Scott King, the FBI has been investigating me," the Senator said. "I want to know what they have on me. You know, if they're making stuff up about me."

Rita breathed heavily into the phone. "I can't do that."

Morse pleaded, "Why not?" Morse asked. "I'm not asking you to do anything illegal. If she won't tell you or can't tell you, then that's the end of it."

Rita paused. "Senator, I'll try. But I need something from you."

"Oh, really?" Morse said coldly. "Pray tell what?"

Rita rubbed her mouth with her left hand. "I want a transcript of the Senate Rules Committee's investigation of Bobby Baker. The day Kennedy was assassinated."

There was a pause on the phone, then Morse asked, "Why do you want that?"

"You know why," Rita replied. "I'm investigating Bobby Baker."

The line went dead.

"What's that all about?" Rita's mother asked as they walked out the front door toward her car. A steady drizzle greeted them.

As soon as they were in, Rita sighed. What would her mother think if she told her it was a United States Senator who helped her get her last job, who now wanted her to do something she didn't think she could do. *I can't tell Mother he wanted me to get his file from the FBI. She would freak out.* "Just business," Rita finally said.

Her mother gave her a strange look.

"I'm going to start working for *Life Magazine* as soon as I return to Washington."

Maybe she needed a vacation. Rita expelled her breath and leaned against the seat back.

CHRISTMAS EVE
LABADIEVILLE, LA

The drive home from midnight mass was chilly. The cool and damp air from the afternoon rain still hung around. Steven, Jeremiah and LaBelle walked into the chilly old house.

Before doing anything else, Steven turned up the old propane stove as they sat down around the sparsely decorated Christmas tree to talk. LaBelle shuffled over to plug in the Christmas lights.

"How about some stories about Dad?" Steven asked with a hopeful grin.

A big smile decorated LaBelle's face. She rubbed the back of her arthritic hand. "At Christmas time, when you boys were little, he'd take you all out and find the best shaped pine tree, cut it, and bring it in to decorate. He and I would pop and string popcorn. And your father was a big fan of bubble lights. I used to knit some decorations—always added a few new ones each year."

Steven stopped her. "Mother, we've been told that story over and over. Tell us something we don't know about you and Father."

LaBelle displayed a sheepish smile. "Oh, before either of you were born, your father and I went to the Mardi Gras every year. To celebrate our first meeting. Your father was doing okay as an IRS investigator, so we could afford to do those things then. We were out watching the parade when one of the entertainers on the float was singing your father's favorite song."

Steven broke into the song.

LaBelle started laughing. "That's it. You know it, child. Anyway, he jumped up on the float with the lady singing, and they finished in a duet."

Jeremiah's eyes grew big. "He would do some crazy things when he had been drinking?"

LaBelle said with a sly smile, "He never had much to do with his family after we got married—they weren't happy I was a Negro woman—so he just adopted my family. At first, he had a hard time adjusting to not having his family around. Once he was very close to them. He had a hard time with that" but She wrung her hands. "*Anyway,* he didn't drink very often, but when he did, he got crazy. When he went to the New Orleans Police Force, he quit drinkin' completely."

The small living room got quiet. Steven was beginning to understand where his brother got his problems with marijuana. He would probably have to fight it the rest of his life if he couldn't keep it under control.

Jeremiah had been staring at the Christmas Tree for a little bit. He looked at his mother. "I'm looking forward to getting back to running. I can hardly wait to leave for Washington. I really appreciate the Howard Track coach giving me a chance to join the track team. Practice starts on January second for a team meeting, then I'll enroll the next day."

LaBelle smiled. "Steven, when you're on your way to the airport to return to Vietnam, take me to the bus station with you. I'm going to my sister's in Norman, Oklahoma."

Steven started to object.

"Listen, Steven, I did what you wanted last year. I went to Uncle Jake's. It wasn't the most fun thing to do. I'm an old woman, and I don't have many years left on this earth. I want to go spend some time with my little sister. I used to write her all the time, did for years. Just like I wrote you. I want to go sit with her while I still can."

Steven knew when to relent, and this was the time. All he could say was, "Yes, ma'am." Then he let out a big laugh.

LaBelle got up from her favorite easy chair, walked over by the Christmas tree to admire it, then turned back around. "Boys, I want you to listen to one more story about your father. It has boiled in my craw through that entire episode of dealing with Marcello that you had gone through, Jeremiah." She looked at both boys, then returned to her chair. "You boys have always known your father was killed in the line of duty while on the New Orleans Police Force on a drug raid. But I want to tell you the story behind the story. You both know he was an I.R.S. investigation agent before moving to the police force. While he worked for the I.R.S., he was sent to do a forensic investigation into a mobster in Miami—Santos Trafficante, Sr. As he investigated this activity, he uncovered what he always believed was a tie between the mob and the CIA moving drugs into poor black neighborhoods in Miami. He didn't tell anyone at the I.R.S. about it out of fear of reprisal against him. It was all speculative. Then, on his last day on the case, he found more evidence to show the drugs spread out to New York, Chicago, and New Orleans. He came home very upset. I had to drag the story out of him."

"Why didn't he turn this evidence in, Momma?" Steven asked.

LaBelle frowned at him. "Let me finish. He took a few days off from work, just went away. I know he went to spend some time just fishing with Jake. They were close, you know."

Both boys nodded as they sat on the edge of their chairs.

LaBelle swallowed hard as she pulled a handkerchief out of her purse. "When he came back, he said he was going to apply for a job at the New Orleans Police Department. See if they would hire him as a detective. Naturally, they jumped at the chance to hire someone with his credentials. He asked to be put on the Narco beat, they agreed. He wanted to see if what he thought was correct. Was the CIA behind putting illegal drugs into the poor black community? I don't know what he discovered on the last raid he conducted, because he was killed. That entire event has been shrouded in misinformation. All I know, he believed this somehow tied into—what was it he called it?—I think the term he used was *blackbag operations*."

Steven stared at his mother. Why had he never known about this?

Jeremiah jumped to his feet and paced the floor.

LaBelle took the handkerchief and dabbed her eyes. "I never wanted you boys to know that, because it was a story full of speculation, but with all that has happened, I decided you both needed to know the truth, since it's about your father. He was a good man."

The room got quiet for a little while. Steven looked at the clock on the wall. It was now after midnight. Perhaps some hot chocolate was appropriate. As he got up, he looked under the Christmas tree. No presents, but they had all received a much greater gift than any material things could have provided—being together as a family and learning more about their father.

As he walked into the small kitchen, he glanced out the window over the sink. There was a flashlight off in the distance. Then it went out. Steven was certain he'd seen it. He called to his brother to come into the kitchen.

Jeremiah walked into the kitchen. "What do you want?"

Steven waved for him to come over to where he was standing next to the window. "Count to fifty backwards, then flip on the kitchen light."

Jeremiah lowered his voice. "Why?"

"Someone's out there. I'm going to try to catch them." He started back through the house.

Steven picked up his M1911 gun, then grabbed his knife and went out the front door. He slipped through the trees and brush. *I will go to their parking place, then wait for them to come to me. The perfect trap.* Just before he slipped into the place he expected to find a parked car, he heard a motor start, so he ran faster. As he got back to the dirt road leading to his mother's house, the taillights of a car pulled away.

CHRISTMAS MORNING

MARIETTA, GA

Rita Sullivan tiptoed out on the porch and picked up the morning *Atlanta Constitution*. As she walked back into the house, her eyes became fixated on a story about the Vietnam Conflict. She glanced over the article about the truce the Viet Cong had agreed to for Christmas Day. The article stated there had been a Viet Cong mortar attack on Christmas Eve. Didn't that count as a violation of the truce? She sat down on her mother's couch and continued to read another article. *President Johnson called for a second pause in the bombing of North Vietnam.* The article stated Johnson was hopeful this would entice the North Vietnamese to return to peace talks. Rita mumbled, "Peace on Earth, Good will toward men. I just want Meredith to be safe."

CHAPTER TWELVE

FEBRUARY 10, 1966

WASHINGTON DC

Rita sat near Antoinette Bradlee's home, reading last night's *Washington Evening Star*. She had just finished the column about the Honolulu Conference regarding the Vietnam Conflict.

Rita was ready to explode. *Damn, the Johnson administration must still be spoon feeding my old boss Petit and his newspaper everything to puff them up in the eyes of the American public.* The article frustrated her. Same old, same old.

Antoinette Bradlee's car pulled into the street. Rita raised the newspaper as she drove by, then quickly looked over her shoulder to make a mental note of the license plate number.

Rita struggled to keep Antoinette Bradlee's car in sight as she drove across Washington. Not to mention she was very uncomfortable in trying to get another conversation with Antoinette. *How do I approach her? What do I ask?*

Despite being unsuccessful in her previous attempt to get Antoinette to talk about her sister, Rita remained persistent. *I need answers.* Their phone call last week hadn't gone well at all. After Rita identified herself, Antoinette boldly stated she didn't want to talk to any reporters. Strangely, she stayed on the phone for the next question, which was if she had remembered Rita. She stated she knew Rita had interviewed her sister regarding the Washington Cherry Blossom Festival, plus she'd shown up every day in the trial. When Antoinette found out what she wanted to discuss, her answers grew short, only offering to meet her at the Quorum Club. Rita had quickly rejected that site. *That would not be wise.* Antoinette had said, "Then I'm not interested in talking to you," and hung up.

Antoinette parked near a high-end clothing store

Rita parked nearby, then walked close enough to discreetly watch Antoinette inside the boutique. Rita waited for almost thirty minutes. Finally, Antoinette walked out with a couple of bags in her arms.

Rita walked up to her.

Antoinette huffed, "What do you want? *I told you* I wasn't interested in talking to you. Can't you take no for an answer?"

"Give me just a couple of minutes of your time. You may not know this, but your sister actually got to like me. Your sister's murder remains unsolved."

Antoinette drew a deep breath and looked around. "Okay, a few minutes. Let's go there." She pointed down the street to a little café.

Rita nodded as Antoinette put her packages in her car. The chill in the air caused them to walk quickly but silently down the street. As soon as they were inside the café, Rita pointed toward a table. "Could you put us in a quiet corner where we can talk?"

The waitress nodded and led them in the direction Rita had pointed.

Once seated, Rita thanked her again for giving her a couple of minutes.

Antoinette just stared.

Rita gritted her teeth. "On that morning your sister was murdered, we were supposed to go for a walk together." She tried to read Antoinette's reaction, but there was none, so she continued. "She had something very important to tell me—and give me. From the tone of her voice, she was desperate."

Rita's dialogue only brought a look of skepticism from Antoinette.

Rita stopped talking when the waitress brought over two cups of coffee and set them down. Rita took a sip from her cup while Antoinette put cream in hers.

Rita bit her lip. *It was time to get into this, despite the little voice in her head telling her to just get up and leave now.* She put both hands around the cup of coffee as she set it down. "I should tell you on my drive over to your sister's, I was tailed by someone in a black Cadillac. At a traffic light they purposely rear-ended me."

Antoinette still sat stoically.

"They hit me so I couldn't make it to your sister's. So I couldn't get what I have come to believe was her diary." Rita stared at her. "You weren't aware that your sister was going to give me a copy of her diary?"

Antoinette shook her head, scowling.

Rita pushed on. "She was genuinely scared that morning. She didn't want to talk on the phone and believed they were listening in."

Antoinette pressed her lips tightly together.

This was going nowhere. *Pay attention to the body language.* "Did you know anything about the diary?"

Antoinette didn't move or respond.

She was not going to get any cooperation. Why? "Don't you care that your sister's murder is unsolved?"

Antoinette sat completely still.

Rita leaned her head back and closed her eyes for a second to think. "What was the relationship between James Jesus Angleton and your sister?"

Antoinette stared straight at Rita, her face impossible to read.

"Did your sister have anyone she was seeing who I could talk to?"

Antoinette's face reddened.

Rita's frustration hit the wall. "Don't you want your sister's murderer found?"

Antoinette looked at her for a moment. "Please stop harassing me and my family. Don't contact me anymore—or I'm going to the police." She bolted out of the café.

Rita sat there, dumbfounded. She reached into her purse and pulled out her personal note pad. She was now a seasoned reporter, but Antoinette Bradlee gave her absolutely nothing. Even her body language was impossible to read. As she thought, she made notes in shorthand. *Mary Meyer had a boyfriend. Find the boyfriend. He'll know something, and he will talk. But how do I find him?* She flipped through her notes. When she was at the *Star*, she'd learned he was an aspiring artist. *Look at the list of art displays in the coming Cherry Blossom Festival. Compare it to the old list Mary gave her. He could be there.*

Also, Antoinette didn't want to give her anything on Angleton, the family friend. She knew more about Angleton. CIA brotherhood. Angleton and her husband. Rita put the pad back in her purse and the pencil behind her ear.

A cold chill ran down her spine. She'd made a huge mistake—she'd told Antoinette about the car accident.

CHAPTER THIRTEEN

SAIGON

Edward Lansdale and Pham Xuan An sat in a corner of a quiet restaurant discussing events in South Vietnam after their late lunch. When the waiter returned to the table, Lansdale ordered a whiskey on the rocks and An ordered beer. Lansdale hoped to learn what An knew about the situations around Saigon. With An's now a reporter at *Time Magazine*, the top news magazine in the world, he had access to more information than ever before. Lansdale wanted to play on that. He was pissed off at President Johnson, who had already moved him into a different position in the Pacification program after only six months in South Vietnam. He'd barely been able to get his teams into the field. His teams had had some success, but more on the clandestine side than the counter-intelligence/pacification side. Also, their accomplishments were not necessarily ones he could brag about to Ambassador Lodge.

After the waiter brought over their drink orders, An took a chug from his beer. "So you have been sidelined by Ambassador Lodge."

Lansdale was stunned. *How did An know that already?* "Lodge is on my side," he snarled at his old friend. "It was Johnson and McNamara. Johnson and McNamara are bringing in someone they can control and put him under Lodge."

An nodded as he lit a cigarette. "Word out of D.C. it's William Porter. They are giving him the title of Deputy Ambassador. I hear Lodge is thrilled to have the man running the Pacification program in the Embassy." An held up his hand, ordering another round be brought to the table.

Lansdale downed his whiskey to give himself time to think. He believed An knew more than he was saying. "I wanted a South Vietnamese over the program. It would be more effective."

The waiter returned to the table with the beverages. Lansdale swirled his whiskey before taking a sip. "Do you think the tunnels the Marines discovered at Ho Bo Woods will impact the Viet Cong?" Before An could answer, Lansdale continued. "According to the report from my first team in the field, Cu Chi was one of the VC's key headquarters."

An shifted in his chair as he took a drag off his cigarette and a long drink of his beer. "Clearly, Westmoreland believes it was a significant discovery. I'm not so sure that it was as important as they wanted the press to believe. You know Westmoreland needed to tout some military victories."

Lansdale glanced down at his drink. "I have it on good word that General Nguyen Duc Thang is going to appoint Tran Ngoc Chau to head up the South Vietnamese program. I would try to find a role for US Colonel John Paul Vann. Chau should be over all Pacification programs—that is, if they don't want me."

Pham Xuan An changed the subject. "Lansdale, are you going to stay over here, or are you going back to the US?"

Lansdale glared at An. "As long as I think I can still make a difference over here, I'm staying. I want to work with Chau." He pried for An's opinion. "What do you think about Chau's potential appointment?"

An shook his head. "The Buddhists will be the key. They may not respond well to this appointment since he worked so closely with Diem. I don't know."

"Really? He'd supported the Buddhists in Da Nang after the army attacked the celebration several years ago, which is what started all the problems between the Buddhists and the Diem Administration."

An nervously picked up his pack of cigarettes and tapped it on the table. "I have my sources. Don't bet on Chau being well received with this appointment. Naturally, it depends on how he implements this program. I have even heard that Thieu and Ky may not accept his nomination."

"You're aware the US military just started Operation White Wing, a search and destroy mission to ferret out the VC? What do you hear about the progress so far?"

"They're having little military success, and they're driving many of the residents away from their homes because of the fighting, particularly in the Binh Dinh Province." An took a big draw off his cigarette.

Lansdale hadn't heard this. His information was just the opposite—that they were disrupting the VC activity. "Did you know Johnson changed the original name, Operation Masher, to Operation White Wing? He felt like it would get him bad press?"

An cracked half a smile on that.

Lansdale looked down at his watch. "I've got an appointment. Let's stay in touch."

An nodded as he took a big drag off his cigarette.

Lansdale patted An on the shoulder as he walked out of the restaurant.

Lansdale arrived at his villa just a few moments before his scheduled meeting. He'd enjoyed the drive on a beautiful day. His mind was quiet. He sat and put his head down. He believed Johnson had micromanaged this conflict from the moment he'd become President. *What does Porter know about the South Vietnamese—or pacification, for that matter? He's just another diplomat, just another crony of Johnson and McNamara's.*

There was a knock on the door. Lansdale let Bohannan and Tao into his villa. Tao looked almost despondent as he flopped down on the couch. Before anybody could say anything, he mumbled, "I got orders today from Langley."

Another knock sounded on the door. Lucien Conein strolled in. "What's this meeting all about?"

Lansdale told them that he'd been moved out of the US Pacification program to just liaison with the South Vietnamese government. More specifically, those working in their Pacification program were now to report directly to Deputy Ambassador William Porter.

Tao slapped his hand down on the couch. "That explains my new orders from Langley. I'm being sent back to Laos to answer to Shackley, going back and forth to Vang Pao's camp and helping assign strike targets on the Ho Chi Minh trail."

Conein spoke up. "Johnson needs to grow some more fingers so he can get more into the pie. Him and McNamara trust nobody but themselves."

Lansdale steamed even more with that comment. "Bo, you're being quiet."

Bohannan leaned forward. "My new orders are to continue doing what I'm doing, but I'm supposed to answer to Porter. I didn't even know who that was until you told me."

Lansdale looked at Conein. "Those orders are consistent with Ellsberg. But he's one of McNamara's boys anyway."

Conein took off his Aussie Bush Hat and pounded it on his leg. "That figures. Damn. The way things are going, I may just move back to the States. This is just one big cluster—"

Lansdale put his hands on his hips. "I have one last plan I want us to try to pull off. It comes at great risk. This is a volunteer mission."

Conein waved his arm around. "Well, come on, let's hear it."

"As you know, Tran Ngoc Chau is about to be put in charge of the South Vietnamese Pacification program. Both he and his brother worked with Ho Chi Minh in the forties and fifties. According to Chau, his brother said Ho told him that Le Duan is the one making all the hard line military decisions. He said Mao is ramping up support, and they're now even sending Chinese Red Army volunteers in to fight the US. While Le Duan is unwilling to negotiate with the US, Ho quietly told Chau's brother he was willing to negotiate but has been pushed aside."

Conein looked at the men. "I believe that. You know Ho Chi Minh wrote a letter to President Truman back in 1946 to get American help to establish an independent government. Truman ignored the letter."

Lansdale waved his hand. "Yes. But who knows what kind of government they would have wanted? Ho was a communist way before World War II—plus that was before the Chinese Civil War. Mao may not have let it stand." He paused as he looked from one man to the next. "So, between now and the end of monsoon season, I want to go into North Vietnam and capture or assassinate Le Duan. I need each of you because of your various talents. Plus Hebert. He'll be our sniper if we fail to capture him."

Conein rubbed his mouth with the back of his hand. "It's going to be very difficult to get close to him. Things have changed a lot in North Vietnam since we were sneaking in and out in the fifties. He has tons of security around him at all times. Hell, I hear he's more scared of some of the more moderate commies than he is of anyone in the South." Conein laughed. "Aren't we about in the same situation here?"

Tao shook his head. "How are you going to get Hebert out of the Embassy?"

"I've been told by a very reliable source that Captain Jefferson is going home," Lansdale replied. "He has decided to retire at the end of this month. This will add undue stress on Hebert. The State Department has implemented a new program providing security for embassies around the world. They work with the Marine Corps security guards, and I would guess some movement will be made soon, but for now all of that stress will fall on

Hebert. He may not like it, and he may want out. Next year, he will have in fifteen years of service and may consider retiring. Lodge has already told me I could have Hebert for my personal security." Lansdale raised both hands palms out. "Obviously, I would need him on this mission."

Bohannan rubbed his chin. "What's the plan?"

"I'm formulating one now. I just wanted to see if all of you were in. Again, this is a voluntary mission. We could be killed. Or court-martialed."

Everyone nodded.

Lansdale smiled. "Good. Not a word of this conversation leaves this room."

Conein and Bohannan both got up to leave.

"Just let me know when you want to meet again," Conein said.

After they had left, Tao asked, "How was your meeting with Pham Xuan An?"

Lansdale licked his lips. "Good. I learned a lot from him. He knows more about the day-to-day mission stuff than I do. Can you believe it?"

Tao patted his hand on the couch. "I can explain that. Hebert was at a military briefing last year. He said An had full access to the military plans. Have you ever heard of letting a member of the media see advance battle plans?" Before Lansdale could speak, Tao continued, "You know Westmoreland is trying to be more friendly toward the press."

"Why would Westmoreland do that? It's a little too trusting for me. But I guess it all makes sense now." Lansdale sat down for the first time. "Also, he wasn't a big fan of Chau's appointment."

Tao looked at Lansdale. "But Chau is a Confucian Buddhist. Why would the Buddhists be against him?"

Lansdale nodded. "Peculiar, isn't it?"

Tao shook his head. "What can you tell me about Theodore Shackley?"

Lansdale jutted his jaw. "I worked with Shackley on a couple of projects. He was with me in Operation Mongoose. He was stationed in Miami at the time. He has good contacts but some of them are mafia." He shrugged. "Shackley is all right. We might have succeeded in Cuba, but McNamara called off the air support at the last minute, completely screwing up the mission. Everybody took the fall but McNamara. McNamara and I have our issues—"

Tao interrupted Lansdale. "My concern with Shackley, what will be his new role with Vang Pao's drug operation? Seems to me that the CIA is as interested in poppies as they are saving South Vietnam."

Lansdale stared at Tao.

"So how do you feel about not being given a chance to complete the Pacification program?" Tao asked.

Lansdale stood and paced around his living room. "I knew not to trust Johnson and McNamara. The Pacification program for South Vietnam is complex." He sat back down and gestured with his hands. "Once the military clears out the VC and the NVA, giving the people some semblance of security, it will take time to set up a functioning local government— maybe years. Washington's meddling is not helping. Only the South Vietnamese can administer this to their own people. How can men sitting in Washington DC have a clue what is in the minds of these people? An told me something very troubling—people were fleeing Binh Dinh province where fighting was going on. That happens in every war." Lansdale stopped again. "My point is, when it was the South Vietnamese fighting the VC, the people had a chance. The battles were minor. Now, since the US put troops in here, the North Vietnamese have been countering by sending in army regulars. It may be evolving to a conventional war. Still a guerilla war, but a more conventional one."

Tao got up to leave.

As he walked toward the door, Lansdale continued, "Before this, I believed the South Vietnamese people could have handled the VC with this Pacification program and our style of fighting the VC. Our ground troops changed everything. The NVA is in here, the Red Army is in here. I believe if Kennedy had sent me before Diem was killed, our program coupled with what de Silva was doing with his teams, we could have pushed the VC out. The South Vietnamese people could have done things and felt good about themselves."

Tao stopped and turned around. "While I agree wholeheartedly, the South Vietnamese Army did nothing. I mean, they literally were waiting for the US to do whatever they were going to do to help them."

Lansdale rubbed his chin. "True. But they would have been emboldened by our successes. They may have tried harder then."

Tao stopped near the door.

Lansdale spoke again, "How can we change this, now? The die may already be cast. That's why I think getting Le Duan may be our only hope."

FEBRUARY 22, 1966

WHITE HOUSE

WASHINGTON DC

Secretary of Defense Robert McNamara looked down at his watch. 11:10 a.m. He walked briskly toward the oval office. He was running late for a quick meeting with the President. The meeting topic focused on whether or not to resume the bombing of North Vietnam. He'd spent the morning reviewing a letter written to his assistant, McNaughton, by Harvard Law Professor Roger Fisher, who had proposed an elaborate anti-infiltration barrier across the DMZ. McNamara had made several notes from his additional conversations with McNaughton. The more he thought about it, the more intrigued he became with the idea. Professor Fisher suggested that McNamara hand pick a group of scientists to focus on the project. One thing was beginning to sink in—the bombing of the Ho Chi Minh Trail hadn't shut down the flow of troops and supplies. It was becoming a real dilemma. Nothing seemed to ebb the tide of movement along this trail.

11:20 AM

McNamara walked into the oval office

"Sit down," President Johnson said.

"What the hell is going on with Robert Kennedy?" the President demanded before McNamara could even make it to the couch. "I'm doing exactly the same things Jack was going to do in Vietnam, and now Robert is criticizing my execution of Vietnam."

McNamara slipped down on the big yellow couch. "I'm deeply trouble by his criticism myself. I feel betrayed by the Kennedys. I agree with you, Mr. President. We are doing everything just the way Jack would've handled the Vietnamese. I was involved in virtually every decision." He looked down at the coffee table. "I thought they were my friends."

The President walked to the couch opposite McNamara. "I believe we have found our man—William Porter—to handle the South Vietnamese Pacification program. He has done so well, so fast."

McNamara took off his glasses and cleaned them with his tie. "I think Lodge is on board now, too. He likes the idea that Deputy Ambassador Porter is under his supervision. It really softened the blow of removing Lansdale. How long do you think it will take Robert Komer to get up to speed on the Pacification program?"

"Not long. We need more quick studies like Komer. With Komer here, we can stay fully briefed on the Pacification program." The President leaned back into the couch. "While I had high hopes for Lansdale in overseeing the Pacification program, some of Lodge's correspondences caused me concern. If Lodge couldn't keep his eyes on him in Saigon, it would be impossible to do so in Washington."

"Even Westmoreland now acknowledges the importance of Pacification in South Vietnam for the first time. Westmoreland has been so focused on getting his troops in place and his intelligence rounded into shape he hasn't had an opportunity to focus on the destruction and construction long term plans for South Vietnam. Naturally, Westmoreland needs some battle victories and is gaining some ground so the Pacification will have a foothold to build on," McNamara said.

President Johnson jutted his jaw. "Despite Kennedy's comments about handling Vietnam, I want to restart the bombing of North Vietnam. Once again, we gain nothing from the halt. I mean, for the North Vietnamese leadership to come out and call our actions a 'ploy' is ridiculous."

"I concur."

"Can you believe the North Vietnamese are forcing women and children to repair the Ho Chi Minh trail at night after we bombed all day? It's unbelievable."

"You know, I had a study done over the last year by a Harvard law professor, Dr. Roger Fisher, about possibly building a fence along the DMZ. I think this project has some real merit to study further. It might be just the thing to shut down the Ho Chi Minh Trail."

CHAPTER FOURTEEN

LATE EVENING, MARCH 10, 1966
SAIGON

Nguyen Tao sat at the back of his Honda moped shop, waiting for Steven Hebert to show up. He walked nostalgically through the old shop he'd called home off and on for almost three years. Tao was selling the shop to the two boys who had worked so hard to build up his business. They had no clue it was a front for the CIA. All the money for the sale was going into the CIA account in Bangkok.

There was a light rapping on the back door. Tao let Steven in, who turned a chair backwards as he sat down at the old desk. Tao thanked him for coming by, as he had several things to talk about.

Steven sat attentively, waiting to hear the reason for the late night meeting.

Tao ran his finger across his desk, then tapped it several times. "I had a meeting with Pham Xuan An earlier this evening. You know, to tell him I was selling the shop and going to a new assignment. He'd long since figured out that I was still working with Lansdale."

Steven raised his eyebrows. "Was he surprised?"

Tao pursed his lips. "Not really, but he had a big surprise for me. He told me a lot about the battle at A Sau Valley. Apparently, the North Vietnamese Army attacked our South Vietnamese camp there. Our military set up that camp to gather intelligence and disrupt the Ho Chi Minh Trail. The Civilian Irregular Defense Group camped there, supported by US Army Special Forces."

"Wow, that was one of our highest level intelligence gathering camps."

"Right," Tao continued. "That's why the NVA put a full effort into pushing them out. Here is what is wild—that camp had several VC defectors come in and tell them about the impending attack. So our guys moved in several Special Forces men, but they still couldn't hold the camp."

Steven stuck out his chest. "How did that even happen?"

"Guess the weather got bad so they couldn't get resupplied. As they were running out of ammo, our choppers tried to drop some, but they landed where they couldn't be retrieved. When the weather started to clear, they decided to extract just the US personnel." Tao hung his head for a few seconds. "Here is the sad part. When the choppers came to extract the US Special Forces, they got so overloaded they had to shoot at their South Vietnamese allies to lift off. An thinks all of them escaped, but he didn't know for sure."

Steven sat in shock. This was a very disturbing development. He'd been aware of this camp since early 1964. It had a strategic location and a high level of functionality. It was a huge loss. "How does he know this stuff? Neither you nor the Embassy staff had any notification of this."

Tao just shrugged. When he was composed, he changed the subject. "I'm picking up Shackley tonight at the Continental Hotel. We're flying out to Long Tieng to go to Vang Pao's camp."

"Shackley flew into Tan Son Nhut?" Steven considered. "Stopping in to see Conein?" He rubbed his mouth with his hand. "Didn't sneak in this time?"

Tao laughed. "Yeah. Beginning my new assignment—to escort him back and forth between Bangkok and the general's camp."

Steven got up from the chair and frowned at Tao. "So, taking Conein with you?"

Tao nodded. "Your guess is as good as mine. I wouldn't doubt it."

Steven started toward the back door. "You still going to be part of our mission for Lansdale?"

Tao looked up at him. "Of course. You?"

Steven reached the back door. "I'm ready now. Wish Lansdale would get his plan done."

"The Buddhist protests are going to get real bad. Don't you think?" Tao got up from the tiny desk. "What do you think Thich Tri Quang is going to do next?"

Steven stopped as he grabbed the door knob. "Lodge thinks this is going to develop into a real problem. Prime Minister Ky screwed things up royally by firing General Nguyen Chanh Thi. The area he was over is a total mess. Da Nang and Hue have had some violent protests today. Lodge had me increase the security, as he's expecting trouble in Saigon."

121

"Will they let you get into combat?" Tao asked.

"At the moment, Lodge has agreed to allow me to work with Lansdale, so I can take some mission assignments. I'm going to see how this works until my fifteen years of service are in, then I'll make some decisions. My mom needs me back home, but I've been here so long, I feel like this is my home—here." Steven grabbed the door handle, opened the door, and left.

Tao watched the door close. Under his breath he mumbled, "Be safe, my friend. Be safe."

SAIGON

4 AM

Tao pulled onto the abandoned air strip. He flashed the headlights of his Peugeot. The startup of the waiting C-47's motors pelted him with dust, then the landing lights illuminated. Tao parked his car under the camouflaged canopy. Without even so much as a glance at Shackley, he got out. *I'm done trying to get along with this caustic man. Clearly, he has no respect for me. That's fine.*

Without a word, Shackley went to the trunk and removed his suitcase. He brushed back his blond hair, then checked the nine-millimeter handgun in his shoulder holster. The two men didn't speak as they walked toward the plane. About halfway between the plane and Tao's Peugeot, another set of headlights pulled up behind them. Both Shackley and Tao pulled their handguns as they pivoted toward the unknown vehicle and crouched down. A man in an Aussie bush hat boldly walked in front of the headlights. Both men re-holstered the guns. They knew it was Lieutenant Colonel Lucien Conein.

"Boys, good to see you on this fine morning. You boy scouts couldn't go camping without me." Conein turned around, took off his hat, and waved it. "Come on."

The passenger door opened, and another individual got out and began walking.

Tao looked around. Shackley had already turned toward the waiting airplane. Tao followed in pursuit. *Well, this is going to be a real circus— plus, somebody new is going along.*

Once on board, Shackley spoke to the unidentified man but didn't call him by name nor introduce him to Tao. Conein, Shackley and Tao all buckled into the jump seats. Conein shouted at the unknown individual to do the same thing, as the plane was picking up speed along the dirt runway. The CIA didn't like to fly in and out of this old airstrip, but sometimes it was necessary, particularly when they didn't want to have people see key personnel moving around inside Vietnam. The flight to Long Tieng, Laos, was very quiet, as the men all tried to catch some sleep.

Once on the ground at Vang Pao's encampment, Tao glanced at the sun breaking over the mountain range. The humidity was already building for the day. He led Theodore Shackley, Lucien Conein, and the other man into General Vang Pao's headquarters. *Who is this man traveling with Conein?*

Shackley and Conein seem to know him. He didn't look CIA. Maybe Mafia. Maybe he's a Corsican. This meeting with Shackley and Conein was critical for the General Guerini.

The five men gathered around the general's desk with the large map on top. Vang Pao began with a description of what his Hmong soldiers were battling. The effort to hold off the Pathot Lao while also engaging North Vietnamese and Viet Cong was becoming insurmountable.

Vang Pao pointed at the Plaines des Jarres. "It is imperative that we focus on retaking this strategic point." He paused and looked up at the three other men. "It is imperative to all our operations. My army has been fighting and dying now for almost five years of intense battle."

Shackley grabbed Conein's arm. "The CIA has got to ramp up."

Conein jerked away from him. "Why are you telling me this? You have rank in the CIA, not me."

Vang Pao continued, "The US Marines were supposed to take some of the load off my stretched and stressed fighting forces. Most of my fighters are nothing but a bunch of boys."

Tao knew what the general was talking about. The CIA was now in the villages recruiting boys as young as fourteen to pick up automatic weapons and go fight. The country of three million people was losing their youth. Tao glanced at Shackley and Conein. Their expressions were solemn during the general's presentation. Clearly, every time someone came to Long Tieng, the story was worse. Tao had also periodically glanced at the other man, who seemed disinterested in what was being discussed.

"I assume the fall of the Special Forces Camp at A Shua Valley has added to the strain?" Conein asked.

Shackley looked at the general, then Conein. "You know President Johnson has refused General Westmoreland's request to send troops into Cambodia and Laos. The US is fighting a conflict with rules made in Washington by bureaucrats."

Tao stepped back. His breath left him. His homeland was falling to the communists before his eyes.

When the general had finished, Shackley pushed his glasses back up on his nose, slicked back his blond hair, and then leaned over the map while looking directly at Vang Pao. "General, as you know, I'm going to be appointed station chief in Laos. I will be taking over in July. The CIA sent me to bring you some help. We will work to provide you with better supplies and military support. Colonel Singlaub has been reassigned to upgrade OPLAN 35. He has two thousand US Special Forces assigned to him, and they will ramp up their operations here, in Cambodia, and in North Vietnam. Unlike the bureaucrats in DC, we understand the importance of shutting down the Ho Chi Minh Trail."

General Vang Pao frowned as he sat down, leaned back, and folded his arms. "My request is the same that it always is. We need more food, particularly rice, and medical supplies for our men and families. The air support has improved now the US Air Force is bombing over Laos and North Vietnam."

At that point, the other man tapped his finger on the table, then nervously glanced at Shackley and Conein. "Well, General, let me introduce myself. My name is Gino DeLuca. I come here representing the Trafficante family to offer some opportunities to make real money, some very quiet money, through mutual cooperation."

When Tao heard the comments from DeLuca, it became obvious to him why Shackley had gone to Saigon before coming here. He'd worked with Conein on the drug network. *I bet they had to buy off some South Vietnamese generals or political officials. They were putting the finishing touches on their deal. With Lansdale's power fading here, Shackley was stepping into the void—but Conein, he's still the man with the connections in South Vietnam.*

Shackley put his hand on DeLuca's shoulder to interrupt him. "Yes, General, I met Mr. DeLuca and Mr. Trafficante before I left the States. They have completed their network. The CIA will handle the movement for both Trafficante—"

"*And* the French Corsican Brotherhood," Conein said.

Shackley didn't flinch or look at Conein. "We believe they can help enhance your poppy growing. Unlike the Corsicans, we will pay your new prices."

Tao glanced at Conein. His poker face hadn't changed one bit. *Conein makes money either way.*

Shackley continued talking. "Your bank accounts we're managing continue to grow. I'm here to oversee." He stuck out his chin. "My patriots within the CIA remain ready, willing and able to assist your farmers grow more. We just wanted you to meet our new financial partner here." He patted DeLuca on the back.

Conein took off his Aussie bush hat and wiped his brow. "Our planes will continue in and out of this landing strip. But since few men in Air America are aware of our little operation to accommodate the increased growth, we're going to get you your own airplanes."

DeLuca glanced at both Conein and Shackley before continuing. "Mr. Trafficante and a few of his friends back home have agreed to modernize your labs. We even opened new markets here in Asia, including Saigon, complete with the blessing of, ahhh, certain needed key individuals." DeLuca looked at Conein. "We aren't here to cut out any of your other business partners. We just wanted to tell you face-to-face that we have no problem paying your new prices."

Shackley leaned forward. "The CIA has spent the last year preparing to work with Mr. Trafficante, General. We believe this will only enhance all of your operations. They have no issues with the Corsicans."

DeLuca smiled smugly, folded his arms on his chest, and winked at Shackley. "More money for all of us, including the Corsicans, if they choose to go along."

Conein reached in his pocket and pulled out something. He tossed it on the table, then put both hands on his hips. "You boy scouts better get a good look at that man."

Everybody leaned forward and looked at the picture.

Conein continued, "That's Federal Bureau of Narcotics Agent Bowman Taylor. He's working from Bangkok to Vientiane to Saigon. Plus, the FBN is feeding some information to the FBI." He reached forward to pick up the picture and stuff it back into his shirt.

Silence fell over the room for several minutes.

General Vang Pao placed both palms on his large map. "Gentlemen, this is all well and fine, but we must find a way to increase our war effort. We must remove the Laotian government all the while making an increased effort to take down the Pathot Lao, while fighting the North Vietnamese

Army. Mr. Shackley, I ask you again, what can you do to help me accomplish this? We're fighting Laotians, North Vietnamese, Chinese and Cubans. The communists have increased their military effort considerably since the US Marines landed. This is no longer a battle against some young NLF idealists."

Shackley put both hands on his hips. "As soon as I get in here as station chief, I'll make positive things happen. We'll get some better resources in here for you."

With that comment Tao glanced around at the four men, he hoped this would not be another unfulfilled promise to the Vang Pao.

5:00 PM

MARCH 13, 1966

US EMBASSY - SAIGON

Steven Hebert sat opposite Ambassador Henry Cabot Lodge. He was about to go off duty for the evening, but for the first time since he had been assigned to the Embassy, he no longer had anyone filling the role on the nightshift. Now, the highest ranking Marine Guard was in charge until he returned to duty in the morning.

Lodge shook his head in disgust. The ambassador was reading a report from intelligence agents. His face turned red as he finished. He took off his glasses and tossed them on his desk. He looked like he was about to explode.

"Well, this is a report." Lodge pointed repeatedly with his index finger. "US Intelligence agents in Hue and Da Nang regarding the violence between the Buddhists and the South Vietnamese Army. Can you guess who's behind these protests?" The Ambassador pursed his lips. "Thich Tri Quang." He sat at his desk. "Tri Quang has instigated this Buddhist protest because Premier Ky fired the highest ranking Buddhist general, Nguyen Chanh Thi. With the chaos already in I Corps, particularly Hue and Da Nang, and the constant insurgence of the Viet Cong, this is absolutely the last damn thing we need up there. And there is Tri Quang in the middle of all of this."

Steven was astonished. Tri Quang had been on the side of the US and their fight against the Viet Cong and the communist movement. His support of the Buddhist general would be misinterpreted.

Ambassador Lodge drew a deep breath. "I have no choice but to side with the South Vietnamese government on this. Tri Quang has finally pushed me too far. I've wanted to remain neutral on him, but I fear his actions, intended or not, is playing straight into the hands of the VC."

Steven nodded. He understood where the ambassador was coming from.

The Ambassador looked at Hebert. "You have been with me through all of this with the Buddhist Roshi. I just wanted to tell you before you heard it somewhere else about the mess this man has created. You're dismissed, Major."

Steven went into the outer office and stood before Meredith Brown's desk. She had a worried look on her face. Before he could say anything to her, the ambassador stepped through the door and asked her to take dictation for a letter to the President. He also told her to have Sergeant Tim Mitchell come up to the office and wait so that he could transmit this document to the President.

Steven sat in the outer office, waiting for Tim Mitchell to come up and pick up the memo Lodge was dictating to the President regarding the situation in Hue and Da Nang. Just as Steven checked his watch, Tim popped into the office.

A quick display of disappointment etched across Tim's face as he glanced at Meredith's empty chair, but he quickly returned to his happy self.

"What's so exciting?" Steven asked. "Came to see Meredith, who won't give you the time of day? Or did the Beach Boys just release a new album?"

Tim gave him a sarcastic half smile. "As a matter of fact, the Beach Boys *are* releasing their new album, *Pet Sounds,* next month."

Steven shook his head as he folded his arms across his chest. He was afraid to laugh because the ambassador might overhear. Lodge was all business, all the time.

Tim took a seat. "I can't wait to get out of the service. This place has changed so much since I arrived in April sixty-three." He looked around Meredith's office. "When I get out next year, I'm going to go to as many Beach Boys concerts as I can."

Steven understood. The changes in Vietnam had been dynamic since he'd arrived in 1956. *Tim should be in my shoes, seeing the changes in the last ten years.*

Tim again looked over at Meredith's desk. "No doubt, Lodge has me on stand-by to transmit an urgent message to the President"

Steven smiled sarcastically. "It's why we serve, Tim. It's why we serve." He stood at attention, saluted, and left. The major slowly walked down the hallway to check on the MPs before leaving duty for the evening. *Ten years.* A wave of emotion came over him. Tim's comment opened his mind to something Steven had worked hard to repress. *I've been in Vietnam for ten years. When I got here to serve on Lansdale's team as a sniper for the Saigon Military Mission, this whole territory had a chance to become free. It was what the government sought. Now graft and corruption seemed to have permeated the government. Freedom feels like an afterthought. Now we have our soldiers in here to correct all of this. The general population, for the most part, couldn't care less, and the government officials just want American money for their own pockets.*

Steven realized he was conflicted himself. On one hand, he'd been here so long it sometimes felt like home, while he had an elderly mother at his real home who could use his help. Maybe it was time to decide where his real home was.

CHAPTER FIFTEEN

APRIL 12, 1966

CHERRY BLOSSOM FESTIVAL - WASHINGTON DC

Rita Sullivan remembered the first year she came to the festival with Mary Meyer. So much had happened in the last two years. *I had no clue who Mary Meyer was at that time, and now she's almost an obsession in my life with more tentacles than an octopus.* After walking through the first art exhibit, she was unable to uncover anyone who knew the name of the artist who was dating Mary and where he might be found. Rita walked outside into a blustery wind and ran to her car as best as she could in high heels. She tried to straighten her bun, but it was useless. She pulled the list out of her purse, then drove off toward the second art display on her list for this year.

She was more determined than ever to find Meyer's boyfriend. She entered the next exhibit a large one, only stopping where artists were setting up their exhibits. After inquiring of several artists and coming up empty, finally, the last woman there, adjusting one of her paintings was all that was left. Rita flashed her credentials. "I'm a reporter investigating the unsolved murder of Mary Meyer. Did you know her or anyone in the art community who I could speak with?"

The woman met Rita's eyes. "Yes."

"Would you be willing to sit down and talk about it?"

The woman glanced at her exhibit, then back at Rita. "For a few minutes."

Rita invited her to join her for a cup of coffee.

A few minutes later, they sat at a table. Rita was just starting to warm up after her first sip of coffee. "Did you know Mrs. Meyer?"

The woman shook her head. "Not really, but I knew her boyfriend, an artist by the name of Kenneth Noland."

Rita pulled out her notepad and pen. "How can I get in touch with Mr. Noland?"

The woman pulled out a business card. "We did several exhibitions together. I won more awards than he did, so he wanted me to critique his work, you know, so he could improve. I tried to get him to ask me on a date, but he was never interested in me. He said I wasn't his type. I decided I wasn't interested in helping him anymore."

Rita didn't need more meaningless information. All she wanted was that business card.

Finally, the woman handed her the card.

Rita quickly wrote down his address and phone number, then handed it back to her. "Thank you, I appreciate it. By the way, is he displaying at the festival this year?"

The woman took the card back and put her right index finger on her chin. "Yes. Show me your list."

Rita pulled the piece of paper out of her purse and held it out to her.

The artist pointed at the fourth name on the list. "He should be there setting up this afternoon."

Rita thanked her for her assistance.

The exhibit was just a few blocks away, but due to the blustery day, she decided to drive. By the time she found a place to park, it was almost as far away as her earlier parking place. As Rita walked, she thought about the morning news that the US Air Force used B-52s for the first time in North Vietnam, targeting power, war support, transportation, military, fuel and air defense. She wondered if these new targets would make a difference in how the conflict was going.

When she stepped into the exhibit, Rita was still shivering. She pulled a mirror from her purse and tried to get her hair back in place. It was a lost cause. She scanned the large room. The exhibition wasn't open to the public yet, so she flashed her press credentials.

Several artists were still placing their works of art, while others sipped glasses of red wine. Rita walked toward two men. "Are either of you Kenneth Noland?"

Both men looked her up and down, then said simultaneously, "Yes. Who is asking?" They laughed.

Rita became flustered. She knew her good looks got her places, sometimes not exactly where she wanted to be. "So, then—which one of you dated Mary Meyer?"

Both men's eyes grew big. "Okay, you got us." The taller of the two men pointed across the room. "There's Kenneth Noland."

Rita gave the men an exaggerated wink, then turned and strutted toward the man they singled out. As she approached the good-looking man, she said, "Kenneth Noland."

The man turned around and smiled. "Why, yes. Who is asking?"

"My name is Rita Sullivan. I'm a reporter investigating the murder of Mary Meyer."

Noland's smile disappeared. "Why do you want to talk with me?"

"Did you know Mrs. Meyer?"

Noland put his hands on his hips. "I knew her a little, but I doubt I can give you any information."

Rita pulled out her pad and pen. "Did Mary ever express to you that she was scared of anyone?"

Noland raised an eyebrow. "What are you talking about? She never said anything at all like that. All we ever talked about was art. I tried to help her improve her paintings. Get a better use of color. That's all we *ever* talked about."

Rita thought for a minute. *Is Noland telling me the truth? This is really a dead end.* "Is there anyone else you could suggest I talk to?"

Noland didn't hesitate for a second. "You want to talk to someone who knows, talk to Professor Timothy Leary. He was her confidant. If anybody knows anything, it's him." He folded his arms over his chest.

Rita tried not to smile. Noland was obviously jealous of Leary. She'd heard of Timothy Leary. But would he talk to her?

Rita turned and walked out of the exhibit and thought about all she'd learned. She needed to get back to the *Life* office and write her feature on the Vietnam Conflict. Two days ago, the *New York Times* printed a large column with the headline "Crisis in Saigon." Rita wanted to write an overview of the conflict comparing the situation in Vietnam matched against the growing youth protests throughout the United States. This would be her first big article for the magazine. She wanted to be right down the middle, presenting both sides.

Soon she was back in her office and sitting at her typewriter. As she reached for two sheets of paper and a sheet of carbon to put between them, her hand diverted to her purse. She couldn't start on the article until she made a personal note. While up until now every page had been written in shorthand, Rita flipped to a blank sheet and wrote one word. *Leary.*

APRIL 13, 1966 - 01:00
US EMBASSY - SAIGON

The phone rang in Steven Hebert's room. "This is Major Hebert"

"Major Hebert, Tan Son Nhut is under attack."

"I'll be down immediately."

Steven moved swiftly around his quarters. He dressed, then grabbed his M1911. He double-timed it toward the US Embassy First Floor.

He went to the front of the facility to check on the status of all security positions. The night duty officer had already put the Embassy on full alert status. Steven ran to Meredith's office. Ambassador Lodge was not there. He grabbed Meredith's phone. "Ambassador Lodge, Major Hebert. Tan Son Nhut is under attack."

After a long pause, the Ambassador spoke. "Keep me apprised of any new developments. Meet me in the office first thing in the morning, so we can review the report from MACV and assess the current situation at the Embassy."

"Yes, Ambassador." Steven spent the rest of the night monitoring all stations and sending extra personnel to each critical station.

Steven blew over his cup of coffee to cool it off. He glanced up at the clock on the wall. 0500. *The ambassador should be headed into his office any minute.* He sat down on the metal chair. About the time he was almost finished with his coffee, a Marine Guard stuck his head in the room and said the ambassador wanted to see him, asap. Steven took another long sip of coffee, then dumped the remainder and headed out.

Steven walked into Meredith's office. *Too early for her.* The ambassador's door was open. He shouted for Steven to come on in.

Ambassador Lodge put his hand over the receiver as he raised his other finger up to his lips. Lodge continued writing notes without a word. After a couple of minutes, the ambassador finished his call, then looked over his notes, raising his eyebrows several times.

Ambassador Lodge jacked his lower jaw. "That was one of the colonels at MACV." He read his notes. "At zero-thirty, the Viet Cong began a twenty minute attack. They estimated seventy-five rounds of eighty-two millimeter mortars plus seventy-five millimeter recoilless rifle rounds were fired. They focused on the headquarters for the Seventh Air Force and the Army, plus the Vietnamese Air Force. They destroyed twelve helicopters and nine aircraft, plus set a fuel tank on fire."

All Steven could do was look down. *This was the first time the VC had attacked Tan Son Nhut—the airbase just outside of Saigon. In the last year, the VC had also attacked the Embassy and Tan Son Nhut.*

Lodge continued to read his notes. "The total casualties are now listed at one-forty. We were able to get armed helicopters and a few gunships in the air to attack the Viet Cong positions, but no ground forces were able to engage the enemy."

Steven wanted to believe that any assault on either the Embassy or Tan Son Nhut should have been a suicide mission for the VC, yet the enemy wasn't engaged on the ground. This wasn't the fault of the US military. The South Vietnamese military had taken responsibility for security of the base and were ill prepared. Because of the lack of preparedness, it was up to US troops to push the VC and the North Vietnamese army out of not only the South, but now Saigon.

Lodge tossed his glasses on the desk. "We need to review our security and our evac plans here, Major." He squinted. "The enemy is clearly all around us."

Steven had believed for a long time the Viet Cong were literally among the citizenry of Saigon. He was more confident than ever they were employed by the Department of State. Yet, there hands were tied—and Washington held the keys.

CHAPTER SIXTEEN

APRIL 15, 1966

WASHINGTON DC

Rita Sullivan stared at her phone. Her only solution was to call her old confidant, Oregon Senator Wayne Morse. She'd avoided him since Christmas Eve. She knew all too well the price of her phone call. The minute she asked for the same favor she had previously asked from him, he was going to ask the same of her, but she'd exhausted all other avenues. Rita picked up the phone and dialed his office number.

Within a few minutes he was on the phone. "Yes, Miss Sullivan. What do I owe the pleasure of the overdue phone call?"

Rita bristled, but she'd expected some such snarky comment. "Senator Morse, I need a private face-to-face meeting with you."

"Miss Sullivan, it will be a pleasure. And perhaps you can get me the information I requested of you on Christmas Eve?"

Rita slowly shook her head. "Yes, Senator Morse, I'll try to get the answer to your question." She bit her lower lip. "I'll call my contact today, then call you back to set up an appointment. It has to be out of the office, somewhere we can talk privately. I want something... ." She took in a deep breath. "I want a transcript of the Senate Rules Committee's investigation of Bobby Baker. The day Kennedy was assassinated."

There was a long pause, then Morse replied, "Miss Sullivan, I'll be waiting for your call. Goodbye for now."

She really wanted to read that transcript. She was ready to make another run at FBI researcher Stephanie Keeton. *Here's hoping on hope that she'll take my call.*

Rita pushed the button down on the top of the base of the switchhook, then slowly placed the receiver down on top. She reached inside her center drawer and pulled out the letter FBI employee Stephanie Keeton had sent to her back in January. She'd written down her home phone number in the letter. Rita made a note of the number so she could call her from a phonebooth somewhere after work. Stephanie's letter provided no new information on Mary Meyer, Angleton or Baker. Rita wasn't surprised about the lack of information on Angleton, but the Mary Meyer murder and Bobby Baker's illegal activities had to be on the FBI's radar.

Rita got off at her bus stop, but instead of going straight down the side street to her apartment, she went on up the street to the closest phonebooth. As she walked, she looked down at her wristwatch. 6:45 PM. Stephanie should be home from work. Rita took a deep breath, opened the glass door, then closed it behind her, picked up the handset, pushed a dime in the slot, and dialed.

"Hello?" Stephanie answered.

"This is Rita Sullivan. I'm calling you from a phonebooth." All Rita could hear was Stephanie breathing into the phone.

Since she had not hung up on her, Rita told her what she had learned over the last few weeks on the Meyer murder. "Mary Meyer's confidant was Timothy Leary."

Stephanie remained silent.

Then Rita asked, "Can we meet again? I have some more information to share."

"I'm not interested in being involved in the Meyer investigation."

Rita's heart dropped into her stomach. Yet, she had to continue. "Is the FBI investigating Senator Morse, Senator Gruening, or any other anti-Vietnam congressmen?"

Stephanie breathed hard into the phone. "So, that's why you called. Look, if I knew anything about it, and I don't, I couldn't tell you a single thing about an on-going investigation. That would get me fired."

"Since when is it wrong to have a dissenting opinion in the United States?"

There was a long pause. Finally, Stephanie said, "Lose my phone number and don't call me again." There was a loud bang in Rita's ear, then a dial tone.

Rita looked at the handset and placed it back on the receiver. "That went well."

She leaned against the glass. Here goes. She reached in her purse for another dime and dialed the Senator's office. He agreed to meet the next night at the little restaurant on the other side of town where they had met before, when she'd asked for the Senate study. Rita remembered the place. Once they agreed on a time, all was good.

WASHINGTON DC

At 8:45 PM, Rita's cab pulled up to the small, out-of-the-way Italian restaurant. She paid the cabbie, then walked in and sat down at the same table where she'd met Senator Morse in August 1963.

The waitress came to the table and brought a glass of water, then asked for her order. She decided to order a glass of sweet tea and wait on the Senator and his entourage to show.

A little past nine o'clock, Senator Morse walked in with two aides, who took seats on either side of her. After some small talk, Rita said, "My FBI employee wouldn't tell me anything. She acted like she didn't know anything about you being investigated."

Senator Morse looked at his aides. "Well, this meeting is no help for us. We know the FBI is after us. I believe since calling for the vote to repeal the Gulf of Tonkin Resolution on March first, they have turned up the heat on me. And in the Senate—well, only one other brave soul voted with me. I'm not too well received anywhere in Washington."

Rita looked at all three men. "Senator, I have some things I need to discuss with you that may be important to you."

The waitress returned to get their orders. Everyone sat quietly until the waitress left the table. Rita leaned forward. "Senator, I've been investigating the murder of Mary Meyer. Do you know who she is?"

The Senator looked at his two aides. Clearly, Rita had his attention. She was surprised they hadn't just gotten up from the table and left. Rita placed both hands on the table. "I need to tell you some things and see if you can answer some of my questions. This may have some impact on you, I don't know."

Senator Morse nodded for Rita to begin. Rita decided to start light and work her way up. "As I said, I was investigating the murder of Mary Meyer. So I will assume you know who she is."

Everyone at the table nodded.

Rita continued going through the entire scenario dealing with the journal, black Cadillac, and the police investigation—or lack thereof.

Senator Morse's aide asked, "Do you know who was driving the black Cadillac?"

Rita shook her head. "Still to this day, I have no idea." She had the fake name, but was afraid to divulge even that information. "At first, I thought the driver worked for Bobby Baker." This caused everyone to exchange glances. "But now I need to know who Bobby Baker is working for— besides the President. That's why I wanted a copy of that Senate Rules Committee transcript."

Again, the three men exchanged glances. Senator Morse said, "Is this why you brought us here?"

Rita sat back in her chair. "CIA Agent James Jesus Angleton and an unnamed FBI agent were both watching Mary Meyer. What was she doing that caused both the CIA and FBI to watch her? I believe she was murdered because of what she knew and had documented in her journal. Why was her journal so important that it had to disappear—and she had to die?"

Rita looked directly at the Senator, who seemed genuinely surprised. She pushed on. "I'm going to meet with Timothy Leary, who may be Mary Meyer's confidant or boyfriend or both."

The waitress returned to the table to bring their drinks. They waited for her to leave.

Senator Morse cleared his throat. "As you know, Professor Leary has a jaded reputation. While all of this is very interesting, why did you want to meet with me? And without bringing me the information I needed?"

Rita looked down at the table. "It wasn't for the lack of trying. I have been stonewalled by my contact at the FBI." She reached into her purse and pulled out her notepad. "What can you tell me about James Jesus Angleton?"

Senator Morse rubbed his chin. "I've heard rumors that Agent Angleton is in charge of an unofficial mission—you know, one of those illegal CIA operations inside the United States to investigate dissidents. Similar to the FBI program I wanted you to get me information about."

Rita's heart almost stopped. "Was Meyer investigated by the CIA because she was a dissident? I mean, her sister is married to Ben Bradlee, former CIA, her husband is CIA, and Angleton, a family friend, is CIA. Why was she watched? At the moment, I don't know for sure that it was the

CIA or Baker that was after her—and me, but why?" She continued. "By the way, I'm trying to get your information, but so far I've gotten turned down."

Senator Morse looked down at the table. "I'm here for you. But with me being a target of the FBI, I'm not sure I can get you any more information on Angleton, since I'm likely a target of the CIA, too." He nodded at the aide sitting on the left.

The aide pulled out an envelope and pushed it toward Rita.

Morse folded his hands on the table as Rita picked up the envelope. "That's the transcript. You're really in dangerous territory, Miss Sullivan."

As the waitress placed their meals in front of each of them, Rita realized how daunting her task was to uncover why Mary Meyer had been murdered and her journal disappeared. The word

Rita put the envelope in her purse and took out her personal steno pad and wrote in shorthand. One of Morse's aides peeked over her shoulder to see what she was writing. *Angleton. Find out about the CIA program to spy on US citizens. Investigating dissent—that's illegal. FBI running a similar program? Did Stephanie know and not tell me? Maybe, probably.*

Rita looked back up at him and smiled as she put the steno pad back in her purse. *I guarantee that aide can't read shorthand.* She took a sip of water, then picked up her fork and started to quietly eat her dinner. Hopefully, the transcript would lead to something about Baker.

APRIL 16, 1966
WASHINGTON DC

Robert McNamara pulled out a sheet of official Secretary of Defense stationary and grabbed a pen from his breast pocket. It was time to respond to the two doctors from Harvard and the two doctors from MIT. He wrote: "Your objective focus of your initial proposal of building an electronic fence, complete with warning systems; night reconnaissance methods, including night vision devices; defoliation techniques, and area denial weapons. Please provide a detailed follow up to your initial proposal for our upcoming summer seminar. Include an agenda featuring the top engineers and scientists to discuss these hypotheses of the technical possibilities in relation to our military operations in Vietnam."

When McNamara finished writing, he leaned back in his chair. As he proofread the letter, he sat back in his chair. *This could be the biggest scientific operation since the Manhattan Project.*

CHAPTER SEVENTEEN

APRIL 17, 1966
BOSTON

Rita Sullivan was drowsy as she rode the train. Between reading over the research into James Jesus Angleton—which wasn't much—and the rhythmic click-clack of the train on the tracks, it was an effort to stay awake. These CIA agents really kept what they were doing buried deep. *I guess that's what they're supposed to do.* She was hoping Timothy Leary would shed some light on Mary's life, her journal, and what she was scared of. *I've struck out every other corner. This is really my last hope.*

As the train pulled into the station, Rita picked up her overnight bag and her purse, then started toward the platform. As she stepped down on the ground, she looked at her watch. She barely had enough time to make it to her hotel, check in, and then meet Leary for dinner. He wanted to be interviewed over dinner and a bottle of wine. Rita was hoping enough would come out of the interview that she could write an article for *Life Magazine.* Otherwise, these expenses would be on her, and that would just about wipe out her cookie jar money. She'd received a nice raise going to work for *Life,* but it hadn't shown on her paycheck just yet.

After checking in at the front desk, she set a direct course for her room. Rita plopped down on the bed for a minute. She was exhausted from the train ride, her eyes were dry from reading too much, and now she had to freshen up and be ready to conduct an interview. She'd made a list of questions in case an interesting article emerged from this, but it was secondary in her mind. She hoped to resolve Mary Meyer's murder. Rita pushed herself off the bed.

Rita walked into the quiet little restaurant and came face to face with Professor Leary. He greeted her with a smile, grabbed her hand, and walked her to a corner booth. Leary was absolutely charming. He was open talking about LSD and smoking marijuana.

After dinner, he asked, "Is *Life Magazine* trying to get their article out before his *Playboy* magazine interview?"

With those words, Rita sat straight up in her seat. After another hour of conversation and half a bottle of wine, he asked her to go back to his place and drop some acid. Rita declined. It was time. "Professor Leary, I have a story to tell you, and I'm hoping you can fill in a lot of blanks for me."

Leary got a puzzled look on his face. "Go on, Rita. Let's hear it," he said with a smile as he reached out for her hand.

Rita told him the story of her relationship with Mary Meyer through the trial. The longer she talked, the more he fidgeted in his seat, frequently looking around at the adjacent tables. When she finished, he sat in silence for a long time. Finally, he signaled to the waiter. Rita thought he was going to blow her off and send her packing. When the waiter brought the bill, she picked it up and placed enough cash down for the bill and tip.

Leary stared at her hard. He still had not said a word.

I hope he's just thinking.

Leary sat back in the booth. "Will you take a walk with me? What I'm about to tell you, I have never said—nor do I want any other human being to hear."

Rita blinked. This wasn't what she expected. "Sure, let's go."

Leary didn't move. "Rita, I'm going to say this once before we get up. I'm not sure you will want to hear what I'm about to tell you. So if you think you can't handle it, perhaps we should part ways right here and call it a wonderful evening."

A series of chills ran down her spine. Rita believed she was on the edge of the truth, but the tone of his voice had clearly changed. *Was he behind this? Am I going to be killed tonight too? No, he was obviously just emotional.* She pushed the negative thoughts from her mind. Professor Leary was in love with Meyer. She picked up her purse and coat. "Let's go. I have waited too long to walk away from answers. I can handle anything you tell me."

They walked on the tree-lined street of beautiful homes. Leary didn't say a word for most of the block. Rita's feet were getting numb from the chill in the air. Leary stopped and grabbed her arm, pulling her to a stop. There was fear in his face. "What I'm about to tell you is strictly off the record. It could get us both killed—which is why I have been silent since her death. Do you understand?"

Rita felt the chill of death. Her mind said *no*, but her heart said *yes*. It was time to finish this story. "I walked out here, didn't I? If this is off the record, its off the record. But I have to know."

Leary started walking again. "Because you have information I didn't know, let's close this circle."

Rita nodded. "I'm ready, I think."

Leary looked around, stopped, and whispered, "Mary Meyer was having an affair with President Kennedy."

Rita froze. Her legs wouldn't move. She didn't think she'd get scared, but she was. She gulped hard but could barely swallow.

Leary continued. "Mary said they would occasionally do LSD or smoke a joint before sex. She believed they would eventually get married. She told me on numerous occasions that after his second term, he would divorce Jackie and marry her. I don't know whether that's true or not, but she believed it, and I didn't question it. I was in love with Mary."

Leary had nothing to do with her murder. She'd known all along, but this confirmed in her mind what her heart told her.

Leary picked up the walking pace. "A little over a week after Kennedy's assassination, Mary called me. She was scared, real scared. She may have been drunk or stoned or both, but she was scared. She said they killed him because they could no longer control him. 'He was changing too fast. They covered up everything. I gotta come see you. I'm afraid.' That's almost word for word what she said."

Rita looked around. She had to make sure no one had heard what she'd been told. "So, you're saying it wasn't Oswald who killed the President?"

151

"No, I'm not saying anything. I don't know anything about that. But you were here to discuss Mary's murder. Knowing what you know now, why do you think they killed Mary?"

Rita picked up on one thing immediately. Leary said *they* not *he*. "It was a professional hit. I don't think they will ever find the murderer. She was shot twice, point blank. What the Mafia calls a double tap. Even the FBI expert's testimony came to the same conclusion. Then, after the man the police arrested was acquitted, not even the FBI wanted to investigate any further. It doesn't make sense—unless they were told to stop."

Leary stopped again. "Did you talk to any of her family members or close friends?"

Rita raised both hands palms up. "Totally stonewalled. Her sister met me but barely talked to me."

Leary started walking again. "That figures. It makes me think the CIA was behind her death. Why, you ask?" He stopped and grabbed her arm. "It just hit me. You said the FBI was investigating her. From what you have found out, it sounds like her family and friends in the CIA were watching her. They must have found out she was going public with her journal, and they killed her."

What could be more revolutionary?" she mumbled.

Leary frowned at her. "What?"

"When I talked to her, she said what she had could be more revolutionary than Khrushchev being ousted. It had to be the story of her affair with Kennedy and using LSD. They couldn't let that story out. She had to die—and the journal disappear."

Leary asked, "Who has the journal?"

152

Simultaneously, they both said, "Angleton."

"At least, he took it," Rita continued. "We'll never know who has it now. I don't believe for a minute he destroyed it."

Leary picked up the pace. They knew why she had died, and if either of them spoke of it, they wouldn't see the next day. They walked maybe another block without a word.

Finally, Rita realized she was chilled to the bone. "I need to go. I have to get back to my hotel and warm up. Now that we know this, do you think that's why I'm being followed?"

Leary ignored the question. "Are you sure, after all of this, you don't want to go back to my place and smoke a joint and drop some acid?"

Rita burst out laughing. "I don't know anything about pot or acid, but after what we have put together, I can't imagine me having a good trip, even if I did want to try it—*and I don't.*" She reached out her hand for Professor Leary.

Leary grabbed her hand, then pulled her close enough to kiss her cheek.

Rita pulled back away from the professor.

Her gesture startled him for a moment, then he reached in his pocket and pulled out a card. "Call me if you need to talk, my friend. But for God's sakes, don't ever tell anyone what we have figured out. I already have enemies in the government because of my knowledge and their use of LSD, particularly the CIA. They know I know too much. I have kept my end of the deal and kept quiet."

Rita turned and started back toward her hotel. *Why did she want me to have a copy of the journal? Why wouldn't she give to one of her friends? I get why she wouldn't want to give it to her family or Cicely Angleton, but why me?* She was shivering all over now. She tried to walk faster to warm up, but that was almost impossible in high heels. The more she walked, the more paranoid she got. What she'd learned tonight was powerful—and extremely dangerous. She looked around the vacant street for people watching her.

Rita walked into her hotel room and tossed her purse on the bed. She went to the bathroom and turned on the faucet to wash her face. She raised her head up and looked directly into the mirror. *That's it. Mary Meyer wanted to give me a copy of her journal because I'm a reporter. So if anything happened to her, her story would survive. Damn it. They knew. They couldn't let me meet her.* With her makeup half off, she went to the hotel bed and sat down. She pulled out her steno pad and made some notes about her conversation with Professor Leary. For these pages, since she was a lefty, she decided to write the shorthand in reverse. If this information fell into the wrong hands, she would end up just like Mary Meyer—dead in a ravine. *Do I have enough information to tie the hit man to Baker's thug? I believe in my heart of hearts Baker's thug was working with the professional hit man on the day Meyer was murdered, but I can't find any evidence to tie it together. Baker, mob, hit. All makes sense. It was too well-timed to be a coincidence.*

For a few seconds, she stared at the small lamp on the dresser. *I never felt like we were watched or followed tonight. Why not? Was nobody following Leary? Strange. I meet with a controversial figure like Leary, and no one's tailing me? Nobody is tailing him? That makes no sense.* She went back to writing. Leary worked with the CIA on the use of LSD in the secret MK Ultra Program ran by them. Leary didn't tell her this—her research into

154

the professor did. He *had* to be watched by the CIA. *Was that why Angleton was watching Meyer? Is that why he had to get her journal? The President of the United States was dropping acid, smoking pot, having an affair—it was a revolutionary story, to be sure. You tie in the CIA?* She'd been able to find virtually nothing on Angleton, which made sense—a top operative for the CIA. The man could probably hide in plain sight. There must be a tie-in on the professional hit on Mary Meyer. Were there any connections between CIA Agent James Jesus Angleton and Bobby Baker?

She flipped back to her notes. The transcript she'd received from Senator Morse revealed Baker was involved in kickback and bribery schemes between businessman, Don B. Reynolds, and President Johnson. How ironic. The day Kennedy was assassinated, there was a hearing on Baker. It died down for a while but didn't go away. Now the "heat" was on Baker's shady dealings. Baker had to shut down his strong arm tactics; he had to clean up his act. She flipped back a couple of pages. Stephanie Keeton remarked about Baker's ties to the mob—Lansky, Giancana, Trafficante and Marcello—but still hadn't tied in that connection. *Professional hit and mob, it sure goes together.* Rita had turned up a lot of information on him, but nothing tying him to Angleton.

She got off the bed and returned to the bathroom to finish removing her makeup. Her mom had taught her that when working jigsaw puzzles, work all your knowns first to see if that reveals a clue on the unknowns. *Finish investigating Bobby Baker. You have got to learn his ties to the mob and if he or his thug had a relationship with the hit man. But the role of Angleton and the CIA in all of this was still baffling. Come on, girl, you got this.*

CHAPTER EIGHTEEN

APRIL 23, 1966

CONTINENTAL HOTEL TERRACE - SAIGON

Neil Sheehan had been out on the front lines as an embedded reporter and was looking forward to a good meal, which he'd not had for a while. As Sheehan strolled across town to his dinner meeting with Pham Xuan An, his thoughts drifted to one of the most vicious battles he'd witnessed as an embedded reporter. He compared his most recent experiences on the front line to that day last November watching Charlie Company fight off the NVA attackers trying to break their defense at Ia Drang Valley. Those in Charlie Company fought and died like lions holding their ground, driving back the NVA. While Sheehan still preferred the tactics of Edward Lansdale, he was impressed with the US military.

He stepped into the restaurant at the Continental Hotel and looked around for An. Sheehan had a pending deadline for a column with the *New York Times* on his latest assignment. An had always been a great source of information. Perhaps a dinner would reveal some of the little details his column may have been lacking.

Sheehan sat down with An, who was enjoying a cigarette and beer. "What are you currently working on for *Time* Magazine?" Neil asked.

An blew out smoke. "I just came from a military press conference detailing their new mission, Operation Birmingham. Westmoreland plans to open up the area north of Saigon and Route 13 so troops have access to the north. It's an extension of the Search and Destroy battle plans the US military has been pushing over the last year." An provided significant detail to what Westmoreland's bureau chief had explained for the operation. About halfway through An's sentence, the waiter appeared with a fresh beer for both and took their dinner orders.

They continued chatting for several minutes until the waiter brought their meals.

"So what article are you working on Neil?" An asked.

Sheehan, between bites of his meal, said, "I don't know at the moment. I'll come up with something, but I wanted to tell you what I witnessed last month up in Hue."

An took a drink of beer and nodded for Sheehan to continue.

Sheehan picked up his napkin and wiped his mouth. "I was in the middle of the protests right after Ky fired Thi. The Buddhist crowd was crazy. A student leader in the middle of about twenty thousand protestors stood up on this big scaffolding and shouted, 'Do you want the general to stay with us?' Naturally, the students and Buddhists all replied, 'Yes, yes.' The crowd got real rambunctious. I'm here to tell you, it left no doubt the ruling Saigon junta was in trouble."

An lit up another cigarette, then leaned forward in a low voice. "I've said all along that Thich Tri Quang will be the downfall of the South. Even more than the enemy."

It was a strange thought. But from what Sheehan had seen and the conflicts that Tri Quang had created in the north, it was hard to argue with. "Well, then General Thi appeared before the crowd and tried to calm things down. He said, 'Think about our country, not about me.' I was near Thi when he gave an interview to a South Vietnamese journalist. I overheard him say something like he would take any position that was useful to the country."

An winced with that remark. "You know as well as I do that neither Ky nor Thieu will ever let the general back in power."

Sheehan nodded as he finished his beer. "I understand that Ky and Thieu are negotiating with a more moderate Buddhist monk here."

An waved his cigarette. "Only because Lodge, Komer, McNamara and Johnson are telling them to do so."

Sheehan leaned on one elbow. "Seriously, what choice do they have? Hue and Da Nang are a total mess. It can't be helping the fighting."

After they finished their dinner, An asked, "Have you seen Lansdale since he was removed from the Pacification program?"

Sheehan pursed his lips. "No. I heard Daniel Ellsberg was assigned to Porter." He looked down at his watch. "Uh-oh. My deadline is approaching to get my article in. I better go." He waved to the waiter to bring over the dinner check. *You always learn something speaking with An. Well worth the price of dinner.*

MAY 24, 1966

HUE, SOUTH VIETNAM

Nguyen Tao's last week had been a virtual whirlwind. When Theodore Shackley left Thailand to return to the United States, Tao received new orders from CIA Analyst George Allen to leave Bangkok and report to the US Embassy in Saigon. Tao had operated in such deep cover for years, he was surprised Allen even knew about his existence.

When Tao arrived at the US Embassy, he was met by a surprised Major Hebert, who was doing his rounds. Tao asked, "Could you walk with me to George Allen's office?"

As they walked, Tao mentioned his concerns about how Allen knew about him.

Steven said, "Lansdale gave your file to Allen several weeks ago. Allen stopped by and talked to me about your file."

Tao sighed. Surely, nothing should surprise him. But why would they investigate his background?

Too soon, they arrived at Allen's office, and Steven bid Tao good afternoon and good luck.

Tao entered and was greeted by Allen, who offered him a seat across from him.

Allen got right to the point. "Tao, I'd like you to accept an undercover assignment into Da Nang and Hue for the purposes of preparing a report on the Buddhist situation in those two critical cities. Lansdale says you're one of the best deep cover agents, which is exactly what I need."

Tao was flattered but said nothing.

Allen continued to describe the proposed assignment. "Three weeks ago, Premier Ky told General Westmoreland the Buddhist Struggle Movement controlled the three northern provinces of South Vietnam. Ky believed the Buddhists were negotiating with the Viet Cong. I have direct orders from CIA Director Vice Admiral Rabon to get good intel from that region." Allen looked at Tao.

Tao gave no reaction.

Allen finally spoke, "Look, Tao, the situation has deteriorated so much the Buddhist ARVN troops are fighting with the Ky loyalists. They finally start fighting, and they fight each other."

Tao leaned forward. "Since you have read my file, you know I'm a Catholic, and the Buddhists were protesting the Catholic leadership in this province."

Allen laughed as he countered. "Being Catholic was part of the reason for your selection. Moreover, you'll understand both sides, having grown up here."

"I'm from that area," Tao said. "There's a good chance I could be recognized."

Allen smiled as he spoke. "I was prepared for you to say that. If you are recognized, then you say you've retired and simply moved back home.

Tao raised both palms. "I'm not worried about all the residents—just the ones that are VC."

Allen raised an eyebrow. "Tao, you have your assignment. I'm being transferred back to the United States with a promotion. My new position is to advise George Carver, the Special Assistant for Vietnamese Affairs, who answers directly to DIA Raborn. You will answer directly to me."

Tao bit his lip. Whether he liked it or not, the CIA had expectations for him. He had no choice but to accept the assignment.

Allen smiled again. "I thought you'd see it our way. Now, I have some other news. Richard Helms, who you indirectly worked for when you were assigned to Lansdale, is going to replace Raborn as the Director of the CIA. Keep that under your hat."

Tao smiled. Helms knew the situation in Vietnam very well. He'd been one of the decision makers in Laos in the "secret" war. This could be the last chance for Lansdale and the CIA's involvement in the Vietnam Conflict.

Allen reached in the desk drawer, pulled out a file, and handed it to Tao. "These are the individuals we want you to keep track of, plus any others you deem necessary. Lansdale said you were the only man who could handle this mission and remain in the weeds. I want you up there immediately. You will report back to me directly. No one else. Is that understood?"

Tao reached for the file. "Yes, sir." He stood up to walk out.

Allen leaned back in his leather chair. "I'm not naïve. I know you'll brief Lansdale, but that's all. No one else is to know about your mission. You're dismissed."

Tao plodded methodically to the doorway. *Man, this agency and this war is changing so rapidly I can barely keep up.*

The first person Tao ran into was Steven. The two men walked out of the Embassy without so much as a word. As they walked toward Tao's Peugeot, he told Steven about his new top secret assignment. "What can you tell me about Tri Quang?"

Steven shrugged. "A lot and nothing. I've never been able to get a real feel for the monk. Everybody else here seems to think he's conspiring with the VC or the North. That doesn't make sense to me. He believes the Buddhists will lose their rights to worship if the Communists win."

Tao shook his head. "I'm still not convinced he isn't a communist. The Buddhists in the North get to worship. Maybe not openly, but still..." He looked Steven in the eyes. "If we were playing chess, I'd say Tri Quang's next move is a Bishop Desperado." He didn't wait for Steven's response. He just got in his Peugeot and drove off.

Tao boarded the Bell helicopter for his ride to the secure landing zone at the base camp at Dong Ha in the Quang Tri province. This was the home of the Third Battalion, Fourth Marines of the Third Marine Division, a site near Hue. It was unusual to be in a bird and not be flying it himself. About three-fourths of the way through their flight, the pilot spoke into his com-set. "Jack Rabbit here."

Tao continued to look out the window. He saw his old stomping grounds where he'd grown up and his family lived. He shoved his family's horrific fate out of his mind and tried to focus on how little the geography of the countryside had changed over the last decade.

The pilot reached over and switched the control head from red to green. He was about to get new orders. Then he looked at the co-pilot and frowned. "Commander, we have a package with an expiration date."

Despite hearing only one side of the conversation, Tao leaned forward to listen, as the radio discussion was about him—he was the package.

The pilot listened for a few more minutes. "Roger that." He looked over at his co-pilot, who was writing something.

The co-pilot nodded to the pilot. "Jack Rabbit. To new coordinates, then on to the base. Understood, sir."

After the pilot finished his conversation, he leaned forward but said something through his mic to the co-pilot. Then he turned back and looked at Tao. "New orders. We have to do a pick up, then proceed to Dong Ha."

Before Tao could give the pilot a thumbs up, the bird made a hard turn away from Dong Ha. There was nothing to debate. Tao sighed. "Can you tell me where we're off to?"

The pilot leaned back and put his hand over the mic. "Not too far out of your way. Going to an ARVN outpost near the DMZ."

Tao closed his eyes. *Must be picking up some Re-Con Marines.*

Thirty minutes later, the Bell helicopter swept out of the sky to a large opening. Two jeeps were parked in the opening with five Marines and a Vietnamese man in black pajamas. The pilot waved out the window, and the contingent walked two Marines in front and two behind, with one on the side of the man in the black pajamas. The co-pilot shouted back for Tao to open the door on the side of the approaching Marines. He flipped the handle and gave it a push. The Marines still had green and black grease on their faces, as though they had just returned from a mission.

The Vietnamese soldier was pushed into the bird while one of the Marines got in beside him. Tao leaned over to make eye contact with the Marine as the bird lifted back off the ground with a lurch.

The Marine winked at Tao. "Somebody from the NVA wants to have a conversation with us—and, he brought us some maps...plans."

Tao cracked a smile as he looked at the defector, then back at the Marine. "Do you know his rank?"

The Vietnamese soldier looked at Tao. "Thủ quân"

"Ah, a captain."

The Vietnamese captain leaned forward. "I know you."

Tao kept his poker face as he stared at the man. *Who the hell is this man?*

The rest of the helicopter ride was quiet to the Dong Ha base.

The chopper dropped out of the sky toward the postage-stamp size landing pad. A number of US Navy Seals emerged from cover so they would be on all four sides of the bird when it landed. As soon as they were on the ground, two Seals walked up to the helicopter door on Tao's side. They escorted the NVA Captain and the Marine to the closest building, which Tao assumed was the command post. He glanced at his watch. 1730. The best thing to do was bed down there for the night, then get up before daylight, get into character, and then proceed into Hue.

One of the Seals gave Tao directions to the barracks.

Tao sat down on a bunk, pulled out his mission file, and studied the information the CIA wanted. Naturally, the top sheets in the file pertained to

Thich Tri Quang. No surprise. There were several pages of background on what they characterized as the militant monk. *How can he blame President Johnson for the unrest in the area?* The mess started on March 10 when Ky fired General Thi, a Buddhist responsible for I-Corps, the northern districts of South Vietnam. The official reason for his dismissal was his loyalty to the Buddhists in the north. Thi was an aggressive field commander and was credited with planning the very successful Operation Starlite. The real reason for his dismissal, Ky feared him as a rival for political power in South Vietnam. Some in the CIA believed that Thi was negotiating a peaceful settlement with the communists. *I don't believe that.*

In April, the unrest in the region worsen with students joining the Buddhist protests. Then Premier Ky sent in the military without consulting with President Thieu. Within the last couple of weeks, the situation had deteriorated to the point US troops were sent to the region. Ten days ago, the US Marines confronted the pro-Buddhist ARVN soldiers outside of Da Nang.

Tao shook his head in disgust as he read. To make matters worse, after being fired upon, an American helicopter returned fire on the hostile crowd and killed an ARVN officer. Naturally, the protestors blamed the Americans for interfering with internal affairs.

Tao sat back. *This situation is a tinder box. I see why the CIA wants me in here. The Buddhists are blaming America.*

There was a knock on his door. Tao opened the door to a US Navy Seal commander. "The North Vietnamese captain would like to talk to you. It would help us if you were to sit in on the last of our interrogation."

165

Tao secured his file and followed the commander toward the interrogation area. He inquired if they had obtained the information from the deserter they had hoped for. The commander was quick to say the man seemed to want to cooperate, but the results were less than satisfactory.

Tao looked over the notes produced by the two Seals, who had been interrogating the captain.

The two men entered. The Seal sat down hard on the chair then leaned forward into the face of the Viet Cong Captain.

Tao calmly sat down without the bravado on the same side of the small table. The Seal pointed to Tao. "There he is. Now, let's pick up where we left off, shall we?"

Tao had seen one of the best interrogators in action. Santa Romana, also known as Father Diaz, had taught him many things about interrogation two decades ago. His techniques worked. If Tao had to get rough, he knew how to produce results, but he didn't believe it would be necessary. The man had surrendered and wanted to cooperate. Tao wanted to present himself as someone from the country. Make him believe in a strange sort of way they were kindred spirits. Plus, in the back of his mind, he wanted to find out if the man really did know who he was. This had weighed on his mind since he'd heard the NVA soldier speak to him on the helicopter trip over to the base.

Tao quietly asked the defector in English, "What is your name and rank?" Then he repeated it in Vietnamese.

The captain nodded out of respect and answered.

Tao went on, calmly asking the enemy captain questions for the next hour or so. He stopped to have fresh water and crackers brought in for everyone. He was almost finished with his questioning, which had revealed details of the planned operation of NVA 324B battalion's battle plans, strengths and locations on a map.

Tao leaned up on the table. "How do you know me?"

The enemy smiled. "I was one of the invaders who burned your home in the village Hoa Ninh. We took the other villagers prisoner and marched them back to the North. Most were put in work camps."

Tao struggled to listen intently to the detail. If he lost his temper, the man would become uncooperative and stop talking. This was the break he'd wanted for almost a decade. Finally, when the man finished talking, Tao bit his lip, then asked, "Who was responsible for burning my home? What happened to my personal items?"

The captain shrugged.

Rage climbed Tao's body. He gripped the seat of his chair to suppress his desire to pull his Colt 1911 and kill the man on the spot, but he was able to focus on his missing information. "Captain, we're Vietnamese. Family is dear to us—above all other things. My wife and daughter burnt up in my home. I want to know who ordered the fire and what happened to my things. I have no photos of my wife of daughter. You, above all, understand why I want them returned?"

The captain looked down for a long time. Just as Tao was ready to explode, the captain replied, "We took all your personal items to one of our top officers, who planned the attack on your village and ordered your house burnt, to send you a message. His name is Nguyen Van Trung."

Tao jutted his chin and snarled. "Does he still have my chalice?"

The defector shrugged. "I don't know. It's been many years."

Without another word, Tao looked at the Seal, then got up and walked out of the interrogation room.

Tao returned to his bunk room and tried to refocus on his current mission. He picked up the file he'd been studying two hours previous. He found what he thought was one of the key elements for why he'd been sent to Hue. Just a few days ago, the combined US and ARVN troops regained control of Da Nang from the Buddhists and students, but there were deaths on both sides. It all made sense now. The CIA wanted Tao in Hue because the day after tomorrow was the funeral for the ARVN officer killed by a soldier who fired from a helicopter. If there were protestors, he was to report who was leading them. Who was agitating this situation?

When Tao had completed his review of the file, he let his disciplined mind flow to what he'd learned. He had confirmed one of his secret concerns. The chalice. *His name, plus his son, Luc, and that of his deceased wife and deceased daughter were engraved on the chalice, as well as the names of his deceased friend, Danilo Quezon, his wife, Catherine, and his son Franco. In the wrong hands, that information was very dangerous.* He closed his eyes and lay back on the bunk. This evening he had learned the name he'd sought for years—Nguyen Van Trung.

CHAPTER NINETEEN

MAY 26, 1966
HUE, SOUTH VIETNAM

Tao walked around the ancient city of Hue, wishing he could take in the architecture, but this was not to be. Hue was, in essence, the Buddhist capital of the country. Few people were out on the streets in the early hours. Most of those who were out kept their heads down, unwilling to make eye contact. Tao assumed they were the residents, and those making eye contact were likely either the antagonists or the spies. He made another assumption—that the passive residents were out gathering in the necessities before the protests and violence broke out so they could hunker down at home.

One of Tao's personal missions was to sort out which spies might be there representing either the Viet Cong or the North Vietnamese Army. They had to be in the midst. Their roles would likely either be observers or maybe even part of the antagonists. As Tao continued his excursion through the older portion of the city, he saw ARVN troops guarding certain buildings while others moved about in military vehicles. There likely would be some protests today, as the funeral for the ARVN officer was to take place later. Tao was surprised at the minimum presence of US troops. He assumed they were lying low in an attempt to minimize confrontation.

He made his way to an area near the Dieu de Pagoda. If there were going to be trouble, it would start in that area. *I need to be close enough to observe, but obscure enough to not be obvious. Once again, I'm spying on my own people rather than the enemy.* It was an uncomfortable position.

Tao entered a small café that appeared to be open and sat at a window table. He ordered breakfast and coffee, then stared out the window, sipping his steaming coffee. Allen had obviously given up on trying to convince McNamara, Lodge, and Westmoreland that Thi was a good commander for the area, an opinion held by US Marine Lieutenant General Lewis Walt, the man in charge of US forces in this area, designated as I Corps.

No sooner had he finished his small breakfast then students ran down the street toward the Pagoda. He paid the proprietor, then strolled in the direction of the students. As he followed, to his surprise, they didn't go to the Pagoda. Instead, they were met by a large number of monks. The leader of the students talked for a few minutes with one of the monks, then the group took off in a different direction. As they walked, more students and monks joined the crowd. The last ones to join carried bottles, rags and gasoline—to make Molotov cocktails, no doubt.

A few blocks later, the crowd started chanting as they approached the United States Information Service Library. They set the building on fire, making sure it burnt to the ground. Fortunately, no one was injured, but by now the crowd had worked itself into a frenzy. Tao remained in the area observing the Buddhists and the students, who seemed satisfied carrying out their protest at this location.

Before he left the streets for the night, Tao had witnessed protestors in the streets rioting and worse yet, he witnessed several monks immolate themselves.

Tao went to a cheap hotel and checked in under an assumed name. He sat down on the dirty bed and prepared his report for George Allen. In essence, there were gangs of students with some Buddhist monks. They were trashing everything. He speculated they may have been led by left-leaning students or maybe even the VC. Their trashing of the library, Tao speculated, was more than it seemed. It kept momentum building for the Buddhist protest, all to keep the focus on the American who killed the Buddhist soldier.

After he finished his report, his mind drifted to the burning monks. It has been a long time since he'd had the nightmare of watching a monk burn, only to realize it wasn't a monk, but his wife. He wouldn't sleep this night.

May 27, 1966

Columbia Restaurant - Tampa, Florida

Theodore Shackley parked his car in a space at the far end of Santo Trafficante Jr.'s Columbia Restaurant in the Ybor City district of Tampa, Florida. Before he got out of his car, he placed his nine-millimeter in the glovebox and locked it, and then headed to the entrance of the lavish restaurant.

Just inside the door, he was met by the receptionist. "Do you have a reservation, sir?"

Shackley glanced around the restaurant. In a low voice, he replied, "I have an appointment with your boss."

The receptionist pulled his reservation book from the podium. "What is your name, sir?"

Shackley calmly gave him a steely-eyed stare. "Mr. Appointment to see your boss."

The receptionist nodded. Without a word, he snapped his fingers. Within seconds, a waiter appeared at the tiny podium. The receptionist whispered to the waiter, who disappeared for a moment. When the waiter returned, he waved for Shackley to follow.

Shackley looked around at the extravagant structure as he walked behind the young man.

The waiter opened the door to the private dining area. Shackley walked straight toward to Trafficante, but two bodyguards intercepted his path.

Trafficante snapped his fingers. The bodyguards stopped and looked back at Trafficante. "It's all right. Leave us."

Shackley sat down at the round table. To his left was the mafia kingpin, while Gino DeLuca was to his right. He adjusted his glasses back up on his nose. "Gentlemen. I wanted to deliver the news face to face. Just in case our friends at the FBI are listening in." He cracked half a smile.

Trafficante waved a waiter to come take orders. "Bring up a bottle of Louis Roederer, crystal vintage."

Shackley leaned back in his chair. "I'm to report to Vientiane in July. As you know, I'm the new station chief for the CIA. All arrangements have been made on our end to be ready within two weeks of my arrival. The rest of my team from Miami will be in place by the middle of August."

Trafficante nodded. "Did you inform Marcello?"

Shackley sniffed as he wiped his mouth. "No, I'm leaving that to you. The FBI is getting ready to crank up the heat on Marcello. I can't take any chances. I figured you have a way to get him a message. I'm sure his phone is hot."

Trafficante frowned. "What makes you say that?"

"He gave me some names to slip discreetly to the FBI for a bust. But the DOJ is still pissed off about Marcello's obstruction of justice and bribery from two years ago. His help didn't take the heat off. There are three FBI agents who have been watching him for a couple of years. The situation has gotten bad enough that now even Hoover can't ignore it."

Trafficante sat back and was quiet for a few moments. "Carlos got sloppy buying off that juror . . . ." His voice trailed off. "He regrets that."

DeLuca cleared his throat. "Boss, when can we get started with Vang Pao's labs? I think that's going to be critical to our operation."

Trafficante snarled at DeLuca. "I know what you promised. We'll do it on *my* timetable." He leaned back. Trafficante pointed at Shackley. "We'll be in there before Shackley arrives in Laos."

The waiter with the Louis Roederer returned to the table, followed by another waiter bringing fresh salads to each of the three men.

The conversation became mostly about family, which kept Shackley out of the conversation. The waiter brought a second bottle of wine.

"Take it to my office," Trafficante barked.

The three men got up from the table. When Trafficante's bodyguards started to follow, once again, he waved them off. They retired to his office. He reached into his humidor and pulled out several Cuban cigars. "DeLuca."

DeLuca took one.

Trafficante held the box toward Shackley. "Ted?"

Shackley refused.

The three men sat down in oxblood-colored leather chairs away from his desk. Trafficante pulled out his clipper, then cut and lit the cigar. He passed the cutter and lighter to DeLuca. Then he reached into the ice bucket for the wine and poured three glasses.

Once Trafficante and DeLuca had taken several puffs off the cigars, Trafficante leaned forward. "DeLuca here tells me everything went well with Vang Pao. What do you say?"

Shackley ran his hand over his blond hair. "Very well. Vang Pao was pleased you and your friends are willing to meet his new prices. According to Conein, the Corsicans are not going along at the present. Conein is a little nervous about the position he's in."

Trafficante blew out smoke. "It's just business. I'm willing to pay. I'm not cutting Guerini out—he's in trouble. I have it on good word there's a turf war coming. Guerini and his brother have their hands full. I like the man—hope he wins. I—we—owe him big time. But, like I say, it's just business. Hell, if he wants back in at Vang Pao's prices, fine."

Shackley took a sip. "Conein is concerned about his cut. I think that's part of what he's nervous about. He doesn't want the Corsicans to find out he's still getting paid."

Trafficante looked at DeLuca. "You know that's not my concern." He took a draw off his cigar, then sipped his wine. "Conein's all right. Perhaps he has an aunt we can cut into the deal. You talk to him. I think we need him—for a while, anyway. What do you think?"

Shackley nodded as he leaned forward. "Conein is an invaluable asset. He knows everybody that's worth knowing. We'll keep him happy." He sat back in his chair.

The room fell silent for a while.

Shackley tapped the table. "Let's see what the Corsicans in Indochina do. Are they going back to Italy and France and get in the middle of the turf war, or will they stay where they are? If they stay, well, who knows— maybe another outlet. They may pay these new prices, plus we can step on the product and put another mark on them. Since there's no transportation fee, if you know what I mean."

175

Trafficante took off his glasses and waved them around. "You know that's not such a bad idea. Our O and H business is getting real big. We're going to make some real dough here. Then I want to move on the Corsicans' morphine labs."

DeLuca raised both hands. "Wow, I think the timing is wrong for that."

Trafficante smiled. "Let's see how all this plays out."

Shackley finished his wine. "I think we're done here. I need to get back to Miami."

Trafficante stood. "Get in touch, if you need me. We got this deal dicked."

Shackley left. Relief swept over him as he drove off. This Laos mission was taking shape. Now, to get his team in place and assist Vang Pao in getting his troops ramped up to fight better was his next task.

After Shackley left, Trafficante looked at DeLuca and smiled. "This is working out better than I had planned."

DeLuca leaned to the right in the high-back leather chair and took a big draw off his Cuban cigar. "Boss, I agree. When I was meeting with Shackley and Conein, they were all over themselves to keep Vang Pao happy."

Trafficante took off his glasses and looked at them. Then he grabbed a napkin from the table to clean them. "Furci told me he had up to seven sergeants lined up in Saigon who were in charge of NCOs and USOs' procurement. A really ballsy move. They'll take over in July about the same time Shackley gets to Laos. Perfect timing."

DeLuca took a sip of wine. "Conein took me around Saigon before I went to meet with Vang Pao. I was really surprised at the number of places for the enlisted and officers to hit."

Trafficante leaned forward in the chair. "Frank Furci has done an excellent job setting up this network, but, Gino, I don't trust him for a minute. This is why I wanted to talk to you privately. I'm putting you on him, too."

"Wow, Boss, he set up a network for you throughout Southeast Asia."

"I know, I know. But I'm telling you, I just don't trust him. You I trust, you're my aunt's kid. You love money and power, in that order. You screw up, all I have to do is call her and you're out of the will and I'll take away your power. Your ass is grass. Furci—" Trafficante snapped his fingers.

CHAPTER TWENTY

MAY 29, 1966

HUE, SOUTH VIETNAM

The last three days in Hue had been relatively calm, eerily so. Tao was surprised the Buddhists hadn't participated more. Further, he hadn't been able to see Thich Tri Quang. Odds were he was residing in Dieu de Pagoda. Tao couldn't gain access to the monk. He had to wait for him to come out, then attempt to find a way to talk to him. Access to the monk was key to Tao's mission.

Today, Tao decided he was to make a move on the Pagoda. His idea was to get in to worship—a considerable challenge—but he knew the Buddhist traditions well from his own family's heritage. As he approached the Pagoda, a large gathering of monks emerged from the religious structure and poured into the street. Tao stopped. Had he just been presented an opportunity to enter the building without having to get past too many monks? Perhaps have direct access to Tri Quang?

The monks in the street marched and chanted. The students, who had been such a large part of the weeks of demonstration, quickly joined the chanting.

Tao slowly and methodically moved toward the entrance of the Pagoda. Just as he was about to head up the long path leading to the entrance, the chanting in the street changed. He turned his attention in that direction. Something was different. Tao tried to refocus.

The door to the Pagoda opened, and a Buddhist nun ceremoniously stepped out the door. She didn't give Tao so much as a glance as she solemnly placed one foot precisely in front of the other toward the street.

Her appearance mesmerized Tao. A cold chill crawled down Tao's spine. He turned and slipped from pillar to pillar, discretely following the nun toward the street. What was she up to? Would she create a big enough distraction to allow him to get to Tri Quang? Tao snuck along the path, but keeping his distance from her. As he stood at the last pillar, he realized following her had taken him away from the entrance.

As the nun approached the street, the chanting changed again. The monks moved to seal the street as she entered. One of the monks leading the chants with a megaphone stopped momentarily. Two other monks approached her.

Tao was spellbound by the process, as was the crowd. *Was she going to speak?*

This was the moment Tao had waited for. He turned and slinked toward the front door of the pagoda. As he hurried toward his destination, the crowd let out a collective gasp. Tao stopped. His heart overruled his head. He knew what he would see when he turned, but he had to look.

There in the street, the Buddhist nun had set herself on fire. She sat there peacefully in the middle of the street, burning. Tao dropped to his knees. Images of his deceased wife and daughter flooded his mind. He struggled to get up, to get his emotions back under control. The door was so close. Tri Quang had to be on the other side. All he had to do was get up and move in that direction.

Tao lay in bed, staring at the ceiling. He was physically exhausted, but he feared the sleep he desperately needed. Today, he had failed his assignment. He didn't make contact with Tri Quang, despite a perfect opportunity. His emotions were destroyed along with his mission. He didn't even know how he made it back to the sorry hotel. He didn't remember anything. The last thing he remembered was seeing his watch. 2:45.

Tao sat straight up in bed. He—and his bed—were soaked in sweat. Tonight was the most intense the nasty dream had ever been. The Buddhist nun sitting in the street on fire . . . that look on her face . . . so peaceful while she was consumed by fire. . . . Then the nun turned into his deceased wife, wailing in anguish as she burned, trying to protect his daughter, who sobbed. The dream ended as his wife screamed, "Why didn't you save us?"

Tao could smell burning flesh, just like he had earlier. He got up and went to the tiny bathroom, sipped water from his palm, and splashed water in his face. When he looked in the mirror, he asked himself if his CIA career was over. Had he lost his drive to complete not only this mission, but any other assignment given to him? If one would come? He went in and turned on the low wattage light bulb above his bed and stared at the wall.

JUNE 5, 1966

LIFE MAGAZINE BUREAU OFFICE

WASHINGTON DC

Rita Sullivan was told to check out an advertisement in the June 4 edition of the *New York Times* by her chief editor, Cal Singleton. It was a list of 6400 professors and teachers who were against the Vietnam war. Rita's second major article had appeared in this past month's issue of *Life Magazine*. Her topic was the impact of the ongoing Buddhist protests in Da Nang and Hue upon the Vietnamese Pacification program. Her conclusion was the Buddhist chaos had resulted in a huge setback for the Pacification program in the two largest cities closest to the DMZ. Instead of US troops confronting the ever-growing Viet Cong presence in this region, called I-Corps, they were having to focus on policing confrontations between the South Vietnamese Army and the Buddhist militants. Moreover, it was driving a wedge between the United States and the South Vietnamese governments and militaries.

Her column presented the facts, providing the readers with as much information as possible. Singleton had told her to check out this ad so she could write an article about the growing anti-war sentiment and the associated protests. She could use any of her previous sources, no holds

181

barred, for a hard-hitting column. Additionally, she could include any recent or current photographs. The chief wanted the column for the July publication.

As Rita began drafting her column, she struggled to keep her personal views neutral. Her early writings, her best columns, came with leads on anti-war protests or left-leaning politicians, yet she'd viewed herself as neutral. Perhaps she wasn't as neutral as she'd believed. *I wish I had a way to get in touch with her confidant, Billy now with the SDS.*

Rita retyped her introductory paragraph. It lacked the zing to capture the reader. She ripped the paper out of the Smith-Corona and tossed it into the wastebasket.

She refocused on her column. *Hey, look at the changes in the music industry.* Document the changes in the music industry. How it had begun a little over a year ago with Malvina Reynolds' song "Napalm." Then there was the sell-out "Sing-in for Peace" concert at Carnegie Hall on September 24, 1965. Rita made a list of the protests around the United States, beginning with the December 19, 1964, one she'd attended, through the most recent world-wide protest on March 26 that included the US cities of Boston, Chicago, Philadelphia, New York, and San Francisco. She wrote several paragraphs on the May 15 protest in Washington DC with 10,000 demonstrators marching between the White House and the Washington Monument. The final portion of Rita's column was devoted to heavyweight boxing champion Muhammad Ali's refusal to be inducted into the US military on March 9. Ali, never one to lack words for any occasion, nor one who had any concern of being controversial, made a public statement that since he was a Black Muslim, he was a conscientious objector. Ali didn't stop there. "My conscience won't let me go shoot my brother, or some darker people, or some poor hungry people in the mud for big powerful America. And shoot them for what? They never called me *nigger*, they never lynched me, they didn't put no dogs on me, they didn't rob me of my nationality, rape and kill my mother and father . . . . Shoot them for what? How can I shoot them poor people? Just take me to jail."

Rita had picked out several pictures of protests from *Life's* vast file of anti-war photographs. She included one of a recent heavyweight fight and another of Ali appearing in public with other Black Muslims. Just before she finished her column, a picture came across the AP wire of a Buddhist nun, Thich Nu Thanh Quang, setting herself on fire in front of the Dieu de Pagoda in Hue, South Vietnam. Her act of suicide protested the Catholic regime in that province of South Vietnam. Rita decided she should go talk to her editor before she changed her column. She wanted to include the story about another Buddhist religious figure, this time a nun, emulating herself.

Rita grabbed the photo of the Buddhist nun, then started down the hallway to the chief's corner office. She knocked on his door. When she heard a "Come on in," Rita opened the door and stood in the doorway. "Mr. Singleton, I have a picture from the AP of a nun self-immolation in Hue." She held it out for Singleton to see. "Should I change my column to take in the Buddhist protests in South Vietnam?"

Singleton seemed fixated on the picture. "Let me see your column first, but I'm inclined to say let's make this a separate story. I think the Buddhist protests are too big to be included here. Plus, it would be good to follow your last column with a follow-up on the Buddhist protests with this photo." He spun around in his chair to glance out the window, then turned back.

"Rita, without even seeing it, let's go with your column, as is, right now. Let's just finish what you have on the US protests first. For your next one, go back to the Buddhist. By the way, good work, Sullivan."

Rita lowered her arm, then held the picture out in front of herself. She smiled, then quietly closed the door and started back toward her Smith-Corona. *I'm so happy here. Chief Singleton is so good to work for.*

CHAPTER TWENTY-ONE

JUNE 14, 1966 - 1:45 PM
WASHINGTON DC

President Johnson had just about finished reading over the long memorandum from Special Assistant Robert Komer. His desk phone buzzed. Gerri informed him that Robert McNamara, Dean Rusk, and Walter Rostow had arrived for their lunch meeting. The President requested Gerri make enough copies of the memorandum and provide one to each man. He laid the copy on her desk as he headed off.

As soon as the President was seated with the other gentlemen, lunch was brought in and Gerri delivered the copies of Komer's memo. Johnson asked them to read as they ate.

McNamara acknowledged he'd received an advanced copy. He pulled his notes out of his pocket; Westmoreland's troop build improved the chances of the program working.

Rusk added that he also believed the military couldn't "stoop to the guerilla strategy" of the North. The Pacification program was critical for the people of South Vietnam so they could feel at ease and get involved in their own governing.

McNamara looked at the President. "I have a question. Why did Komer want you to review this before discussing it with Porter?"

Johnson shrugged. "He sure seems to want to get bigger and go faster. Which I don't see how we can in the middle of the damn Buddhist crisis. What's the latest on Tri Quang and his antics?"

Rusk rubbed his chin. "According to Lodge, they have declared martial law in Hue. Tri Quang doesn't have many moves left."

As they finished their meeting, Johnson felt they had covered all the matters he believed were important. Westmoreland got his new troops for implementing Phase II of his strategy of pushing the North Vietnamese back. While he was not big on the Pacification program, he did believe that with Komer and Porter reporting directly to him, it had its best chance of succeeding.

JUNE 25, 1966

HUE, SOUTH VIETNAM

Tao had struggled to stay focused on his mission over the last month. He'd spent many nights staring at the ceiling out of fear of falling to sleep, only to drift off in the wee hours of the morning. He was back on the street early each day. The protests had calmed down some. He thought some of the calming was based on the highly-publicized hunger strike of Tri Quang, now in its third week. The only big issue was that the protestors had taken over the US Consulate, despite it being defended by ARVN troops, and set it on fire. Tao had submitted several reports to Allen. He had a clear reason why Allen had sent him on this mission for the CIA—the powerbrokers in Saigon and Washington DC had fed the press a narrative that wasn't the complete picture of the situation in northern South Vietnam. Lodge had met with Tri Quang before all of these protests began. Now, Lodge was working with the moderate Buddhist leader Thich Tam Chau in Saigon, who called for peace and support of the country's constitution.

Finally, the ARVN had regained control of Hue, returning control of both Da Nang and Hue to their government.

Now that Tao's mission was coming to an end, he was going back to his home village of Hoa Ninh. At the rate his career and the conflict were going, it may be his last opportunity to return there. It would soon be ten years since his home had been burned out.

As he ate breakfast, he had overheard talk that Tri Quang was going to be arrested today. *Change was coming faster than ever. Just a few months ago, Tri Quang was still considered a friendly when he sided with the Embassy against Thich Quang Lien's supposed peace offering to the Viet Cong.*

After eating, Tao walked through town toward the Dieu de Pagoda. There was little evidence of the three months' protests. In the last couple of days, the military had removed all the monks and their altars from the streets—the last vestige of the Monk Tam Chau and Tri Quang's protest.

When he got to the pagoda, it was very quiet. Perhaps he'd been misled. Tao stood near the pagoda and watched. He'd been told that once Tri Quang was in custody, his mission here was complete. His new assignment was to report back to Bangkok to meet Theodore Shackley and escort him to Vientiane. Shackley was to officially report as CIA station chief at the US Embassy. He was now in command of the "secret" war—and Tao was reassigned to him.

After about an hour, two military vehicles pulled up in front of the pagoda. Several officers walked in while a few others stood outside with weapons drawn. Within a short period of time, they walked out with the gaunt, weak Thich Tri Quang. A long procession of silent monks in white robes followed him out of the pagoda. *It was over.*

CHAPTER TWENTY-TWO

JULY 1, 1966

SAIGON – TAN SON NHUT AIRBASE

Tao sat next to his small suitcase at the Tan Son Nhut Airbase CIA office, waiting on the government plane carrying Theodore Shackley to land. He read over the latest CIA intelligence reports. The bombing of the oil tanks and loading docks at Haiphong Harbor had destroyed eighty percent of that facility. This may have been the best news in the conflict yet—with no fuel, there could be no movement of equipment.

Tao's orders were to board the plane to continue the flight on to Vientiane. Shackley's flight landed. It taxied to the end of the runway, toward the hangar, and shut down. No one exited the plane.

Tao got up and walked toward Shackley's plane and boarded it. When he stepped in, Shackley picked up his briefcase. "We're taking another plane to Vientiane."

The two men walked side by side to the Air America C-47 sitting next to the hangar. The gangway was pulled over to this Air America plane, and both men hustled up the steps.

Tao sat his suitcase down near the front of the plane, flopped down in a convenient seat, and watched his new boss. After Shackley settled, Tao nodded toward the door. "Should I pull it closed?"

Shackley looked over his glasses and shook his head.

Tao tried to get comfortable. Just as he leaned back and closed his eyes, the plane vibrated as if someone were climbing the steps. Within a couple of seconds, Lucien Conein popped his head through the doorway. "Glad I caught you all before you left."

Tao glanced up for a second, then closed his eyes again, trying to get some rest.

"What do you need?" Shackley asked Conein. "We got to get wheels up."

Conein took off his Aussie bush hat as he walked through the plane. He slapped Tao on the shoulder as he moved past. "How the hell is my little Gook friend?"

Tao opened his eyes to glance up at Conein, then closed them to try and get comfortable again.

Tao listened intently to the conversation behind him. Conein spoke in a low voice, still audible to Tao. "Helene sent me to talk to you. They wanted to get back into Vang Pao's network. Even though their don, General Atonine Guerini, has refused to pay Vang Pao's new prices."

Shackley whispered, "I think I can make it happen."

Conein continued, "There's a gang war in Marseille between Guerini and the Francisci family. It's really hurting their business. People cutting their turf." He spoke slightly louder. "Some of the Corsicans who remained in Vietnam wanted to break from their boss."

Shackley whispered again, "Let me get settled in at the Embassy in Laos, then I'll get with Vang Pao to try to work something out." After a few seconds of silence, he asked, "Are we putting ourselves at risk from the Corsicans if they win the turf war?"

"Big-titted Helene told me they didn't care. They had users they couldn't supply at the moment, and they were afraid to lose them to new suppliers from China."

"Is everything was good with the South Vietnamese government?" Shackley asked.

Tao's ears perked up. *What was that about?*

Conein lowered his voice more. All Tao heard was, "Ky." *I can't believe it. Premier Ky is getting bought off on these drug deals. Nothing has changed. The leaders are more concerned with their pockets than our country.*

The pilot and co-pilot stepped through the doorway. the co-pilot went straight to the cockpit, while the pilot waved his arm in a circle. "We're fueled up and will be wheels-up in less than fifteen minutes."

As the two motors fired up, the rest of Shackley and Conein's conversation couldn't be heard.

Tao closed his eyes again and tried to get some sleep. Just as he was about to fall asleep, Conein walked by and slapped him on the shoulder again. "Hope I didn't wake you up, old friend." He guffawed as he exited the plane.

Tao looked over his shoulder at Shackley, the man they called the "Blonde Ghost," who was staring out the window. *I'm ready for retirement. It's time for me to go.*

July 6, 1966

Washington, DC - *Life Magazine* Bureau Office

As Rita Sullivan walked through the *Life Magazine* office, several reporters next to the teletype gasped in unison. She moved in and out between the desk to the journalists. She lightly touched the girl in front of her to inquire about the commotion. Without turning around, the girl and another man spoke loudly without making eye contact. Hanoi Radio was saying the North Vietnamese were parading US pilots through the streets and the crowds were jeering them. Rita seethed with anger. *How can they treat our pilots like that? They will probably take them back to prison, then torture them.*

Rita stomped away from the crowd. As she was about to reach her desk, Chief Singleton entered the large room and moved in the direction of his office. He pointed at her, then gestured toward his office. Rita stopped, drew in a deep breath, then turned in his direction. She was behind on preparing her article for next month's publication. *Well, I guess I'm about to find out how Singleton pushes his journalists. Can't be as bad as that ass Petit.* She slipped into the office. A handsome young man sat at the opposite side of his desk. Singleton pointed to an empty chair. Rita bit her lower lip as she sat down.

The chief placed his hands on top of his desk. "Rita, this is Denny Shaffer. He's going to become your new best friend. He's a photographer. I'm assigning him to work with you. We just stole him away from *Look*. He does great work. So we're going to put him to the test—with you."

The young man reached across and extended his hand to shake Rita's.

The chief pointed at the young man. "Denny is going to go with you when you cover protests. While I'm not solely assigning you to write about them, I believe these events are going to get bigger, likely more radical, and maybe even more violent. I hope not, but I want pictures, lots of pictures, to choose from. You've done such a good job covering them so far, I want something better than file photos. These protests are going to start shaping our country, for better or worse, and I want my readers to feel like they are there." He pulled out a folder and handed it to Rita. "Check out these photos."

Rita sifted through the photos. *Very Impressive.* She put the folder back on the chief's desk.

Singleton pointed at Denny, then raised his same hand and pointed his thumb toward the door. The slender young man got up, slid through the tight space behind Rita, and disappeared out the door. When the long haired photographer had left the room, Singleton leaned back in his big chair. "I know we started out with you trying to go back and forth on protests, you know, covering both sides of that story. But your contacts are so good on the anti-war side of Vietnam, that's where we want to keep you. But you're doing so well here at *Life*, we don't want to lose you, so do you have a problem with being focused on just one side?"

Rita bit her lower lip and sat silently. *All these years, I've fought not to be pigeon-holed, and now I'm being asked to do just that by Life.* It was time to lay her cards on the table. "I don't know where I stand. I've tried to keep an open mind to everything, but as I've watched some of these recent developments—"

Singleton interrupted her. "Okay, *okay*. Irrespective of where you stand, I want you to be our go-to journalist on this subject, but presenting only the facts. I don't want you to editorialize."

Rita fidgeted in her seat. "Yes, I can do that. I can keep my emotions and opinions out of it."

Singleton nodded, but sat for a minute as though he were in deep thought. Just about the time Rita was ready to speak again, Singleton folded his hands on the desk. "Now, go get your final version of your latest article to me. Hurry up, you're behind."

Rita hustled back to her Smith-Corona. Time to finish her article on the Buddhist protests in Vietnam and its impact on the South Vietnamese government, and, more importantly, the US war effort. She had the photo of the Buddhist nun Thich Nu Thanh Quang self-immolation lying beside her to keep her focused. This was going to be her best article yet.

July 8, 1966
Saigon

Neil Sheehan was strolling back to his hotel when he spotted Pham Xuan An walking down the other side of the street. Sheehan had hoped he would run into his old friend before he returned to the United States to take his new *Time Magazine* assignment at the Pentagon. Sheehan shouted out.

An looked over his shoulder and waved, then turned and joined Sheehan. The two men walked into the Continental Terrace and sat down at An's favorite table.

Sheehan went straight at An. "Give me your synopsis of the Buddhist situation up north. Is it over?"

An fidgeted with a pack of cigarettes, tapping them lightly on the table, then pulled one out, lit it, and took a couple of puffs before he glanced around. He leaned forward and spoke in a low voice. "As long as they keep Thich Tri Quang under house arrest, the situation is over. He was and has been the leader of the radical side of the Buddhist movement for years. While I anticipate more unrest, without a leader, it will die down quickly."

Sheehan agreed with An's position. He just wanted someone else to articulate it. The waitress brought unordered drinks to the table. *Wow, I guess I come in here too much that that waitress knows my order. I'm too predictable.*

Then she asked what they wished to order for meals. Neither man wanted to order at that moment.

Sheehan took a long sip of his cola. "I'm being assigned to the Pentagon. I'll be returning to the States in a couple of days. I was hoping to catch up with you before I left."

An raised both eyebrows. "You must be looking forward to going home. You have covered a lot of ground in the last three years between here and Indonesia."

Sheehan nodded. "Yes, I have. I'm ready to leave. I'm frustrated with the South Vietnamese leadership and military. They have done little since I arrived. I'm working on a story, and I stumbled onto the desertion rate within the South Vietnamese Army, and you can already guess it's not good. But I was surprised how high it was."

An smiled as he took a drink from his beer. "I just came from a briefing. Westmoreland is planning a big attack along the DMZ. He has named this mission Operation Hastings. It is a joint operation and will focus on trying to take down the NVA 324B Division. They will be fighting in pretty rugged country. It should be easy for the NVA to escape."

"Isn't this in the area where all of the Buddhist problems occurred?"

"Yes, as a matter of fact—" An tried to continue his statement.

"The VC or NVA must have had spies in there watching and waiting. It doesn't surprise me that Westmoreland has planned this operation."

An frowned as he tilted his head. "How do you know they were planning an attack?"

Sheehan leaned forward and spoke in a low voice. "One of my sources said they got a VC defector who gave them some key information on the NVA. I pressed for more information, but he didn't know."

An looked down at his watch. "Oh, look at the time. I'm late." As he stood up, he reached across the table to extend his hand to Sheehan. "Be well, my friend. I shall miss you."

Sheehan was surprised by An's sudden rush. "I'll miss our conversations, too. I'll take care of the tab."

CHAPTER TWENTY-THREE

AUGUST 10, 1966
SAIGON - US EMBASSY

Ambassador Lodge called Meredith into his office. She stepped through the door and sat down with her steno pad and pencil. Lodge took off his glasses and placed them on the table. "You won't need those."

Meredith looked down at the items, then placed her hands on her lap. "Yes, sir, Mr. Ambassador."

Lodge wiped his mouth and chin with his hand. "Miss Brown..."

Meredith bit her lower lip and looked down at her steno.

"I've been in discussions with the State Department over the last few days. You have been here in Saigon, what? Just a little more than eighteen months? You have served your apprenticeship here well, but it's time for you to get a promotion to utilize the skills for which you have been hired by the State Department—and that means returning to the States."

Meredith almost started to wiggle in her chair, she was so happy.

Lodge continued. "If you accept—"

Meredith blurted out. "Oh, I accept, believe me."

Lodge raised an eyebrow and continued. "We want you to return to the States, get some guidance and training, and move into Public Relations immediately. This is where we believe—I believe—your strengths are."

Meredith beamed. She wanted to climb the ladder and had begun to worry it wouldn't happen.

"I'm going to call your father. I haven't talked to him for a while. I want to catch up with him, but I wanted to tell you so you could tell him first. Congratulations."

Meredith smiled. "Is that all, Mr. Ambassador?"

"No, Meredith. I've been talking with my old friend, Vice President Nixon. You know, just yesterday, he came out wanting to ramp up the war effort here. He talked about more troops and more bombing. He's not at all happy with what Johnson is doing and how he's doing it."

Meredith started to ask a question, but Lodge held his hand up stopping her. "I know Richard pretty well. He hasn't told me anything, but I suspect we've not heard the last of him. There's nothing official, but I know he wants to be President. Anyway, that's not what this is about. When you're in the States, he wants to meet with you and your father sometime soon. So discuss that with your dad. I'll notify the State Department to get a secretary in here to replace you as quickly as possible. So go make your arrangements. Please have Major Hebert come into my office. Oh, and again, congratulations."

Major Hebert stepped into the ambassador's office. Lodge looked at him as he pointed toward a chair. He pulled out a file from his desk drawer. "I have a file I want you to take to Lansdale as soon as you're off duty this afternoon. It's the after operation report on Operation Hastings and a new plan, Operation Prairie—the next one Westmoreland has planned. I want his feedback on these, their impact on the Pacification program, and an update on where the South Vietnamese government is on their portion of the program. We may finally have begun to clear some areas where our program can get a foothold."

Steven reached across the desk and grabbed the file. As he started to get up, the ambassador stopped him. "I want to tell you, you're about to lose one of your friends. Miss Brown just got a promotion and she's going home."

Steven smiled. "She's very deserving, Mr. Ambassador. But we will all miss her."

Lodge nodded and put his hands on his desk. "Such is life in the State Department. You are dismissed."

Steven stepped into Meredith's office. She was bouncing around in her chair with a big smile of her face as she spoke to someone on the phone. He mouthed, "Congratulations."

Meredith nodded and held up her index finger.

Steven stepped to her desk as she finished her call.

She placed the handset back down on the switchhook. "I'm so excited I can hardly handle it."

"You deserve it. Your talents have been underutilized here."

"Not really. My father told me I needed to understand every facet of how the Department of State works, particularly going into Public Relations."

Steven smiled. "Perhaps you're right. This was sort of your boot camp."

"Well, I never quite thought of it that way, but you're right. You better let me break the news to Tim. I don't know how he'll take it."

Steven stuck the folder he was carrying under his right arm. He raised both hands in front of him and shook them. "No way would I take on that task. It's *all* yours." He saluted Meredith with a big laugh, then left.

Steven picked up a letter from his mother, stuffed it in his back pocket, then continued to the carpool. The letter was on his mind as he drove toward Lansdale's villa. He was tempted to pull over to read it, but his time schedule was too tight. He hadn't heard from her in a while—those once-monthly letters were becoming far less frequent.

Steven pulled up to the villa. Before he could knock on the door, it was opened by a waiting Lansdale. As he passed through the door, he stuck out the file in Lansdale's direction, who mumbled something at Steven about sitting down on the couch. He sat down on a rickety chair opposite Steven and started sifting through the file.

Steven sat quietly for about ten minutes while Lansdale read and mumbled inaudibly. Finally, he looked up at Steven. "Westmoreland has finally started attacking with all those soldiers. He has left so many of our camps as targets for NVA and VC mortar fire. We put in troops, then they send in more. Plus, bomb the shit out of our bases at night—just like I predicted." Lansdale leaned back on the chair, now on two legs. "I wonder what the ARVN desertion rate is. Chua told me it has gone up considerably since we started bringing in our troops—maybe something like one in six South Vietnamese soldiers are just walking off."

Steven shook his head. "I haven't heard anything official, but George Allen has said it's high."

Lansdale let the chair drop back down on all four legs. "Chua is doing the Pacification program the way it ought to be run. He's down at Vung Tau, and he's having a lot of success. Just like I said, it takes a Vietnamese person for the people to buy in—the people will pay more attention to one of their own." Lansdale paused as he looked down at the floor. "Hell, even John Paul Vann likes the guy. But, you watch. With Johnson's micromanaging, he's going to fill every position with an American he can keep under his thumb."

Steven nodded. "Do you talk to Colonel Vann often?"

"Often." Lansdale nodded. "He can get with me anytime he needs my advice, but for the most part, with all of his background, he doesn't need much coaching. He just needs everyone to get out of his way."

Lansdale picked up a file from the coffee table and handed it to Steven. "Take this back to Lodge. It's my report on the Pacification program."

"You heard anything from Tao?"

Lansdale got up and walked into his small kitchen. "He contacted me shortly after he got into Vientiane. I don't think he likes working with Shackley, who won't tell him anything."

Steven ran his hand over his short cropped hair. *Boy, that's like the pot calling the kettle black.*

Lansdale came back in, carrying a glass with two fingers of brown liquid—bourbon, probably. "Tao is going to be all right. He's a warrior. He'll get along with Shackley, whose management skills are a little different than mine."

Steven shook his head. "Permission to speak freely, sir?"

Lansdale squinted at Steven. "Go ahead."

"I think the thing that bothers him the most is all the drug activity. I agree with you he'll get along with Shackley. Tao is all about keeping the South free."

Lansdale took a sip of his drink and stood. "Well, it's a necessary side of our efforts in Laos. You know me, I don't like it but—"

"When are we going to go into North Vietnam and try to kill or capture Le Duan? I'm getting tired of the Embassy."

Lansdale paced around the room. "Colonel Singlaub has OPLAN 35 working on a mission in which he may need our services. He has asked me to stand by. He isn't sure about taking you on that mission."

"Why? I'm still the best sniper in Vietnam. He needs me, and I'm wasting away in the Embassy."

Lansdale slammed his drink down. "Singlaub says he still has reservations about your dependability since you weren't in your room that morning in Dallas when you were supposed to go hear Kennedy speak at the Trade Mart. You let a lot of people down that fateful morning. I'm tired of you not telling me what happened that day."

Steven bristled. "I'm protecting my family. That's all I can say."

Lansdale folded his arms across his chest. "Can't or won't? I've talked to Hunt. He said everything was fine when he dropped you off at the hotel. I need to know what happened to you."

Steven sat and stared at Lansdale. *He has opened the door for me to talk.* "All I'll say, don't believe everything *E. Howard Hunt* tells you. Someday… someday, I'll tell you the story."

Lansdale sat back down, picked up his glass, and finished his drink. "I'll tell you this, Major Hebert. That incident is keeping you from getting a promotion. I saved your ass from getting dishonorably discharged from the service. So who is protecting your family?"

Steven picked up the file for Lodge. "Do you have anything else?"

Lansdale just stared at him.

Steven got up and walked out the door without another word.

When Steven sat down in the jeep, he looked in the rearview mirror. *What was I thinking walking out on my boss? That was really dumb. That man has done more for me than anyone I know. Should I go back in and apologize?* Steven sat for a minute, started the jeep and drove off.

LATER IN THE AFTERNOON

Steven was running late to meet with Ethan Graham for dinner downtown. He drove around to cool off after his conversation with Lansdale. Plus, he had stopped and read his mother's letter. Her handwriting was very bad now, whereas she used to write in gorgeous script. Further, it wasn't filled with much detail. Her age was starting to catch up with her. The one thing he learned from her letter was Bill Russell was named basketball coach of the Boston Celtics, the first Negro to hold that position. *The all-time great had been part of the Negro rights movement. His role in the movement had put him at odds with some in the public and a few in the press, but, thank God, he was a man of principal.*

Graham's unit, Third battalion, Third Marines, was being sent to Okinawa. *Who knows what condition he'll be in when I catch up with him?* Ethan had now been back in Vietnam two and a half years. Steven was disappointed their time together would be cut short, since he was running late. *I figure that will be okay with E, since he'll probably want to party out the night carousing, drinking, and grabbing girls.*

As Steven walked toward the restaurant, a commotion erupted in front of it. A big Marine was fighting with several Vietnamese, but it was hard to see through the growing crowd. Steven feared for the worst—that it was E in the middle of the scuffle. He jogged up. Sure enough, Ethan was fighting two Vietnamese. Despite their kicking and punching, E was getting the better of the two men.

Just as he was almost to Ethan, a jeep with two MPs pulled up and jumped into the fray to stop the fighting. Steven knew he had to get in there fast to prevent Ethan from getting arrested. The two MPs pushed their way through the three-deep crowd of Vietnamese civilians. Steven arrived at the same time as the MPs, who picked up Ethanl, which appeared to be a task at that particular moment. Steven recognized the older MP, who was about to put the cuffs on Ethan.

Ethan slurred, "Hebert, get me out of here, buddy."

Steven stepped into the older MPs line of sight to be recognized before he stepped any closer. He glanced at the older MP, leaned over toward his right shoulder, and looked Ethan in the eyes. "Calm down, E." Then Steven spoke to the MP. "If I get him out of here, will you turn this soldier over to me? He's being sent back to Okinawa tomorrow. It would be best for all concerned, don't you think?"

The older MP didn't acknowledge what Steven had said to him. He looked at his younger counterpart. He barked, "Get this crowd dispersed while I put him in the jeep." The younger MP started moving the crowd. The older MP pushed Ethan, who was resisting, toward his jeep. He put Ethan in the back of the jeep forcefully, then turned and winked at Steven. "Sit tight for a minute, Major. We don't want the Vietnamese to think we aren't punishing your friend."

Steven nodded, then looked at Ethan with disgust.

After the young MP cleared out the crowd and helped the two Vietnamese that Ethan had been pummeling, he walked back over to the older MP. "They say he—" The younger MP pointed at Ethan in the back of the Jeep. "Wouldn't take no for an answer about being admitted to the club without paying a cover charge. Then he started pushing them around, and they didn't like it."

The older MP turned around and looked at Steven as the younger MP stepped alongside. "You see the dilemma we're in here. This is not the first disorder tonight by the men from this unit. Several of them have already been taken back to the base, just to get them out of Saigon. The relationship between our soldiers and their civilians hasn't had a good evening."

Steven rubbed his chin. "I understand. This is my best friend. I'll keep him under control. You have my word. I'll make sure—"

The MP's radio chirped. The young MP stepped over and grabbed it. It was another incident they needed to answer. The older MP turned and grabbed Ethan, pulled him out of the jeep and took off his cuffs. "He's all yours. We got to go." The two MPs jumped in the jeep and sped off.

Steven looked at Ethan. *"What's your story, man?"*

Ethan wouldn't make eye contact with Steven. "I offered to pay them, the first guy. Then the second guy wanted me to pay him, too. I turned and said I paid him and pointed. He said, 'You American. You can pay me, too.' I refused. Then the other man wouldn't give me my money back so I could just leave. That's when I got pissed and all hell broke loose."

Those words cooled Steven. He knew the environment around Saigon all too well. Most of the residents of the city liked Americans. Naturally, there were exceptions, but they were few and far between. However, since the US troop numbers had increased substantially, several things had happened that Steven had picked up on. The countryside of South Vietnam was becoming a battleground everywhere, so there had been an influx of country people moving to the city to avoid the ravages of the conflicts. Also, as had been predicted, there was some resentment toward US troops. As the numbers had grown, some did view the American as occupiers, not liberators, which was natural and predictable.

Steven walked Ethan down the street to a quiet little out of the way restaurant where he'd taken Tim and Meredith over two years ago.

They sat down at a table. Steven inquired if Ethan was ready to go to Japan.

Ethan shrugged. "I suppose. I was tired of just sitting, guarding the airbase. All the fighting going on in the area, and I'm stuck guarding the damn airbase. Not at all what I signed up for."

Steven expected that answer. Ethan was always true to his Irish heritage—a good fight was a good thing. "So, you haven't engaged in any of these search and destroy missions since Operation Starlite?"

Ethan put both hands on the table. "A couple of little missions, but for the most part, we've been sidelined. The last time we were out was at the end of March—out southwest of Da Nang."

Steven was surprised. He was aware of a large number of search and destroy missions. He wondered why Ethan's battalion was sidelined.

Ethan waved for the waiter to come to the table. "As usual, I have a weird story. We were out on a mission called Operation Kings. In March, we went out on this search and destroy mission in an area near An Hoa, to protect the industrial area outside of Da Nang." He raised his eyebrows. "You know, fighting in the rice paddies, then picking off leaches. Then the Buddhist protests started, and we got called back to the base. I mean, we

208

were going out into a VC stronghold. Just as we were starting to make contact with the enemy, we get called back. Timing...."

The waiter returned to the table with their meals, along with a glass of Irish whiskey for Ethan and sweet tea for Steven. Ethan took a big swig off his whiskey. "Let me tell you something—and I've heard this from other Marines—those of us who are trained in jungle warfare techniques, we are kicking butt to the point the NVA has to escape back across the DMZ or into Laos or Cambodia. Damn, for whatever reason, we can't continue to pursue the enemy. We could inflict some tremendous damage."

Steven knew from sitting in on his meetings why they weren't allowed to pursue. He decided it was best not to tell. He was weary of politicians holding back the battle plans with rules of engagement and disengagement.

The two men ate their dinner over chit-chat, discussing old friends and family. Steven told him how proud he was of his brother, Jeremiah, who was getting ready to start his fall semester at Howard University and was a member of the track team. Steven omitted telling how his brother had overcome drug issues, as it was no longer a part of his life. He expressed his concerned about his mother, who was living in Louisiana. She was elderly, but still insistent on living by herself.

As soon as dinner was over, Steven looked down at his watch. It was late. He'd had all he could take of this day. He told Ethan he was heading back to the base and could drop him off somewhere to keep him out of trouble until morning. Ethan agreed it was probably in his best interest to take a ride back to his barracks on the base since they were flying out early in the morning. Steven obliged.

CHAPTER TWENTY-FOUR

OCTOBER 8, 1966
PENTAGON - WASHINGTON DC

Secretary of Defense Robert McNamara sat in his office reading over the report from the Jason Division, as the select group of scientists had affectionately named themselves, on their findings on new innovations for the war in Vietnam. The Jason Division had been given full access to high officials at the Pentagon, the CIA and the Department of State. Their September report had been eye-opening, ranging from opinions on the current state of the Conflict to potential innovations. Many of these scientists had been "think-tank" members of the Military Industrial Complex from World War II to the present.

McNamara let out a deep breath as he stopped reading, took off his glasses, and stared out his office window. The Jason Division had just eviscerated Operation Rolling Thunder. The US focus on continuous bombing of North Vietnam had proved to be useless. They concluded there were few industrial targets in a predominately agrarian culture, plus what was destroyed was quickly replaced by the Red Chinese and the Soviet Union. Moreover, their "flexible transportation system"—i.e., the rugged Ho Chi Minh trail and other comparable routes—were easily repaired. One of their conclusions was the bombing program would do nothing to reduce the North Vietnamese will to stay engaged in the Conflict.

This was at least the third time that McNamara had studied this revolutionary report, which he'd received back in September. He'd shared it with several of the Pentagon and CIA officials, who had participated in the top-secret operation. He paused to take off his glasses and cleaned them before reading the harshest part of the report. Glasses back in place, he continued. McNamara put his finger on each word in the report as he read:

"...that there is currently no adequate basis for predicting the levels of US military effort that would be required to achieve the stated objectives—indeed, there is no firm basis for determining if there is any feasible level of effort that would achieve these objectives."

McNamara despised those words. The Jason Division had cut him personally, attacking the very plan he himself had designed, advocated and implemented. Again, he went back to reading the assigned objective, some form of electronic barrier. They determined that it was feasible to build it in two parts, an anti-troop system made up of small gravel mines set to damage the enemy's feet and legs. Plus, an anti-vehicle system composed of acoustic sensors that would direct aircraft to the targets. Then there was the most difficult part of their recommendation. While a large part of the system could be dropped from planes, it would have to be checked by ground troops. This would be a non-starter. From the very beginning, McNamara and Johnson had set up ground rules. If they didn't go outside of South Vietnam, the Red Chinese and the Soviet Union would stay out of the Conflict.

McNamara took off his glasses again. *Despite our efforts to keep them out of the Conflict, both have been in since the beginning and both have recently publicly announced they're in the Conflict with aid to the North.* He drew a deep breath, then went back to reading. The total to build the system, which was already etched in his brain, was $800,000,000 a year. Which didn't include the price of maintaining it.

McNamara decided he had to swallow his ego and pass the report to Army engineering expert Lieutenant General Alfred D. Starbird. All in all, McNamara was satisfied with the report and wanted his feedback on the feasibility of implementing this radical project. McNamara laid the report on the edge of his desk and called his secretary to make a copy for the general. Then he reached back on his credenza for a notepad. He began making notes for his upcoming trip to Saigon and a critical meeting with General Westmoreland, who had just made another request for more troops. After reading this report, he'd already soured on the request, but still it was his obligation to go and have the conversation.

OCTOBER 11, 1966
SAIGON

Lucien Conein tucked his pearl-handled .357 Magnum into his belt. As he walked toward the front door, he told his wife he would be home when she saw him. Tonight, he was going to the Duc Hotel to catch up with his team members, who rarely left his side. The hotel was the residence of many bachelor military officers serving in the Vietnam Conflict. Conein would stop by there on occasion to hear first-hand stories of how the war effort was going, talking to some of the officers returning from field duty.

As he drove through Saigon, he realized how much the city and the area had changed over the last decade. When he'd first arrived, he helped the Vietnamese and the French get rid of the Japanese. That was easy. It was the Allies against the Axis powers.

At the next stop light, he watched the people hustle and bustle on the street. It hit him. *The people hadn't changed. What had changed was who was on whose side. It was a microcosm of the Cold War. The enemy of my enemy is my friend. Now it was different, more personal, at least to many of the Vietnamese, in its simplest form Vietnamese against Vietnamese.*

He drove past an ARVN army vehicle. His mind flashed back to the good news that Shackley had given him, that their network with Vang Pao was functioning very well. That would keep his funds flowing. Additionally, Shackley informed Conein about Operation Irving. The US Air Cavalry was attempting to clear the mountainous area from Bong Son to Qui Nhon. It was a significant battle, and the US strategy focused on one of the eastern ends of the Ho Chi Minh Trail. If only they pinched the trail from this side, perhaps Vang Pao's army could come in and re-take the Plaines de Jarres.

After parking Conein hustled inside, busted into the bar and glanced around. His men were there—it was time to get rambunctious. He shouted at the top of his lungs, "Bartender, get me and my friends a round immediately." He kicked over a couple of empty chairs as he hurried toward the bar. Patrons scattered to get out of his way.

This particular evening, several Marines who knew about his colorful background came up to tell him about recent missions. They had been part of the team that followed up the advancing forces in Operation Attleboro. The sergeant among the three Marines spoke first. "Colonel, we went into some shallow cave. Man, you wouldn't believe the cache of Viet Cong weapons we found. Me and my men here were responsible for documenting the find."

This got Conein's attention. "Where did you find them?"

The sergeant pounded his fist on the bar. "Colonel, it was after a battle with the Viet Cong about fifty miles north of Saigon toward the Cambodian border. Our boys were hoping not only to liberate the region but catch the enemy before they could sneak into Cambodia, where the Marines weren't allowed to pursue."

However, the sergeant's comment, succinctly defined the conflict, a "war with borders" plus, "not holding captured territory". Those phrases pissed off Conein, *damn politicians*. These stories only confirmed what he already knew—the military wasn't making the final call on how to fight. All decisions were made in the White House. By the same token, he blamed the military brass for not fighting back. He tried to imagine what Patton would have said or done in these circumstances.

Still, Conein loved these war stories. It kept him involved in the war effort. Not to mention, it fired him up. In a strange sort of way, it kept him young. When the sergeant finished elaborating on the sophisticated weapons, both Chinese and Russian, they had found, Conein leaned over to the bartender. "Seven beers, immediately." He handed each of the Marines one and nodded to his own three team members. He held up his beer and shouted at the top of his lungs, "To the best damn fighting force in the World. The US Marine Corps."

Everyone in the bar cheered and took a drink of beer.

Once they finished, naturally, Conein had some new Marines to talk to, so he told them some of his old stories in the French Underground days. His team members all looked at each other. Conein leaned against the bar after downing a beer. "Gather around, boys. Now, this one is the double truth. When I was with the French Underground, we were constantly sneaking around right behind those crack German troops. They were clueless we were there. We were relaying messages to the Allies in London. There was this one time we were in the middle of transmitting troop positions when the Krauts showed up at our cover's front door. They banged on the door. We sent some *fraulein* to answer the door. She unbuttoned her top two buttons—enough to distract the damn Krauts. They lost their mind over big-titted Paithoon. Boys, she was a looker, now." He turned to the bartender. "Set up a round for me and my boys."

The bartender set four beers up on the bar for Conein and his men.

Conein held up his beer. "To our Allies."

The three other men clinked their glasses with Conein. Just as they were about to down their beers, another voice shouted, "Here, here. To the Allies."

Conein spun around to canvas the large barroom. Immediately, he focused in on another CIA agent seated at a small table. "Hey, hey. Come on over and join us." He waved his free hand at the man to join his friends. He turned to the bartender again. "Another round. Add one more for my friend, here." As the man joined the group, Conein put his arm around him. "Just return from an assignment?"

The man nodded. "Yes, Lucien. I was parched. Heard this was the place."

Conein turned to his other men. "Boys, say hello to an old friend of mine." He knew he couldn't give out the man's real name, since he was a deep cover agent. "Let's just call him John Doe."

All of the men pounded their beer mugs together, spilling some. Conein shouted out, "*Salut!*"

He turned back to his old friend. "Let's take this party up on the roof. Bartender, hand me a bottle of whiskey." Conein yanked the bottle from his hand and the group of five men headed toward the stairway to the roof top. "Come on, let's get some fresh air."

Once the five men stepped through the service door to the roof top, damp humid air hit them. Conein stomped to the edge of the roof, swinging the whiskey in one hand, then looked down on the street below. The other four men stepped alongside. Conein took the top off the bottle, took a big swig, then passed it down the line to the other men. "John Doe" wiped his chin with the back of his hand, then took another drink and passed it back up the line. By the time the bottle got back up to Conein, he looked at the half empty bottle, then set it down. He walked over and grabbed a large concrete pot with several overgrown plants in it. He pushed it, and over the edge it went. When it crashed on the sidewalk below, all the compatriots on the roof cheered. *It sure feels like old times.*

Two of his team members went over to another planter and pushed it over the edge. When it shattered on the street below, they all cheered again. This caused the men to pass the whiskey bottle around for another swig. Conein moved over to the largest concrete pot, but it wouldn't move. So he pushed again, falling down trying. All his buddies started laughing. He joined them in their laugh as he leaned against the pot. "Bring me that damn whiskey bottle. We're going to get this done."

"John Doe" took a swig off the bottle, then they passed it like a water bucket line with each man taking a swig before it reached Conein. He looked at the almost empty bottle, turned it up and finished it. He waved at the men. "Help me up. Let's finish this."

All three men got low on the pot and started pushing.

A South Vietnamese policeman stepped through the rooftop door. "Stop!" he shouted.

But it was too late. The three men finished the task and off the roof it went, crashing on the street. The policeman stepped up to the five men. "Look, you all need to stop before somebody on the street gets killed. Now, I want all of your names."

Conein closed the distance between him and the policeman. "You don't need their names. My name is Lucien Conein. That's all you need to know."

The policeman looked at Conein. "You all need to leave the roof now and go home. Sober up."

Conein waved his right hand, knowing he'd pushed as far as he could without getting arrested. "Come on, boys. Let's go. We've almost run out of planters, anyway."

OCTOBER 27, 1966
WASHINGTON, DC

E. Howard Hunt was awakened by a ringing telephone. He drowsily reached over and picked it up. "Yes?"

"We got big problems."

Hunt looked over his shoulder at his wife, who'd just rolled over in bed. "Give me a minute. Let me pick up my office extension. Call me back in two minutes." He hung up the phone.

He pulled on his pants and a shirt. He tip-toed out of the bedroom and went to his office. In precisely two minutes, his desk phone rang. "What is it?"

"I'm at the Naval Medical School in Bethesda. I came out to the first payphone I could find. Lieutenant Commander Pitzer is making a movie out of autopsy photos."

Hunt snarled. "Who the hell is Pitzer? That's impossible. There were no autopsy photos taken. We didn't want any visual evidence." Hunt ran his hand over his head. *Damn pictures of Kennedy's autopsy.*

"He was the morgue photographer. He took photos, but they were never officially recorded. Apparently, they were private photos. No one knew about them—or, at least, no one ever spoke about them."

"That's bullshit. They were under strict orders. No photos. Hell, I've never heard that name before."

The voice on the other end of the phone said, "Sir, I'm telling you I just stumbled onto him coming out of the theater late one night. He acted kind of weird, but I didn't think anything of it until I heard him in there tonight. So, I inconspicuously snuck into the theater and saw for myself what he was doing. He's was watching a film of those photos."

Hunt stretched his jaw. "Okay, I'll handle it from here." He pushed down the button to hang up the call then dialed another number.

The voice on the other end said, "Odd time for a phone call from you. Must be important."

"Shut up and listen. I have a sanction. Meet me in Langley early in the morning."

Hunt was waiting in the parking lot when a man pulled up beside his car. Hunt signaled for the man to get into his car, then handed the man the keys. "This is an official Navy vehicle, tags registered. Gets you past the front gate." He reached into his breast coat pocket and pulled out a Navy identification, complete with a picture matching the man with a rank of

219

commander. He held it up next to the man's face and nodded. "Damn near perfect. Your custom fit uniform is in the trunk of the car."

The man took the Navy ID and looked at it. He slipped it into the inside pocket of his sports coat. "Information on the target."

Hunt reached his hand inside his jacket pocket again and produced a picture of Pitzer. He looked at it, then passed it to the large man. "You must make his death look like a suicide."

The man looked at the photo, then handed it back to Hunt.

Hunt continued, "He's assistant head of the Graphic Arts Department and chief of the Educational Television Division of the Naval Medical School. Gather up all photos, negatives, film, and film cannisters. *Anything* that has to do with pictures. I want them. They're autopsy photos that were never to be taken—they must never get out. *Got it*? When you have completed your mission, call me and say, 'Soup is done, dinner is ready.' I'll meet you right here to get them. You hand me that information, I'll hand you your payment."

CHAPTER TWENTY-FIVE

NOVEMBER 10, 1966

WASHINGTON DC

Rita and Denny were working on an article for the December *Life* issue about the protest against Secretary of State Robert McNamara at Harvard University. Just a few days ago, she had received a call from Billy, the young man who always gave her tips about upcoming protests of the SDS. On November 7, McNamara was going to give a speech to a small group of students at the university, and the SDS was planning to protest the event. Despite the call coming the day before, Singleton gave her permission to take Denny. Rita scrambled to get to Boston with Denny in tow.

Rita was becoming uncomfortable with receiving so many notices from Billy about SDS activity. She figured she was on the watch list now at the FBI, same as Senator Morse. She still couldn't make up her mind whether she was for or against the Vietnam Conflict. Things weren't good from her prospective. US bombs where killing North Vietnamese civilians at a high rate, and the US had started spraying chemicals to defoliate the jungle in the DMZ. Rita was against the use of chemicals, as she couldn't differentiate in her own mind the difference between a defoliating chemical and the use of chemical warfare on people. This felt the same. Conversely, she'd seen what Communism had done in East Germany compared to West Germany and North Korea versus South Korea.

Rita and Denny sat sorting over the pictures he'd taken. His appearance—long hair and newly grown mustache—allowed him to get right in the middle of the protest. There were photos from a distance to show perspective, and close up photos of some of the individual protestors, signs and all. Some of the photos reminded Rita of how scared she'd been at that protest when it turned ugly. She pulled out a photo of Billy and stared at it. He was no longer the inexperienced young man she'd first met in December 1964. He'd become a very vocal radical. *When I first met him, I believed I could trust him. Now his face has changed—he's almost scary.* Rita continued to leaf through the photos.

When McNamara had exited the building, most of the demonstrators closed in on him, demanding they debate him over Vietnam. When McNamara attempted to engage with the group, they shouted him down. He was hustled to his limousine, only to be surrounded by twenty-five of the more radical students who refused to let him drive off. Finally, the police arrived and dispersed the crowd so he could leave with a police escort. While Rita wasn't a fan of McNamara, she thought the students' treatment of him had been more than rude when he'd at least presented some willingness to talk.

Denny's pictures were dynamic. They really tied into the rough draft of her article. Rita struggled to keep her own emotions out of this article—her fears and her opinions regarding the protests. She believed in the first amendment rights and all, but lately more and more protests nationwide had become confrontational.

When they finished picking the final pictures, Rita realized she'd just enough time to meet Meredith. She dismissed Denny with a quick background story on meeting her friend, finishing as she slipped off to the bus station to head into the heart of Washington DC. Rita hadn't seen her best friend, Meredith, since she'd left for her assignment at the Embassy in Saigon right after Christmas in December 1963. She'd returned to the States at the end of August and was given time off to be with her family in Boston. Now she was at the State Department in Washington.

Rita stepped off the bus and took a few steps. Meredith ran up from behind to surprise her. They hugged, then continued on to the restaurant. It was in a high class part of the city—an area out of Rita's reach.

When they sat down at a private table in the corner of the restaurant, they caught up on the three years since they'd seen each other. A waitress, dressed in a starched white shirt, black bow tie, and black slacks, arrived and asked for their orders. Rita looked at Meredith and shrugged. Meredith ordered some French-sounding wine.

Wow, I can't believe it, if I can't pronounce it, I know I couldn't afford it.

They discussed what they'd heard about old friends from the University of South Carolina. Lastly, they discussed their families. "How is your mother?" Meredith asked.

Rita drew a breath. "Mother is doing well—healthy and still living in Marietta, Georgia." She took a sip of her water, then continued. "I was up near where your mother and father live on assignment at Harvard covering a big protest. The protestors really went after McNamara."

"Why didn't you go by and see my parents? You know they would love to see you."

Just as Rita was about to speak, the waitress showed up with a bucket of ice and the wine. She offered the cork to Meredith, who giggled. "Please, just pour us each a glass."

Rita smiled. "Meredith, it was a last-minute assignment. Plus, I had my photographer Denny Shaffer along with me.

Meredith raised both palms. "You know my parents wouldn't care. They would want to see you. You're family."

Rita smiled. *I sure have missed my friend.* "So what's it like working around all of the diplomats and elites of the government?"

Meredith took her first sip of wine. "Not to sound arrogant, but because of my family, I grew up around many of them, so it doesn't seem like that big a deal."

Rita's eyebrows raised on that remark. "Surely someone or something stands out?"

Meredith looked around to make sure no one was close enough to hear. "Richard Nixon wants to meet with me and my dad. Can you believe it?"

Rita rolled her eyes and laughed.

Meredith finished her first glass of wine and poured another for herself.

Rita realized she had been so busy talking she hadn't sampled the drink. So she did. It was the best tasting wine she'd ever had.

Meredith leaned forward. "Tell me what's been going on with you? I've read some of your newspaper and magazine clippings. Are you totally against our war effort in Vietnam?"

Rita reached back and let her hair out of the tight bun. She ran her fingers through her hair as she pondered how to answer. "I have mixed emotions about both sides. I'm not trying to be vague. I have leanings against the war, but in my most recent assignment, I watched the Students for a Democratic Society really mistreat Robert McNamara. A week later, they were still trashing him at school. Then there is you working for the State Department, so I have to support my friend. The chief at *Life* wanted me to work the protest angle because of my contacts. But that's the only reason. I have worried over the last year that I was going to be pigeon-holed into the anti-war side." Rita took another drink as she looked at her friend to gauge her unspoken reaction. "I want to stay in the middle and be objective to everything, despite my assignments."

"Are you dating any one? Do you have any private life? Come on, Rita, give me some good gossip."

Rita froze. Her best friend was asking—and here was the one person she could tell everything. She desperately wanted to talk about the Mary Meyer-President Kennedy stuff that continued to pile on her, but the words stuck in her throat. "I don't have time for a boyfriend. I did just started working with a cute photographer, but I don't want to mix that into work and mess things up."

Meredith looked down, then made eye contact with Rita as she smiled. "I'm sorry I never answered your letter about being interviewed on the

Lodge election vote in New Hampshire, but I was scared. You know, new at my job and all."

Rita laughed. "Well, I found out I had jumped the gun a little myself."

The formally dress waitress returned to the table with menus and placed a dish of hors d'oeuvres in front of the two women. When the waitress walked away. Rita asked, "What's your fascination with Richard Nixon?"

"My dad has always said the man had more connections than most politicians. Ties into the military and CIA. You know me, it has always fascinated me how the world really works."

Rita frowned. "What do you mean, how the world really works? I don't understand."

Meredith picked up an hors d'oeuvres in one hand and her glass of wine in the other, then held them out. "The world exists at two levels. Elites like my family can move around the world without any issues. Don't take this wrong, but the elites and diplomats have always had the press and media in their back pocket."

Rita looked away. *What is Meredith telling me? I'm the media—am I being manipulated?*

Meredith leaned across the table. "I've seen it. My family and their friends were tight with Nixon and Eisenhower. But now that I've been around Ambassador Lodge, he and Nixon are tighter *still*. All I can say is, I have seen things, things I can't talk about, and clearly a bunch of things I don't know but can guess about. Nixon came into Vietnam two years ago and was on some kind of secret mission. I have no idea what it was, but it was some kind of big deal. I could tell. It really piqued my fascination even more."

Rita smiled as the waitress returned to take the dinner orders. As Meredith ordered her meal, Rita stared at the menu.

After they had both ordered dinner, Rita inquired, "Do you know anything about your new assignment?"

Meredith refreshed Rita's glass of wine, then poured the remainder into her glass. "Well, yes. Just to show you what I've been telling you. I'm going to do PR for the Ambassador at Large Averell Harriman"

Rita blurted out. "Uncle Averell!"

Meredith giggled as she nodded.

"I thought he'd retired?"

Meredith shrugged. "Well, MacArthur said, 'old soldiers just fade away.' My dad added his own little saying when he found out, 'State Department diplomats never fade away.'"

Rita was beginning to comprehend what Meredith had tried to tell her. "Meredith, you're amazing."

Meredith waved her hand around and continued. "We just sent over a memo to President Johnson about the divisions between the NLF and the North Vietnamese regarding peace talks."

Rita got a serious look on her face. "Yes, but in the meantime, many more soldiers will die."

After dinner, as they were walking out of the restaurant, Meredith stopped in the doorway. "Do you want to have another drink? I'll take us to the Quorum Club. My treat?"

Rita was floored. For two years she'd wanted to get back on the inside. Go find out who Jack Armstrong—the thug who had wrecked her car—

really was. This was her perfect chance, but she had a deadline on the McNamara protest article. "I'll take a raincheck. I'd really like to go. Please ask me again, *real soon*."

Meredith smiled. "Of course. Maybe next Thursday night? It's always a big night. Lots of big shots in there. I'll introduce you to a few."

Rita was ready to jump out of her own skin. She had time to prepare to go. No one would mess with her if she were with Meredith. "We'll get dressed u to the nines. Be really flashy. We'll be the best looking females in there—a hot blonde and a hot brunette."

Rita bounced out the door and headed to the bus stop to go back to her apartment. *This is the break I've been looking for.*

NOVEMBER 11, 1966

WASHINGTON DC - *NEW YORK TIMES* BUREAU

Since Neil Sheehan had returned to the United States, there had been a flurry of activity in South Vietnam. US troop operations had intensified substantially with the increased number of divisions assigned to the theater. Sheehan was happy to be reunited with his family, plus his assignment at the Pentagon had kept him busy preparing articles for the *New York Times*. Currently, he was researching the US Navy's shelling along the fishing coast of Vietnam. His bosses were constantly pushing him to write faster, but his desire to research all angles slowed him. He took another sip of his morning coffee as he read the *Washington Post*. This was becoming the "newspaper of record" in the DC area. He got up to go to the coffee pot and glanced out his back window at the yard. The cold drizzle made the entire backyard look dank and dreary. Quite a contrast to the weather he'd never grown accustomed to in Vietnam.

Since Sheehan had been assigned to reporting at the Pentagon, he'd encountered several officers he'd met in Vietnam. They were much more willing to discuss subjects off the record with him. He believed if he didn't abuse this, they could become valuable sources in the future.

Sheehan sat back down with his freshened cup of coffee. He picked up his yellow pad and flipped back several pages. When he found what he was looking for, he slurped his cup, then re-read notes he'd made to himself. President Johnson's trip to Cam Ranh Bay in late October was designed to shore up his mid-term elections. It had worked. While the Democrats had lost three seats in the Senate, they maintained their large majority in both houses. Sheehan hadn't been back in the States long, but it was obvious the American public was teetering on a fulcrum regarding the Vietnam Conflict. The draft had turned the youth of America against it, but there was still enough World War II and Korean veterans who understood fighting Communism. The middle class was still on board with Johnson and the effort. He thought former President Eisenhower and Vice President Richard Nixon's criticisms of President Johnson's policy, which they characterized as "hesitant, indecisive and timid," would have a bigger impact on the election results. The Republicans were still trying to overcome the damage from Goldwater's devastating loss, and the party had really not coalesced around a new leader—but Nixon was pushing for that role.

Tomorrow, the *New York Times* was breaking a story that forty percent of the US economic aid sent to South Vietnam was either stolen or wound up in the black market. He'd seen it up close and personal. Sheehan believed if that article had run before the election, the Republicans could have won a few more seats. He was unsure whether or not the *Times* had "sat on their research" purposely until after the election, as they had a close relationship with the White House.

To make matters worse from his perspective, the US troops were engaged in most of the fighting while the South Vietnamese Army had been pushed into providing local security for all of the communities and cities. *This was Westmoreland's doing. The South Vietnamese had to take or receive a more active role in their own freedom effort.* He watched the situation change in his time in the country from 1963 until now. From the beginning, the South Vietnamese were unprepared or unwilling to fight off the Viet Cong. Their government officials seemed more concerned with power and filling their pockets with US dollars. He'd sat with David Halberstam and Malcolm Browne while they were all in Vietnam discussing the issues and the problems of the country. Halberstam, in particular, had been the first to point out the corruption in the South Vietnamese government, which had grown worse since he'd left in 1964. They had all seen things, but generally chose not to write about them—until Halberstam started. Plus, he considered his relationship with Pham Xuan An to be invaluable. That man had insight into the South Vietnamese government and an uncanny ability to break down battle plans.

One of the things those "unnamed confidants" at the Pentagon had told him was that drug usage in Vietnam was on the rise. While he was there, he'd noticed it had picked up as more of the regular forces, the draftees, began to show up in Indochina. The professional soldiers, the enlisted men, seemed to avoid drugs. Marijuana grew wild in the country. It was used by the North and South Vietnamese soldiers. Sheehan had been told by several of the US soldiers that they had captured NVA soldiers with large amounts in their backpacks. It was troubling that the harder drugs, opium and heroin, in particular, were brought into Saigon in much greater quantities since the US soldiers had arrived. Before Sheehan had left, there were rumors circulating that the drugs were coming in from Laos, Burma and Southern China. *Did this correlate to the corruption issue? Were US supplies being exchanged for drugs? Was the government involved in this? There were rumors of the Mafia being involved.*

Sheehan finished his cup and flipped over to a clean sheet of paper. *Come on. Focus on my article before my chief editor jumps on me again. I need to make some more notes before I go to my typewriter this morning.* From the intelligence information that had been provided to him, the US fleet had been sailing up and down the Vietnamese coast shelling fishing villages. According to this information, six hundred civilians had been killed, the wounded likely numbering at least that many, out of an estimated population of 15,000. Clearly, there was strong intel that these villages were populated with a high number of Viet Cong. Sheehan ripped the sheet of paper from his yellow pad and headed off to work. This information alone would be the backbone of his next article. He believed it was a hard sell to the South Vietnamese that US were liberators with these death totals. There had to be a different way. The US seemed to be pushing the South Vietnamese out of the way at every turn—in the military battles, the pacification programs—even dictating directives to their government. All decisions were being made by the White House or Westmoreland.

On the drive over to the Washington bureau of the *New York Times*, it dawned on him that he'd gone to Vietnam believing in the Conflict. Now he wasn't so sure anymore.

CHAPTER TWENTY-SIX

SAIGON

Edward Lansdale sat down to review the latest report on the South Vietnamese Pacification Program as submitted by Tran Ngoc Chau. Tran was making real progress working in the Vung Tau area, southeast of Saigon. In the past, this coastal community had little influence from the Viet Cong. Lansdale believed the US Pacification Program, now run by Porter, had thus far been a failure. Now McNamara was renewing his push on the program. *He should've left me in charge or put some Vietnamese in there. Look at the job Chau is doing.* He continued to read Chau's report. His program was dealing with census grievance, social development, security, and counterterror, but his open arms policy to Viet Cong was the only facet Lansdale didn't like. He set the report down and went over to the cabinet, pulled out a bottle of Jack Daniels, and poured three fingers. As he returned to his chair, he looked at Daniel Ellsberg, then at Major Hebert. "So what do you have to say, Hebert?"

233

Hebert rubbed his hand over his mouth. "What do you want me to say? I don't even know what you've read."

Lansdale swirled the brown liquid and took a drink. "What it's in the Porter report?"

This time Hebert shrugged and handed him a sealed envelope. "Since you have arrived in Vietnam, all I have become is a glorified courier. I work for you, General. Why would I read it?"

Ellsberg laughed. "I can tell you what's in there. Platitudes."

Lansdale nodded, cracked half a smile, then frowned. "Hebert, you think you've been sidelined. I'm the one who has been stalled and sidelined." He opened up the Porter report. It was filled with reasons things hadn't been accomplished. Komer's oversights, plus Westmoreland's lack of clearing areas for him to incorporate the program. Now, McNamara was wanting to focus on this Pacification Program and wanted Westmoreland to be more involved. Lansdale shouted, "What the hell does Westmoreland know about Pacification? This is the kind of stuff that makes McNamara such a *genius*."

Hebert jumped in his chair.

Ellsberg only laughed louder.

Lansdale went back to reading Porter's report. It was infuriating. He pointed to Ellsberg. "What do you know?"

Ellsberg leaned forward in his chair. "McNamara has had an epiphany on the war—at least, that's what Porter called it."

Lansdale downed the rest of his whiskey, then slammed the glass down. "I would love to know what it is that McNamara really knows about fighting a conflict. Both he and General Taylor have had it in for me *forever*."

Ellsberg folded his arms on his chest. "Lansdale, this isn't always about you. This country desperately needs help. Do you know we got more American military involved in pacification than civilians? That's ridiculous." Ellsberg got out of his chair, walked over to the same cabinet, and helped himself to the whiskey. "I still don't understand why they didn't give you more time. You understand the people here. I'm really disenchanted with my new role." After pouring his drink, he turned and stared at Lansdale. "I've been writing a report on the disaster the US Pacification Program is. I'm going to take it straight to DC and shove it into McNamara's face, real soon."

Lansdale laughed. "You sound frustrated. You must not be getting any relief from that big-titted Corsican's boss's girlfriend?"

Ellsberg emptied the rest of his drink. "Touché, Lansdale." He put the glass down on the coffee table and glanced at Hebert, who was trying not to laugh. "Are you enjoying this, Major?"

Hebert looked down at the ground.

Lansdale decided to go back to the Chau report. *I want to read about someone actually accomplishing something here.* He picked it up from the table and went back to reading. He waved the report around. "Chau told me that last time we talked, his commie brother told him the North was running out of volunteers to go into the South. They have been conscripting their population. They even have women and children working on fixing the Ho Chi Minh trail when the bombing stops."

Hebert raised an eyebrow and both hands. "So the military is finally getting ahead?

Lansdale nodded as he went back to reading.

235

After a period of silence, Ellsberg winked at Hebert. "Hey, Lansdale, did you hear about your buddy Conein?"

Lansdale held on to the report as he twisted his mouth. "No, what?"

"Conein and some of his buddies got drunk the other night and started throwing concrete ornaments from the top of the Duc Hotel. The South Vietnamese police showed up and sent them home. However, after the CIA got wind of it, and they're transferring him to Phu Bai."

Lansdale went back to reading the report. "Conein isn't going to be happy at Hue. Wonder who made that call? I can't imagine Colby doing that. He, more than anyone, knows how connected Conein is. Must've come from above him. I bet McNamara or Rusk has something to do with it. I can't believe the CIA would do that, but whoever is making the call sure seems to be sidelining all of us with experience in Vietnam." Lansdale looked at Hebert.

Hebert's face showed surprise.

Lansdale asked, "Didn't know how to take Conein's new assignment?" He picked up the empty glass, tipped it in his mouth.

Hebert got a sheepish grin. "Conein has always had it in for me, but you're right. When Conein wants to be valuable, he can really contribute. However, truth be known, no one has ever been able to rein him in."

Lansdale pointed at Hebert with his empty glass, then went back to reading.

Ellsberg mumbled, "I'm going to try to get transferred back to the States."

Lansdale looked over at him. "So the French girlfriend dumped you? Went back to her rich Corsican man?"

Ellsberg raised his eyebrows. "I moved on from her a long time ago, after you and Conein kept them from killing me." He shook his head. "No, I'm just ready to go home. The situation here is not getting any better. Nixon and Eisenhower are right—Johnson and McNamara have no real plans. It's all about political optics." He got up, glanced at Hebert and Lansdale, then left.

Lansdale pointed his glass toward Hebert again. "What's going on with Lodge?"

Hebert shrugged. "I don't see him that much, but when I do, he seems to have pretty much the same attitude as you. Even with Porter at the Embassy, he feels the Pacification Program is unproductive..." Hebert leaned back. "While he doesn't seem to blame Porter, I think he feels Westmoreland hasn't cleaned up enough areas to really get anything to work."

Lansdale flipped over another page on the Chau report. "I hear McNamara has changed his tune on Westmoreland since his trip here in October. I hear he went back to the States and told Johnson *no more troops*. He now believes this is going to be a long war."

Hebert reached for his glass of iced tea. "Lodge hasn't said much, but that's what he seems to believe. I don't think Lodge talks to Rusk very much. At least, he doesn't seem to rely on him." He sucked an ice cube. "The last time I spoke with Tao, he said that Westmoreland, McNamara, and Johnson have misjudged the North Vietnamese—you know, their will to fight. He believes that defeating them is going to be more difficult than the Japanese during World War II, for two reasons. The Communist Soviet Union and Red China are resupplying them, plus the North Vietnamese believe they're fighting to defend their homeland. All while the US is playing by the rules, not going outside their self-imposed boundaries."

Lansdale continued to read the Chau report. "Did he tell you that Shackley brought in all of his CIA operatives from Miami? Carl E. Jenkins, David Morales, Raphael Quintero, Felix Rodriguez and Edwin Wilson—all of them are now in Laos."

Hebert replied. "Tao told me that Shackley is as focused on Vang Pao's poppy operation as he is their war effort."

Lansdale sucked his teeth. "You know, Tao is right. That's why you need the South Vietnamese more involved than they are. I talked to him several weeks ago. Shackley is pushing Vang Pao to make another attempt to retake the Plaines des Jarres." Lansdale tossed the Chau report down. "When does Lodge think the new Embassy will open?"

Hebert shrugged. "No idea. Summer? Who knows? The idea of using Vietnamese labor has been a disaster. Why they didn't bring over union laborers from the States, I'll never know."

Lansdale glanced around his living room, then inquired. "You hungry? I'm hungry. Let's go to the kitchen and rustle up something to eat."

The two men entered the kitchen. Lansdale opened the small refrigerator.

Hebert asked, "Whatever happened to our mission to go capture or kill Le Duan?"

Lansdale spun around. "When the government took away all my money, it pretty well kneecapped me. I went through the channels to try to get in contact with General Singlaub to work with some of the OPLAN 35 teams. Well, then I found out the real story. All those teams of OPLAN 34A men the CIA sent into North Vietnam several years ago got captured by the North Vietnamese. However, we didn't figure it out until one clever radio operator used some code language that he was operating under duress."

Hebert sat on the edge of his chair. "*What?* I can't believe it. The OPLAN program was supposed to be an improvement on what we did in the 1950s. Our operatives were training Vietnamese how to go into the North and blend in—something we couldn't do—and carry out missions."

"Yeah, some US soldiers have gotten out. And, of course, you saw where we bought the freedom for several. I guess it got so bad that some of them were captured on the ground when they parachuted in. The NVA was standing there, waiting on them."

"Is there a spy somewhere in this tipping them off?"

"Of course, Major." Lansdale scowled. "We have known for a long time that the North has a better spy network than does the South."

Hebert leaned back in the chair against the wall and ran his hand over his head. "So you had no choice but to kill the mission?"

Lansdale sat down at the table across from him. "No choice. I couldn't just send you, Tao, and Bohannan in there without some support. I have another source of money, but I need to send a ten-to-twelve-man team without the knowledge of anyone but our tight circle—which now is all but impossible."

Hebert stared at Lansdale. "So the Nixon mission—"

"You guessed it. That was the last time. The rest of our operatives are in prison up North. Here's the bad part. When we have listed the captured, the powers-that-be only have listed the Americans, not the South Vietnamese."

"Whose idea was that?"

Lansdale shrugged his shoulders. "I haven't been able to find out, but I'll get to the bottom of it. I just learned about *obvious, purposeful, oversight* in the last few months."

Hebert shook his head. "I can't believe it."

Lansdale got up from the table and went over to turn on the oven, then leaned against it. "So when are you going to tell me what happened in Dallas?"

Hebert turned a steely-eyed stare at Lansdale. "I've told you all I'm going to tell you. Get the truth out of Hunt. And, by the way, considering your relationship with the Corsicans, I'm protecting you, too."

Lansdale walked back over to the table and sat back down. "Conein would never tell me anything about it. And I know now that Hunt has withheld the truth from me."

Hebert nodded. "Well, someday you may get the real story."

Lansdale bit his lip. "You've lost a promotion over this."

Hebert pounded his fist on the table. "But my family is still okay. That's what's important to me. I'll have my fifteen in a little more than one more year, and then I can go home."

Lansdale rubbed his mouth with his hand. "Have it your way. You sure are taking the hard way out. You're dismissed."

No sooner was Hebert out the door than Lansdale's phone rang.

"I've got a question for you from an important man here." Lansdale recognized his old friend's Santa Romana's voice.

"Calling me on an open line?" Lansdale asked. "You know they're likely listening."

"Can Marcos trust making a deal with Johnson?"

Lansdale paused. "You tell Marcos, he hasn't made any deals with me that I counted on." He paused again. "But if he needs him, he'll honor the deal. He may be in a different position than I've been lately. He can probably bargain for more, if he wants."

"You doing okay, Edward?"

"Fine, I guess." Lansdale hung up the phone. *Oh, how times had changed. We used to run operations. Hell, we ran countries.*

THURSDAY - NOVEMBER 17, 1966
WASHINGTON DC

Rita Sullivan looked at herself in the mirror. It seemed like it had been years since she'd dressed up and put on makeup to go out. She remembered what it was like going out on the town with Meredith back in their college days. It was real work to keep up. She was confident they would be the best-looking women in the Quorum Club. If the club's reputation were close to accurate, there would be a number of older, wealthy men "sniffing around" their table. Rita strutted into her living room and sat down by the window to see the cab when it arrived. *Feeling good, looking good. Now, what do I want to accomplish in that club? Jack Armstrong is a fake name. Can I identify him, if I see him?*

The cab pulled up. Except it wasn't the usual yellow cab—it was a black Cadillac limousine. *Oh my.* Rita grabbed her purse and headed out the door. As she ran down the stairs, she considered the irony of going to the Quorum Club in a black Cadillac to try to learn about the individual who had chased her in a black Cadillac. *Obviously, Meredith had no idea. How could she?*

Meredith was already in the limo. On the drive to the club, she said, "Since I have been assigned to work for Averill Harriman, it's been boring compared to being at the Embassy in Saigon. It seems all we ever do is meet diplomats going in and out of the country and understand their various assignments."

Rita was trying to stay focused on her friend's stories, but it was difficult. *I'm going to the Quorum Club.* What started out as anticipation had quickly changed to anxiety. It was good Meredith was talking so fast she didn't notice Rita hardly responded with anything more than a head nod now and then.

As the black limousine drove through the parking lot to the front door entrance, Rita's anxiety cranked up a notch or two. Meredith still didn't seem to sense her duress. Meredith had her compact out, doing a last-minute check of her makeup. Rita thought perhaps she should check hers, too.

The two women stepped out of the black limo and strutted up to the door. When the door opened, the security man looked at Meredith then at Rita.

Meredith said, "Meredith Brown, State Department, we have reservation."

The handsomely dressed security man pointed at Rita. "What's her name?"

Meredith snapped, "Rita Sullivan, she is my guest this evening."

The man looked down at his clipboard containing a list of names, then looked at Rita twice, then waved her in as he handed a table reservation to Meredith.

Meredith nodded to individuals who waved as they made their way to their table. As they sat down, a waiter stepped to the table to get their orders. Rita noticed immediately that it was close enough to the bar that the lights over it illuminated their table. Being in the spotlight caused her nerve to start letting her down. The club was intimidating. Meredith ordered a bottle of red wine from the NAPA Valley Cabernet Sauvignon. This time, Rita could pronounce the wine, but knew it was expensive.

Just as the waiter returned to the table with the Cabernet, two older gentlemen walked by and gave the two women the lookover. Meredith snickered after they had passed and informed Rita of the club's reputation. Surprisingly, she knew a good bit about the Bobby Baker story, which Harriman had filled her in on. Rita was intrigued, as she'd only known a small portion of the "drama" from Stephanie Keeton and what little Mary Meyer had told her.

The Quorum Club was no longer run by Baker, as his legal problems had become quite cumbersome, but he was still around.

After both glasses had been filled, Meredith called for a toast. "To renewed best friends."

Rita clicked glasses, smiled and replied, "Friends 'til the end."

A gentleman stopped by the table to speak with Meredith. Rita assumed she knew him from the conversation. During that time, Rita scanned the room, her eyes locked on "that corner" where the man had watched her and

Mary Meyer. As she looked in the corner, it came to her. The man who'd sat in the corner watching them was not the same man who had driven the black Cadillac. *Wow. Why had it taken so long to figure that out?*

When the gentleman left the table, Meredith took a long sip of her wine and looked at Rita's still full glass. "Rita, you haven't even sipped your wine yet. Are you okay? You seem distant or something."

Rita tasted her wine. It was delicious. "Oh, I was just looking around while you talked to that man. Who was he, anyway?"

"He works in the State Department, several offices down from our office. Seems like a nice guy. He's in charge of security of all State Department offices here and around the world. That's the first time we've had a conversation."

When they finished their respective glasses, the waiter returned to the table to refill them and asked if they wished to see dinner menus.

They both nodded.

After they finished dinner, a different waiter brought another bottle of wine to the table. Rita looked up at him for a minute. *Was there something familiar about him?* He popped the cork and freshened each glass. He smiled at both women as he left the table, and then looked back at Rita for a long second.

Rita excused herself and left for the bathroom.

When she emerged from the bathroom, a man stood directly in front of the door. She stepped around him. As she passed him, he said, "Miss Sullivan, it's a pleasure to have you and Miss Brown at the Quorum Club."

Rita turned around and found herself inches from Bobby Baker. She tried to maneuver out of his space gracefully and move away, but another man bumped into her. Baker grabbed her arm and squeezed as the other man held his position without showing his face. Baker pulled her close. "Yes, ma'am, it's a *real* pleasure meeting you face to face here. I never thought I would get to meet you."

Initially, Rita was stunned by his grip on her arm, but then she leaned forward. "Mr. Baker, it's a pleasure to meet you, too. I was hoping to meet Jack Armstrong, you know, your driver of the black Cadillac," she whispered. "But we both know that's not his real name." She tried to pull free as she snarled, "I have extensive research on you. Including some of your current legal troubles. Perhaps you should let me go before you add to those problems."

Baker's grip increased in pressure on her forearm. "Miss Sullivan," he said in a low voice. "You're on thin ice. I have a nice thick file on you, too, complete with candid pictures taken all around town. I must say I love looking at them." He raised an eyebrow. "Tread lightly, girly. You're being watched by more than me. Alphabet Soup."

Rita tried for a second time to pull her arm free. "Why the hell are you watching me? And threatening me?"

Baker released his grip and flung his arms in the air. "I don't know what you're talking about." He laughed boisterously.

Rita stepped forward. He simultaneously stepped backward. "You damn well know what I mean," she said. "Sending a man in a black Cadillac after me, the hit and run, then trying to run over me at the protest. Not to mention the late night telephone calls."

A few of the patrons standing nearby turned and looked. Baker took another step back and leaned away as he shook his head. A camera off to the side flashed as Baker leaned back away from Rita and opened his mouth as he gasped. "Again, I will tell you in front of all these witnesses, you're on thin ice with those false accusations. That would make you guilty of slander and defamation."

Rita knew she'd walked into a trap. He had a picture of her confronting him with a bunch of witnesses—likely his employees. She had been played and Baker had won.

Rita returned to the table. On the inside, she was shaking, but on the outside, she tried to be calm. Her glass had been filled again with wine while she'd gone to the bathroom. She wanted to tell Meredith what had happened, but it was too much for her current state of mind. She worked to finish her fourth glass of wine. *I'm feeling tipsy.* "I'm ready to go, as soon as we can. I have a big day of work tomorrow."

Meredith tilted her head as she looked at her. "Sure, okay. I'll call for our limo now." She left the table and walked toward a phone booth in the corner.

Rita glanced around the room. It felt like everyone was looking at her. It had been a huge mistake coming here. She was an amateur playing in a professional's game.

CHAPTER TWENTY-SEVEN

NOVEMBER 18, 1966

SAIGON - US EMBASSY

Steven was awakened by a ringing phone. "Hello?"

"I can't get ahold of Mother." Steven recognized his brother's voice.

He sat straight up in bed. "Be calm. When did you call her last?"

"The day she was getting home from Oklahoma," Jeremiah replied. "I called night before last at five o'clock. No answer. Didn't think anything of it. Thought she may be doing somebody's laundry, hanging it out, or something. Called at nine o'clock. Still no answer."

Steven got up from his bed and paced as far as the telephone cord would allow. "So did you try today?"

"Yeah, that's why I'm calling. Still no answer."

Steven methodically paced.

Jeremiah shouted, "Steven! Steven, are you there?"

"Shut up, I'm thinkin'"

"Should I try again?"

Steven sat down on the edge of his bed, put his hand up to his mouth, then ran it over the top of his head. "No. Do you have the telephone number for the LeBeau Family?"

"Of course not. Why would I have their number?"

"Call directory assistance and put in a person-to-person call for Bill Bob LeBeau. Ask Bill Bob to go over to the house and check on Momma. Then call me back after he lets you know. I don't care what time it is."

"I got class in a half hour. What should I do?"

"*Get the number and make the call.* Tell Bill Bob you will call him back between classes. Got it?"

"Steven, I'm worried."

"Me, too. Now, do it." Steven hung up the phone. His mother had just returned home after being at his aunt's home in Oklahoma. He'd only spoken with her once. She was obviously very tired. The trip had been good for her soul, but bad for her body.

Tim Mitchell jogged down the hallway as Steven was doing his rounds. "Your brother said to call him in his dorm room, asap."

Steven knew immediately it wasn't good. He followed Tim into the communications area where he picked up the phone and dialed his brother's dorm room.

The phone rang and rang, but finally, Jeremiah picked it up. "Hey."

Steven took a big gulp. "What did Bill Bob say?"

Jeremiah's voice cracked. "She's gone, Steven."

Steven didn't understand. "What do you mean *gone*? Not there?"

"No, Bill Bob found her dead on the floor. Apparently, she'd been there for two or three days. Bill Bob called the police. They didn't call back until they had taken her body to the funeral home."

Steven sat with his head down as he listened to his brother. He'd just been handed a logistical nightmare. His brother was in college, but Thanksgiving break was this coming week. Steven had to figure out a way to get home and get his brother there as well. "Okay, I'll send you the money to buy a plane ticket home and back. You need to call Aunt Jeannette and let her know. I'll meet your flight, unless you hear otherwise."

Steven had known this day would come. He'd spent the last two years preparing himself. It was still devastating. Finally, he looked up at Tim, who stared at him.

"Steven, I didn't mean to listen, but I assume your Mother has passed? I'm so sorry. Is there anything I can do?"

Steven shook his head. "No, thanks, my friend." He got up and walked slowly to the door. "I've got to talk to the Ambassador."

Steven looked down on the Bayou as the plane flew in the direction of the Belle Chasse Naval Air Base. He realized he still had to take a boat ride out to Uncle Jake's. Uncle Jake wasn't going to take this well. According to LaBelle, they had become very close.

He looked down at his watch and turned the hands to re-set the time. He was to pick up Jeremiah at the airport in about four hours, if his math was correct. It was way too much time to think.

Steven and Jeremiah drove away from the funeral home after making arrangements. The secretary advised them that their mother's obituary would run in the local newspaper, as well as Baton Rouge's and New Orleans'. Steven was numb. He looked over at his brother, who was just staring out the window of his military-assigned truck. Steven wanted to relax and just think. However, he knew that was not going to be possible. The day after tomorrow was the visitation, with the service the next day.

As they pulled onto the dirt road leading to his mother's home, it no longer seemed like the same place. The place where he'd grown up was just a wooden structure. *A home is a home where you're comfortable. Mom and Dad made this place comfortable, a place of rest. It's not the same.* Steven and Jeremiah walked into the house and looked around. After Steven set his duffle bag down, he walked into the kitchen. His brother stood, looking at the place on the floor where Bill Bob LeBeau had told him he'd found his mother. Steven walked over and put his arm around his brother. "She's in a better place, reunited with Pops."

Jeremiah nodded. He shivered.

Steven said, "Go light the propane stove."

Jeremiah didn't take his eyes off the spot. He just walked out of the room toward the living room. Steven went over a made a pot of coffee.

Steven and Jeremiah stood in front of their mother's casket. Jeremiah was dressed in a suit and tie, while Steven was in his Marine dress blues. Steven looked at the closed casket and thought of how hard she'd worked—sewing, doing laundry, anything to make some money for her family. Their mother had barely enough money from their father's pension to supply her family with their basic needs.

After the two of them stood there for a few minutes, they walked away and went to the front of the small showing room. They didn't expect many people. Jeremiah told and retold the stories of his track career at Howard College, while Steven did the same with the stories from Vietnam, more particularly, the US Embassy. Steven looked down at his watch. The visitation period was just about to end. He let out a sigh of relief. He glanced down the hallway and watched three older men walk in his direction. They signed the registration book, then walked over to them. The three men introduced themselves, saying they had worked with their father at the NOPD. They moved over to the casket to pay their respects. The men didn't spend much time, then walked out.

The funeral home owner walked into the room and reviewed the schedule for tomorrow's service.

Steven and Jeremiah slowly ambled out the door. The air seemed unusually crisp for this time of year. When he got to his truck, he leaned back on it, closed his eyes, and tried to enjoy some of the serenity of the moment. He heard footsteps scuffing gravel off to his right. He pushed himself off the vehicle and turned to face one of the old NOPD gentlemen.

The former detective looked at Steven. "Would you boys like to buy me a cup of coffee, down the road at the Lafayette Diner?"

Steven looked over at his brother, who shrugged. "Okay. Lead the way."

The man pointed to an old Buick. "That's what I'm driving."

Once Steven and Jeremiah were in the truck, Jeremiah looked at Steven. "What do you think he wants?"

"I have no idea."

They made the drive less than a mile down the road to the diner and parked. The old man steadied himself on the rail leading up the two steps to the diner door. They were the only ones in the place. They sat down in a booth in the corner. The old man said, "As I told you back at the funeral home, my name is Charlie Lott. I was on the raid where your father was murdered. At the time, I was a lieutenant and the lead detective. I had asked your father to come along because of his knowledge about the business we were raiding from when he worked as an investigator for the I.R.S." The conversation continued while the waitress brought over a coffee pot and filled each cup. "I have kept my mouth shut for too long about what happened that night. I was ordered to keep the truth quiet. I always wanted to tell your mother. I didn't know she still lived in the area. When I saw the obituary, I decided I needed to get some things off my chest. Before I die."

Steven looked at this brother, then back to the old man. "Okay, go on."

Lott slurped his hot coffee. "Your father was on the Narco squad. I was on the Vice squad. We were raiding a business with illegal gambling machines..."

252

Steven could feel Jeremiah's eyeballs staring into him, but he ignored him, not wanting to tip Lott off that what he said wasn't adding up with the story he knew.

Lott continued to tell his story of that night. "We thought we would find illegal drugs."

Steven asked, "What time of day was the raid?"

Lott looked at him. "It was a little after two a.m. They had just closed, and we made sure the last players were out. We didn't want any civilians hit or taken as a hostage if there was a gun fight. We entered the facility from two sides, making sure every exit was covered. Your father was second to my command and came in the back door. I came through the front. Nobody was there. Everything was gone, including the gambling machines."

Steven interrupted him while still refusing to look at his brother. "Let me guess. Both of you figured they were tipped off."

Lott nodded.

"And it was Carlos Marcello's place," Steven added.

Lott's eyes grew large. "Why, yes." Lott looked at Jeremiah. "We wanted to get him in their raid. He'd been working with Meyer Lansky of Chicago for several years, bringing gambling machines into New Orleans. When your father worked for the I.R.S., he investigated Santos Trafficante and knew a lot about the mafia drug business and their connections. He'd studied our files on a bust in 1938 of Marcello, and believed he had a lead on their network. We really wanted to get the goods to take him down that night."

Jeremiah started to speak, but Steven kicked him under the table.

253

Lott continued. "There was six of us on the raid. Anyway, while the other detectives went through the place looking for any evidence, your father and I found a false floor in a back office. In there I found some cryptic notes. They didn't mean anything to me, but when I handed it to your father, he asked me to hold my flashlight on it. He was thrilled. I'll never forget what he said next. He said, 'This is exactly what I've been looking for, for years,' and that there were several names from his Miami days and places. Then he said something that still to this day doesn't make sense. He said, 'So that's the agency connection. I never would've figured it was him.' Then he mumbled something just as the other detective stepped over to the two of us. 'He's the CIA connection.' He was thrilled with these papers, I'll tell you. He stuffed them in his jacket."

Steven asked. "What happened after that?"

Lott rubbed his chin. "Nothing much. There just wasn't much there at all. I mean, they had stripped the place clean."

Steven looked at his brother. "What happened to the other detective who walked in on you guys?"

"Well, he left shortly after that. I mean, there really wasn't much else to do. After a few minutes, we all started to leave."

Jeremiah blurted out, "So my dad was alive when you all left?"

Lott looked down at his cup of coffee for a few minutes. "As we walked out of that building, four cars pulled up. Their headlights were on us, and they opened fire. We were sitting ducks. Your father was the only one killed in the ambush, but we were all shot up pretty good."

Steven jutted his jaw. "So what happened to the cryptic notes?"

Lott pursed his lips. "When we got to the coroner's office to go through his affects, they were gone."

254

Steven glared at Lott. "What happened to the detective who left early?"

Lott rubbed his forehead. "He turned up dead later that night. I always believed he'd been the one who tipped off Marcello's boys, but I have no proof of that."

Steven frowned. "So you couldn't lay a hand on Marcello. No evidence. Plus, none of you could identify the shooters in the ambush?"

Lott nodded. "Yeah. The same caliber of rounds they pulled out of us, they pulled out of the other detective. So I always figured they silenced the snitch, and they came and got us."

Steven nudged his brother. "We need to get home. We have a rough day tomorrow."

They all walked out of the diner together.

As Lott got in his car, he turned to the two of them. "That's what I wanted to tell your mother. I just figured she'd moved away."

Jeremiah started to say something, but Steven put his finger to his lips. "Not until we're in the truck."

Once in the truck, Jeremiah punched his brother in the arm. "You didn't thank Mr. Lott."

"You're correct. Something about the story didn't feel right. We didn't get the whole truth."

CHAPTER TWENTY-EIGHT

TWO DAYS LATER
LABADIEVILLE, LOUISIANA

As the funeral home's assigned minister finished the gravesite prayer, Steven, Jeremiah and Uncle Jake got up from their chairs and went to their mother's casket one last time. Each laid a red rose on top of the casket and turned away. The jazz band began to play "Just a Closer Walk with Thee," which was one of the songs their mother had requested. It had been played at their father's funeral. As they moved toward the limousine, two of the retired policemen from the night before came up and expressed their condolences. Uncle Jake continued on slowly, while Steven and Jeremiah stopped to talk to the two retired policemen. They told Steven and Jeremiah that Charlie Lott had died in a car accident the night of the visitation— he had apparently fallen asleep at the wheel driving home. *Steven was so sure about him falling asleep after they had been drinking coffee.* Out of the corner of Steven's eye, he saw a Lincoln Continental waiting at the edge of the cemetery. Steven nudged his brother and lowered his head. "They're watching us."

Tears ran down Jeremiah's cheeks. "Mother and Father, of course."

Steven jutted his jaw. "*No*, the men who kidnapped you."

Jeremiah stopped, then lowered his head and whispered, "You mean Marcello's men are here?"

Steven said. "Keep walking. Act natural."

The two young men stopped at their limousine and leaned against it as the band played "When the Saints Go Marching In." Steven burned with rage. *Can't I mourn for my mother? Must I deal with this riff raff?* As the song was finishing, Steven looked at Jeremiah. "It ends here once and for all."

"What are you going to do?"

Steven scowled. "I don't know yet. But I'll figure it out."

As darkness sat in, Steven went into Jeremiah's bedroom. "Are you ready?"

Jeremiah rubbed sleep from his eyes as he awoke from a nap. "Let's get this over with."

They walked into the kitchen, going straight to the window. Jeremiah asked, "Mr. Night Vision, can you see anything?"

"Not yet."

"What makes you think they're coming? Are you sure that was them this afternoon? Did you see their faces?"

"It was them. They showed up at the funeral to get a fix on us, not pay their respects."

"How did they know we were here? We've been gone for more than a year."

Steven walked away from the window and sat down at the kitchen table. Jeremiah followed suit.

Steven picked up the salt shaker. "I don't know for sure, but, remember, Mom's obituary would have run in the New Orleans newspaper. However, I bet they were tipped off by someone. I'm betting it was somebody on Marcello's payroll on the inside of the police force."

Jeremiah seemed stunned by Steven's opinion.

Steven snapped his fingers in front of his face. "We have to stay focused." The two sat there in the dark for a few minutes before Steven got up and went back to the kitchen window. "They are out there. I just know it. We'll wait a few more minutes, then we start."

Steven walked out to his car, carrying his M1911. It was his back-up gun that he'd always left at his mother's home, hidden in his bedroom. He checked his knife in his right boot. He started the truck and drove up the driveway. On cue, Jeremiah flipped on the light in the kitchen, illuminating his presence, so the thugs would see Steven driving away, leaving him alone.

Steven turned onto the county road and drove away to make sure the thugs would believe he'd driven away. *It's weird. I didn't see any cars. Was I wrong?* He stopped after the designated five minutes, and then pulled his car off the road so it wouldn't be seen. As he got out of his car, he stuck his handgun in his belt and started running back toward his mother's home. *I've got to get where I can see the house. Make sure the trap works.* He ran to the spot where he believed they would be watching. When he got to that clearing in the woods with a view to the back of the house, he could perfectly see the illuminated kitchen. There was no one in this spot, and Jeremiah was moving around in the kitchen. He stopped and looked around for fresh evidence that the thugs had been there. *Nothing.*

Twigs snapped, the sounds growing closer. Steven pulled out his handgun.

A huge man ran into the opening at him.

Steven fired two shots at the man, hitting him in the chest and jaw. But the man kept coming. The big man hit Steven with a roundhouse, driving him to the ground. His handgun flew off about five feet from him. When he landed on the ground, the big man dove on his chest and pummeled him with lefts and rights. Steven didn't have the strength to lift the strategically placed giant. This was the same man he had grappled with to free Jeremiah in the house in New Orleans two winters ago. *So he wants some more.*

He heard graveling being thrown up against a car speeding down the long driveway toward his mother's house. Steven had fallen into a trap. His hands were pinned under his body, plus the man sat on his legs so that he couldn't raise them either. He was getting severely beaten.

Rage climbed inside. Steven was able to free his right hand. He pushed on the bullet lodged in the man's chest. The big man yelled as he grabbed Steven's hand and pushed it to the ground. But this shift in the big man's weight allowed Steven to hoist him off.

Steven rolled toward his gun. The big man was able to get his hands around Steven's trunk and pull him back. Then he dropped his elbow down hard on Steven's back, driving him into the ground. But once again, the big man's balance was off, so Steven was able to roll and deliver a half forceful kick to the three-hundred-pound man.

Steven kipped back up on his feet before the big man regained his balance. He jumped on offense, delivering a right-hand roundhouse to the bullet hole in the big man's face, driving him off balance in pain. Steven kicked toward the bullet in the chest, but landed lower. The big man charged him. But his kick stopped his charge temporarily. Steven jumped into the air and delivered a hard punch to the man's head, driving him backwards again. Blood sprayed everywhere.

Steven turned back and leapt toward his handgun, landing with one knee on the ground. Just as he reached the gun, the big man stomped down on his hand, crushing the bones and driving the gun into the ground. The giant threw a hard punch toward Steven's head. Steven swung his left hand so he could pull his knife out of his right boot and stuck it in the big man's calf. The man reached for the knife with his right to pull it as he grabbed for Steven's broken right hand. This was his fatal mistake. He was bent over for Steven to deliver a hard jab with his left hand to the big man's jaw. This caused him to stand up as he staggered backwards. Steven stayed on the attack, delivering another left jab, followed by a right foot kick to the stomach. Then he reached back with his left hand, picked up his handgun, and fired one shot, right between the eyes. He held the gun in position to fire again. *I only have five rounds left. Save them. Two more thugs.* He checked to make sure he was dead.

As Steven ran toward the house, adrenalin kicked in. There was no reason to try to sneak around getting to the house. He stuck the gun in the belt behind his back. Just as he reached the house, the two thugs walked out onto the porch with Jeremiah's hands behind his back and a man on each side, yet partially shielded. Jeremiah's face was puffy, and his lips and nose were bleeding. Steven moved between the thugs and the Lincoln.

The bigger of the two men spoke. "If you don't want your brother hurt, you'll move away from the car." He wrenched Jeremiah's arms behind his back, causing him to winch.

Steven stood his ground. Surely, those thugs heard him shoot the gun. Did they have a gun behind Jeremiah?

The two thugs seemed surprised that Steven didn't respond. They started to backpedal into the house. Steven walked toward the men. Then one of the thugs pulled a gun and waved it in the air. "I wouldn't do that, if I were you, nigger."

That was all that Steven needed to see and hear. He pulled his M1911 and shot both men between the eyes before they could take a third step. Jeremiah dropped to his knees, then looked up at Steven. "You should have shot them sooner."

Steven nodded. "I didn't know if they had a gun behind your back."

"I'll go call the police?"

"Not yet." Steven walked over and sat down on the porch. His brother slipped over on the steps beside him. Steven looked at him. "I got to think about this. It will be daylight in a few hours."

Jeremiah gave him a funny look. "What do you mean, you have to think about this?"

Steven rubbed his good left hand over his swollen lips, then wiped blood from his nose. He was in a lot of pain from the beating he'd taken from the huge man. "The story Detective Lott told me didn't add up.

Someone in the police department tipped off the owner of the gambling joint a raid was coming. I'm not sure it wasn't Lott or one of the other two men."

Jeremiah looked at his brother like he'd been shot himself. "Are you sure? What do you mean?"

Steven felt his right hand. It was busted up pretty good. "Well, some of these police may not be on our side."

Jeremiah lowered his head. "Steven, remember Momma said Dad believed the CIA was involved with the Mafia. What if they're the ones behind all of this and not the police?"

Steven got up from the steps and grabbed the legs of one of the bodies and started dragging him. He didn't want to address Jeremiah's statement. "Remember, Lott said he didn't know Mother still lived in the area or he would have come and talked to her? Well, Mother contacted some of Pop's old friends when you got in trouble at Southern Miss. They had to know she still lived here."

Jeremiah got up and started to grab the man's arms. "Where are you dragging him?"

"Don't touch him." Steven dropped the man's legs. "I'm getting rid of all three of these bodies. These thugs got no one that will come looking for them."

Jeremiah pulled back. "Wait a minute. I'm going to call the police."

"No," Steven said sternly. "We're two Negros in the South who just killed three White men. If we call the police, it will lead to too many questions. Do you want to go to trial and defend that in court?"

Jeremiah raised both arms. "Steven, what about all the evidence?"

Steven sat back down on the steps and Jeremiah sat down beside him, again. "You said the other day you thought you would settle in Washington, DC. So, you don't consider this your home any more. As for me, this was my home when Mother and Father were alive, but now it's just a wooden structure."

Jeremiah frowned at him. "What are you saying?"

"I'm going to put these bodies in that Lincoln and dispose of them in the Bayou. Then I'm going to torch this house."

"Are you crazy, Steven? Get away from me! I'm not going to help you do that. I'm not going to be a part of that. I'm going to go call the police."

As Jeremiah started to get up, Steven put his left hand on his shoulder and pushed him back down. "Listen to me. You're right, you're not going to help me. That would make you an accessory to the crime. If you call the police, they might be on our side, but if we got the wrong bunch on the jury, we could end up in jail. Forever. These bodies will get eaten up on the Bayou, and I'll take away the license plate and the serial number from that Lincoln. If I do this all by myself, they can't touch you—if we were to get caught." Steven removed his hand from Jeremiah's shoulder and pointed at the Lincoln.

Jeremiah looked down at the ground for a few minutes. "What about Mr. LeBeau? He heard your gunfire. What if he turns us in? Isn't anybody going to wonder why these men never came back?"

"Listen, Old Man LeBeau knows I'm in, and we'll just tell him I found our father's old gun, and I cleaned it and fired it. As to those thugs, do you really believe their mommas know anything about them now? Case closed."

Jeremiah got up and shook his head. "Okay, let's go, brother. I want to get this over with. I'm going to help you."

"No. Look at the facts. I killed all these men. *They* were ready to kidnap you, *again*. You're clean. Let's keep it that way. You go in and gather up the things you want to take from this house. I'll deal with this."

After Steven finished dragging the bodies into the car, he took off the license plate, then took off all the serial numbers he could find on the car body and engine. He went to the small shed and got a can of gasoline and a six inch piece of two by four laying in the shed. While he was putting the two thugs in the car, he realized Jeremiah would have to follow him to the old deserted pier to pick him up.

He started the Lincoln and went to get the three hundred pound man from the woods. He struggled mightily to put his body into the trunk. Afterwards, he sat down on the ground for a few minutes to get his breath. Finally, he got up and went around and started the car. *If Jeremiah doesn't witness me doing anything, he should be in the clear.* He drove straight to an old abandoned dock he knew about in the Bayou. Fortunately, he didn't pass anyone on the road as he was driving.

He started to drag the two bodies out of the car, then realized he'd nothing to tie them down so they would sink. *Damn, can't tie them down.* He went to the trunk and pulled out the gas can. Steven started the big Lincoln, then got out and dumped the gasoline on the seat. He pushed down on the lighter, then set the seat on fire. When the fire was going strong, he reached in and put the car in drive and propped the piece of wood against the accelerator. *Good riddance to bad rubbish.*

Steven walked slowly back to the hard road where Jeremiah was sitting in the truck and climbed in. He looked down. He'd burnt his left forearm, hand and the left side of his face pretty good putting the car into gear.

After an hour of driving silently, they arrived back at the house. Jeremiah sat in the car while Steven went back to the shed, picked up another gas can, then entered the house and grabbed a couple of things for himself, including a picture that hung on the wall of his mother and father's wedding day. Next, he yanked the curtains off the windows and threw them on top of the propane stove. He lit the stove and poured gasoline on the curtains.

He walked outside and got in the military truck with Jeremiah. They drove a few hundred feet up the driveway and stopped. Both of them got out, leaned on the hood of the truck, and watched the family home become engulfed in fire in about five minutes. It was done. Their lives in Labadieville, Louisiana, was over. Neither would ever plan to come back here. After watching the building burn for a few more minutes, they got back in the truck and drove off silently. About a mile down the road, they heard a huge explosion. The propane tank had finally blown up.

CHAPTER TWENTY-NINE

DECEMBER 16, 1966
WHITE HOUSE - WASHINGTON, DC

President Johnson looked at his watch. It was 9:56 a.m. as Justice Abe Fortis walked in to discuss the rumors regarding Press Secretary Bill Moyers' resignation. Johnson had been preparing for this for more than a month. George Christian was coming in to replace him. However, with all that had gone on in the last couple of days, Johnson, as usual, needed to create a positive spin on the news.

The North Vietnamese had publicly rejected his proposal for better treatment of US Prisoners of War, while flat out rejecting his proposed exchange. Despite Operation Rolling Thunder flying more sorties and inflicting more and more damage on the North, their leadership remained "stiff legged"—steadfastly willing to wait out the war effort. The report from the Joint Chiefs documented 148,000 sorties this year, compared to 55,000 in the previous year. The bomb tonnage had increased almost 400%, and despite McNamara's comments that they were running out of targets, the Joint Chief listed an increase of 185 fixed target strikes this year, again an increase from the previous. However, with that there always comes bad news. In the last couple of days, US bombing leveled the village of Cau Dat outside of Hanoi. Once again, the international press had come out with strong criticism of the Johnson administration. And Johnson couldn't control them like he could the US press.

Fortis sat down across from the President and drummed his fingers on his crossed legs.

President Johnson bit his lower lip to try to control his anger. "Abe, I need to get a letter out from Moyers, words to the effect that he still supports this administration and believes in our efforts to keep South Vietnam free." Johnson ran his hand over the top of his head as he continued. "We need him to say that he's leaving for an outstanding opportunity to take over as publisher at *Newsday*."

Fortis scratched his chin. "What about Moyers writing something? I think it would have more impact."

Johnson leaned forward. "No, I want it to come from me, but it just needs to be a brief statement in the letter—and the letter will cover other things so that it will look like I don't consider it to be a big deal."

Fortis nodded. "I'll get with Moyers and get some notes from him and draft something up for your signature later today."

Just as Fortis was getting up to leave, Johnson's desk phone buzzed. He picked it up. "Mr. President, Assistant Director Deke DeLoach is here for your morning FBI briefing."

President Johnson held the phone against his chest. "Abe, get that ready for my signature." He put the receiver back up to his ear. "Send DeLoach in." He sat back down at his desk. The morning briefing would certainly include information regarding Operation COINTELPRO. Johnson's concerns were climbing regarding the subversives working in the United States—a position that J. Edgar Hoover shared. Over the last couple of meetings, more and more names were showing up on the list. Johnson was particularly interested in any update on the *Life* reporter, Rita Sullivan, and boxer, Muhammad Ali. This female reporter had written some particularly hard-hitting articles with compelling photos, but what she was up to behind the scenes was more concerning. Word came to Johnson that she'd had a public confrontation with Bobby Baker at the Quorum Club. She was meeting with some of the wrong people behind the scenes trying to uncover things that were best left buried. But Johnson wasn't going to bring her name up in hopes she would be covered in the briefing.

DeLoach entered the office and passed the morning briefing to Johnson. The President put his glasses back on and took a couple of minutes looking over the document. *Nothing new on Sullivan. Good.* Johnson had as much trust in DeLoach as Hoover did. He was an excellent choice as the highest authority in the FBI behind Hoover and Tolson. The man could get to the bottom of things and was loyal to the FBI and its deeply held secrets. Johnson asked, "So what is the latest on Ali?"

DeLoach handed the President separate report on Ali.

After Johnson completed reading the briefing, he asked DeLoach. "So the FBI believes while Ali definitely has a voice in the black community it appears that he has had some disagreements with Martin Luther King.

Reverend King doesn't believe he is as engaged as he should be with the Civil Rights movement."

DeLoach nodded.

Johnson got up to show him out. "Tell Hoover to keep a close on eye on this situation."

7:10 PM

MANSION ON THE WHITE HOUSE GROUNDS

Ambassador Henry Cabot Lodge walked away from the podium after finishing his press conference and headed to what he considered a working dinner in the Mansion. He was proud with how it had gone.

He smiled as he walked. Earlier in the day, Walt Rostow had tried to pick his brain for what he was going to say at this dinner meeting, just so President Johnson would be prepared with his rebuttal, but Lodge was unwilling to say much. He greeted the secret service agents as he walked into the hallway where he was met by Vice President Hubert Humphrey, U.N. Ambassador Arthur Goldberg, Secretary of Defense Robert McNamara, and Ambassador at Large Averill Harriman. A white coated waiter walked among the five diplomats with glasses of white wine. Lodge continued to casually visit with everyone, particularly catching up with his old friend, Harriman. "How is Meredith Brown working out?"

Harriman smiled. "She's a real trooper—going to be great." Then their conversation went off to each of their families.

Two secret service agents led the President into the hallway. The President suggested they all head into the dining room. Lodge took his designated place at the dining table, next to Harriman. He realized he was the only Republican in the room—which may be about to change. Lodge had become as disillusioned with the Republican party, just as he'd been with the Democrats. Since the mid-terms were over, and knowing how much micromanagement Johnson had with the Vietnam Conflict, Lodge realized he was likely to be replaced soon, if he didn't resign first. As Lodge chit-chatted with everyone seated around the table, he thought about the mistake he'd made by not resigning sooner in order to come home and campaign for the Republican representative in the 1964 primaries. It likely had been his last chance to become President, as he didn't support or campaign for Goldwater, which would prevent him from being supported by the Republican party. Because he didn't support Goldwater, he'd been given his ambassadorship back in South Vietnam. Lodge still believed in the South Vietnamese people, and his vision for keeping the country free was getting steamrolled by Johnson's policies. The promises Johnson made when he'd reappointed Lodge were barely kept six months before Johnson started backtracking.

When the waiters brought in the first course, the room got quiet. President Johnson took that opportunity to start the informal meeting with a question to Ambassador Lodge: "Give me your opinion about the latest developments in Vietnam."

Lodge took a sip of water. "President Johnson, in the summer of 1965, you made a commitment of placing more troops in South Vietnam and Asia in general. I believe we're seeing good results from that commitment. General Westmoreland has made great progress. I can tell you, today we no longer fear that the Viet Cong will cut South Vietnam in half. Also, the regionalism as prescribed by the Buddhists hasn't torn the country apart, and the South Vietnamese government keeping Thich Tri Quang under house arrest has really helped. Lastly, I don't believe we have to worry any longer about a communist revolution or coup from within South Vietnam. Despite the corruption of Thieu and Ky, the South Vietnamese government is finally stable and functioning."

"What about inflation? Their economy?" Vice President Humphrey asked.

Lodge finished a bite of cottage cheese. "Inflation is under control. We still believe the communists are bringing in counterfeit currency, so it's an endless struggle. The agriculture industry has been impacted greatly by the effects of war, but no one is starving."

McNamara jumped into the conversation. "Westmoreland has had so much to manage, what with the inefficiency of the South Vietnamese Army. Still, he has cut the Viet Cong down to size. Therefore, he believes the terrorism of the Viet Cong is down. The downside is that we're now facing better-trained North Vietnamese regulars."

Ambassador Goldberg, who had joined the group just before the President, changed the subject. "We need to get more countries participating."

"So, Arthur, you mean you will be asking the French for assistance ?" Harriman grinned.

Everyone laughed.

Humphrey raised his right hand. "US AID needs more personnel in the country, but they are having problems getting people trained in language and culture skills to go there. As Abe said, we need more foreigners assisting."

Lodge bristled with this comment. *Everything is about more US people or foreigners going into the country. More micromanagement. The South Vietnamese people need to be more involved in their fight for freedom. They will do it. Lansdale and I had the correct plan. I wonder if they're even aware of the success of Chau's South Vietnamese Pacification program. But now we're barely supporting the man who has been the most successful.*

President Johnson turned to Lodge. "Do you think we should have President Thieu be more involved with the Pacification program? Go into the field and work with the regional leaders?"

Lodge had been waiting for this. He was aware from an earlier conversation with Walt Rostow that the President would be asking this question. "If he isn't going to run for office again, maybe. In my conversations with him, we both believe the South Vietnamese military should assume a greater role, but they're barely able to provide security to the population centers they control. Ky and Thieu do not allow strong generals around them, out of fear of another coup. As to the Pacification program, Thieu isn't going to remove his brother-in-law, Chin, who has a large role. Chin is corrupt. It's a culture issue we can't overcome."

The President seemed to lose interest about halfway through Lodge's response. Instead, he asked Harriman, "Are you having any luck with your feelers out to the Algerian diplomats regarding my peace proposal?"

Lodge couldn't believe his answer was ignored. While Harriman answered the question about the potential role of the Algerians in the peace negotiations, Lodge's mind wandered off. *The President has been more concerned about his peace effort and ending the war than winning the peace.*

Goldberg turned back to Lodge. "Can the North Vietnamese maintain their ability to infiltrate? Can the VC maintain their ability to conduct terrorist operations?"

The white-coated waiters returned with the meal's main course.

Lodge replied to Goldberg, "I expect brilliant results in 1967 . . . ." Lodge grabbed his left index finger with his right hand. ". . . in conventional military operations." He grabbed his middle finger. "We would move South Vietnam ahead politically." He grabbed his ring finger. "We can hold inflation, although it would be a great struggle." He grabbed his little finger. "We would make limited progress in Pacification." Lodge took a sip of wine, then finished his point. "Ho would not decide to end the war until, in his own phrase, the 'guerrilla infrastructure' was destroyed. This embraces about 150,000 people. It might take five years to complete the job. But it ought to be clear during 1967 that we can be on a winning track. I expect US casualties to be way down by the middle of 1967." Lodge looked at both Johnson and McNamara as he made the last statement.

Lodge continued with his points, despite feeling he wasn't being listened to. "The people don't like the ARVN. The preferred pattern was the kind of combined force I have witnessed outside Da Nang, with twenty-five US Marines and fifty local Vietnamese working together in local security operations. The regional forces and the popular forces killed more VC than the ARVN. We should be moving to convert the ARVN to a police force. That was the only way to disengage them from bad habits derived from their training under French colonial rule."

President Johnson looked at McNamara. "Bob, give me the report on the bombing situation in North Vietnam."

"Two targets outside Hanoi were attacked on December second, third, thirteenth and fourteenth—a railroad yard and a vehicle depot. Some photos were available from the fourteenth, which showed the railroad yard had been hit, with some but not extensive damage. Some civilian buildings near the railroad yard were hit. There were no photos of the area within the city limits. There's some possibility that a SAM fell in the city limits."

"Is there any evidence?" Johnson quizzed.

McNamara shook his head. "I doubt that US bombs fell within the city limits; but there were probably some civilian casualties near the targets."

"What about the claim from Hanoi and Red China that we hit the Chinese and Romanian embassies in the city?" the President asked.

McNamara pushed his glasses back up. "As for the Peking Embassy, we have no evidence that we hit it. Nor the Romanian Embassy. It's exceedingly difficult, however, to prove a negative. A great deal of anti-aircraft debris fell on the city during our attacks nearby."

The waiters returned to pick up the dishes and serve coffee and wine.

President Johnson leaned against the table. "I think we have resolved a lot of issues."

McNamara nodded. "But I don't think we let Westmoreland have any more troops. It has been like a game of chess, and it's a stalemate. We add troops, they match."

Goldberg placed both hands on the table. "At some point, they're going to run out of North Vietnamese and mercenaries. The Cubans are done supporting, and the Red Chinese are running out of money to support the North and their men."

Lodge remained silent. At this point, all he wanted to do was get back home for a few more days before he had to return to Saigon. He had made good points, but no one wanted to run with his thoughts or ideas.

DECEMBER 29, 1966
SAIGON

Nguyen Tao sat in Lansdale's small living room surrounded by Daniel Ellsberg and Steven Hebert. They had just stopped by to catch up on the latest developments, since they were all off in different directions. None seemed particularly happy with where their roles had placed them.

Hebert spoke up. "In several months, I'll have my fifteen years in. I'm seriously thinking about getting out."

Tao leaned forward. "Really?"

Hebert nodded. "I haven't heard from the Marine Corps about my options. All I know is I want out of the Embassy. Being around politicians is no fun." He pointed at Lansdale. "You're here now. You have a great relationship with Lodge. I'm worthless. I need to get back into the fighting, or I'll just go back to the States."

Lansdale looked at him. "The Marines will get with you. They always wait until the last couple of months to offer a deal."

Hebert shrugged at Lansdale and Tao.

The phone rang. Lansdale went to pick it up.

After the conversation continued for a few minutes, Hebert said, "I better get back to the Embassy. It's quiet with Lodge gone, but we're light on staff." He waved at everyone as he left.

When Lansdale finished his telephone call, he went back over and sat down. Lansdale had a smile on his face as he got cozy in the easy chair. "That was William Colby. The CIA is working on a new program, which I hope he asks me to join. It's to run parallel to the Pacification Program. Colby and I have always worked well together."

Ellsberg got off the couch and paced. "I have been offered a job going to work for the Rand Corporation. I'm just so fed up with the US Pacification Program." He pointed at Lansdale. "You were right, this program must be run by either you or a Vietnamese."

Tao glanced at Lansdale, who half-smiled with that comment.

Ellsberg wasn't done with his frustration. The more he paced, the redder his face grew. "The only reason I went to work for McNaughton was to study high-level decision making in the government. I figured he was about as close as you could get to McNamara. Now that I see how it works, it's just a total mess." He paused and raised both hands up from his side. "McNaughton told me when I took this assignment, 'You want to study crises; Vietnam is a continuous crisis.' Well, he was right. McNamara and Johnson have micromanaged this to the point that it's beyond comprehension. We're on the verge of winning the fighting despite ourselves, but have no clue how to win the peace."

"Of course," Lansdale said and looked at Ellsberg. "I was the exception to bad decision making."

Ellsberg stopped long enough to frown at Lansdale.

Lansdale reiterated his point about the Pacification Program. "I told Johnson after he and McNamara took me off it, he would have been just as xenophobic if Canadians or British or the French had moved into the United States and took charge of his dreams for a Great Society." Lansdale waved his right arm around. "I told him to imagine how he would have felt, if these foreigners then would spread out by thousands throughout the US to see that it got done."

Tao nodded. "Hey, Ellsberg, can you get me a job? I feel like I'm wasting away in Laos. I'm just a glorified chauffeur for Shackley and his staff, particularly Edwin Wilson. Lansdale, anyone who thinks that you, Bohannan and Valeriano Napolean were out of control here in the 1950's, Wilson makes you all look like nuns."

Ellsberg shook his head, as he looked at Tao. "You can't really mean that."

Before Tao could say anything, Ellsberg's face grew red, again. He stomped out of the villa.

Lansdale scratched his head and raised his eyebrows. "I guess Ellsberg is leaving. Goodbye."

Tao chuckled.

Lansdale looked at Tao. "What exactly is the Blonde Ghost up to?"

Tao leaned back into the couch. "Shackley and Trafficante are getting pretty chummy with Vang Pao. I overheard a conversation I wasn't supposed to—something about some sergeants in Saigon distributing drugs for them. I think Shackley offered to set up some banking for Vang Pao."

Lansdale shook his head. "Shackley always has something going with Trafficante."

Tao continued, "While I was in the US, there was a tremendous amount of bad press regarding civilian casualties in North Vietnam. The Department of Defense had to send one of their spokesmen out to acknowledge that they had accidently bombed an area of North Vietnam. But I think them using Napalm on Viet Cong positions and Agent Orange to defoliate is a much bigger deal. You and I talked about what a bad idea Napalm was over a year ago."

Lansdale folded his arms on his chest. "We're doing absolutely everything possible *not* to win the hearts and minds of the Vietnamese people." He walked over to his liquor cabinet and poured a shot of whiskey. "So you really are thinking about retiring?"

Tao nodded. "Yes, I really want to spend more time with Luc. As you know, you don't retire from the Agency, but they did offer me a desk job. I served as senior analyst last year. I'm thinking about it."

Lansdale downed the whiskey. "Has Shackley ever asked you about our time in the Philippines?"

Tao laughed. "He has fished a couple of times. But I didn't tell him anything."

"Shackley can never know about what we did there, Santa Romana—" Lansdale grimaced. "If he gets in the wrong place, he could open a real can of worms. Keep me posted about him. Our old operation can never be revealed."

Tao got up from the couch. "I need to head out. Got a flight going to Vientiane."

CHAPTER THIRTY

JANUARY 9, 1967

WASHINGTON DC

Rita Sullivan couldn't pull her raincoat tight enough to keep warm in the driving rain, as she left work. The damp air was penetrating. As she arrived at the bus stop, one other individual was already seated under the burnt-out light at the shelter. His hat indicated he was a Navy man. Rita glanced farther up the street—no sign of her bus. She sat down as far away from the man as possible.

Despite being in the lighted area, Rita was uncomfortable. She placed her purse on the opposite side, then rubbed her hands together to try to warm herself.

The man looked up slightly, but his face was still hidden within the darkness. "Miss Sullivan, I need your help."

Rita's eyes darted for a second in his direction but didn't acknowledge his question.

The man reached inside his coat. As he did, Rita scooted farther to the very edge of the bench.

The man pulled out a newspaper clipping and laid it down on the bench between them. "Miss Sullivan, I need your help. Please look at this."

Rita glanced down at the clipping. It was an old obituary. "I don't do that kind of writing—obituaries."

"I'm very aware of that. Please pick up the obituary and read it. I need your help, and his family needs your help."

Rita's curiosity got to her. She picked it up and read it. It was an obituary from Monday, October 31, 1966, for a Lieutenant Commander William B. Pitzer. When she finished, she laid it back down. "I don't see anything about anybody needing my help."

The man continued to shield his face in the darkness as she tried to get a glimpse. "His death was ruled a suicide. It was confirmed by NIS and the FBI joint investigation, but I knew that man. He was a fine officer getting ready to retire, not commit suicide."

Rita drew a deep breath. She leaned out again, looking for her bus. It was now two blocks away. "I would go back to the NIS or the FBI with your thoughts. There, I helped you."

"I can't. It will get me killed, too. I was with Lieutenant Commander Pitzer that night. No suicide note," the man said. "Besides, this could be related to your research into Mary Meyer."

Rita snapped around and glared at the man. "I don't know what you're talking about."

"It could be the same assassin made this hit, too. Their deaths may be related." He pulled another typed page out of his pocket and slid it under the obituary.

Rita rolled her eyes. "I don't know what you're talking about. Get away from me."

The man stood up, but still held his head so his features would not be seen. "Miss Sullivan, I have been told what you're up to. I was told to talk to you by an aid to a certain senator. Pick up the obituary and those notes. Do yourself a favor. Investigate it."

The bus pulled up. Rita looked at the obituary. The man started to walk away. Rita grabbed the papers and put them in her purse. As she jumped up on the first step of the bus, she turned and shouted, "What is your name? How can I get in touch with you?"

"I'll find you." Then he disappeared into the dark.

Rita stepped into the bus and sat down next to the closest heater. She needed to get warm, but the cold chill running through her body wasn't all from the night weather.

NEXT DAY

Rita proofread her article on Senator J. William Fulbright's upcoming book, *The Arrogance of Power,* before she took it into Singleton's office. She believed it was strong, plus Denny had pulled some file photos to go along with the theme of the book. According to letters sent to *Life Magazine*, her columns were getting as many replies as any journalist. That was a great thing, and the chief knew it. Good comments or bad comments—they were the same. People were reading the columns. The readers wanted more.

Singleton stepped out of his office and shouted across the room, "Sullivan, where's your column?"

Rita smiled as she rolled it off her Smith-Corona and waved it in the air. The phone on her desk rang. She looked up at the chief as she picked up the receiver. "Hello, this is Rita Sullivan."

The voice on the other end said, "Hey, Blondie, this is Ed Boland. Before you go crazy on me, I have good news for you."

Rita didn't say anything, but she didn't hang up either. She continued to make eye contact with the chief as she pointed at the phone. "What do you want, Ed?"

"Blondie, I'm the current local president of the Society of Professional Journalists. You've been nominated to run for secretary for the next term, starting in July. What do you think about that?"

Rita calmed down. She was glad she hadn't blown him off. "Wow, that's good news. Who nominated me?"

"Come on, Rita, you know I can't tell you that."

Rita said, "Thanks for having faith in me, Ed. You really helped me when I was getting my career started," Rita said. "My problem was always with Petit."

Ed replied, "You're welcome, Miss Sullivan. You've come a long way."

Rita fidgeted in the chair as she looked at the chief. "Ed, my chief is giving me that 'look' about delivering my column. So, I have to go. See you at the next meeting."

JANUARY 16, 1967

PHU BAI, SOUTH VIETNAM - 8TH ARMY SECURITY AGENCY (ASA) FIELD STATION

Lucien Conein drove toward the Secret ASA listening post outside of Da Nang. As he approached the compound, he observed it was encircled by two 12-foot-high cyclone fences. Razor wire covered the tops of both fences. He'd been told not to get out, as there was a mine field between the two fences. As he approached the MPs standing at the entrance gate, he noticed other MPs walking around the parameter inside the gate with dogs.

Conein flashed his identification to the MP standing next to the driver's side, while another MP walked around his jeep with the dog sniffing around. He wanted to say something sarcastic, but resisted the temptation. Conein wasn't in a good mood about this transfer—or, as he thought, a sentence for his fun time. He'd done worse, much worse, and never been punished.

When the MP saluted and motioned him forward, Conein looked around as he slowly drove. He knew a little about the secret listening post. The thought crossed his mind to toss something out to set off one of the mines, but thought better of it.

Conein had been advised that the perimeter was protected by the First Marine Division and the One-hundred-first Airborne Division, but he didn't see a lot of evidence of their presence at the entrance he used.

The operation was supervised by the Army Chief of Staff, and he was certainly not affiliated with the Army. He was in the CIA under the Air Force uniform. He failed to see how his talents could be applied. Surely, the CIA would transfer him back to Saigon soon. He figured he'd be hanging out with a bunch of desk jockeys who had no clue of how to directly contact the enemy.

He pulled in front of the building where he was required to check in. As he entered, he bowed gallantly, taking off his Aussie Bush hat. "Boy Scout Lucien Conein reporting for duty, ma'am."

The secretary looked at Conein without any expression, then buzzed the base commander. Within a few seconds, the colonel stepped through the door and offered to show him to his new quarters, followed by a quick tour.

Conein moved about the various monitoring stations with the commanding officer. They discussed the functions and how their monitoring communications protected US troops. They monitored hundreds of communications every day, friendly and enemy. They were literally spying on everyone. It was impressive—and unnerving—at the same time. Conein believed in listening in on enemy communication, but he wasn't so gun-ho on US noise. He was told their operation picked up when the US Marines landed in '65 and was continuing to grow. It had helped Westmoreland plan strongholds to attack since his offensive had begun to finish off the Viet Cong.

The colonel stopped behind one station. "Our assignment is to track the enemy. Our goal is when General Westmoreland sends out his troops, they are in the field waiting for the enemy to arrive. Literally, every transmission we pick up is translated, then sent to Military Assistance Command. From there, it's sent to wherever it's needed, including your boys at Central Intelligence."

As they walked out of the communications area, the colonel pointed at a picture on the wall. "That's SP4 James T. Davis. He's listed at the first official US Combat soldier to be KIA in Vietnam—December 22, 1961."

Conein looked at the picture and the colonel. "Of course, we know that's not true. What happened to the soldier?"

Colonel gave him a hard stare. "Ambushed by some VC just outside of Saigon. He was placing monitoring equipment."

As the two men walked out of the building, the colonel looked at Conein. "You're not to discuss a word of anything you have seen here with anyone. Is that understood, Lieutenant Colonel?"

Conein couldn't believe he was being talked to that way. *I know more secrets about this country than he will ever know.* He stopped, clicked his heels together, and saluted. "Sir, yes, sir."

JANUARY 28, 1967
SAIGON

Steven Hebert sat in his assigned jeep, waiting for Tim Mitchell to show up. Tim had asked that Steven take him over to the US Headquarters at Tan Son Nhut to show him around and meet some of the "brass." Tim was planning to go home as soon as his enlistment ran out, and wanted to see how the war was administered.

A few minutes later, Tim walked out, dressed in civilian clothes and pressed his face up to the window, then got in. Before Steven could say anything, Tim pulled the door shut. "This is going to be fun."

Steven shook his head. "What are you talking about?"

Tim just looked out the window as they pulled out of the Embassy.

As they drove across the city toward the airbase, they talked about the Beach Boys and the things Tim was planning to do once he was discharged and state-side. Tim had three goals when he got home: one, follow the

Beach Boys on a concert tour; two, learn to surf; and lastly, since Meredith had no interest in him, find a blond beach girl to hang with.

Steven laughed. *Finally, Tim realized Meredith was out of his league.*

Then Tim drew a deep breath. "Major, I'm thinking of going to college and studying criminology. When I graduate, considering my security clearance and role here at the Embassy, I want to try to get into the FBI or maybe even the CIA."

Steven stared at him, waiting for a smile that would say he was joking. But the smile didn't come. He shook his head. "The CIA? You can't be serious after all you have seen and heard! Are you crazy?"

Tim laughed. "Major, how can you say anything, after your career? You worked with the CIA—"

"I never—"

"You didn't have to say it. I knew it from your actions."

Steven rubbed his jaw. He sucked in a deep breath. "So, Tim, what's the deal with the Beach Boys, beach music and surfing?"

Tim grinned. "My grandfather on my mother's side was an FBI agent and supposedly loved surfing. I never met him, but my mother used to tell me stories and show me pictures of him when she was a child at the beach. Seemed like there was always a surfboard in the picture." His smile disappeared and he lowered his voice. "He was killed before I was born."

Steven pulled up to the guard gate at the airbase. Both men pulled out their military IDs and flashed them to the MPs on duty. As they continued driving toward the US headquarters, Steven asked, "How was your grandfather killed?"

Tim shrugged. "My mother never told me much. Just that he died in the Philippines on assignment."

Steven parked the jeep. As he walked to the entrance, he was met by a Marine colonel, who introduced himself as Carter Breyer. Colonel Breyer acknowledged that both men's security levels had checked out, so they could see whatever they wanted. Tim wanted to see the communications area first. They walked around, examining the different communication stations. Steven looked over at Tim, who was leaning over the soldiers manning those stations. He looked up at Steven and flashed a big smile.

When they finished, Colonel Breyer asked if they would like to walk through the ops room. Both men nodded.

They walked through two rooms and past a couple of MPs before stepping into a room with five tables covered with papers and charts. Maps hung from the walls. This time, it was Steven's heartrate that picked up. The colonel pointed toward the first chart, an Air Force map with "Operation Bolo" written on it. "Let me show you two something," Breyer said, "Here's an airstrike over Hanoi." Steven and Tim followed as the colonel moved to the table in front of the map. "On January second, twenty-eight F-4 Phantoms lured North Vietnamese MiG-21s into a dogfight. We took out seven of them." The colonel paused for a moment, then snarled, "The decision makers in Washington DC prohibited us from finishing off the remaining nine MiGs left in the North Vietnamese Air Force."

When Tim started to speak, Steven nudged him and shook his head.

The colonel pointed at the next map. "This was a Marine operation into the Mekong Delta."

Steven placed his finger on the word *Marine*, while Tim looked at the map. The map was titled "Operation Deckhouse Five."

Colonel Breyer pointed at the river. "This was a large joint amphibious operation between the Marines and the South Vietnamese to set up a POW-holding area and possibly take some additional prisoners." The colonel jutted his jaw. "This ten-day mission, while successful in moving all POWs to the area, caused us to lose seven men. Plus, we didn't capture enough additional prisoners to make it a worthwhile assignment."

"Did they know we were coming?" Steven asked.

The colonel squinted at Steven but didn't answer his question. Instead, he walked with them to a third map with the title "Operation Cedar Falls." He said, "This operation included 16,000 US troops with 14,000 South Vietnamese to clear out the Viet Cong from an area the brass had assigned the name *Iron Triangle*."

Steven stepped up to study the map, then turned to the colonel. "This stronghold is only twenty-five miles northwest of Saigon?"

Again, Colonel Breyer didn't respond to Steven's comment, as he led them to a chart on the closest table. He picked up a paper and glanced at it. "Major, those VC wanted nothing to do with us. They slipped over the border into Cambodia. You would not believe the network of tunnels we discovered leading into Cambodia."

Hebert folded his arms on his chest. "How long ago was this operation?"

Breyer laid down the paper. "It just ended a few days ago."

"I used to be Force Recon," Steven said. "Was it those teams who discovered these tunnels?"

Breyer replied, "I don't know how it was first discovered. We have known about them for a while. We're just now starting General Westmoreland's final phase for eliminating the VC and pushing the NVA back. Last year, we did some real damage to them. If we had been allowed to pursue...." Breyer stopped talking and walked back to the door they had entered.

Steven and Tim got the hint. The tour was over. Steven knew the military was frustrated with the ground rules. As he got to the door, he turned. "I have a good friend in the Third Battalion, Third Marines. Do you know what they're up to?"

The colonel nodded. "We just brought them back from Okinawa in the last couple of weeks. We have asked for more troops to finish off the VC, but DC keeps cutting us back."

Steven knew that was bad news for Ethan Graham. They were returning to the battlefield. They stood at the door and thanked the colonel, Steven sensed the frustration oozing from the men on the ground who were executing the war effort.

They walked to the jeep. "What was that all about?" Tim finally asked.

Steven started the jeep, but didn't look at Tim. "Well, you got a real up-close look at not only how operations are conducted. Did you get a sense of the frustration in the military with the leadership in DC."

Tim replied, "Sort of. I guess I don't have the experience you have, Major."

Steven spoke up. "Our troops are doing a phenomenal job fighting, but they're being micromanaged by DC, instead of letting the brass on the ground make the decisions. If the politicians would stop meddling, I believe you would be seeing real military progress."

CHAPTER THIRTY-ONE

February 15, 1967

Washington DC

Rita Sullivan stepped into a staff meeting with several other *Life* staff journalists. She was happy she'd rekindled her friendship with Ed Boland. She'd likely be the next secretary for the local Society of Professional Journalists, with his assistance. It could be a resumé enhancer for her career.

Chief Singleton walked into the room and waved several sheets of paper. "Listen up, people. One of our London correspondents is working on this article."

"Chief," Rita asked, "What's this all about?"

Chief Singleton waved his arms again. "London claims when President Johnson learned former British Prime Minister Wilson was planning a secret meeting with Soviet Premier Kosygin, Johnson asked a state department official to approach Wilson to present three principal points to Kosygin in hopes of re-starting the peace talks with the North Vietnamese. Then get this, the White House sabotaged their own potential meeting by changing their demands. Get me facts, get to your sources that can corroborate this story, I want details. We're in an all-out race with the *New York Times* and *Newsweek* to break this story. *I want this story.*"

One of the other reporters asked, "Is London's source good?"

Singleton replied, "Very solid." Then he dropped the papers on the table. "I will have copies of these notes delivered to your desks, asap. Now, get to work."

Rita meandered back to her desk. She'd been working on several protests. She sat down and pulled out her notebook and went back to reading.

Denny Shaffer slipped into the chair next to her desk. "Singleton wanted me to bring this over to you. He wants us to select some pictures." He flashed his captivating smile and pushed his long hair back away from his face.

They had been working on the column for the upcoming *Life* issue. This month's topic was the favorite chant of the anti-Vietnam Conflict protestors: "Hey! Hey! LBJ! How many kids did you kill today?"

Chief Singleton walked up to her desk.

Denny flipped open the folder. Rita had already seen the series of pictures he'd taken.

Chief Singleton leaned over the desk and stared at Rita. "You need to pick out three or four pictures to go with your article. Denny took some great photos, so we want to encapsulate the story of the pictures into the article."

As Rita started leafing through the photos, her desk phone rang. The voice on the other end said, "Miss Sullivan, what have you learned about Lieutenant Commander Pitzer?"

Rita felt her face grow hot. "Nothing. I'm very busy."

The voice continued. "Meet me in the *Life* parking garage this evening at ten o'clock. I'll be standing next to the exit on level 2A." The line went dead.

She slowly hung it up. *I hope they didn't hear anything.*

The chief and Denny stared at her. "Are you ready to get back to work?" the chief asked.

Rita didn't reply. She just picked up the pictures and looked through them for ones that met her needs. She grabbed five and laid them out across her desk. "These are my favorites. I can't eliminate any more. Your turn."

The chief and Denny agreed on two. Singleton nodded. "Rita, one of the final three goes. Now, pick one, then get to the London story."

Rita knew the one she wanted. Her old friend Billy was in it. His mouth was wide open as he held a sign over his head with one hand and pointed with the other.

With them all in agreement, it was time for Rita to focus on the story from the London correspondent. After Denny and Singleton walked off, she picked up the papers and started reading.

Rita slammed the paper down on her desk. She'd become cynical of the entire Vietnam issue. Half the people who showed up for the anti-war protests had no idea what they were even protesting. They just wanted to smoke pot and protest.

As she focused on this Wilson story, it was puzzling. The US worked behind the scenes to get a British diplomat to go to the Soviets to get the North Vietnamese to return to the table to negotiate a peaceful settlement, and it was working—if the US would stop bombing the North, then the North would stop infiltrating the South. Then, at the last minute, Johnson changed his demands.

When she got home that night, Rita was going to check in with Meredith. Now that she was working with Ambassador Harriman, she may know something about these negotiations.

Rita was nervous meeting someone in a dark parking garage. She was scared she would be abducted or accosted. Pushing those thoughts aside, she walked into the garage, then down the steps to the second level. It was cold and smelled dank. When she stepped through the door on the second level, a voice behind her said, "Don't turn around. Now, what have you learned about Pitzer's death?"

Rita shivered out of cold and fear. It was the same voice from the phone and that night at the bus stop. "Nothing. All I've been able to get is a description of the crime scene; the victim was found dead in a pool of blood with a gunshot wound in his right temple and a thirty-eight caliber revolver lying close to his body. He lay face down with his head under the lower rung of two aluminum ladders.

"You better find out if there was gunshot residue on his hand. I'm telling you it is highly unlikely." the voice said. "You are my last and only hope. I don't want to contact his wife until I have something."

Rita hadn't really thought about it. "Well, yes, I suppose so."

"Think about this. Pitzer had top-secret clearance. He was Assistant Head of the Graphic Art Department and Chief of the Educational Television Division of the Naval Medical School."

Rita shook her head. "What's your point?"

"Let that sink in for a minute with this fact. One week after Kennedy was assassinated, I saw him working with photos of the Kennedy autopsy. He was thinking of making a film. He told me the last time I saw him he was almost finished with the film. I was the only one who knew where he kept it, to my knowledge. As soon as I could sneak into the crime scene area, I looked for the film cannister, and it was gone."

Rita started to turn her head around to get a glimpse of the man.

His feet shuffled. "Please don't try to look at me. I'm safe as long as no one knows who I am, but I *owe* this to Pitzer's family."

Rita stopped moving. "What makes you think it wasn't a suicide? I need some help here, if you want me to do anything. I can't imagine the FBI covering up an investigation."

"The FBI was the back up in the joint investigation. It was a death of a Navy officer on Naval property. That makes NIS the lead investigator. I'm betting the FBI was only involved with lab analysis."

Rita nodded. That made sense to her.

The voice continued. "Here's what else I know. That night, Pitzer was sitting in the theater writing notes to other people when he was murdered. The man was compulsive about writing notes. He was a meticulous note maker. He's sitting there with a pen and pad, but doesn't write a suicide note. One more fact. I learned there was a heel print on a piece of paper taken from the crime scene. It didn't match Pitzer's shoes."

Rita looked down at the ground. "Okay. But that's not much to go on."

The voice implored, "The Navy is pressuring his wife not to say anything or talk to anyone. They have put the fear of God into her. Go find out about the gunshot residue."

Rita heard the second level door open and close behind her. She was now standing alone in the dark, dank lower level of a parking garage. Someone else tied to Kennedy. The only item known to exist had disappeared. Just like Mary Meyer's writings. Both people were dead. Why was she continually being drawn to a story that now more than ever she just wanted to go away?

Rita walked out of the garage toward her bus stop. She felt eyes on her. She looked around for a white Chevy. *Nothing.* She hadn't seen it in a while. Or had she just not noticed? *Am I just being paranoid?*

February 28, 1967
Washington, DC

Ed Boland followed the car until it was driven into a parking lot. He parked his white Chevy across the street and watched as the young woman got out and walked into the FBI parking lot. *What is she doing here?* He sat there for a few minutes. Then he sat down on one of the benches along the outer edge of the parking lot. When another car pulled into the lot, the girl he was observing got up off a bench and walked to that car. Another attractive young woman got out of the car. He pulled up his Nikon camera, zoomed in, and snapped a picture. He didn't recognize the woman. Was she a friend or an informant? Was she giving information—or getting it?

Same Day
Washington, DC

Rita Sullivan parked across the street from the FBI building and walked toward the employee parking lot. This wasn't where the high-level, top security personnel parked. She was hoping to catch up with Stephanie Keeton. Rita decided that trying to get with her face-to-face was better than a phone call. Her only hope was that this would not get her arrested. It was all she had left in her investigation into the Pitzer death. If the man's story were true, there would be something in the FBI report she could use to spur on her investigation.

Rita found a place to sit without being obvious. It was a cold morning, but the sun warmed her a little.

Stephanie pulled into the lot in her old Ford Fairlane. As she got out, Rita made her move. "Stephanie, I desperately need to talk to you."

Stephanie spun around and frowned. "I told you not to contact me. Do I have to go to court and get a stalking order against you? It would be easy to do. Now, go away." She turned to walk away.

Rita bit her lip and ran after her. "I'm trying to help a widow. The NIS and the FBI said her husband committed suicide. I have been advised it didn't happen that way. I believe he was murdered and his wife needs answers. Put yourself in her position."

Stephanie walked faster.

Rita stayed up with her. She had to gamble. "The man had taken photos of the Kennedy autopsy and may have been killed by the same people who had Mary Meyer murdered."

Stephanie spun around. "Let it go. You're trying to create a controversy for your career that doesn't exist. Let...it...go." She twirled away, almost running.

Rita shouted, "I was confronted by Bobby Baker last November. I was in the Quorum Club. He trapped me coming out of the bathroom and told me I was being followed. So I'm already in trouble. I'm already a target. I think I even know why they killed Mary Meyer. Have I written anything about it?"

Stephanie froze in place. She didn't turn around. "Call me at home from a payphone tonight." She took a few steps, then ran, high heels and all, towards the building.

Rita knew this was the best she could hope for, but did she just get blown off?

LATER SAME DAY
WASHINGTON, DC

Rita walked out of the *Life* Building toward her usual bus stop. On her way, she stopped at a phone booth. She pushed a dime into the slot on top of the phone and dialed Stephanie Keeton's home phone. It was answered on the fifth ring.

"This is Rita. I need to know about the joint investigation between NIS and the FBI into Lieutenant Commander William B. Pitzer, who died on October 31, 1966."

"You said the official report was a suicide. What makes you think it wasn't?"

Rita bounced from one foot to the other in an attempt to stay warm. "The man who worked with him said he was getting ready to retire. Was excited about it. He was a meticulous note taker. The night he died, he was in the film room writing notes—but he didn't write a suicide note."

Stephanie didn't say anything for a minute. "You have got to be kidding. That's all you have. You expect me *to get you this file on that*?"

"Stephanie, please help me. I'm telling you, I have a hunch. Why would the white Chevy still be following me, if I weren't on a trail they didn't want me on?" Rita hadn't seen the white Chevy in a long while, but she was desperate and had to say something to try to obtain the file.

There was a long pause. Finally, Stephanie spoke, "You said you think you know why Mary Meyer was murdered? Will did you tell me? Did it have anything to do with me or the FBI?"

Rita's heart sunk. If anyone was listening to their conversation, she was in big trouble. "Not now, but when we're face-to-face again. Yes."

"Wait a minute. Let me get a pen and pad." When Stephanie returned, she asked again for the name and the date of the Navy commander's death. She said she would see what she could do, then hung up the phone.

Rita jumped out of the phone booth and walked on numb feet toward the bus stop.

When Rita got to her apartment, she called Meredith. After catching up for a while, she finally got her nerve. "Hey, I am looking for a lead—or perhaps I should say a *confirmation*—to a story."

Meredith laughed. "So you want *me* to be your inside source?"

Rita fidgeted with the telephone cord. "Our London office got a story that a State Department official asked Prime Minister Wilson to go to the Soviet General Secretary to try to get the North Vietnamese to return to the peace table. Then the White House tried to change the criteria at the last minute, which killed the deal. Do you know anything about it? Or, should I say, anything you can tell me?"

A long pause followed. "All I can tell you is that I have heard the same story. As a matter of fact, there's been a lot of talk about it, but I don't have any more details than you already have."

Unfortunately for Rita, Meredith probably didn't have a high enough clearance to see those papers. *In the end, it was only a confirmation to the story. Good. No new details. Not as good.*

But did Meredith know more?

CHAPTER THIRTY-TWO

April 1, 1967

US Embassy - Saigon

Steven Hebert stepped down from the Embassy front door to meet his old friend, Staff Sergeant Ethan Graham, who had been granted a few days' leave. Steven couldn't get away to meet him in town, so Ethan decided to stop at the Embassy.

The last time they had caught up with each other was just before Christmas, when Ethan was being sent to Okinawa for some R and R. He was part of the Third Battalion Third Marines. They had been called back to Vietnam early to serve in reserve and support for the First Battalion Ninth Marines on a new operation near Khe Sanh. Their new assignment set them in an area with rugged terrain, coupled with aggressive battle plans. It was likely they would be engaging the NVA or VC soon.

As they walked, they talked about the war. Ethan stopped in the middle of the hallway and grabbed Steven's arm. "Steven, I'm telling you they're sending a bunch of kids over here that don't want to be here. They just want to serve their time and go home. They're counting down the days. Some even say they don't think they'll make it out of here alive. You and me are different—we like to fight and we're good at it."

Steven started walking again. "That's not good. Most of those battalions like you're in are good, hard-ass Marines, aren't they?"

Ethan got in stride. "Absolutely. They send bad asses in on the tough assignments. I'm just saying the draft is sending over a bunch of kids, that…" His voice tailed off.

The two men entered the lunch area to finish their brief visit. Ethan chewed his lip. "Have you ever contemplated retirement?"

Steven leaned his chair back against the wall, raised his hands over his head, and clasped them. "It's strange you ask. I'm thinking about it more and more. My fifteen years of military service is up the end of May. Could get a decent retirement."

"What's your plan? I know your mother is gone and your brother is living somewhere back east."

Steven drew a deep breath. "I don't know, E. The Marines haven't made me any offers. I don't—"

Ethan scratched his neck. "They have to be working something up. Surely, they aren't going to let you go home."

Steven dropped his hands into his lap and shrugged. "I really want to get out of the Embassy. My skills are fading. I've been here almost four years, hanging around a bunch of elites and diplomats. It's not been fun."

Ethan looked him in the eye. "With your rank, you don't think they'll return you to the battlefield, do you?"

Steven bit his lower lip. "That's a good question."

Ethan looked at his watch. "I got to go. Get back to the base. We head back to camp early in the morning."

Steven and Ethan walked quietly back to his ride. As Ethan got in, Steven said, "Stay safe, my friend."

APRIL 7, 1967

WASHINGTON DC

Rita Sullivan sat with Denny Shaffer. He was trying to get her to go on a date with him, but she stayed focused on her work. She read over the text from Martin Luther King, Jr.'s speech at the Riverside Church in New York on April 4. "Denny, I'm writing an article on what the possible impact of this speech could be on the American public."

Denny licked his lips. "What are your goals? I think you ought to attack President Johnson in it."

Rita stuck the tip of the pencil in her mouth. "I intend to chronicle Dr. King's changing attitude toward the President since enacting the Civil Rights Act." She quickly scribbled out two paragraphs. When she looked back up, she caught Denny ogling her. *Never date someone you work with. If it doesn't work out, it's always awkward.* Besides, he was more radical than she about Vietnam.

Denny leaned over and looked at what she wrote. "Hey, remember in King's latest speech, he called for the US to stop the war in Vietnam."

Rita leaned back in her chair and dropped her arms. "C'mon. I don't have that much column space. His speech was focused on the poor and the Negro populations in the United States."

Denny was about to speak again when Chief Singleton walked up to the desk and tossed a printout from the teleprinter onto her desk.

Singleton folded his arms on his chest. "Remember back in February, when we were breaking the story about the Soviet's claim? They were about to help with negotiations with the North Vietnamese, then Johnson and McNamara changed the rules? Well, here's the follow up. Our journalist in London just got another tip from someone in the British Embassy that Kosygin said they have lost confidence in our word. Further, the Soviets aren't happy with us bombing Hanoi and Haiphong."

Rita glanced at Denny, then back at the chief. "How good is the source at the Embassy?"

Singleton frowned at Rita. "It's the same as the last time, and it was spot on. Anyway. The Soviets are hinting they may not be able to restrain themselves from staying out of Vietnam much longer."

Denny flung both arms in the air. "So—we're going to be fighting the Chinese and the Soviets both before long? And for what?"

The chief looked down at him. "At the moment, I don't want your unqualified opinion on foreign policy." He turned and walked away.

Denny looked at Rita and laughed. "Works every time. Say something he doesn't want to hear, and he'll go away."

Rita shook her head. "Yeah, someday he could just point you toward the door. This behind-the-scenes Soviet story is going to explode."

"Show me your draft of the King article when you're done." Denny stood and walked away.

Rita was glad he went away, and returned to typing. She reached in her purse for her steno pad. As she leafed through the pages looking for her notes, she passed a page with Stephanie Keeton's home phone number scribbled on it. She stared at it for a moment. She had given up on her help with the Pitzer murder. The Navy man would be calling on her any day to see what she'd learned, and so far it was a great big zero.

MIDNIGHT

Rita Sullivan crawled in bed. *Tomorrow, I'll have to start looking for new sources on the Pitzer murder.*

She'd been asleep for a few hours when her phone rang.

The voice on the other end said, "Sorry to call so late. I'm really upset about what I discovered."

Rita recognized the voice. Stephanie Keeton.

Stephanie continued, "I think you were right. I couldn't remove the file, but I took notes word for word from the file. Are you ready to write?"

308

Rita rolled over on her elbow. "Just a minute. I got to turn on my light and get my pen and pad." After a few moments, she said, "Okay. Ready when you are."

The original FBI lab report mentioned the photos. Stephanie said without preamble. "It stated that the muzzle of the revolver hadn't been in contact with the skin at discharge, nor did they find powder burns around nor powder particles imbedded in the entry wound in the right temple. The gun could have been very close to the head, but not touching it— but so close there would have been no time for the powder to have spread out after leaving the muzzle, and thereby leaving no outside splatter burn or powder particles around the wound. There was an area of charring around the wound that may be interpreted as a margin of soot deposit, yet the autopsy report describes the skin around the entry wound as having 'no deposits of foreign material.' The bullet entry was in the right temporal area, and exit was in the left parietal area, five centimeters posteriorly in a diagonal from the attachment of the anterior helix. In layman's terms, the exit wound was behind the left ear. But, the autopsy report further states that an internal examination revealed a defect in the left sphenoid bone and supra-orbital plate—that means at the left temple. And this is a quote: 'After removal of the brain, a third defect in the bony skull was encountered. This consists of a large defect in the left supra-orbital plate measuring three by one centimeters.'"

"But does that disprove suicide?" Rita asked.

"Hold on. There's more," Stephanie said. "There was no evidence of powder burns on the right side of the head where entry was made. The coroner explained that he couldn't say how far from the head the gun was held, as he was no expert in this field.'"

Rita's ears perked up with that statement.

There was a pause on the phone. Stephanie was still breathing hard into the phone. "There was some follow up. 'The paraffin tests of Pitzer's right palm and back of hand were negative, indicating the absence of nitrate, therefore no exposure to gunpowder. FBI tests indicated that the revolver must have been held at a distance of more than three feet when discharged. Although there were links between Pitzer and the revolver found near the body, the FBI could find no record of Pitzer acquiring live ammunition. The autopsy showed both an entry and exit wound to the head. It also revealed a third wound that wasn't related to the gunshot to the head'.'"

Seconds ago, Rita was exhausted, but this sent a charge of adrenaline through her body. "I got it. Thanks. Are you all right?"

Stephanie paused again before she replied. "No, I'm not. It doesn't sound conclusive. Do you still think you're right?"

"You think the NIS conclusion is flawed?"

Rita wiped sleep out of the corner of her eye. "Probably, maybe." She had uncovered part of the Navy's unofficial story of Pitzer's suicide was due to marital difficulty and having an affair. Despite to this day no 'other woman' being found. *Yeah, total garbage.* Rita laid her head back down on the pillow, but it was no use. She was now wide awake. "I just don't believe it."

Stephanie let out a big sigh. "Well, I want to tell you this. After I got finished making those notes, I went to another file room. I found out that the CIA is running a program spying on the American people. It's called

OPERATION CHAOS." She paused, and then added, "Your name is on the list."

Rita got out of bed and started to pace. What she had believed for some time was now confirmed. She knew that pressure was turned up on her now.

"Are you still there?" Stephanie asked.

"Everything is going to be okay," Rita said. "Thank you so much for your help."

Stephanie finally said, "Did you hear me? Your name is on the CIA watch list. What are you going to do?"

Rita continued to pace the distance of the stretched out telephone cord. She'd guessed long ago that the CIA was watching. However, confirmation was impactful. She tried to downplay it to Stephanie. "Yes, I heard. Nothing I can do about it. I'm in too deep at this point. There's no way out for me. I will say, I believe I'm about to tie together the connection between Bobby Baker, his thug, and the CIA—or James Jesus Angleton."

Stephanie spoke softly. "That still seems like a stretch to me. I don't see the connection. You must know more than you're telling me."

Rita walked back over to the switchhook. "I need to go."

Stephanie blurted out. "The FBI does so many good things for America, but..." Again, she stopped before completing her sentence or thought.

Rita was ready to hang up. She had to process everything she had been told. "But what, Stephanie? I need to get back to sleep." Yet she knew there was no way she would sleep again tonight.

Stephanie ignored the remark. "The FBI is doing the same thing, it's called OPERATION COINTELPRO. Both operations are watching what they call subversives." She sobbed into the phone. "The FBI is spying on innocent citizens. It's just plain wrong. It's all just because Hoover suspects the worst in people. Rita, how can you handle all of this?"

Rita forced a laugh. "I'm a reporter. I see and hear all sorts of things." She looked over at the clock next to her bed. 2:30 a.m. *I need sleep, but it's not going to happen now.*

Stephanie replied, "I'm sorry, but I can't handle this story."

Rita reached back in her purse to pulled out her old notes. "Stephanie, thank you. Thank you very much. Good night. You get some rest, if you can." She hung up the phone.

James Jesus Angleton walked into his office, picked up the phone and dialed. "Boland, I want an update on Rita Sullivan."

Ed Boland breathed hard into the phone. "I have continued my surveillance. She has been meeting with some Navy man from Bethesda, but I haven't been able to identify him."

Angleton slammed the pen down on the desk, sending parts flying in every direction, and snarled. "Don't concern yourself with the Navy man. He's not your assignment. What are you doing with Sullivan?"

Boland continued to breathe hard. "I'm getting close to her again. I will know exactly what she is up to and what she knows soon."

Angleton leaned back in the chair. "Don't screw up like Baker and that dumbass thug of his. Do you understand me? I want to know what she knows, and I want to know *now*. Your time is running out.

CHAPTER THIRTY-THREE

APRIL 14, 1967 EVENING

SAIGON

Major Hebert had been assigned to escort former Vice President Richard M. Nixon, a front runner for the Republican presidential nomination, to a meeting with Prime Minister Ky and Ambassador Lodge. Lodge was traveling with a different motorcade to the same meeting due to a prior commitment. As Hebert listened to the discussion in the meeting, Ky spoke of his concerns about presidential candidate Phan Khac Suu's campaign. Both Nixon and Lodge attempted to calm him, questioning Phan's loyalty and patriotism. They believed it would be a factor for the people to consider when voting. Neither thought he had much of a chance, but it was uncertain whether or not the Viet Cong would attempt to disrupt or create chaos in the election process. Everyone agreed that significant progress had been made in South Vietnam in the last two years. As of now, it seemed that only the pacification programs were lagging behind.

After about an hour, Nixon got up from the table and excused himself with the comment that he had another appointment. Hebert opened the door and escorted him from the room. On the way to the jeep, he advised Hebert to take him to Edward Lansdale's villa.

It was pouring rain on the drive over to Lansdale's villa. When Hebert pulled up at their destination, he got out of the jeep and looked around to make sure his passenger was safe to exit. Once Hebert cleared the area, he opened an umbrella, then the jeep door. Nixon stepped out and walked quickly up to Lansdale's villa. Hebert shielded him at the door until Nixon entered.

Lansdale asked Hebert to wait outside while the two men met privately. Hebert returned to the jeep. He leaned back and closed his eyes. As he got sleepy, he thought about his father's favorite song "Dream a Little Dream of Me."

As the downpour continued, Steven was getting drowsy.

Someone pounded on the window glass. Steven jolted awake. Lucien Conein laughed, then turned and walked up to Lansdale's villa, where he was quickly admitted.

About an hour later, Lansdale waved for Hebert to come back up. Steven hurried to the front door, looked around again to make sure all was clear, then escorted Nixon, under the umbrella, back to the jeep. As they drove off toward the Embassy, Nixon asked Hebert for his opinion regarding the war effort in Vietnam now.

Steven respected Nixon enough to know he wasn't expecting some "sugar coated" response. Steven unloaded his dissatisfaction regarding President Johnson's implementation of the war effort. Quickly, the conversation moved to McNamara and the turnover of personnel so they could incorporate more and more of Johnson's and McNamara's appointees. Steven listened to Nixon's critique of the situation, and then said, "So you want to get all the right pieces positioned in just the right spots on the chessboard?"

Nixon cracked half a smile. "That's an excellent metaphor."

As they closed in on the Embassy, neither individual spoke much. Nixon seemed more interested in taking in the sights along the way. When Hebert stopped the jeep at the entrance, Nixon bounded out of the vehicle and greeted the MP at the front door. Hebert caught up with Nixon halfway down the hallway. The two men arrived at the secretary's door leading to ambassador Lodge's office. At that point, Nixon dismissed Hebert.

Ambassador Lodge jumped to his feet to greet his old friend, Richard Nixon. They visited casually for a few minutes, then both got down to the task of assessing their meeting with Ky. Lodge asked, "What's your opinion of the upcoming elections?"

Nixon stuck out his chin. "Lansdale told me he's been talking privately with Ky. He says there is some conflict between Ky and Thieu. This has also divided the generals. Naturally, Ky said the generals are on his side."

Lodge leaned back in the chair. "Ky hinted around about that, but said he was going to do whatever needed to be done to unite behind Thieu, so he'll get re-elected."

Nixon nodded. "We need our people to win this election. We need Thieu re-elected. It will demonstrate support from the South Vietnamese people support. That's essential. A real message to the North Vietnamese of stability. Then if I can win the presidency, I can work with Thieu and Ky. I'm not sure about the others. What do you suggest to get the generals united behind them?"

Lodge tilted his head back. "I'll do my best to get Thieu on board before I leave here. I'll go see him personally. I may stop by and see Ky again."

Nixon said, "This unity is critical."

Lodge picked up his glasses. "I believe if Ky agrees to come on board as vice president with Thieu, it will unite the military behind Thieu. Plus, they have to get their constitution approved. If all of that happens, then that will put the North Vietnamese on notice that South Vietnam has a stable government."

Nixon wiped his mouth with his left hand. "That's critical, if we can get them to the negotiating table. As Hebert said on the ride over, 'it will put the right pieces on the chessboard'."

Lodge asked, "What all did Lansdale and Conein have to tell you?"

317

"Lansdale said that Tran Ngoc Chau, whose Pacification Program has been the most influential, is getting perturbed with the American intervention with Komer. He's likely to resign and run for office. Lansdale hopes to get involved with the Phoenix Program that Colby is developing, but I don't think Colby will let him in." Nixon leaned forward in his chair.

Lodge glanced at Nixon when he mentioned the Phoenix Program. "Yes, I'm wondering how that Phoenix Program is going to work myself. Lansdale told me he has some concerns about the Phoenix Program's implementation, which was why he wanted in. I agree. I don't see Colby letting him in. He's bucking for the head of CIA. Lansdale would only get in the way of his old friend. Johnson is trying to push Lansdale and me out of here, and it's working." Lodge took a deep breath. "You know Komer is being put in charge of the Civil Operations and Revolutionary Development Support? They call it CORDS. It gives Komer more power, and, ultimately, Johnson more power over Pacification, bringing into MACV control, too. Lansdale's bottom line—he said he's seeing his greatest concern playing out—if South Vietnam wins, they will still be dependent on the United States, not independent, as per his plan."

Nixon nodded.

Lodge raised an eyebrow. "Have you heard about the botched negotiations between the US Embassy in London and Kosygin?"

Nixon scowled. "Yes, a real missed opportunity. Now the Soviets don't trust us and are talking about taking a bigger role, which, as you know, the minute they step up, it will force the Chinese to step up. They can't afford to have the Soviets having a greater role in a country on their border."

Lodge cleaned his glasses. "I don't understand Admiral Sharp and Westmoreland asking for more troops. McNamara has told them no once, and with this going on in the background, you know he will turn them down again."

Nixon replied, "Conein told me that. Conein says that the North Vietnamese and Viet Cong are on their heels. They're losing, and they're afraid of confronting the Marines head on. So, we have enough troops over here. Get this—Conein told me the Air Force is going to start bombing Haiphong any day. They're going to force my hand—if I can defeat Johnson, which I think I can." Nixon paused for a moment. "I think, if I can get enough press in front of me, I'm going to issue a statement that the protests on the streets of the United States are 'prolonging the war.' This could win me some votes with the older American people and get them behind me. What do you think?"

Lodge was keen to give Nixon advice, in hopes of having a future role, although he was looking forward to working with Ambassador Harriman again. *Hmmm, maybe he will ask me to be vice president again.* "I like your idea. The situation at home is turning fast, and the youth are gaining momentum. Something has to stem the tide or we're going to be forced out of Vietnam."

APRIL 24, 1967

US EMBASSY - SAIGON

Ambassador Lodge called for both Steven and Tim to come to his office. While he waited for them to arrive, he read over a statement General Westmoreland had issued that the protests in the United States were giving the North Vietnamese hope of winning politically what they couldn't win militarily. Lodge just shook his head. He'd been told that Westmoreland had privately told Johnson the Conflict could go on indefinitely. Why was he getting political? Lodge knew the reason. In a word, Johnson. Westmoreland had great integrity, but Johnson was ruining him. He was becoming a sacrificial lamb.

When Lodge was advised Steven and Tim had arrived in the outer office, he asked they be showed in. "Take a seat, gentlemen." The ambassador leaned back in his chair and glanced at each man. "Major, I called you here to see if you'd be willing to take Tim to Tan Son Nhut."

Steven glanced over at his friend, then back at the ambassador, and nodded.

Lodge continued, "I have done everything in my power to talk him into re-enlisting, but Tim is adamant. He wants out."

Tim wiped his mouth with the back of his hand. "You know, for the last few years, all I have thought about is getting out. I really want to go back to the States and just kind of hang out. I never got to do that as a kid, so I'm going to go do it now. I'm just not ready to grow up, and I don't want to spend my youthful years in Vietnam."

Steven smiled.

Ambassador Lodge drew a deep breath, then looked directly at Steven. "Tomorrow, Major, you will have a similar assignment. I have resigned my position here, I'm going back to the States. I would like you to take my wife and me to Tan Son Nhut."

Steven and Tim looked at each other with raised eyebrows, then back at the Ambassador.

Lodge continued, "I was offered and accepted a different position in the Department of State. I will be working with Ambassador Harriman and your friend Meredith. I wanted to tell you, since I always considered the three of you my own version of the Three Musketeers."

Tim and Steven both laughed—Steven a little longer than Tim.

"Yeah, maybe someday they will do a movie or a TV show about a white guy, a white girl, and a negro," Tim said.

Everyone laughed at that comment.

Lodge looked at Tim. "You're dismissed. I want to talk to the major for a minute. He'll take you over as soon as we're done talking."

Tim exited the ambassador's office.

Lodge leaned up and folded both hands on the table. "Major, you have been ordered to report to US headquarters. Someone over at Headquarters wants to talk with you about a potential new assignment, after you drop Tim off." Lodge rubbed his chin with his left hand. "You know, Major Hebert, we know you aren't happy here."

Steven tried to show as little emotion as possible as he raised his eyebrows.

"Both General Lansdale and I have put in a good word for you, and we believe the service needs good men like yourself. You're dismissed."

Steven walked down to Tim's quarters to see if he could help him load the jeep. As he approached, he heard Jan and Dean's "Surf City" playing louder than he'd ever heard music played at the Embassy. Steven literally had to pound on the door to get Tim's attention. Both men had a good laugh. Tim handed him two armfuls to take to the jeep. When Steven went out the door, "Ride the Wild Surf" began to play.

The drive to Tan Son Nhut was very quiet. Steven pulled up to the drop off at the waiting area and went around to help Tim unload his duffle bag.

Steven thought Tim was going to cry when they shook hands, then Tim hugged Steven—an action he wasn't expecting. He looked down at the ground for a minute, then back up. "You kept your promise—both Meredith and I left here safely. You're next." He turned and almost ran away.

Steven smiled. He understood exactly what Tim wanted. He wanted to go back to the US and chase girls. Just be a crazy young man. It was something Steven had missed out on. But Tim was different. He was white. The life of a white kid in the States was different than a Negro kid. That was just the way it was.

Steven stepped into the headquarters and was escorted into an office in the back, where Lieutenant General Victor Krulak was waiting. Hebert saluted the man who currently was Commanding General, Fleet Marine Force, Pacific. It came as a surprise to him he was meeting Krulak, considering their volatile meetings almost four years ago. And he'd come in from Hawaii for this face-to-face? *This is not going to go well.*

Lieutenant General Krulak returned the salute. "At ease, Major Hebert. I want to discuss an option for you, to keep you in the Marine Corp." Krulak pointed him toward a chair.

Steven sat straight in the chair. "Yes, sir, General. I would like to hear some opportunities."

Krulak paused as he looked at the Major, then opened a file on top of his desk, pulled out a piece of paper, and pushed it toward Steven.

But before Steven could pick it up, Krulak clasped his hands on the paper. "General Greene thinks outside the box. He has created a new prototype position. He wants an experienced Marine to review Force Recon mission assessments and future planning. You were our first choice. If you accept, you will receive a promotion to Lieutenant Colonel and be transferred immediately to Marine headquarters here in South Vietnam." Krulak paused for a second.

Steven did not flinch as he sat in his chair. His mind was processing Krulak's words. It sounded like an exciting proposal.

Krulak focused the steely-eyed stare that had given him the nickname "Brute," then continued. "There is more. Either way your time at the Embassy is coming to an end. The United States Department of State is changing security protocol. They are bringing in Leo Crampsey to oversee security."

Steven maintained eye contact with Krulak, still unflinching, but his words didn't disappoint.

Krulak added, "Commandant Greene is setting up a top secret project, MarCor 85. He wants visionaries, a few men who can look into the future and imagine what a battlefield will look like in twenty years. Because of your background in Force Recon and serving in the Saigon Military Mission, General Lansdale gave me your file."

Steven still hadn't moved, but he swallowed for the first time. He was still trying to process what he was being told, still wanted to see the paper under Krulak's arms.

"Lastly," Krulak added, "you can be discharged, honorably, and return to the United States. You have also earned that right."

Finally, Krulak pushed the paper to Steven, who quickly picked it up. He scanned the official Marine stationary. His eyes moved to the bottom, and there it was—what he was looking for. "Signed. Marine Commandant Four Star General Wallace Greene." He quickly read the page. Steven's lungs expanded to their fullest. He took in a deep, satisfied breath. "General Krulak, sir. I will likely accept this position."

Krulak said, "You can think about it, but don't take too long. We want you and could use you, but if it's not going to be you, we will find someone else to take this role."

Steven remained sitting straight in the chair, still processing all that Krulak had said. The General added, "If the answer is yes, we will send you to the Pentagon immediately for sixty days of intense training."

Steven knew it was challenging, exciting, and may even allow him to get back into the action. "Lieutenant General Krulak, I would like to talk it over with my brother. But unless there is an issue with him that I'm unaware of, I want the new assignment. I'm honored by the offer."

The General nodded. "Do not delay with your answer, Major. You're dismissed."

Steven stood, saluted and left.

On the drive back to the Embassy, he was barely able to pay attention to the traffic and the traffic lights. *I can maybe see my brother while I'm in DC. That would be great.*

April 28, 1967

Life Magazine office - Washington DC

Rita Sullivan and Denny Shaffer showed up early for a staff meeting called by Chief Editor Cal Singleton. Since Denny had been out of town on a photo shoot, he wanted to see the final layout of Rita's article for the upcoming May 12 issue. The article and photos focused on the April 15 spring mob protests in New York City and San Francisco. Reverend Bevel had gained notoriety leading protests in the South, and then a meeting with Reverend Martin Luther King had taken Bevel to the forefront of the anti-war movement.

On the same day, Bevel's organization held a protest in San Francisco. Then came the written statement issued by Reverend King that the Vietnam Conflict was undermining President Johnson's Great Society program. He claimed, "...The pursuit of this widened war has narrowed the promised dimensions of the domestic welfare programs, making the poor white and Negro bear the heaviest burdens both at the front and at home."

Shaffer also had pictures of a group of Cornell students burning draft cards in a Maxwell House Coffee can. Shaffer wasn't able to get a picture of uniformed Green Beret Reservist Gary Rader burning his draft card. He was shielded and shuffled away from Shaffer and his camera at the last minute.

Just as Shaffer finished reviewing the layout, other staff walked in, followed by Singleton, who closed the door behind him. As he walked over to his chair at the head of the table, he stopped at the corkboard and pinned up three photos. "Okay, people. These are the finalists for the cover of the May 12 issue. Let's decide."

Immediately, Denny sat up as he saw his photo—a shot of Reverend James L. Bevel leading the Spring Mobilization Committee to End the War in Vietnam—from the New York City protest. As usual, it captured the emotion of the crowd as they marched from Central Park to the United Nations Building. Denny nudged Rita. "Isn't that a dynamic photo of Bevel?"

Rita nodded without making eye contact with him, so as not to get the wrath of the chief.

Singleton's secretary stepped into the conference and waved her arm, indicating something big had just come over the wire.

Rita ran out into the journalist area to the teleprinter and crowded in with the other reporters. Muhammad Ali appeared in Houston for his scheduled induction into the US Armed Forces, but he refused three times to step forward when his name was called.

The staff meeting erupted into a chaotic buzz. Rita looked at Denny. "Oh, my God, what's going to happen now? Will they strip him of his heavyweight title?"

Denny shrugged. "The New York Boxing Commission stripped him last month, right after he defeated Zora Folley. The government might arrest him for draft evasion."

Rita whispered, "This is huge news. Ali is both famous and notorious. Who knows what kind of impact this will have on Vietnam?"

Denny frowned. "Notorious? *For what?*"

Rita put her finger to her lips so Denny would lower his voice. "Draft evasion, not to mention his ties to the Nation of Islam. Most people have a hard time accepting his religion."

Singleton herded everyone back to the meeting room, and then let out a loud whistle. "People! People, let's get back to the task at hand. We need a cover for the magazine."

Rita leaned over to Denny and whispered, "They aren't going to pick your picture. The chaos in the room will cause everyone to go with what Singleton wants and get out of here to get more on Ali."

No sooner were the words out of her mouth than Singleton held up the picture of Truman Capote standing in the middle of the road with two actors from the film *In Cold Blood.* "Who else wants this as our cover?"

Everyone but Rita and Denny raised their hands.

"Okay, get me the caption and the title," Singleton said. "It's settled. I want suggestions within the hour. Now, back to work, people."

CHAPTER THIRTY-FOUR

MAY 7, 1967

WHITE HOUSE

President Johnson reviewed Robert Komer's resumé in preparation for their meeting. It was obvious why McNamara liked him so much, as he'd graduated from Harvard Business School magna cum laude. The President had first seen him in action while he was on President Kennedy's National Security Council. He was one of very few men who served under Kennedy he actually trusted. Based on his resumé, he was the man for this assignment.

The desk phone buzzed. Komer was there. The secret service ushered him in. Komer sat down on one of the yellow couches opposite the President.

Johnson, in his typical Southern drawl, said, "I'm putting you in charge of the other war in Vietnam."

Komer tilted his head and frowned. "Other war? What are you referring? I thought we only had one."

Johnson gestured with both hands. "That's part of the problem. I want to have a war to build as well as to destroy. So I want to put you in charge of generating a massive effort to do more for the people of South Vietnam, particularly the farmers in the rural areas, and your mandate will be an extensive one. In fact, I wrote it myself." He pushed the document toward him.

Komer took the document and glanced over it.

Johnson leaned forward and clasped his hands. "I want you to take over the Pacification Program. What do you think?"

Komer frowned. "I'm no expert on Southeast Asia."

Johnson chuckled as he ran his hand over thinning hair. "I've got too many people who claim to be long-standing experts. What we need is some fresh blood."

"Mr. President, we need to have all of the pacification programs under one single authority; we bring in both the South Vietnamese and an American program, answering directly to me and me to you. Therefore, we can disseminate funds and resources more quickly in accordance with their needs."

These were the words President Johnson had wanted to hear. The reputation of Robert Komer—"Blowtorch Bob"—was evident in his opening presentation. "I want you to be over our counter-insurgency program against the Viet Cong—train village militias against the Viet Cong." Johnson drew a breath while reading Komer's body language.

"Ultimately, I want you to be involved with setting up local governments in the villages and the regions."

Komer rubbed his chin. He appeared to be pondering all that Johnson had told him.

Johnson added, "You will be given the title of special assistant to me, but serve directly under Westmoreland. I'll have to get McNamara to sell this to the general, but I can't foresee any problems."

MAY 11, 1967

WHITE HOUSE MANSION SECTION EAST ROOM

President Johnson sat down for lunch with Secretary Rusk, Secretary McNamara, Walt Rostow, George Christian, Vice President Hubert Humphrey, and CIA Director Richard Helms. Johnson had a multitude of items he wished to discuss. First on his agenda was his appointment of Robert Komer to head Civil Operations and Revolutionary Development Support.

McNamara jotted down the initials and blurted out "CORDS!"

Johnson frowned as he looked at McNamara. He nodded at Helms, then began discussing why he had moved to place Komer in charge of the program that would now encompass all pacification programs in South

Vietnam. Komer would be the number two man under Westmoreland, but in reality he would answer directly to the President.

When Johnson finished, he glanced around the room to see how everyone was responding to him. "I'm appointing Komer Special Presidential Assistant over this program. The man is quick and intelligent, plus he's fearless and tireless. All the qualities I need."

After Helms took a sip of water, he leaned forward. "So you have combined Lansdale and John Paul Vann and Tran Ngoc Chau's ideas and placed them under one man."

McNamara briefly glared at Helms, then said, "But this will be the President's man over there, in the field running things. I'm sure none of those men would have been as dedicated to the President as Komer."

"Look, the rural election process is working," Rusk said. "Seventy-seven percent of the population voted, according to official figures. But to show the importance of our program, the Viet Cong killed twelve candidates and kidnapped thirty-one others." He poked his finger on the table. "This…must…stop."

The room fell quiet while lunch was brought in by the White House staff.

Rusk spoke up again. "I have talked with Ellsworth Bunker. He is completely onboard with becoming the new ambassador in South Vietnam, replacing Lodge. I think he will make an outstanding one."

Johnson nodded. *The man is on my side and is for our military effort. I think I can control him much better than Lodge.*

CHAPTER THIRTY-FIVE

JUNE 24, 1967

8TH ARMY SECURITY AGENCY (ASA) FIELD STATION - PHU BAI, SOUTH VIETNAM

Lucien Conein slowly replaced the phone receiver on the base, leaned forward in his chair, and put his head down on his right hand. He'd just received a real gut shot. His life-long friend, his one-time boss, the man he'd fought in the trenches with during World War II, had been killed in a drive-by shooting. General Atonine Guerini was dead. The mafia turf battle in Marseilles had scored its biggest target. The Francisci family had scored big. He reviewed every detail of the phone call in his head; yesterday, two masked motorcyclists caught Guerini at a gas station. Eleven bullets later, Guerini lay dead in a pool of his own blood.

He sat there with his head down for a long time. In war, you lose friends. He'd lost many, but this one hurt. *Was this the end of the French Corsican Brotherhood, or was this just a family change?* He'd known the turf war over drugs coming out of the Golden Triangle was going to get messy. These two families had been going at it for some time. The man on the phone said the fight was over casino revenues, but he knew better—that was only a small part of the turf war. Now, whoever was going to take over the Guerini side would put out a hit on the Francisci family, and on and on it would go. Conein had made his new deal with the remaining French Corsicans in Saigon, so for the moment his deal was tight. Conein picked up the phone and dialed. *I'd better tip off the Blonde Ghost.*

"Yes."

"Shackley, Conein here. Guerini is dead. Killed in the turf war."

Shackley breathed hard into the phone. "How does this affect us? Not much, I say."

Conein jutted his jaw. "I wanted you to hear about Guerini from me. I don't know whether or not we will be seeing Julian Romano coming in and out of Laos. But I wanted you and your boys to know. Be sure to include those other CIA boys, Pop Buell and William Young, too. May have some new operators. Things may be changing fast. Who knows how this will affect the Brotherhood?"

Shackley replied. "I got this handled. I'll take care of it."

Conein picked up his Aussie bush hat and looked at it. "Shackley, I think I'm going to retire. Move back to the States. The CIA has moved on without me. They think they don't need me anymore. I'm too old school for them." He looked around his small quarters, a place he'd given the nickname "Phu Elba." "Shackley, you're the new wave in the CIA."

"Why don't you come here and spend some time with my team before you do? Yeah, we really need your expertise before you get out of here—if you're really leaving. I've got everything pretty well under control. I put Thomas Clines in charge at Long Tieng and David Morales in charge at Pakse."

Conein nodded as he pulled out his pearl-handled, silver .357 and admired it.

Shackley continued. "I was going to call you. We got a real problem. Trafficante needs us to get Frank Furci out of Saigon."

Conein drew a breath. Furci had gotten into the black market currency exchange business and was ripping people off. He had a new competitor, William J. Crum, an old hand at making money in the liquor and drug business. As soon as Crum got wind of Furci's bad exchange rates, he made his move. First, he went to the Fraud Repression Division of South Vietnamese customs service. The authorities had already raided Furci's offices and were getting ready to fine him forty-five thousand dollars, which Furci claimed he didn't have. This was despite accumulating two point five million dollars ripping off the USO. Conein slowly released his breath. "If I were still in Saigon, I'd handle it. You better send Tao to get him out."

"That's exactly what I had intended. If you got any strings, you better pull them. Furci is in deep trouble with the authorities. Someone there in Saigon ratted him out. I just need a little time to get Tao there. Where do we dump him?"

Conein rubbed his chin. "Have Tao take him to Hong Kong. Let Trafficante deal with him from there."

"Why don't you come back with Tao after he takes Furci to Hong Kong?" Shackley asked.

Conein thought about it. *One more trip around Indochina before I get the hell out of here. Sounds like a good idea. Plus, I need to lay out some insurance policies on my payments.* "I think I might just do that. Have Tao pick me up here on his way back."

"Agreed." Shackley hung up the phone.

It was time for Conein to walk around the operation center and see the latest on the Conflict.

He walked out of his small living area toward the operation center. *I think I could still run this place, Indochina. My contacts are as good as ever, even stuck out here in the middle of Phu Elba.* His people had told him about Furci's problems, but he chose not to say a word to Shackley. He'd heard that Crum had paid a high-ranking US Army officer for protection, which was how he had found out about Furci's dilemma. That same officer was one of Conein's informants. Crum was in the process of setting up shop in Saigon. *Perhaps I can set up some business with him in the future. In this line of business, the players change but the drugs and corruption will continue. You just have to be flexible and stay out of the line of fire.* He grabbed the door handle and entered the operation center.

July 2, 1967
Saigon

Tao looked twice at the number to make sure he was knocking on the correct door. At this hour of the morning, he was going to awaken someone. He just wanted to make sure it was Frank Furci. Tao's job was to get him out of town past all the authorities without their detection.

He rapped lightly on the door. According to the Blonde Ghost, he was expected.

The second time, he knocked a little harder. This time, a voice answered from the other side. "Who is it?"

Tao replied, "It's your ride."

The door opened only enough for Tao to slip in. Several suitcases littered the floor. Tao looked around. "Grab one. That's all you get. It's better to look like you're coming back if they break into your place."

"You little gook! I ain't coming back. It your job to get me out safely."

Tao stepped into the mobster's face. "You have two choices—one bag or prison."

Furci looked at the assembly of bags, grabbed one, and started toward the door.

When they got to the old Peugeot, Tao opened the trunk and threw in the luggage. He looked at Furci. "Crawl in the backseat and lie down on the floor."

Furci wiggled his shoulders, then stepped toward Tao. "I'm not getting on the floor."

Tao nodded. "Fine. In the trunk."

Furci stepped closer to Tao.

Tao shoved his M1911 under his chin.

Furci stepped back. "I'll get on the floor."

Tao looked at his watch, then up at the night sky. They had just enough time to make it to the abandoned runway to get out of Saigon unnoticed. He started the car, threw it in drive, and was off before he even pulled his front door shut. Certain parts of Saigon had become a city that never slept—and it was exactly that part of town Tao was trying to escape. It was also the part the South Vietnamese MPs covered like a blanket.

As Tao tried to escape the night club area of the city, it seemed like he passed MPs on every corner. Part of him actually wanted to get caught so the MPs would pick up the scumbag Furci. Yet, he was loyal to his assignment. Plus, he would be arrested for aiding and abetting—until Lansdale came and bailed him out.

As he passed the last traffic light in the night club section, he breathed a sigh of relief. He accelerated his Peugeot.

From the backseat, Furci shouted, "Can I get up now?"

Tao slammed down on the brake, causing Furci to bounce between the back of the front seat and the backseat. "No. Keep your head down until we're completely out of the city."

Furci mumbled something under his breath. Tao figured it was good he didn't hear.

Within a half-hour, Tao pulled up on the abandoned runway and flashed his headlights twice. As they got out of the car, the Air America plane came to life. Tao commanded Furci to get up and get his bag from the trunk. As they walked toward the waiting airplane, another set of car high beams flashed on Tao's right. Tao stopped as a silhouette of a man wearing an Aussie bush hat emerged and approached them. Tao didn't even reach for his gun. He knew Lucien Conein had come for Frank Furci.

Furci looked over at Tao. "Who is that?"

"You'll find out in a moment."

Furci took a step backwards, but Conein was on top of him in a minute. "Furci. I came to give you some advice. You screwed up my deal. Your greed has cost me. Now, I just wanted to show you how easy I could have finished you off right here. Always be watching for me over your shoulder." Conein turned to Tao. "Listen to me, my little gook friend. Come back here and get me on your way back to Laos. I want to tag along. I need to see the Blonde Ghost face to face. Got it?"

Tao nodded. "Hell, if you shoot Furci right now, we can just go straight to Laos."

Conein laughed and slapped his hat on his leg. "Now you know why I love you and your big tizzun friend. You guys have a great sense of humor. No, go ahead and get Furci out of here before I change my mind."

Tao and Furci turned and walked toward the plane. Tao looked over his shoulder as Conein pulled off the abandoned runway. Conein had been banished from Saigon, but he was probably going to check on his wife.

Before Tao even sat down on the jump seat, he raised his right hand over his head and made a circle. The Air America plane lurched forward, throwing Furci down on the floor. Tao looked at him. "You better get belted in before we get in the air or you'll be bounced all over this plane. The weather is bad between here and Hong Kong."

Tao watched the limousine pull away with Frank Furci. He was so glad to be rid of the worthless man who had ripped off his fellow Vietnamese and US military men. All he could think of was getting out of Hong Kong, back to Laos. As he turned to walk back toward the plane, the pilot walked by him. "We'll be wheels up as soon as we refuel and get something to eat. Maybe forty-five minutes?"

Tao nodded. "I'm going to grab something to eat, too." He turned and walked toward the ground station. About halfway between the plane and the ground station, another black limousine pulled up around the corner of the building. It stopped directly in front of Tao, blocking his path to the doorway. The driver rolled down his window. "Get in the back. The Priest wants to talk to you."

Tao placed his hand on his concealed handgun as the back door of the limo opened up. Immediately, he saw his old friend Santa Romana, aka Father Diaz. Tao broke into a smile and slid into the car opposite him. Santa Romana tapped on the glass between him and the driver. When the glass slid open, Santa Romana said, "Pull over to the side and take a fifteen-minute walk."

"Yes, sir."

Everything remained quiet in the limo until it stopped and the driver got out. Santa Romana leaned forward. The large cross hanging around his neck swung free in front of his Cassock as Santa Romana kissed Tao on the forehead.

Tao placed both hands together. "What brings you to Hong Kong? How did you know I was going to be here?"

Santa Romana dropped his hands to his knees. "I came to finish some banking here. I have some accounts, and I wanted to make some changes."

Tao shook his head. "That still doesn't explain how you knew I was coming here."

Santa Romana cracked half a smile. "I always know where you are. You know the promise I made you and Quezon years ago." His smile went away. "I've come to give you a warning. Lansdale has fallen out of power in the CIA, and he can no longer protect our old team like he once could."

Tao leaned back in the car seat. "I have seen hints of that, but he swears if Nixon gets elected, he'll be back in power. Nixon promised him."

Santa Romana crossed his leg and grabbed the cross in his left hand. "Look, Lansdale is still in a powerful political position. He must keep Premier Nguyen Cao Ky in line with the upcoming election—and, aligned with Thieu—not only for the benefit of South Vietnam, but also the United States. Lansdale has been dealt a tough hand of cards on this assignment. This has nothing to do with Nixon winning or losing. I just know that those in power at the CIA will not back Lansdale anymore. There is a real turn over—the young guns are after their own power. Lansdale's time has passed." Santa Romana looked out the limo window for a couple of seconds.

"Oh, Lansdale will still be consulted within the political arena. At the moment, Johnson and the ambassador need him."

As Santa Romana spoke, Tao thought about Conein and Lansdale. He'd seen in it his time around Shackley. Tao jutted his chin. "Santy, I must tell you that Franco Quezon and my son are fighting in a martial arts tournaments this summer. If they win their divisions, they believe they're good enough to start fighting internationally."

"Excellent. I will try to catch on of the tournaments. I'd like to see how those young'uns are doing."

Tao nodded. "Franco has been trying to research his father."

"I knew he was researching his father. I have blocked or destroyed all that information." Santa Romana looked at him with a steely-eyed stare. "You've been offered an assignment back at Langley—and you should take it. It will allow you to keep a better eye on your son and Franco. Something you can't do in Laos. Remember this—there are some in the CIA who have it in for our team and what we accomplished in the Philippines. If you fall into a vulnerable position, the Japanese Yakuza and the Chinese Green Gang will be after you."

Tao sat quietly. How did Romana know about his offer to go back to Langley? He pondered his advice for a moment "What's up with Marcos? I hear through Lansdale that he's giving Johnson fits about public commitments— not to mention money and troops. I hear he keeps raising the price on the listening station at Clark Air Base."

"Marcos is my friend, but he has Johnson eating out of his palm. You know Johnson doesn't like that—he likes to be in control. The US needs the

Philippines' support in Asia, and it needs Clark Air Base and Subic Naval Base. It's critical to Vietnam, but Vietnam isn't critical to the Philippines. All the diplomatic meetings are in Manila. My situation with Marcos is similar to that of Lansdale with Ky." Santa Romana put his hand to his mouth. "You never want to have Marcos hold something over you. He's ruthless—and then you must watch out for Fabian Ver, who is even more ruthless."

Tao thought of his past dealings with Ver.

Santa Romana rolled down the window, waved to his driver to return, and then rolled the window back up. "Take the assignment back in Langley. Get back to the States. It's for your own safety. We know too much."

Tao rubbed his chin. "I will consider your advice. You be safe." He looked Santa Romana in the eyes, then got out without another word.

CHAPTER THIRTY-SIX

July 17, 1967

Tan Son Nhut Air base - Saigon

Lieutenant Colonel Steven Hebert had returned to Saigon late last night. This morning, as he walked down the hallway to his new assigned area in the command center of the US Headquarters at Tan Son Nhut Air Base, he contemplated the time he'd spent in the States. It was really great to see Jeremiah. He'd gotten his life back on track. Doing well in college— Howard College really had been great for him. He was making good grades to boot. On top of that, he got a real thrill to see his brother run in an AAU/Open track meet, the first time he'd ever seen him run. The boy was fast—ran a forty-eight point seven time in the quarter mile and long jumped, first time ever, nineteen feet, nine inches.

He arrived at the door of his assigned office. A piece of white medical tape covered the top, with the letters *OPS* written in black magic marker. He grimaced. *They have really gone out of their way to welcome me.* He entered the room. The only things on the desk were two thick files. Obviously, his assignment was starting at full speed. His first task was to review the fighting outside Khe Sanh, which had received the appropriate nickname "the Hill fighting." General Krulak and Commandant Greene wanted this bloody series of battles reviewed. How were the Marines deployed? What was their strategy for the defense of the Khe Sanh Combat Base? What additional assets could be brought to yield a better tactical advantage?

On the other file was written *OPERATION BUFFALO*, the most recent major engagement with the enemy.

Steven's orders were to prepare a report on the Hill Fighting near Khe Sanh Combat Base, then review Operation Buffalo. He reached in his pocket and pulled out a yellow sheet of paper. On it was written: *look into the future and imagine what a battlefield will look like and how we apply our fighting talents.* He laid it down next to the other thick file, which he opened. He flipped to the last page, the casualty data. It listed the US Marines Killed In Action (KIA) as 155 men, with an additional 425 wounded. The confirmed "official" figure of North Vietnamese Army KIA, 940, seemed really low for the bloody fighting that lasted eighteen days.

He flipped back to the front of the file, which included a map of the area and the hills surrounding the base. This battle had taken place in the valley along the Rao Quan River near an intersection of two roads, including the all-important Highway 9. Next page, a brief history of the base camp; originally established for Green Berets in 1962, over the next five years however, there had been more frequent VC or NVA mortar attacks. In October of last year, the US decided to bring in Marines to encamp there then, just after the first of the year, the Navy Seabees moved in to extend and upgrade the runways. Steven theorized that may have been the breaking point for the NVA.

Steven pulled out a memo pad and pen, *here are my questions:* Was Force Recon sent out to scout the area? How far out were they sent? Considering the bunkers the NVA had built, they had been missed. How quickly could they have dug in and built these bunkers? Later, a five man advance team was sent out, of which four were killed and the only survivor was badly wounded. Immediately, several companies from the US Third, then the Twenty-sixth Marines, were sent out to engage the North Vietnamese Army. His friend Ethan Graham likely would've been deployed. As the fighting intensified, it was estimated the Marines engaged maybe three divisions of North Vietnamese in the area, each covering a different hill, all of which could overlook the Khe Sanh Combat Base.

There was a section in the file describing the three steep, triple-canopied hills. Plus, bunkers had been built from wood in these steep hills, which the Air Force bombs couldn't penetrate at first. As the fighting dragged on, some of the Marines after action reports referenced as they dug in, they were literally digging up NVA dead bodies.

Besides the conditions, the Marines didn't have sufficient food and water, not to mention they may have lacked the best available weapons. This led to him to question if, in the future, could rapid deployment be improved with better long range helicopters, so the camps could be farther away from the enemy?

Still, it nagged at him. How was it, with a base this close, did they miss the build up of North Vietnamese troops? Was this US Marine base in a strategic location? It had emerged that a number of the Marine commanders had questioned Westmoreland regarding the importance of this base near the Laotian border. Westmoreland considered the base critical to combating the movement of supplies and men off the Ho Chi Minh trail.

After Steven finished reading over the entire file and made his final notes, he looked at the NVA KIA—nine hundred-forty seemed really low for all of the fighting. The thing that troubled him the most was the dispute among the commanders of the significant status of the base at Khe Sanh. If you keep the base, you must control the hills overlooking it or else abandon it. Conversely, being this close to Laos and Highway 9 was important to keep the enemy in check.

Perhaps he had made a mistake right off the bat. *Note to self,* he wrote on a piece of paper. *Don't look at the death tolls first. Something doesn't add up. All this intense fighting over this amount of time, I would expect greater NVA KIA.*

Steven concluded the Marines had fought hard under some of the worst conditions, yet they had persevered. He knew Westmoreland and his staff had been defining success in the battle field with KIAs, yet the NVA and VC seemed to have an unlimited supply of men to sacrifice.

As Steven sealed up the envelope, he hoped he'd provided Commandant Greene with the type of analysis he'd sought. While he wasn't back in combat, he was enjoying his new assignment. He felt like he was contributing positively to the Conflict's cause.

Steven reviewed Operation Buffalo. Marines were sent in to take out North Vietnamese Army troops operating in the DMZ near Con Thien. On their first day out, July 2, the First Battalion, Ninth Marines were ambushed, which resulted in the death of eighty-four soldiers, one hundred-ninety wounded, and nine MIA. It was the worst one day loss of Marines. Why?

Hours later, after Steven had been through the detail file a third time, nothing seemed to fit or make sense. He leaned back and closed his eyes. Then he remembered Tao mentioning his suspicions several years ago about a potential spy high enough up in the command to have advance knowledge of operations. It had to be in the South Vietnamese side—surely no one on the American side would set up their own Marines to be killed. *I know that's not part of my new assignment, but this has to stop.*

AUGUST 11, 1967

SAIGON

Lieutenant Colonel Steven Hebert had been invited to General Lansdale's villa. When he arrived, Tao let him in. Lansdale wanted to discuss several items of business, including a new US program.

Steven and Tao sat down in front of Lansdale.

Lansdale rubbed his chin. "We need to watch and see what the impact of the death of Nguyen Chi Thanh has in North Vietnam. Next to Le Duan, he may have been their most important leader. He was close to the Red Chinese leadership and, militarily, was instrumental in leading the Viet Cong and the

North Vietnamese Army in South Vietnam. His death will create a void in a very key role."

Steven sat up straight. He knew this man was an important leader in the North. "The Air Force believes he was critically wounded on a B-52 strike of the North Vietnamese Southern Command Headquarters?" He rubbed his chin. "Who do you think will fill this position?"

Lansdale nodded. "I heard the same thing. But the fact is he is dead."

"You still believe now Ho Chi Minh is only a figurehead in North Vietnam?" Tao asked.

Lansdale leaned forward and looked at Hebert and Tao. "Yes and no. He's a symbol to his people, but these young communists have taken over." He waved his hand. "I had another reason for calling this meeting. I wanted to talk to you about a new program the US is starting."

Tao and Hebert glanced at each other. Hebert thought they had just wanted to get together since he was returning from his brief assignment at the Pentagon.

Lansdale began discussing what he had heard about Colby's new Phoenix Program. Once again, he detailed the need for South Vietnamese to be running all programs like these inside their country. The people needed to have a cause to fight for, their freedom and independence. Hebert sat and listened intently to basically the same history lesson he'd lived through about every time he'd been over to see Lansdale. By the same token, Lansdale had a reason to be upset. He believed Lansdale was mad because despite his insistence that he should be allowed to over see this program for the United States, it was very unlikely at this point in his career. Just like North Vietnam, the new leaders in the CIA were running the clandestine operations in Vietnam. People like Lansdale and Conein were on their way out of power.

When Lansdale finally finished ranting, Tao leaned forward. "I want to tell you, I've heard that SEAL unit Detachment Bravo is working with the PRU in South Vietnam. I think they're training is really paying dividends with the improvement of ARVN Seals operatives. Also, in Laos, we have witnessed several of the South Vietnamese Commandos carrying out insurgent operations very effectively. They were trained by and accompanied by some members of SEAL Team 2."

Steven chimed in, "One of the things I was briefed on for my new assignment was the success of the US Navy Swift boaters. Word around the Pentagon is that they have really shut down the VC in the waters of the Mekong Delta. It's something they wanted me to study for insertion of troops into a battle."

Tao nodded, then looked at Lansdale. "You talked to Pham Xuan An about any of these developments? I haven't had a chance to see him, and I would like to before—"

Lansdale waved his hand. "I have tried to catch up with him a couple of times, but he has been so busy we just haven't had a chance. I'm curious what he's been writing."

Tao leaned back into the couch. "I haven't talked to him in over a year. That's why I want to catch up with him before I go back to the United States for good."

Steven jerked as he turned toward Tao. "You're going to the States? For good?"

Tao drew a deep breath. "Taking a desk job, kind of like your new job. Analyzing CIA missions."

Steven looked down at his watch. Since Lansdale had finished with his rant, he thought it was best to get out of there. When he stood, Tao did too. Lansdale bid them goodbye as they walked out.

Once outside, Tao asked, "Do you have time for a cup of tea?"

Steven shook his head. "No, I've already been gone too long. The military staff is much stricter than the Embassy staff."

Tao laughed. "You're going to have to be much more disciplined now."

Steven frowned, faking being mad at Tao, then burst out in a laugh. "Yeah, you know what a slacker I've always been." He continued to walk to the jeep. "So you really are going back to the States?"

Tao nodded. "Getting a chance to spend some time with Luc."

Steven got to his car and leaned against the jeep. "Yes, while I was in DC, I got to spend some time with my little brother—"

Tao turned toward Steven. "I can't handle working with Shackley. I serve no positive role."

Steven pursed his lips. "I understand."

Tao placed both hands on his hips. "Before you got here, Lansdale told me there's another change over in the power structure in the South Vietnamese government. He's trying to keep Prime Minister Ky and President Thieu from each other's throats. At least until after Thieu gets re-elected. He's concerned about Ky's acceptance of his new role as Vice President. Lansdale said that's all the State Department is worried about at this point."

Steven shook his head. "So Lansdale is now expected to babysit the South Vietnamese leaders and generals?"

Tao glanced at the ground. "Lansdale's role here has changed, but he said everyone in Washington was happy with him keeping tabs on the South Vietnamese leadership." He nodded, then said, "Since you won't go have a cup of tea, I think I'll go say goodbye to Pham Xuan An. I want to know what he thinks about the death of Nguyen Chi Thanh."

Steven reached out his hand to shake that of one of his truly best friends. *I'm going to miss him, but I bet he's back here before long, at least on assignment. You never retire from the CIA, and his knowledge of South Vietnam is invaluable.*

As he drove off, it occurred to him that as long as he'd been in Indochina, he'd never met Pham Xuan An. *An had been associated with Lansdale as long as I have.* He felt like he knew him, probably because the man was a legend in the reporters' world in South Vietnam.

Tao walked into the crowded Continental Hotel restaurant, hoping to catch up with Pham Xuan An. He caught a glimpse of his friend sitting in a corner table. Tao bumped his way through the throng to sit down opposite him. Immediately, An offered him an American cigarette, which Tao accepted. "I'm trying to quit these things again."

An laughed as he took a draw off his cigarette. "You'll never quit."

Tao got serious. "I wanted to stop by and see you. I'm getting ready to head to the US for a while, maybe for good."

An finished off his beer and waved to the waiter, holding up two fingers. "We should celebrate." His words were slightly slurred.

Tao nodded in approval. "I understand you and Lansdale have been missing each other to catch up?"

An snubbed out his cigarette. "Yes, *Time* has been keeping me busy. I know Lansdale has been busy working with the South Vietnamese leadership."

"I just came from telling him I was leaving. Anyway, it appears that the United States is finally getting the upper hand on the communists and VC."

An didn't respond to Tao's statement, Tao continued. "How much do you think the death of Nguyen Chi Thanh is going to hurt the communists?"

The waiter showed up with the two beers and a menu for Tao. As soon as the waiter left, An replied, "Thanh was an important cog to the North Vietnamese Army, too."

Tao noted that An's facial expression changed a little as he answered the question. He remained quiet to see if An would continue to talk, as Tao believed he'd been drinking for a while.

An lit another cigarette, he offered one to Tao. "Thanh worked well with the leaders in Peking. He should have stayed in the politburo rather than coming out of retirement back to the military." An composed himself. "He will be replaced soon. Nothing the US has done has changed the position of the communist leadership in the North. I think it will stay that way until they run out of people."

Tao pondered his answer, as he below out the smoke. There was a lot of truth to it, but it was strange An didn't respond to his comment about the US winning on the battlefield. Just as Tao was about to comment, the waiter returned to take their orders.

Tao smiled. "I want to order one of my favorite dishes, as it will likely be awhile before I will have it again." He looked up at the waiter. "Bún bò Huế."

An smiled. "That sounds good. I'll have the same."

The dinner conversation turned to family. An kept the conversation on Tao's family, asking about Luc. An seemed pleased to hear that Luc and his American friend were competing in Tae Kwon Do tournaments to get on the international circuit. They also discussed Luc's degree from the prestigious Duke University. An proudly talked about attending two years of college at Orange Coast College in Costa Mesa, California, with the help of Lansdale.

After dinner, both men had another beer. As Tao was getting ready to leave, he asked one more question. "What do you think about the current political climate in South Vietnam?"

An replied, "Lansdale has his hands full keeping Thieu and Ky together. There is a lot of animosity between the two, and both have big egos, too. I believe they should win the election, but if their egos get in the way, it may not be so easy. They still have not won the countryside, though."

Tao thought that An precisely defined the political situation. He looked down at his watch. It was time to go. The two men said their goodbyes and Tao left for Tan Son Nhut.

CHAPTER THIRTY-SEVEN

AUGUST 22, 1967

LIFE MAGAZINE HEADQUARTERS - WASHINGTON DC

Rita Sullivan had been writing an article for next month's *Life Magazine* on the upcoming elections in South Vietnam. In the absence of large anti-Vietnam war protests this summer, Chief Singleton had assigned her to the potential impact of those elections. They were critical not only to the stability of South Vietnam, but to the upcoming elections in the United States. President Johnson's political future was defined by one thing—the Vietnam Conflict, nothing else. The last big anti-Vietnam student protest had been in the Spring with several former service men joining their cause. *I wonder why it's been so quiet?* She wished she knew how to reach out to Bobby. He always knew what was going on with anti-war protests.

She was almost finished writing her article. It was a comprehensive article, yet it lacked pizazz—no "catch line, catch paragraph." Tonight, there was a meeting with Ed Boland and several other members of the Society of

Professional Journalists to plan future events. She wanted her article out of her head so she could focus. As the new secretary for this prestigious organization, it was critical she be there to take the minutes of the meeting.

As Rita walked to her desk, she saw the morning *New York Times* on a friend's desk. The headline got her attention—"TWO US NAVY JETS DOWNED IN CHINA; ONE PILOT SEIZED." She pushed her glasses up on her nose as she leaned over and read the first several paragraphs. The four Navy jets from the USS Constellation had targeted the Duc Noi railroad north of Hanoi, then ended up about 75 miles into Red China, where they were shot down. One pilot, Navy Commander Robert J. Flynn, the only survivor, was taken prisoner. *Wow, China is now holding one of our servicemen. Will this change the dynamic of the conflict?*

Rita sat down at her desk. On it sat a plain manila envelope with only her name on it, no address—so someone had to have dropped it off. She picked it up and looked around the large office area with all the desks. *No one seemed to be paying attention to her.* She opened it to reveal a transcript of Defense Secretary McNamara's appearance before the Senate Armed Services Committee. It was obviously from Senator Morse, something he must have wanted her to know. She intently read the transcript. Her conclusions were that McNamara was questioned about the influence of civilian advisors on military planning, but it quickly evolved to harsh questions regarding the expense versus gain of the US bombing campaign against North Vietnam. In the questioning of McNamara, he concluded that short of "the virtual annihilation of North Vietnam and its people" nothing was stopping the North's ability to make war. The word around Washington was that McNamara and a few other key advisors to President Johnson had turned against the bombing campaign, but this was the first time McNamara's position had emerged.

Denny Shaffer plopped down at her desk, startling her, as she hadn't seen or heard him coming. "What's ya readin'?"

Rita calmly laid down the transcript. "Nothing important," she said.

Denny slouched down in the chair and said he was looking for something to do. Rita looked at him. "Are you bored or something?"

Denny smiled at her, then frowned. "If they don't come up with some good on-location assignments, I'm going to look for a job somewhere else. I need some excitement. Some action."

Rita stuck out her lower lip. "Come on. You can't leave me. You like working with me. Anyway, I'm bored, too. I wish I had Bobby's phone number so I could get in touch with him. Maybe he'd have some big protest coming up. But I—"

Denny leaned over and kissed her on the cheek, then left.

She stared after him. Denny wanted a relationship, but Rita didn't. She sighed, then returned to go back over the transcript again, wondering if there was anything in it that she could work into the article she was preparing. Ultimately, despite the powerful admission, it couldn't add to it.

Just before lunch, Rita's mind began to wonder. She was thinking about her own personal pursuits, Lieutenant Commander Pitzer and Mary Meyer. The only thing she had learned about Pitzer was on the weekend he'd been murdered, the Kennedy family had transferred formal possession of all materials and documents related to the late-President's assassination to the

National Archives and they weren't to be released, reviewed, nor read by anyone without consent of the family. Then there was Dr. Joseph Humes, who performed the official autopsy on Kennedy, who made a statement that Pitzer wasn't present during the procedure. However, he did admit there was a closed circuit television camera in that room. Therefore, Rita believed there could be a film or, at a minimum, some photos of the autopsy. *Nothing conclusive.* It was also strange the mysterious Navy man hadn't made contact with her in some time.

The Mary Meyer case had gone cold, too. While she'd learned likely why—the diary—had gone missing, she was no closer to who her killer was. It was like someone had removed every shred of evidence out there to be discovered. She thought she should check in with FBI employee Stephanie Keeton sometime, just to see how she was doing and see if she had any new information. It would soon be three years since Meyer was murdered. *Talk about a cold trail.* Rita felt like she was the only one investigating the murder. *Makes me think they know exactly who did it and why, and that person will never be put on trial. Such an injustice.* With what Rita had learned, she believed Meyer was watched as a part of Operation Chaos, but it was what was in her journal that caused the CIA to call for the hit. *Why hasn't the family ever made any more public statements? All too eerie and creepy.*

EVENING

Denny dropped Rita off at her apartment. She was in a hurry to get to her first meeting of the Society of Professional Journalists, but she needed to pick up something she'd forgotten to bring to work with her. She picked up the thick file that Ed Boland had sent her to bring to their meeting. When she picked up the file, Stephanie Keeton's home phone number was written on the sheet of paper under where the file had been. Rita picked up the phone and dialed the number. It just rang without answer.

Rita glanced at the clock on the end table. She had to get moving to be on time. *I'll try to catch up later.* She put on some comfortable shoes and hurried to the bus stop.

Rita arrived at the hotel lobby where everyone was to meet, then sat down over dinner and drinks.

The five members, including Rita and Ed Boland, sat around the bar having a drink while they waited for their table reservation. The conversation was generic, with the group getting to know one another. Only Boland, the president, was a returning official.

The waitress, dressed in a white shirt with a black bow tie and black slacks, escorted them to their large round table in the corner of the hotel restaurant. Boland had arranged for a chilled bottle of red wine to be brought to the table as everyone ordered their meals.

After dinner, Rita pulled out two calendars, covering this year and next, so as they mentioned events she could give the days and other pending events. By the time their meeting was over, they had the agenda filled with guest speakers and potential speakers, all with tentative dates. Rita said she would attempt to get Meredith Brown to give a presentation on working at the US Department of State.

When everyone was walking out, Ed asked, "Rita, will you go sit in the bar and have a drink with me? I have one more thing to discuss."

Rita nodded as they said goodbye to everyone.

As soon as they sat down at a table, a waiter came over, Rita quickly replied. "Only a glass for me."

Ed ordered both of them another glass of wine. He turned to Rita, "What other projects are you working on at *Life?*"

Rita replied. "At the moment, just working on some small projects. I'm looking for a big protest here in the States or something coming up in Vietnam."

The waiter sat fresh glasses in front of both of them. After they'd had finished their glass of wine, Rita picked up her purse. "I'm going home. I'm really tired."

Ed got up at the same time. "Let me walk you to the bus stop." As they walked out the door together, Rita glanced at Ed. "So has Petit's head exploded yet, because I got elected secretary?"

Ed replied, "No, after I told him he did say a single word."

Just then the bus pulled up, she jumped on. She was glad she got out of the Washington Star, at least she had come out of there with a good relationship with Boland.

As soon as Ed Boland had escorted Rita to the bus station and saw her step onto the bus, he returned to the hotel lobby and picked up a payphone in the long hallway. He inserted a dime and dialed.

"Yes?"

"This is Boland. Meeting went well. I believe I have her total trust."

"Okay, Boland. That's great, but did you learn anything?"

"No. Not this time. I didn't push. Look, the case on the dame is dead. I have talked to the detective, who ran that case. It's unsolved and no one is asking questions but her. I've made sure she has dead ends everywhere. As to the Naval officer, that FBI girl is our only problem. But she doesn't have the clearance to learn anything. In our next meeting, which I'll set soon, I'll get her to open up. I still have that vial you gave me."

"Boland, that's not good enough. Don't worry about the Naval officer—he's gone. I've got everything he was working on. I've got that situation under control but, *we need to know what she knows. She's the only one working on those two cases.* If she breaks them, we're all in trouble. I'm in trouble. And if I'm in trouble, you're in bigger trouble. Someone will be around to visit you, and it won't be to just say. 'Hello.' Do you understand me?"

"Yes, sir. Trust me, I know how to handle this. I'll report in after our next meeting."

"For your own good, it better be soon. I'm losing my patience with you on this. This is your last warning, just like I gave Baker's boy. Notice he isn't around anymore. This has gone on too long." The phone line went dead.

Boland slowly hung up the receiver. *I've gotta keep Angleton calmed down or he's going to ask me to do something I may not be able to do.* He stared at the payphone for a minute, then walked out the main entrance toward his white Chevy Impala.

CHAPTER THIRTY-EIGHT

SEPTEMBER 4, 1967

WASHINGTON DC

Rita sat in the *Life Magazine* office reading the teletype with the South Vietnamese election returns. The ticket of Nguyen Van Thieu, president, and Nguyen Cao Ky, vice-president, won just thirty-five percent of the vote in which eighty percent of the South Vietnamese population participated. This was hardly the referendum that either the South Vietnamese or the United States had wished for. How was this going to affect the public opinion of the war effort? How would the students react?

Rita walked back over to her desk and was joined by Denny, who was singing Phil Ochs' song, "Draft Dodger Rag."

It was the last thing she wanted to see—and babysitting him was the last thing she wanted to do. He was still thinking about looking for another job. But this afternoon, she had a couple of things she wanted to accomplish. Just as Denny was about to say something, Chief Singleton called them to come to his office. They jumped up, went in, and sat down.

Chief Singleton walked around and sat on the edge of his desk. "Here's the deal. As you know, earlier we ran an article regarding the US working behind the scenes to negotiate with North Vietnamese. Well, our staff in London has been tipped that this story hasn't gone away—as we knew it wouldn't."

Rita deadpan stared at Singleton. "So, Chief, what are you asking?"

Singleton leaned forward. "You have a friend who works at the State Department. She works for one of the power brokers in government—Averell Harriman."

"Yes, as a matter of fact, I'm meeting her for dinner tonight."

"See if you can get any inside information. I want this story corroborated. I want to know what things are going on behind the scenes at the highest level. I don't want to break this next story if I can't verify it."

Rita fidgeted with her hair bun. "Oh, so I'm doing the behind the scenes stuff with no credit on the story?"

The Chief cracked half a smile. "What more do you want? This is big, but I don't want my neck—check that, our necks—the magazine's neck—sticking out on this one. You like your job, I like my job." He looked at Denny and pointed. "I think even he likes his job. We have to tread carefully. If this blows up in our faces, we could all be fired."

Rita pushed her glasses farther up the bridge of her nose. "Well, I'll try. But I'm going to be straight up front with you. I want to know what the London staff knows so I can let her know what we're about to go to press with. She won't be able to go on the record about anything, but she may be willing to react or respond to our story."

Singleton stared at her for a minute, then nodded. "Deal. I'll get the London staff writer to call you before you leave today." Then he looked over at Denny. "What about you?"

Denny rubbed his chin with the back of his hand. "I know several cameramen at the networks. I'll check with them."

Rita glanced over at him. She didn't know whether to be happy or sad. *Singleton is sending him to talk to someone who may offer him a job, but at least he would be working on something stimulating.*

The chief looked at the two of them, then with half a laugh said, "Why are you still sitting there? Get out there and learn stuff."

Rita and Denny left Singleton's office and slowly walked back toward her desk, but stopped at Denny's work area. "Who do you know who could be a source for this?"

Denny laughed at her as he brushed back his shoulder-length hair. "Remember, cameramen film—they don't talk. But we see things, usually more things than the reporters. And we hear things you don't hear."

Rita forced a chuckle. "Okay, let's try to chase this down. So—give me a couple of tips who you might know?"

Denny rubbed his bearded chin in a sarcastic manner. "No names, but I have a friend who's a cameraman at the BBC. He works with one of the top field reporters. Another friend works for the NBC team here as the White House assignment."

Her desk phone rang, and she hustled over. It was the London office. Rita nodded, then with the wave of a hand, shooed Denny away.

Rita strolled toward her regular bus stop. It was a warm September evening in Washington DC. As she sat down on the bench in the partially enclosed bus stop, she let out a long breath. It had been a stressful day. While she was used to the normal stress of the daily magazine business, getting Meredith Brown to meet her for a quick drink had gone from being an exciting catch-up dinner to a potentially uncomfortable discussion. Rita didn't like the predicament she'd been placed in by Chief Singleton.

Rita leaned out and saw her bus two blocks away. A man slipped into the opposite side of the bus stop, seemingly out of nowhere. It was the Navy man. "Who the hell have you been talking to?"

"Nobody. I've found nothing but dead ends since we last talked."

The Navy man slapped the bench with his open palm. "Why, then, did the Navy Intelligence agent go back and re-question several people, including the Navy tech who did the x-rays of Kennedy's body?"

Rita tried to get a look at the man's face, but all she could see was his lower jaw. "I don't know what you're talking about."

The Navy man pulled his hat down farther, simultaneously tilting his head lower to shield his face. "I don't believe you. You *have* talked to someone and *all hell* has broken loose. Why would the NIS agent re-interrogate the man who did the x-rays?"

Rita dropped her head. *Was it Stephanie Keeton at the FBI? Surely, she didn't tell anybody.* "I'm telling you, I have done nothing but run into dead ends. But please tell me about the x-ray man."

The Navy man glanced down the street toward the bus now a block away. "I'll not give you his name, but know this. This guy who was involved with the x-rays of Kennedy. He corroborated the story that Pitzer was making a movie from the pictures and that it looked like one of the bullets did hit Kennedy in the front. Their last interrogation made him very nervous."

Rita drew a deep breath, trying to process what she'd just been told. Before she could ask another question, the Navy man snarled. "Mrs. Pitzer had another visit from that same Navy Intelligence agent. The NIS agent said that if he heard one more story, he was going to have her pension pulled."

"I'm telling you, I have not said a word to anyone. All my research has been very quietly. No one knows." She knew not to mention that she'd received information from the FBI.

The Navy man sat quietly for a moment. Rita watched him fidget. She thought he was going to bolt at any moment as the bus approached. Finally, he said, "I told you to be discreet in your search for information. This is getting too deep for me. I—we—can't trust you. Stop whatever you're doing and drop the case now, before you hurt Mrs. Pitzer."

Rita noticed the bus and reached for her purse. The Navy man slapped the bench again and was gone before the bus headlights could illuminate where he sat.

Rita stepped inside the bus, deposited the correct change, and slipped into a seat. *I've got to get in touch with Stephanie.*

When Rita got home, she picked up the phone and dialed Stephanie Keeton's home phone. After the second ring, it went to a recording. "This phone has been disconnected or is no longer in service. If you think you have reached this recording in error, please contact the operator." Despite the fact that her number was blazoned into her brain, she redialed the number with the same results. Rita slumped down in the chair.

When the bus pulled away from the bus stop, Ed Boland sat in his white Chevy and watched the bus drive off. Time to update Angleton.

Boland drove straight to the nearest payphone and parked. He opened the glass door, closed it behind him, dropped in a dime, and dialed Angleton's number.

"This is Boland. She met with our pal in the Navy again."

"That might be a good thing," Angleton replied. "We've cleaned up part of the mess she's created already. We now aware the NIS agent has visited a certain widow to tell her to shut up."

Boland shifted from his left foot to his right foot. "Okay. What's next?"

"Watch the girl, dammit. You have two jobs—watch the girl and do what you're told. That seems pretty easy," Angleton yelled. *"Doesn't it?"*

Boland looked down. "Yes, sir."

"Let's make sure we got one problem put to bed. If we can shut her down on that little ravine investigation, it will all be good." The line went dead.

Boland let out a long breath. *If Rita would just stop digging, she'd be safe. God help me, I don't want to hurt that girl.*

Rita checked her hair in the vanity mirror one more time. It didn't want to cooperate tonight. But it wasn't a date—she was just going to dinner with her best friend. She gracefully danced over to the window of her second floor apartment overlooking the street below and sat down. Her ride would be there in about fifteen minutes. Just enough time to look over her notes. She pulled out her steno pad, along with her glasses. She gently pushed her hair back from her face and started reading. Her mood changed from excitement to concern over asking questions of her best friend. *Would Meredith think that was the only reason they were meeting?* According to the London staff writer, two French diplomats informed Dr. Henry Kissinger their meeting with the North Vietnamese Foreign Minister had been very productive. The North Vietnamese demands had softened. They were willing to meet in secret with the US delegation. They had also softened their position with respect to the Viet Cong. *I have no idea what*

that means, and neither did the London staff writer. The North Vietnamese understood that some US troops would remain in South Vietnam until a political settlement was reached. And, lastly, they seemed willing to accept a "de facto" cessation of bombing.

Just as Rita stuffed the steno pad back into her purse, the limousine pulled up in front of her apartment. She was looking forward to sitting down and having a relaxing dinner with Meredith—which now may not be so relaxing because of her questions. Out the door she went, high heels clicking on the steps and her purse flying behind her.

Rita slipped into the limousine next to Meredith. As they exchanged a hug, Rita began the conversation, "You have been impossible to get ahold of. I have tried to call your suite several times, but no answer."

Meredith smiled sheepishly. "I've been all over the world in the last two months. First off, when Ambassador Bunker went to South Vietnam, they had me assist with the refiling system in the new Embassy building, since I'd worked with both Ambassador Lodge and Taylor. So, I was there for almost a week. Then I met Ambassador Harriman in Paris, and was there for several days."

Rita smiled. "Speaking of which, I was asked to have you fact check an article that's scheduled for an upcoming *Life* edition. I told my boss I wasn't going to put my best friend on the spot."

Meredith cocked her head and gave a frown. "What do you mean, put me on the spot?"

"I told him to give me the article, and I'd see if you can verify it, but I wouldn't ask you to divulge anything that's new or secretive."

Meredith smiled, as she raised an eyebrow. "So…your London office has sources and the State Department has a leak? How novel."

Rita half smiled. She reached into her purse and handed her the steno pad. Meredith looked at it. "You still do George shorthand? This'll be an interesting test. I haven't seen it since college."

Rita started to reach for the pad, but Meredith pulled back. "No, this should be fun. Let's see if I still remember—unless you have thrown in some of your own little quirks." Both girls laughed. Rita felt a little more at ease.

After a minute, Meredith handed it back. "Okay, since the elections are over, some things may have changed. Harriman is unsure of how the election results will impact the negotiations. As you know, the results weren't exactly what our government was hoping for. Don't give this to the London office, but Kissinger and Harriman believe that any agreed-to coalition government, naturally, non-communist, must include Viet Cong representation. They still have so much influence in South Vietnam."

Rita nodded. "I won't say a word. But everything else is correct?"

"Absolutely. Harriman is going to wonder where the leak came from, but by the time your article runs, much of this may be outdated." Meredith looked out the window for a minute. "How's your love life?"

Rita's jaw dropped. "Same. Trying to keep my photographer at bay."

Meredith half smiled. "You always have a little glow about you when you have a boyfriend—and you're wearing your hair a little different."

"No, no. Just wanted a different hairstyle." .

The limo pulled up to the restaurant. The two women got out and strolled in.

Rita was so happy and relieved her questions regarding the secret negotiations hadn't damaged their long-term relationship.

Dinner went by quickly, but the women remained at the table, enjoying the fine wine.

"My parents are getting old," Meredith said with a sigh. "I'm starting to have concerns about their health and them getting around."

Rita loved Meredith's family. She believed because of their wealth, they would be fine well into their later years. Rita shared her apprehensions. "My mother is still living by herself in Marietta, Georgia. We hope Johnson's new Medicare program will be able to take care of her, the remainder of her life. She is getting frail now. You remember, my mother worked two jobs all her life just to make sure my needs were met."

Meredith smiled briefly. "I remember you telling me about all the different second jobs she would take on while we were in college."

After the second bottle of wine was brought to the table, the two girls started talking about old times at the University of South Carolina.

Halfway through the second bottle of wine, Meredith said, "Harriman has proposed to McNamara to tie the bombing targets to negotiations. He believes the military has run out of high value targets anyway. The idea of including the Viet Cong in a new coalition government was actually the proposal of the Norwegian ambassador to a Chinese diplomat. Needless to say, the State Department and White House are deeply divided over this proposal."

"Do you think all this behind the scenes negotiations is going to work?" Rita asked.

"I think if the US agrees to stop bombing Hanoi, there's a real chance." Meredith swirled the wine around in her glass. "I'll be going to Paris for an extended period of time." She smiled at Rita, then continued, "I'll have to let you read between the lines on what that means."

Rita raised her eyebrows. "Wow, I can't imagine how nice it would be to stay in Paris for a while. Particularly on someone else's dime." She finished off her glass of red wine. "DeGaulle has had it in for the United States for years about Vietnam. Despite losing in Vietnam, he's fighting to make Vietnam communist, just to get back at the United States."

Meredith appeared to ponder what Rita said, then she said, "I thought you were for ending the conflict in Vietnam."

Rita nodded. "Honestly, I'm still trying to understand Vietnam and everything involving it. The more I know about it, the less I understand it."

CHAPTER THIRTY-NINE

SEPTEMBER 5, 1967

LANGLEY, VA

Nguyen Tao strolled into his office at CIA headquarters. Today, he was starting his new assignment, assessing data coming out of Vietnam. There were two documents stacked on his otherwise clean desk to get him acclimated. The first one was a two-page memorandum that DCI Richard Helms had sent to President Johnson on August 29 regarding the bomb damage in North Vietnam.

By the time Tao finished reading the memorandum, he was nodding. Helms had shown the stepped-up bombing program had been effective. The industrial base in North Vietnam had been brought to a complete halt, and they were strictly focused on rebuilding and repairing. Particularly important was the damage to the Doumer Bridge, which gave direct rail access to Red China. North Vietnam's support from the Red Chinese and Soviet Union was the only thing keeping them going, and it was now almost solely coming from Haiphong Harbor traffic. The big "however" in Helms report was that North Vietnam continued to fight. *I never would have believed we would have to completely destroy the country to win freedom in the South, but that appears to be the case.*

He reached over to the second memorandum from Ambassador Bunker to Walt Rostow, also written on August 29, regarding the current strength of the Viet Cong operating in South Vietnam. Bunker and Robert Komer re-analyzed the latest MACV military intelligence, putting the enemy strength at an estimated four hundred thirty to four hundred ninety thousand. Bunker expressed concern. If this figure were leaked to the press, it would be devastating news to the Johnson Administration. They had inflicted huge losses in fighting, yet enemy strength had increased. *The US press would have a field day with this.*

The interoffice courier knocked at the door. He carried an envelope, which he handed to Tao.

Tao opened the memo from William Colby, the Chief of CIA's Far East Division, who wanted Tao to review an old memorandum. Tao opened the enclosed memorandum. The CIA was wanting to set up a leftist political party in South Vietnam to attract the National Liberation Front members or the Viet Cong. At first, the thought infuriated him. The more he thought about it, the more he actually liked the proposal. When he finished, he believed it might work, but it had to be run by the Pacification Program, not the CIA.

Tao leaned back in his chair. Welcome back to the United States Central Intelligence Agency, where chaos always seemed to be the word of the day. *Think about it. If this doesn't show the factions in the CIA, nothing does. On one hand, the CIA is trying to set up a left-leaning political party to draw in the Viet Cong, and on the other hand, they are setting up the Phoenix Program, run by the Agency, to root out and eliminate the Viet Cong.*

Before taking the bus to work, Rita decided to call Stephanie Keeton's desk phone at the FBI. Stephanie had told her not to call there, but her home phone being disconnected changed that. Before the first ring had completed, it was answered, "Federal Bureau of Investigation, Michelle Galloway speaking."

Rita paused, then asked, "May I speak with Stephanie Keeton please?"

There was a long pause on the other end. "Whom may I say is calling?"

Rita replied, "This is a friend. I know I shouldn't call at her office, but her home phone is disconnected."

"Whom may I say is calling?"

"My name is Rita Sullivan."

Again, there was another pause. "Well, Miss Sullivan, I would not classify you as a friend of Stephanie's. You're the reason she's dead." The line disconnected.

Rita slumped back into the chair. She placed the phone back down on the receiver, then said out loud, "What happened?" She sat there for several minutes, not knowing what to do.

Stephanie Keeton was dead.

When Rita arrived at her desk, she felt trapped. She needed to prepare a report on her notes from Meredith for the chief. However, her heart wasn't into it. She wanted to figure out what had happened to Stephanie. First, she needed to go through the Washington newspaper archives back to the last day she'd spoken with her. This would be her lunch hour assignment. But for now, it was time to report to the chief on what she'd learned last night from Meredith Brown. She'd put it in memo form.

She pulled out a sheet of paper, rolled it into her Smith-Corona, and began typing. Rita was able to recall her conversation from the previous night. After about ten minutes of typing, she rolled it backward to proof it. She nodded in approval as she finished reading the last paragraph. Just as she rolled it out of the typewriter, she looked up to see the chief leering over her shoulder and Denny sitting in a chair beside her desk. Rita held the memo over her head. The chief grabbed it and walked away without a word.

October 18, 1967

Tan Son Nhut Air base - Saigon

Steven was about to get off duty for the evening and decided to go to one of the Military Press Briefings. *Boy, I must boring if this is what I choose to do in my off time.* One of the younger generals, filling in for General Westmoreland, had invited him to attend. He was conducting the Presser today, as Westmoreland had left to go back to the States to meet with the Joint Chiefs and the President. The young general had been trying to buddy up with Steven to find out more about his assignment, but Steven had seen about every move on the chess board played on him over his years in the military. His mission was top secret, and no one was going to break him.

He walked into the back of the large room and peered around. Lately, the press in Vietnam had started to turn adversarial to General Westmoreland or other presenters, despite their openness. Just a few minutes later, a junior Army officer entered through the rear door. He took a seat in the back near Steven. The officer was trying to keep a low profile. *Strange. What's he up to?*

Steven only recognized a few journalists from his Embassy days. He surmised there was as much turnover there as in the CIA and military. He did notice General Lansdale's confidant and friend, Pham Xuan An, seated on the right side of the room. Today, the presentation was on developments at Dak To.

The generals and a colonel gave their presentations and opened up the floor to questions.

One of the members of the press stood up. "Colonel, can you tell us about any up and coming operations?"

Before the colonel could say a word, one of the generals put his hand over the microphone, whispered in the colonel's ear, and then said, "You know we aren't able to comment on anything coming up. Any more questions?"

Now that he was assigned to the base, Steven was going to look harder at the potential spy coming out of the military. There were just too many times the Viet Cong and the North Vietnamese Army seemed to know US moves. In the past, he'd been advised that Westmoreland had divulged more than he should. Steven decided to hang around for a few minutes after the briefing to observe the interaction between the military officers and the press. *It might be informative, if someone in the military were a spy. The spy is likely a South Vietnamese officer. Unfortunately, today there weren't many in the room. I just can't imagine any of our officers causing their own men to be killed.*

As the room slowly cleared out, he noticed a few of the lieutenant colonels remained in the room. Some reporters talked among themselves, while a few moved toward those officers. There were always two sets of clipboards for each of the main US Press Corps—one was for the stories the US allowed to be printed, while the other was for limited distribution to the top editors at *Time Magazine, Newsweek*, the *New York Times* and the *Washington Post*. He observed the reporters that reviewed each.

Steven was hoping to introduce himself to Pham Xuan An, who was among those reporters milling around after the press. However, he seemed to be heavily involved in a conversation with another reporter. *As animated as he is, I don't want to interrupt him. The little man seemed pretty feisty.* Steven's focus moved back to the clipboards.

When the remainder of Westmoreland's staff exited the room, An sauntered toward the clipboards. *Here is my chance to catch up with him.* Out of the corner of Steven's eye, he noticed the junior Army officer trying to slip into a more discreet spot. He was still watching the few remaining reporters. Steven looked back to see An had disappeared among the taller American reporters as they congregated around those clipboards. Steven glanced back at the junior officer. He remained fixated on the reporters as they took turns flipping through the clipboard data. Now, he was bobbing his head back and forth trying to get a clear view of the clipboards. *What is he watching?*

By the time the crowd cleared, An was gone. Steven slipped outside to see if he could catch up with the reporter. He looked up and down. *There he is.* An was talking to a Vietnamese woman leaning against an old dull green Renault, gesturing and pointing in the direction of the front gate while he was talking. Steven studied the woman, then glanced at An. *Must be his girlfriend or something.* The woman pointed at the old beat up car she was leaning against. When An paused his conversation long enough to glance around, his eyes stopped past Steven but off to Steven's left.

Steven looked in that direction but saw nothing. Then An pointed at the Renault, and it looked like he said something. The woman scurried around and got in. The two of them drove off. Steven still wanted to meet Lansdale's old friend, but he didn't feel compelled to go chasing after him.

As Steven turned to walk back inside the headquarters, he noticed the same junior Army officer in a military jeep speeding off in the same direction as An.

OCTOBER 18, 1967
CIA HEADQUARTERS - LANGLEY, VIRGINIA

Nguyen Tao walked out of the office. He was stunned by what he'd just been told. America had a saying, "the icing on the cake." He'd just experienced its sarcastic side. Early in the year, Assistant Secretary of Defense John McNaughton had been asked to prepare a top secret report documenting all the historical activity to-date in Vietnam. The report was ordered by none other than Robert McNamara, who was submitting his resignation as Secretary of Defense. *Why?* The word around the Agency was that Johnson and McNamara were at odds over implementation of the war effort in Vietnam. This was almost comical. McNamara had been the architect of the Conflict since 1961.

McNaughton had passed away this past July. Had he completed the report? When Tao had returned to the States, he'd been contacted by Daniel Ellsberg, who only said he was working on a report but didn't elaborate. Tao assumed now that Ellsberg had assisted McNaughton. Fortunately for him, Tao had never received written papers or orders. All of Lansdale's instructions over the years dating back to the Saigon Military Mission were either done face-to-face or over the phone. There were no paper trails, period.

Upon arriving at Langley, Tao was given two old memorandums; one told the true story of the conflict while the other discussed the on-going clandestine activity of both sides. The first was written by Robert Komer to the President, wherein among other things, he believed that the Viet Cong in South Vietnam were being decimated to the point where Le Duan and General Giap were having to send North Vietnamese regulars into the South to keep up the fight. Moreover, with the exception of the northern I Corp, the NVA was avoiding direct contact with the US Marines due to their losses.

The other memorandum concerned OPLAN 34A, now run by MACSOG and General Singlaub, regarding clandestine missions into North Vietnam and the North's suicide missions against our fast patrol craft. This interoffice State Department memo detailed failed missions attempting to land teams in North Vietnam, yet they continued to use the same method of trying to get South Vietnamese into the North to spy on them. Tao was thoroughly disgusted by this continued failed effort. *What was the definition of insanity? "Doing the same thing, over and over, but expecting different results."*

OCTOBER 19, 1967
LIFE MAGAZINE OFFICE - WASHINGTON DC

Rita Sullivan had exhausted about every source she could check. There was no information on the death of Stephanie Keeton. Was this death being investigated and the obituary being kept from the newspaper? Rita knew sometimes the police withheld information from going public. Rita surmised she could either try to get Michelle Galloway to talk or she could go to the police, off the record. She wasn't confident that Michelle would tell her anything.

Rita decided to reacquaint herself with Lieutenant Brodie, the lead detective of the Mary Meyer murder. He might provide some information. She dug through her desk looking for the now three-year-old business card. *Thank goodness, reporters never throw away any contacts.* As soon as she found the card, she dialed the number. Brodie agreed to meet her at the station for a few minutes. It was good to be a pretty blonde. Sometimes you could get away with not divulging your potential subject yet still get an appointment.

Just as Rita was about to leave for her appointment, her desk phone rang. She looked at it for a minute, then picked it up. It was Bobby, her contact for protests in the DC area. As Bobby started talking, Rita put her hand over the receiver and shouted. "Denny, come here"

Rita attempted to slow Bobby down so that she could pull out her steno pad. Finally, the exuberant protester stopped, while Rita prepared to take down the pertinent information. By the time she was ready to write, Denny stood over her shoulder. Bobby re-started his reason for the call—a large protest was planned for October 22 at the Pentagon. It was being sponsored by National Mobilization Committee to End the War in Vietnam.

Denny mouthed the words, "Radical group—as is their leader."

Bobby said, "Their organization had been planning and organizing similar protests around the US and in Europe for several months."

When Rita finished taking down the details, she replied, "Bobby, thanks for the tip."

Bobby replied. "We can meet in the parking lot near the entrance to the main gate at the Pentagon at about nine o'clock." Then the line went dead.

Rita looked up at Denny, who nodded.

Rita and Denny swiftly moved to the chief's corner office to brief him.

The Chief listened. "Both of you need to be onsite. I want complete coverage, a big article. Lots of pictures."

"Their leaders are very radical," Denny said. "They have a lot of celebrities supporting them. I expect just about anything at this protest."

Singleton put his hands on his hips. "Denny, you have to look after yourself and more particularly Rita." He pointed at her.

Rita glanced at both of them. "Bobby is supposed to get with us and let us know what celebrities may be speaking. Oh, by the way, I have an out of office appointment, so I'll be late getting back from lunch. Denny and I will get together and finish making out plans."

As Rita picked up her purse and headed for the exit, apprehension regarding this protest surged through her veins. If Denny were even partially correct about this group, this protest could turn violent and dangerous quickly, and she and Denny were going to be right in the middle of the action.

Rita went home to doll up her appearance, hoping it would get the detective to be more open with information. Then she called a cab. She tried to calm herself and get focused on the ride to the police station.

The desk sergeant eyed her up and down when Rita walked into the station. Rita told him she had a scheduled appointment with Lieutenant Brodie. The lieutenant sent up a detective to escort her back to his office.

Rita walked through the door into Brodie's office and closed it.

Brodie looked up from his desk. "I didn't ask you to shut the door."

Rita flashed a big sexy smile. "I have something private to talk about. Maybe you wouldn't want everyone to hear?"

Brodie picked up his cigar out of the ashtray, leaned back in the chair, and put his feet up on his desk. "I can't wait," he said sarcastically.

Rita leaned forward. "Is the local police holding back information on the death of Stephanie Keeton? She worked for the FBI."

Brodie stared up at the ceiling for a second. "Never heard of her. Nothing from this office. I stay in close contact with other precincts, and I'm not aware of anything like this in the city. An FBI employee dying, I would remember that."

Rita was puzzled by the answer. "Her shift partner said she was dead, and I haven't been able to find out any information. Read all of the newspapers back several months, nothing."

"Did it occur to you that she could have died somewhere else?"

While Rita hadn't given that thought much credence, she nodded. "Of course."

"Are we done here?"

Rita chewed her lip. "Whatever happened to the Mary Meyer murder investigation? After Crump was acquitted, three years have passed and nothing seems to have happened. No one has been arrested." Rita decided not to mention the journal. *Let's see if he mentions it.*

The lieutenant quickly dropped his feet to the floor and leaned forward, chomping his cigar. "Miss Sullivan, this is none of your business."

Rita started to speak, but Brodie raised his hand and continued. "Be very aware, we let *you* off the hook. *You* were the last person to speak to Mrs. Meyer. *You* would have been the first witness we would have come back to." He stared at her. "So, do you want this opened back up? I can have a detective come in here right now to retake your statement? You knew more than you told us. So, do I call in the detective?"

Rita frowned at the lieutenant, then she blurted, "I'll tell you what I think. Someone told you to stop this investigation, to let it die. That's what I think." She calmed herself quickly, got up out of the chair, and started to walk out of his office.

Brodie stood up and bellowed, "Tread lightly, young lady. You are on very thin ice."

Rita turned back and sarcastically replied, "Thanks for your help." She bolted through the door, slammed it, and moved across the detective's office as quickly as she could. When she got to the door exiting the detective area, she turned around. Everyone was staring at her. As she walked, she realized that Brodie had used the exact same words as Bobby Baker at the Corum Club—*thin ice*. She blinked hard a couple of times to fight back the tears.

Rita decided to push her luck. She went back to her apartment and called Michelle Galloway's number at the FBI office. When she picked up, Rita pleaded, "Please don't hang up on me. I want to know what happened to Stephanie Keeton."

There was a pause that seemed like forever on the other end of the phone, then Michelle replied, "I'm willing to meet you after work for a minute to explain."

Rita closed her eyes tightly. "Where? What time?"

"There's a little diner over in Georgetown, Clyde's on M Street. I'll be there a little before six o'clock—a quarter of six. I'll give you five minutes."

"Got it. Thanks."

Rita had just finished her research on the background of the National Mobilization Committee to End the War in Vietnam. They were as radical as Denny had claimed. She started writing her background information for the article. They were formally organized two summers ago during a teach-in conference in Cleveland, Ohio. Their focus was to organize an Inter-University Committee for Debate on US Foreign Policy, specifically Vietnam. The goal was to bring together political groups, including anti-

Vietnam and Black Civil Rights. In the spring of this year, they had hosted large protests in New York City and San Francisco simultaneously. Their New York protest included an estimated 400,000 participants and featured speeches from Dr. Benjamin Spock, Stokely Carmichael, and Dr. Martin Luther King, Jr. Rita pushed her research newspaper articles into a blank folder, she glanced up at the clock. *Just enough time to make it to Clyde's.*

Rita got off the bus, walked into Clyde's about five minutes early, and sat in a corner booth where she could see out but was secluded. She ordered a sweet tea and waited for Michelle to show up. She had no clue what she looked like, and at this time of day, the diner was starting to get busy. After a few minutes, a nicely dressed lady walked in and looked around. Rita studied her briefly and guessed it was Michelle. She stuck her hand in the air, waved, and forced a smile.

The lady acknowledged the wave, walked over, and sat down. She looked at Rita for a minute before speaking. "You're a reporter, and I don't trust you for a minute. No notes, no recordings."

Rita raised both hands, then placed them on the table as she raised her eyebrows. "No problem. I just want to know what happened to Stephanie. You're right, I suppose, we weren't what you would call friends, but she and I bonded over several similar, scary experiences."

Michelle frowned. "Let's cut to the chase. What do you want to know? Maybe I will answer, and maybe I won't."

Rita chewed her lip, then spoke softly. "I just want to know what happened to her. I've been hounded by some of the same characters who were after her."

Michelle leaned forward and spoke in a low voice. "Her death scared the bejesus out of me." She glanced around, then spoke in such a low voice that Rita could barely hear her. "About four months ago, some higher-ups questioned her about being in a restricted area. She wouldn't tell me anything. I just know she was being grilled. She told me she thought they were going to fire her. Then about three months ago, they offered to transfer her. She wanted to go to San Francisco and work with an agent we had worked with before, but they said no. They told her she could go to New Orleans or Miami. She picked Miami. By that time, she was scared and depressed. But she wasn't taking anything, *understand*? Right after she was transferred to Miami, she didn't show up for work. They found her dead in her apartment, with pentobarbital by her bed. They ruled it a suicide, since it's a common drug for that."

Rita processed what she had been told. "What makes you think I'm the cause of her death?"

"She mentioned your name once regarding a conversation you'd had. All she would tell me was you'd had some experiences similar to what she and I did when we took the assignment to go undercover. Later, she mentioned you'd told her about some very bad things. She wouldn't tell me anything more—she said it was better I didn't know. It was after that she started getting depressed."

Rita looked out the window of the diner for a minute. "I'm sorry. I'm very sorry. But, I'm sure it wasn't suicide."

Michelle stared at her for a minute, then picked up her purse and ran out of the diner.

Rita knew better than to pursue. She'd gotten the information she needed. It was best that Michelle didn't know any more. She didn't seem as strong-willed as Stephanie. She watched Michelle drive off. As she continued gazing out the window, she caught a glimpse of a white Chevy parked across the street that had just pulled out into traffic. She strained to get a good look at the driver, but it wasn't to be. Her paranoia was off the charts. There were white Chevys everywhere.

CHAPTER FORTY

SAME DAY
WASHINGTON DC

James Jesus Angleton read over the last report he'd received from field agents working on OPERATION CHAOS, including Ed Boland's. *I can't trust Boland to carry out his assignment. He has gotten weak. He likes Sullivan too much, which will only get in the way.* He leaned back in his leather chair and closed his eyes. *Next step, next step.* He'd laid out his game plan very well. *Better check in with my back-up plan.* He picked up the phone and dialed the number of the man who always took care of his "special needs." Angleton asked, "Everything set for tomorrow?"

"If the opportunity presents itself. In that big of a crowd, I can't be too obvious. Surely, with this radical group, I'll be presented with some opportunities of chaos. I'll just have to react to what works at the time. I'll report back. This time, I want half my money now, the other half when I'm finished."

Angleton hated discussing money over the phone. "When did you stop trusting me?"

"I haven't, but if I have to make a run for it, I don't want to be looking for cab fare. Get my drift?"

His hit man was right. This time was different. In the past, the hits were all in controlled environments, but this time was different. "Same account? Cayman Islands?"

"Yeah."

Angleton snarled, "The transfer will go out in the morning. If you are successful, call me so I can pick up the package."

The phone line went dead.

OCTOBER 21, 1967

Rita Sullivan and Denny Shaffer parked in the lot between Arlington Cemetery and the Metro Mall entrance. While Denny unloaded his camera equipment, Rita grabbed her notes, scanned them quickly, then stuffed them back in her pocket. She'd hoped to hear from Bobby last night to get more details on this protest, but the call didn't come. *Maybe he'll find me before we set up.* Denny tried to give her a kiss on the cheek but she ducked away.

One of the three cameras hanging around his neck swung and hit Rita in the arm. "Hey, you trying to hurt me?"

Both laughed. Denny added, "If that's as hard as you get bumped today, we'll be okay."

Rita raised both eyebrows, then took off walking toward the Pentagon entrance. Denny ran to catch up. Rita asked, "Why did you insist on parking so far away that it would take several minutes to get to the protest?

As Denny continued to walk, he said, "You remember how terrified you were when McNamara's car was surrounded?"

That scene flashed through her mind, but the chanting in the distance brought her back to the present. They picked up their pace. The closer they got, the larger the crowd appeared.

Denny grabbed Rita's arm. "Are you ready for this?"

Rita nodded.

As Denny walked, he sand the Buffalo Springfield's "For What it's Worth"

Even though Denny had a great singing voice, Rita continually punched him in the arm, telling him to stop singing. "You're freaking me out!" she said. She was already nervous about this protest. She bit her lower lip as they walked even faster.

She repeatedly attempted to suppress Denny's almost continual remarks about the potential violence of this protest. As they approached the Pentagon Metro Entrance, protestors chanted and marched ahead of them. The atmosphere felt different as they approached the large crowd. Rita surmised it was because they were in front of one of the main entrances to the Pentagon.

Just as they caught up with the protesters, Bobby jogged up to Rita. The first thing he did was apologize for not telling her their protest had started earlier in the day at the Lincoln Memorial. They had then marched here to finish their demonstration at the Pentagon, confronting the warmakers. Rita was disappointed when Bobby told her there had been several speakers at the protest—it would've added depth to her report.

Denny frowned at Bobby, then gently grabbed Rita's shoulder. "It's all right. It's all right. We'll get plenty here."

How did he know what I was thinking?

Bobby dropped his head. "Come on. Let me help you get to a good set-up location."

The three of them hurriedly maneuvered through the moving mob, arriving just as the leaders appeared to have reached the Metro Entrance of the Pentagon. As they moved, Bobby was able to shout over the crowd noise that Norman Mailer was among the guest speakers at the Lincoln Memorial. Rita inquired if he was still in the crowd, as she would love to interview him. Unfortunately, he didn't know. Before Bobby could get away, she scored several good quotes for her article. He advised her the more radical members of the US Committee to Aid the National Liberation Front were in the front of the protestors.

By the time Rita and Denny were able to push their way to the front of the crowd and set up, several North Vietnamese flags had appeared. Rita was still looking around for Mailer—to interview as this iconic writer would be a "huge get."

The protestors pushed toward a line of US Marshals and MPs, but they were unable to break the defensive line.

Rita was jostled by the crowd. She almost fell. Fear crawled up her spine.

Denny looked at Rita and nodded. She assumed he meant he had his wanted shots. He held his camera over his head and snapped off a string of photos. He slipped around to the side of the line, then snapped a picture of a girl trying to hand a flower to one of the MPs.

Cheering erupted behind the protestors. Rita grabbed Denny and pulled him as hard as she could to get out of the pushing crowd. As they moved against the grain, they were finally able to see what the crowd was cheering about. Young men held their draft cards above their heads. Before Rita and Denny could get there, each of the men held lighters in their other hands. Again, Denny stopped, raised his camera, and started snapping as the men set the draft cards on fire. Rita couldn't count the number of men igniting those cards.

"Hell, no, we won't go!" the crowd chanted. "Hell, no—"

Another commotion occurred near the Metro Entrance. The crowd pushed toward the Pentagon entrance.

Rita and Denny bumped their way through the surging crowd, calling out, "Press!" as they moved. Within minutes, they jostled their way to the Pentagon's Metro Entrance. The protestors had breached the marshals and MPs, and were now inside the Pentagon and moving forward. Almost as soon as they were in, they were pushed back outside. Rita grabbed Denny's right arm and squeezed it hard out of shear fear.

They were able to weave their way almost to the front of the crowd. Denny looked down at his camera. He had just a few shots left on two of his cameras. He stopped and hit auto rewind. He quickly put new rolls in each and handed Rita the old rolls. As soon as he finished, there was another yell from the crowd. Denny slipped into the flow of the crowd and was separated from Rita. The last glimpse she got of him, he held the camera over his head snapping several photos.

The crowd surged toward the front entrance again.

A scuffle broke out. Just when it looked like they would be able to penetrate the defensive line, a number of troops carrying rifles with sheathed bayonets and wearing gas masks came up from behind to shore up the Pentagon's line of resistance.

Someone grabbed Rita from behind and held her back. It was Bobby. "You don't want in that fracas."

Rita pushed away from Bobby and lunged forward into the crowd. She had to keep Denny out of trouble. But he had disappeared inside the Pentagon entrance along with the frontline of the protestors.

Something was tossed in their midst. When it hit the ground, gray smoke billowed out, and some of the protestors closest to the tear gas coughed and gasped. The protestors surged forward again, penetrating the line of the MPs and US Marshals.

Rita was moving behind the front line of the protestors, when the troops rushed forward into them. Another tear gas grenade came into the crowd. Within seconds, the protestors were met with butts of rifles and threats of the sheathed bayonets. Rita scrambled to force her way toward the back of the mob, but her actions were futile. She tried to stand her ground, as now she was being bumped and pushed by protestors rushing out of the way of tear gas and soldiers. The protestors fought back, swinging signs and fists, but it was a losing battle. As the protestors were knocked to the ground, marshals and MPs cuffed and dragged them from the fight into the interior of the Pentagon. As Rita finally was able to move behind the fighting still inside the entrance, she still couldn't find Denny. Again, she was trying to resist being pushed backwards, but it was useless.

Rita jumped into the air a couple of times to try to see better, until she realized it was futile and endangering her own wellbeing. She struggled to push forward. *Still no sign of Denny.* As she finally got to the front of the protestors. *Still no Denny.* She scanned the individuals on the ground, mostly protestors. *Still no Denny.* She then glanced at those seated against the wall. They were mostly soldiers, MPs and one or two marshals. *Where was Denny?*

She was grabbed from behind. This time it wasn't Bobby—it was an MP, who immediately yanked her arms behind her and cuffed her on the spot.

Rita turned and screamed, "I'm Press! Look at my credentials." She was swept toward the area where other protestors were taken.

Rita repeated over and over, "I'm a reporter. Look at my credentials."

The only response she received was harsher shoving toward the interior of the Pentagon. Rita's eyes darted around for Denny. *Still no sign.*

Finally, she was uncuffed, then pushed hard into a small room, the police detaining area. She asked the other twenty or so individuals if any of them had seen her cameraman.

One of the guys replied, "Yeah, I saw him. He was taken away by two plain-clothed men. He was passed out."

Rita leaned toward him. "Are you sure? Absolutely sure?"

The guy squirmed to get Rita out of his space. "Yeah. Man, like it was rad. The MPs had him for a minute, then two plain-clothed men took him away from them."

Rita leaned against the wall and slowly slid down it.

CHAPTER FORTY-ONE

NEXT MORNING
WASHINGTON DC

The jailer walked Rita through the door to meet Chief Singleton face-to-face. Singleton wore a fake, forced smile. As they walked out the door, Rita began to speak, but Singleton raised his finger to his lips.

As soon as they were outside, Rita again tried to speak, but Singleton grabbed her arm. He almost dragged her, shaking his head. When they got in the chief's car, Rita tried to speak through her parched throat. "Where's Denny? Did you already bail him out?"

The chief leaned toward her and put his arm on the back of the bench. "No, I didn't bail him out. He wasn't arrested."

"Damn it, yes! He was grabbed before they grabbed me. I was told—"

The chief's eyes narrowed. "Yes, I know all that, but he wasn't arrested, and I don't know where he is."

Rita pounded the door. "That's BS. I saw them grab him."

The chief nodded. "Calm down. I know. But I'm telling you, he's not in jail. He wasn't taken into custody by the US Marshals and I have checked the Washington DC and Arlington jails. He's just not there."

Rita jumped out of the car and started to run. The chief caught up with her in a few steps and grabbed her.

She turned around, a stream of tears running down her face. "Where is he, then? One of the protestors said he saw him lying there unconscious. Did you check the hospitals?"

"How would I have known that? No, I don't know."

She dropped down on the grass.

The chief reached out his hand to pull her up. "What were you thinking, getting arrested? No story in that."

Rita jerked away from him. "Well, believe it or not, I was trying to get Denny out of the fray. My goal was to get an interview with Norman Mailer."

Ed Boland walked into the dark room with James Jesus Angleton. He flipped on the light switch, illuminating a twenty-five watt bulb. A man sat in the middle of the room with a black bag over his head. Boland nodded to

Angleton, then started toward the man to remove his hood, but Angleton grabbed him and jerked him back. With a sinister smile, he walked close to the man and looked at him for a minute.

"Who's there?" the man with the bag over his head said groggily.

Angleton looked back at Boland and nodded. "Welcome back, Mr. Shaffer. Did you enjoy your little nap?"

Boland ran stuff his hands in his pockets. *What is Angleton going to do to Shaffer?*

"Who are you? What am I doing here?"

Angleton paced in front of Denny Shaffer. "We just wanted to have a polite little conversation with you."

"Who are you?" The level of frustration and anxiety raised in Denny's voice.

Angleton motioned for Boland to hand him his notes.

Boland stayed as far away from both Shaffer and Angleton as he could but extended his hand with the papers he held.

Angleton grabbed the paper, then a flashlight out of his pocket and flashed it on the page. "Mr. Shaffer, are you assisting Miss Sullivan in her private investigations?"

"I don't have any idea what you're talking about."

Angleton stuck the flashlight in his pocket and pulled out a cigarette, lit it, and took a big drag. He offered it to Boland, who declined. Angleton took another drag off from it. "Are you sure you don't know what I'm talking about?" Angleton pressed the cigarette into Shaffer's forearm.

Shaffer screamed out in pain. He jerked around, trying to get loose. "No, I don't know what you're talking about."

Angleton pulled out the flashlight and glanced over the paper again. He tossed it back at Boland. "Well, Mr. Shaffer, let's assume I believe you." He paused for a long time as he paced. The only thing audible was the footsteps around the hooded man. "I'm going to let you go. But I want you to deliver a message to Miss Sullivan." He paused again.

"What?"

Angleton pulled out his switch blade and slipped behind the hooded man. He put the knife to his neck. "Are you ready?"

"Yes, yes, tell me. Just let me go. *Don't cut me.*"

Angleton put the knife blade on the cigarette burn and pushed down.

Boland flinched as he backed away from the two men.

Denny screamed out again in pain.

Angleton flipped the switchblade closed, right next to Shaffer's ear, and put it in his pocket.

Boland breathed a heavy sigh of relief. He moved back in front of Shaffer. "You tell Miss Sullivan to stop investigating Mary Meyer and Lieutenant Colonel Pitzer. Do you understand?"

Denny nodded.

Angleton pushed his thumb down hard on the cigarette burn.

Denny screamed out again. "You bastard! Stop, please."

"Do you really understand? I'm just getting warmed up!" Angleton yelled over Denny's screams. You tell her—or both of you will find yourselves in a South American prison convicted of drug possession."

Boland stepped toward Angleton and grabbed his arm as he spoke. "That's enough. He gets it."

Angleton shoved Boland away. He reached in his pocket, pulled out a small packet, then pulled out a syringe. He held it up in the air and squirted out some liquid, then jabbed it into Denny's neck.

Denny was out in thirty seconds.

Angleton pointed at him. "Take him back into DC and leave him somewhere. I don't care where. That will wear off in two hours."

Boland moved over to grab one side of Denny. Angleton stepped in front of him, nose to nose with Boland. "Don't ever question me and my methods again."

Boland tried to step away, but Angleton closed on him again. He understood.

Each man grabbed one of Denny's arms, dragged him back outside to Boland's white Chevy Impala, and pushed him into the trunk. Boland drove off.

Boland sure hoped Rita would listen to her boyfriend's warning and stop her investigations. He blinked hard. He really hoped she'd listen.

Two Hours Later

Midnight

Rita tossed and turned in bed. She hadn't slept well for the last two days. Her phone rang. She grabbed it before the ring was complete. "Hello?"

"Come and get me."

"Denny! Where are you?"

"I'm not sure, it looks like . . . ." There was a long pause.

"Denny, are you still there?"

His reply was barely audible, "I think I'm on the National Mall grounds."

"I'll call a cab and get there as fast as I can." She pressed down on the button and released it to call a cab. When she had completed her first call, she decided she'd better call Chief Singleton while waiting on the cab, no matter the time.

Rita dialed the number.

There was a groggy, "Hello."

"Chief, I'm on my way to get Denny. He just called me."

"Is he all right?"

"I don't know."

"Where shall I meet you?"

"Go back to bed, Chief. We'll report in as soon as we can. Two of us don't need to be running around on the National Mall grounds."

Rita's cab pulled up at the closest end of the National Mall, and she asked the cabbie to wait. She got out and started walking, then jogging. She got into the darkness and realized this was a waste of time and moved back toward the street. As she jogged, she called his name over and over. "Denny! Denny!"

Finally, about a half a mile from the cab, she heard him.

He stood near a park bench along the street. She ran over to him and gave him a big hug.

Denny kissed her, then held her at arm's length. "What have you been up to?"

Rita tried to hug him again, but he pushed her away.

"What are you working on, privately?"

Rita stepped back. "Nothing that's any of your business."

"Who are Mary Meyer and Lieutenant Colonel Pitzer?"

Rita pushed herself away from her broken photographer. "I don't want to talk about it. It's nobody's business but mine."

Denny put his hands on his hips. "The men who grabbed me told me to tell you to stop researching Mary Meyer and Lieutenant Colonel Pitzer."

Emotions overcame her. She tried to fight back her tears.

Denny grabbed her arm. "They said next time, we'd find ourselves in a South American prison convicted of drug possession."

Tears streamed down her cheek. Rita grabbed Denny's hand and dragged him toward the waiting cab. Neither of them spoke another word.

However, Rita's brain was on fire. *What do I tell him? I can't drag him into this mess.*

As they slipped into the cab, it finally dawned on Rita—Denny was already involved in her private research. Still, they didn't say a word to each other. When the cab stopped in front of Denny's apartment, Rita got out, too.

Denny looked at her. "What are you doing? I'm tired and need rest."

Rita grabbed his arm.

"Ouch!" he screamed and jerked away from her.

"What's wrong? What's the matter?"

"The SOB burnt me with his cigarette—and then cut me."

"Oh, Denny!" Rita dropped to her knees. "I'm so sorry. So sorry." Tears streamed from her eyes.

"I have no idea what's going on," Denny said.

"I'm so sorry. I must tell you the whole story."

Denny turned around without saying a word as he walked to his apartment door.

Rita waved the cab on. She followed him inside and spent the next two hours telling him every detail of the Mary Meyer and Commander Pitzer stories. By the time she finished, Denny was wide awake. Finally, he said, "You believe the CIA had them both killed by professional hitmen?"

Rita didn't answer. It was a relief to finally tell someone.

Denny sat there for a minute, waiting for her answer. Finally, Denny walked toward the front door. "You need to leave so I can get some sleep."

"May I just sleep on the couch?" Rita asked.

Denny shook his head and opened the door.

Rita called a cab. She walked past Denny, her eyes straight ahead, and waited outside for the ride.

Once in the cab, the city lights cascaded by. It was mesmerizing—no, it was hypnotizing. She had spent 36 months investigating the murder of Mary Meyer, and she had been stonewalled every step of the way. Anyone—except for Timothy Leary, who scared her for other reasons—who had tried to help was dead.

Then there was Lieutenant Commander William B. Pitzer's death. Again, she was thwarted every step of the way. Not even his widow would help. The Navy man who asked her to start the investigation came back and told her to stop. Immediately.

And it was obvious she was going to be the next one in the obituaries. Whoever had grabbed Denny sent them both a message. Stop investigating Mary Meyer and Lieutenant Colonel Pitzer or both of you will find yourselves in a South American prison convicted of drug possession. Who had that kind of power? Angleton and the CIA.

When Rita began her career as a journalist, she promised herself she'd never let fear stop her from getting to the bottom of a story. But this was different. She was genuinely scared. All of this to quiet the assassination of President Kennedy and his affair. They had removed every shred of evidence. *I can't go any farther. I don't want them to frame me to put me in some South American prison on drug charges, and I certainly don't want innocent Denny involved. They have found my buttons to get me to stop. Or, maybe as the anonymous phone caller said, I'll end up dead in a ravine.*

Tears puddled in her eyes. Little Rita Sullivan couldn't defeat the CIA by herself. She had tried.

The cab driver snapped his fingers in her face.

Rita snapped back into the present. The cab was parked outside her apartment.

She wiped her eyes with the back of her hand, paid the cabbie, and, looking around for the white Chevy Impala, walked inside.

It was over. A good reporter knows when they didn't have enough facts to finish the story, and that was where Rita found herself. Even though it hurt the very fabric of her being, she had no other choice. Her investigations were over. She was finished.

CHAPTER FORTY-TWO

EVENING DECEMBER 7, 1967
PENTAGON - WASHINGTON DC

Lieutenant Colonel Steven Hebert and the other Marines assigned to the MarCor 85 project walked out of the conference room after completing their fourth consecutive day of long meetings. Until these meetings, Steven was unaware others were working on this top secret project. They had each come from different assignments around the globe in various phases of service. There was one other Marine with fighting experience, while the others were full bird colonels—the "think tank" kind of Marines. *These guys probably haven't had dirt on their boots since boot camp, but they're sharp, Naval-Academy types.* This caused Steven to laugh as he walked down the hallway. *He had just described himself over the past few years working at the Embassy.* At the end of each day, the Commandant had reviewed their work, then provided them with notes as they started to work the following morning at 0600. Yet, they hadn't seen the Commandant since the first day, when he'd harshly reviewed each Marine's preliminary reports. Since then, they had been locked in the conference room and expected to brainstorm.

Today was different. General Greene had conducted the morning meeting. "I want your final report on what the Marine Corps will look like in 1985 by noon. We will work together to put the finishing touches on the report draft." He passed some papers. "This just hit my desk, this morning. Marines, this is a new study, it says seventy-five percent of M16 rifles had pitted chambers leading to misfires. Study it. I welcome your comments. But the MarCor85 is your top priority."

Steven had been aware of those problems, but as he glanced over it quickly, something popped out. *Seventy-five percent of the rifles could misfire. If this report is validated, then we're equipping frontline fighters with inferior weapons.*

Once he restarted the meeting, General Greene poked his finger at the report. "I want this to be my retirement present to the Marine Corps. What the Marine Corps will look like in 1985. Our goal is to have a futuristic vision of what the battlefield will look like and what a soldier might need. Many of these assets may not be invented yet, such as the ability to look down on a gridded battlefield from far above with satellites."

While they were all pleased with their collective future vision, it was obvious to Steven some immediate problems needed addressed. The Marines understood how important this project was to the general. But these last six intense hours of "fine tuning" and revising was mentally draining.

Steven was proud with what this team had accomplished, but the finality of the report, coupled with General Greene retiring in a little over a week caused him to contemplate his own future. He'd known that working on

MarCor 85 was a short term assignment, but the excitement of getting out of the Embassy and back in the war had caused him to ignore this until today.

Greene stood up, saluted, and dismissed everyone with the orders to return to their previous assignments except for Steven, whom he asked to stay behind for a moment. Once the room was clear, the general jutted his chin. "I am assigning you to General Krulak's ground staff in Vietnam. Krulak was the Commanding General, Fleet Marine Force Pacific stationed in Hawaii. You will report for duty at 0500 at your new assignment at the III Marine Amphibious Force, at Da Nang on 30 December 1967."

Steven stood up and saluted. This would likely be the last time he'd be serving under Greene, whom he'd come to respect so much. The man had an insight and a vision like few men he'd ever met.

Greene continued, "It's likely Chapman will issue you new orders, but I want to keep you with General Krulak as long as possible. He says you've been a real asset to him."

This made Steven happy. He'd learned from General Krulak over the last several months that Westmoreland and Johnson had reined in General Greene on many of his operational plans and futuristic visions.

It was time for Steven to head off to dinner with his brother Jeremiah, since it was the only day they could catch up. He hadn't talked to his brother in several months, nor had he seen him since last summer. That had worked out well, as next week Jeremiah started finals at Howard University, and he didn't need any distractions. As soon as finals were over, he'd be a junior in college.

Steven's cab pulled up in front of the dorm at Howard University. Jeremiah jogged out, wearing his track warm-up.

"Where do you want to go eat?" Steven asked, jumping out and giving his brother a quick hug. "It's on me, but don't hurt me too bad with your choice."

Jeremiah smiled. "Anywhere not on campus."

"What do you suggest?" Steven asked the taxi driver.

"There's a great little Italian bistro not too far from here," the driver answered.

"That sounds great. Thank you."

Jeremiah punched Steven. "What do you think about the anti-war protests? There's a lot of talk on campus about them."

Steven considered, but before he could answer, Jeremiah asked, "What do you think about baby doctor Benjamin Spock joining the protestors?"

The cabbie turned around and looked at Steven. "What the hell are we doing in Vietnam anyway?"

Steven swallowed hard and clinched his jaw as he looked at the cabbie. "We're in Vietnam because we're helping the Vietnamese people keep their freedom from a communist invasion." Then he turned to his brother and scowled. "I'm sworn to uphold and defend the Constitution, which includes everyone's rights to free speech." He folded his arm over his chest. "That includes the good Dr. Spock."

As soon as they were out of the cab, Jeremiah faced Steven and said quietly, "Have you heard anything about the three men you did in back home?"

Steven forced a half smile, then without a word turned and walked into the restaurant.

Jeremiah lightly punched him in the arm.

Steven stopped and pivoted toward him, raising both hands palms up. "Did *you* see anything?" Steven continued without giving him time to answer. "No, of course not. You didn't see anything. You don't know anything." He turned back around and walked into the restaurant.

After sitting down at the table amidst the noisy setting, Steven picked up his earlier conversation. "So how are you getting along with your finals?"

Jeremiah raised both hands. "I have all As and Bs going into next week."

Steven was really proud of his brother. As the waitress handed them menus, he looked at his brother. "I'm not sure what to think about my new temporary assignment at Da Nang." I wish I knew what was next for me. It is unsettling."

After placing their food and drink orders, Jeremiah asked, "You don't seem too happy about that."

Steven nodded and leaned forward. "Krulak and I got off to a bad start four years ago. Things have improved since then, but—" He jacked his jaw and ran his hand over his short, cropped hair. "Now, he was just overlooked appointed Commandant. If he decided to retire, which I think he will, then where does that leave me?"

Jeremiah frowned at him. "What are you going to do?"

Steven had contemplated that question for the last couple of hours. His career was in limbo and he had no answer. He shrugged. For now, he was going to enjoy this lunch with his brother. "My rank is too high to get back into combat assignments." He paused, then raised both hands palms up. "I want to do something adventuresome."

Midnight December 30, 1967
Da Nang - III MAF Headquarters

Lieutenant Colonel Steven Hebert placed the phone back on the receiver after a brief, static-filled conversation with his brother, Jeremiah. Steven's sleep pattern was fouled up; when he was in the United States, his brain was on Vietnam time. Now he was back in Vietnam, he was on US time. So, he'd called Jeremiah to see how he was doing. He'd just received his final grades earlier in the week, and he'd actually raised two of his grades with his finals.

Next, Steven read a note from Ethan Graham saying he'd survived a bad case of malaria. Obviously, Ethan had too much time on his hands, as he'd never written a note before. Since Ethan's parents had passed away earlier in the year, Steven was the closest thing he had to a family. He looked at the date of the note and surmised he must have returned to his company in Khe Sanh. *Depending on how long he would be assigned here, he might be able to catch up with his best friend.* Still wide awake, he decided to go to his office and see what would be waiting on him in the morning.

The only thing on top of his desk was two after-action reports on recent Marine engagements with the North Vietnamese Army. One was at Dak To, and the other at Tam Quan. While he was in the United States, he wasn't able to keep up with the day-to-day operations. However, he quickly learned about these vicious battles against the North Vietnamese Army. Dak To was along the Cambodian-Laotian border, while Tam Quan was along the coast.

He picked up the Battle of Tam Quan. He wanted to study a battle where the U. S. allied forces, composed of Marines, ARVN and Koreans, came in from the sea behind the NVA. He leaned back in his chair for a minute. *I'm happy to be back in Vietnam. The constant news of Civil Rights unrest and anti-Vietnam coverage was difficult to stomach while home. Drugs now seemed to be everywhere. On top of that, the US and World Press continued to make disparaging remarks about US soldiers, even going so far as to calling them "baby killers," yet they barely mentioned the Viet Cong murdering 252 people in the hamlet of Dak Son. Is the US still my home these days?*

He refocused and went back to reading. About halfway through reading this file, his eyes got so heavy he couldn't keep them open. There was a cot behind his desk, and it was inviting. *A quick nap, and I should be good.*

Steven opened his eyes and looked around, wondering where he was. Finally, he was able to focus on the tiny clock on the corner of his desk. 0730. Could it be that he'd slept almost seven hours? He made a beeline for the coffee pot in the command center, then quickly returned to his office.

He went back to reading the Tam Quan report. Excellent strategy—US forces established a blocking force on the West, while troops landing from

415

the South China Sea attacked. It was a pincher strategy on NVA enemy position. However, the troops attacking across the rice paddies attempting to get into position in the woods came under heavy attack by the NVA. The remnant of the NVA escaped down the Bong Son River. This was the only flaw in the strategy—the river should have been covered to the south as well as the north.

Upon completing his notes on Tam Quan, Steven picked up the Dak To file. This was more or less just an on-going confrontation between the NVA plus some Viet Cong regulars and US forces at the southern end of the Ho Chi Minh trail where Laos, Cambodia and South Vietnam met. Several Marine Force Re-Con scouting missions revealed the NVA troop buildup, thus Westmoreland devised Operation MacArthur to try to displace the enemy. Contrary to Steven's vision for the future battlefield, much of this fighting at been close, brutal. The terrain was mostly Central highlands covered with triple canopy jungle plants. Steven envisioned his old friend, Ethan, in the middle of this, although his battalion were only reserves.

Steven pulled out a map to examine the placement of the various skirmishes between Hills 875, 823 and 882. Numerous battles were fought among these three hills over a period lasting a month. While the US forces won these battles, they came at a large sacrifice of troops. He finished writing his report, highlighting two big issues. The first was the loss of six helicopters trying to deliver supplies to pinned down troops. The second was the number of troops lost by "friendly fire," including bombs dropped on US positions. This was and always would be a product of war, but it had to be addressed every single time.

Steven got up from his desk. It was evening and time for a real meal. He headed to the base mess hall. When he'd finished dinner, he realized how tired he was. Time to get some sleep to try to get back on Vietnamese time. Perhaps he could get some real rest. After all, Pope Paul VI had declared January 1, 1968, to be a day of peace. Both the United States and South Vietnam decided to observe a truce. Supposedly, the Viet Cong agreed to a thirty-six hour ceasefire. Steven didn't believe it for a minute. There would likely be an ambush somewhere by morning.

CHAPTER FORTY-THREE

JANUARY 30, 1968
LONG BINH, SOUTH VIETNAM

Steven put the finishing touches on his quick trip up to Long Binh to gather additional intelligence at the Army Operations Center, as he had a few loose ends to tie up on his reports before his scheduled meeting with General Krulak. He hoped Army personnel would share some of their findings. He was to be in Hawaii for that face-to-face meeting on January 31. It was purposely scheduled for the beginning of the Vietnamese New Year of Tet, thus a good time to meet to discuss roles and strategies. The South Vietnamese government had negotiated another truce, just as they had done last year. Since there would be no fighting, Krulak thought it would be a good time to meet, despite the military's lack of trust of the Viet Cong and the North Vietnamese Army. Just last year, they had moved troops and supplies around while the South Vietnamese Army stood by and watched. This had left a bad taste in the mouths of the US Marines, but there wasn't much they could do since the truce was officially called by the South Vietnamese government. He could only wish they'd wise up.

He looked at his watch. His helicopter ride back to Da Nang would be landing in several minutes. He picked up his reports and notes, then started toward the landing strip. As he walked through the Operations Center, he paused as he glanced around the large room for a minute. Everyone was intently working at their stations. He continued toward the exit. As soon as he was outside, someone grabbed his arm from behind with authority. Steven spun around, ready for a confrontation, only to find a black woman standing there. He relaxed as he looked down at her name tag. *Allen.*

She saluted. "Lieutenant Colonel Hebert, I'm Specialist Seventh Class Intelligence Analyst Doris Allen."

Steven frowned. "What do you want?"

"Lieutenant Colonel Hebert, may I show you something, sir?"

Steven nodded, as he glanced at his watch.

"I'm fairly new at this base, but I know my job and I do it well. I analyze gathered intelligence data—you know, reconnaissance photos and the like."

Steven scowled. "If you have something to show me, let's go. I got a chopper coming for me at any minute."

She marched inside with Steven following in step behind her to her desk. She pulled out a folder with several photos and some notes, and shoved it his way. "Look at this."

Steven rapidly flipped through the materials in the folder. He stopped when he got to her report. He then slowly pulled out the chair and sat down. He looked up at her. "Allen, are you sure about this?"

Allen glanced around the room. "Can we step back outside?"

He nodded. They walked away from the intelligence facility. Once outside, she said, "Yes, I have a high degree of certainty in all of my conclusions." She paused and looked down at the ground. "I don't want anyone here to think I'm breaking rank or protocol. There are fifty thousand Chinese troops joining the Viet Cong massing throughout South Vietnam. They have been coming in since the first of the new year."

He put his hands on his hips. "have you presented your findings? Have you run this up the ranks?"

Allen glanced away for a second, then remade eye contact with Steven. She raised both hands palms up and jerked them up and down. "Yes, I have. No one cares." She paused, but as Steven was about to respond, she continued, "Think about it. I'm a forty-year-old woman, not an officer, and I'm new around here. Plus, there is this." She pointed at her hand.

Steven jacked his jaw. "Skin color or not, I have seen your file. This is a game changer. With what has happened over the past couple of weeks, it should not be ignored. We know our enemy is building up to something big." He looked at his watch as a chopper flew overhead. "There's my flight back to Da Nang. I will contact General Krulak as soon as I'm on the ground."

Steven turned and jogged off toward the landing zone. Then he turned back over his shoulder and shouted, "Good work, Allen!"

He double timed it up to the helicopter, blades still turning. He grabbed ahold of his camo hat and slipped in. Steven put on the headset so he could communicate with the pilot. "Let's go."

After about an hour and a half in the air, a radio transmission came in. "Go Green." Steven glanced over at the pilot, who returned his look. The pilot flipped the switch on his radio to a secure channel. "Bat70, this is Vampire Ops."

The pilot glanced on both sides of his chopper. "Roger that."

Vampire Ops replied, "You are a no go. Repeat, no go to your destination."

The helicopter pilot clicked his microphone. "Roger, pulling SOI now. Bat70, authenticate whiskey x-ray."

Vampire Ops replied, "I authenticate Zebra"

The pilot pointed to Steven. "Pull out the classified document."

Steven reached for it, covered the microphone, and then read the response. The pilot repeated the response over the radio.

They both listened intently. When Vampire Ops replied back, Steven looked at the SOI and mouthed with the microphone covered, "Tan Son Nhut."

The pilot acknowledged and pushed the joy stick hard to the right to change directions. The pilot looked over at Steven. "We will be flying into Tan Son Nhut in the dark. I don't like this. Shit. We were fifteen minutes from your destination. *Shit.*"

If they couldn't land at Da Nang, the base was likely under attack. Now, they would have to fly back over potential enemy territory, in the dark—when the Viet Cong did their best work.

As they flew toward Tan Son Nhut, flashes of automatic weapons fire decorated the night. When they drew near Saigon, the gunfire picked up considerably. The North Vietnamese, Viet Cong and Chinese were moving throughout South Vietnam in mass. Within a few seconds, some of that automatic fire was focused on their helicopter, including some rocket fire. The pilot pulled back on the stick to push them above the fire—or so Steven hoped. They could see Tan Son Nhut ahead. However, the west side of the perimeter was coming under mortar fire.

The radio crackled again. "Bat 70, this is Vampire Ops."

"Roger."

"Go Green"

"Roger." The pilot flipped back to the secure channel.

Vampire Ops replied, "Bat 70, you have not been given clearance to land at destination." Then came what neither of them wanted to hear. "Base under attack. We're searching for an alternative."

The pilot pointed repeatedly at the low fuel gauge. Steven kept a stone-cold face. The last thing he wanted was a more panicked pilot.

The pilot looked over at Steven. "I'm not a combat pilot. We need to get on the ground. And fast." Then he keyed the mic. "Vampire Ops. Bat70, bingo. We're landing now, before we drop out—or get shot out of the sky."

There was no response for several seconds. It was an eerie quiet. More automatic weapons fire missed them by inches. However, the next rounds of automatic gunfire did not. Direct hit on the gas tank, plus two up through the cab, but all missed Steven and the pilot. As the helicopter turned away from Tan Son Nhut, the radio sputtered. "You are ordered to deliver your package to the US Embassy."

Steven nodded at the pilot and mouthed, "Let's go."

The pilot pushed the stick forward and headed toward the heliport on top of the new US Embassy. As they flew over Saigon, more automatic fire surrounded the chopper. The pilot shouted to be heard by Steven. "I never believed it was this far between base and the Embassy." The pilot pointed down at the fuel gauge; it was dropping fast from the direct hit. It seemed like more rocket fire was aimed at the helicopter. Flashes of red and yellow struck all around. Within a few minutes, they rapidly dropped. A few flashlights were waving around on the heliport in an attempt to illuminate the landing pad. "I've never landed on something this small," the nervous pilot said. "I've never landed on something this small—and it's dark."

I hope this soldier can put this bird down before he pisses his pants.

In what seemed like an eternity, the helicopter finally swooped to the building top, landing so hard Steven's teeth rattled. He grabbed his camo hat as he jumped out before the blades stopped turning and ran down the stairway to the Embassy entrance.

A Marine guard stood at the entrance. He saluted. "Lieutenant Colonel Hebert, Ambassador Bunker, Captain O'Brien and Leo Crampsey must speak with you immediately."

Steven hesitated for a moment. *Wonder why they want to see me?*

The Marine Guard waved for him to follow. "Lieutenant Colonel, I have my orders. Of course, you understand."

Steven glanced down at his watch. It was just after midnight. He followed the Marine Guard, looking around as he passed through the new Embassy, built since he'd been re-assigned. The building was awesome.

He was escorted into a large conference room. At the far end of the table sat Ambassador Ellsworth Bunker. "Lieutenant Colonel Hebert, Saigon is under attack. I have been advised by my assistant and your former boss, General Edward Lansdale, that you have a scheduled meeting with General Krulak in Hawaii. Obviously, you can't safely get out tonight. We have notified the general, and we will get you out of here as soon as we possibly can."

Steven nodded.

"But before you head out to that appointment, we need to know what you've learned over the past month," Ambassador Bunker said. "I should tell you that General Krulak has approved you discussing your findings with me."

Steven remained at attention until the ambassador nodded for him to take a seat. "Yes, sir." He'd never met Bunker, nor did he know anything about the man. He was uncertain whether to discuss his findings.

Before he could answer the question, the ambassador continued, "Lieutenant General Weyand has put sufficient number of troops around the city to defend it, but what is unfolding is much more than General Westmoreland expected." He folded his hands on top of the large ornate table.

Steven didn't have proof that Krulak had given him permission to speak, so he decided to speak in generalities. "Well, most of my time at Da Nang has been to review After Action Reports from the field. As to the current developments, however, I can say it's my opinion that the North Vietnamese have been building up to the offensive since before the New Year. Force Re-Con patrols had documented the NVA build up since the middle of December. They need to keep the Ho Chi Minh trail open and halt the building of McNamara's fence."

Bunker sat with his chin in his hand as Steven spoke. When he'd finished, he replied, "Just a little more than two weeks ago, I sent a memo to the Department of State praising how well our effort was going against the NVA and the Viet Cong. I even commended General Westmoreland. Plus, I complimented the South Vietnamese people of their own efforts to implement the Pacification Program, which I had deemed successful. Robert Komer and I discussed that very fact on our way over here to the Embassy just a little bit ago. But tonight—seems to have changed everything."

"Yes, Ambassador Bunker, it's much bigger than just Khe Sanh. In my flight tonight, we got halfway to Da Nang and had to turn back because the base was under attack. Then on our flight back into Saigon, it seemed like half the countryside was lit up with gunfire. Then we couldn't land at Tan Son Nhut, which was also under attack. I was pretty happy we received clearance here, as we were extremely low on fuel and the pilot was getting a little nervous. The NVA is really up to something on Tet."

Ambassador Bunker replied, "Lansdale says you can be trusted. What I'm about to tell you is top secret." He sat straight without so much as a twitch of a muscle. "General Westmoreland had requested permission from President Johnson, if needed, to use nuclear or chemical weapons at Khe Sanh. That's how determined Westmoreland is to holding that strategic location."

Steven was stunned. The use of nuclear or chemical weapons that close to our own troops?

A knock sounded at the conference room door. "Come in," the Ambassador said.

Leo Crampsey and Captain O'Brien stepped into the large room. O'Brien saluted the Lieutenant Colonel, then spoke. "The shift change has been made. We have doubled the guards at all one-man posts and have guards posted on the roof. I'm going to the movie room and lie down for a bit."

Crampsey glanced at the Ambassador. "I have secured a sedan equipped with a radio tied into Dragon Net. Everything has been secured throughout the State Department side." Crampsey looked at Steven. "Lieutenant Colonel Hebert, we have prepared quarters for you and your pilot to bed down for the night."

CHAPTER FORTY-FOUR

0243 January 31, 1968

US Embassy Grounds - Saigon, South Vietnam

At 0243, Steven was awakened by an explosion somewhere outside. "Signal three hundred!" someone shouted. Heavy footsteps ran in the hallway.

Steven hadn't been in bed more than an hour, but he knew what "signal three hundred" meant—the Embassy was being overrun. He jumped up, dressed as fast as possible, grabbed his only available weapon—his personal M1911—plus the only three magazines he had, and ran out the door with the intention of going to help wherever needed. Everyone was running. Steven ran for the front gate.

When he got there, Sergeant Harper and Sergeant Schuepfer saluted him and then quickly briefed him. They'd seen a Vietnamese man standing next to the main building just a few minutes earlier giving orders, but had lost sight of him.

"Could he be associated with the Embassy?" Steven asked.

Harper looked at Schuepher. "Is he a guard?"

Schuepher shook his head.

"Let's fan out, see if we can spot him," the sergeant suggested. "We'll meet at Guard Post 12 at the Norodum Compound." Harper looked at Steven as though expecting approval. Steven nodded.

Before they exited, though, the ground shook with several explosions, in concert with AK-47 automatic weapon fire in front of them.

Still, the three men separated and ran in search for the Viet Cong. Steven unholstered his M1911 as he sprinted across the parking lot, seeking not only the Vietnamese man but also some cover. He crouched down near a concrete barrier and looked back for either Harper or Schuepher.

Harper stared at a Vietnamese man running toward the Generator Building. Harper pointed to his eyes, then toward another Vietnamese in an Embassy vehicle near the rear entrance of the Chancery Building. The driver reached into the backseat.

Steven got the message. He scanned the area. There were no MPs at that gate.

Automatic weapons fire exploded from the gate area.

Harper pointed toward the Chancery Building and signaled he was going to secure it. Steven moved cautiously toward the automatic weapons fire in the direction of the back gate.

Another large explosion shook the ground.

Two MPs fired M16s in the direction of a freshly blown hole in the Embassy wall. Automatic weapons fire was immediately returned from that same hole as VC attempted to enter the compound. The MPs dropped several VC.

The automatic gunfire caused Steven to hunker back down at his current position.

The Vietnamese man that Harper and Schuepher had described reappeared, pulled out an AK-47, fired, and struck the MPs.

Steven zoomed in on the Viet Cong—a lieutenant, likely the leader of the assault team. He fired his handgun. Missed. The VC Lieutenant ducked away and disappeared. He looped back to the MPs. *They were dead. Damn, all these men had were handguns.*

He ran in the direction he'd last seen the lieutenant, desperate to find the VC assassin.

As Steven moved around the compound, the battle raged between the MPs and the Marine Guard against the VC. Harper checked the doors around the Chancery Building. Steven wished he had more than just his 1911 handgun, but he had to pursue the VC Lieutenant.

He glanced in the direction of Harper, who checked the service entrance. He signaled it was locked. Then Harper checked the stairway door. Also locked. Steven remained crouching, but believed his back was covered, and continued his search for the VC Lieutenant. He remained focused on the parking lot entrance and cautiously moved toward it.

Harper headed to the open gate and locked it, then turned and shouted to Steven. "I'm going up front. Try to secure the rest of the building."

Steven had a single goal. Kill the VC Lieutenant—take out their leader.

0251-0325

As Steven moved stealthily through the back of the Embassy compound, constant automatic gunfire surrounded him.

The gunfire lessened as he approached the Generator Building. But no VC Lieutenant. *Damn. He has to be back here. He couldn't just disappear.* Too many places to hide. But he had to be somewhere.

Another loud explosion rocked the front of the Embassy. Steven jerked around. *Sounded like a rocket strike.* Then automatic weapons fired all around him. He resisted the urge to go around front and find out what had been struck, believing if he could kill the lieutenant, the leaderless VC attack would fall apart. *I'm trapped. The sniper has a bead on me, and I don't know where he is.*

Steven remained crouched, scanning the area as best he could. He focused on a couple of trees at the back of the parking lot. He waited for what seemed an eternity—about ten minutes. It was a game of chess and he was in check. He couldn't move, but neither could the VC Lieutenant. Steven needed MPs or Marine guards to change his odds. Hopefully, no more VC would come to aid the lieutenant.

After another fifteen minutes, two Marine guards, one a lance corporal and the other a corporal—rounded the front of the Embassy, heading for the rear gate. Steven whistled, but they couldn't hear him.

The VC Lieutenant jumped out from behind a blue sedan and aimed his AK-47 at the Marines.

This was Steven's chance. He took aim—it was about a thirty yard shot. He fired off four quick rounds. The VC started to fire at the Marines when Steven's shots hit all around him. *How did I miss? Or did I?*

The lieutenant spun around, his rifle aimed at Steven. Just as the Viet Cong man was about to fire, The Marine corporal unloaded his .38 caliber revolver.

The lieutenant was hit somewhere in his lower body, but he was still alive—and he dove behind another car.

Steven fired off several shots, emptying his magazine, to provide cover for the Marines. He quickly dumped the magazine and inserted another.

0332 – 0355

Steven hadn't seen the VC Lieutenant move for several minutes. He made eye contact with the Marines, signaling for them to cover him. Steven didn't know how many rounds they had, but he was determined to get this lieutenant.

Red and green tracers illuminated the sky over the French Embassy to the west. So now the French Embassy was also under attack?

Steven darted toward the last known position of the VC Lieutenant. Simultaneously, the Marine corporal ran toward the motor pool in the Generator Building. This wasn't what Steven had hoped for.

Now, Steven was forced to not only try to get to the enemy's position, but also cover the Marine corporal.

The VC lieutenant raised up and fired his AK-47 at the Marine corporal. Behind Steven, another AK-47 fired toward the running Marine, who was sprinting for his life. Steven fired twice at the lieutenant, then spun around in time to empty his handgun toward the AK-47 fire from behind. Then he dove behind the closest car. He dumped his empty magazine and quickly inserted a new magazine and chambered a round.

0400 – 0402

After no movement for almost five minutes, the Lance Corporal emerged from the motor pool, running for Guard Post #12. *What was in the motor pool that required him to run there in the first place?* Whatever it was, it greatly interfered with Steven's personal mission.

The Lance Corporal sprinted toward the Chancery Building. Just as he made it to the door, several Viet Cong appeared with their hands in the air. The MP who had remained behind stepped out to accept their surrender.

The VC Lieutenant stepped out from behind a tree and fired at the MP. *How did he get to that tree?* From behind Steven, another rocket was fired at the doorway where the MP stood. The rocket exploded against the wall, sending shrapnel everywhere. The MP didn't seem injured. The VC soldiers who had pretended they were surrendering opened fire on Steven and the Marine Lance Corporal.

Intense gunfire erupted from all around Steven and the Marines. Once again, Steven and the lance corporal were pinned down by the VC Lieutenant—as well as by automatic weapons fire from behind them. They had nothing more than handguns.

Two minutes later, the Lance Corporal who had escaped returned with three Marine guards and two MPs.

0405 – 0412

The Viet Cong in the area momentarily stopped firing. They gathered near the VC Lieutenant.

With the lull in gunfire, the Lance Corporal joined the corporal, the Marine guards and MPs. More reinforcements came up from behind, with Lieutenant Ribich bringing a Military Police Patrol, which included an M-60 machine gun capable of firing a 7.62mm round at a rate of 600 rounds per minute. Steven smiled. The odds had finally shifted in favor of the Americans.

Steven wanted to join forces with the newly assembled team with the intent of sweeping and killing the VC. Just as he started to move in their direction, he saw the VC Lieutenant ordering his assembled team.

Steven waved at the Americans, then pointed to his eyes and then at the VC position. A Marine sergeant sprayed M-60 rounds toward the huddled VC.

0412

Several more enemy ran up and joined the VC Lieutenant's team. The newcomers attacked from across the parking lot. They were immediately killed by Sergeant Jimerson's machine gunfire. However, the VC weren't done fighting. Rocket fire again attacked the American team, followed by substantial automatic weapons fire. *Where the hell is that coming from?*

The VC Lieutenant sprinted away from his hiding spot. AK-47 fire from behind them was directed at the American team and the M-60 machine gun. Jimerson was hit several times, but he was able to slip back into a safe position.

Surprisingly, no one fired on Steven's position. Another sergeant saw to it that Jimerson was moved to safety as the American team returned fire again on the VC positions with the M-60. Steven looked at his watch. 0415. He remained crouched down, but reached into his pocket for two more magazines. *Fourteen more shots.* He took a deep breath, then ran off in pursuit of the VC Lieutenant.

0417

As he looked up to the sky, he guessed it was almost three hours before daylight. The advantage clearly belonged to the VC Lieutenant, who was dressed in black pajamas. However, unless he could get more magazines or an automatic weapon, he was limited in the number of shots he could fire. He moved along the outside of the Generator Building away from the direction of the enemy's fire—and, he hoped, in the same direction as the VC Lieutenant.

Steven peeked around the edge of the building. Automatic gunfire from the roof of the Generator Building rained down on several of the VC pinned behind vehicles at the back of the lot. Because of that gunfire cover, he was able to slip behind a large planter and wait.

As he scanned the area, he caught a glimpse of the VC Lieutenant in his black pajamas slinking along the Generator Building, so as not to be seen.

Steven ran in pursuit, determined not to let him out of his sight again. These were not ordinary VC—they must have been a part of an elite force. *He must be trying to find a way onto the French Embassy grounds. I can't let him get there.* As Steven pursued the VC Lieutenant, the automatic gunfire intensified substantially. Both men continued to move stealthily around the compound, avoiding gunfire. Just as the lieutenant was about to climb over the wall, he looked back in Steven's direction. Then the lieutenant rapidly scaled the wall.

Steven fired off three rounds from his Colt, all missing the climbing lieutenant.

Now, Steven had to scale the wall at the same spot, knowing full well the VC Lieutenant could be on the other side waiting for him, either to shoot him or fight him. It was a chance Steven had to take. By the time he made the top of the wall, he spotted the VC Lieutenant almost to Trong Nhat Street. Steven's hand landed in a large puddle of blood at the top of the wall. Obviously, the VC Lieutenant was wounded more severely than he'd previously believed.

The VC Lieutenant turned toward Steven once in the street, outside the US Embassy compound. He pulled up his weapon, but for some reason decided not to fire. Instead, he continued running. Within seconds, he found out why. Sniper fire rained down on Steven from the apartment building across from the Embassy. He jumped down from the wall. The lieutenant sprinted two blocks up the street, headed toward the South Vietnamese Presidential Palace.

Damn, if I'm going to kill this VC Lieutenant, I have to run down this street with all these snipers above me. Steven sprinted down Trong Nhat Street following the VC Lieutenant, who was still running in the direction of the Presidential Palace. Sniper bullets soared by his ears. Some tinged into concrete in front of him. Then searing pain went through his right calf. Burning lead also slammed through his left shoulder, driving him to the ground. *Damn it.* He quickly scrambled to his feet out of fear he would be killed, and continued his pursuit of the VC Lieutenant. *I'm not going to die here.* However, he was limping severely. Now, he was not only trying to catch the lieutenant, but also out-run the apartment snipers and get out of their range. But he was finally gaining on the VC.

The lieutenant swung around, simultaneously pulling up his AK-47 to fire at Steven.

Steven continued running, closing ground to make sure his handgun was in range. If he stopped running, there was nowhere to hide from the sniper rounds, and he would be killed. He pointed his handgun straight in front of him and fired four rounds—until the magazine was empty. Those last three weren't necessary, as the first shot hit the VC Lieutenant right between the eyes. His AK-47 rounds went off straight up in the air.

Steven dropped his empty magazine, inserted his last one, and chambered a round.

He was significantly fulfilled from killing the VC Lieutenant, whom he believed was the commander of the attack force on the Embassy. With the lieutenant dead, now he had to escape the apartment snipers. He ducked under several trees along the street.

Another VC Commander ran away from the South Vietnamese Presidential Palace.

Despite the pain, Steven was able to run in pursuit from behind the tree sheltering him from the snipers above. This VC Commander was a good two blocks ahead of Steven. *I got seven rounds, that's it. Be sharp with your shots.*

Within a few steps of taking off after the enemy, a hail of bullets from automatic weapons came from the Presidential Palace. Fortunately, he slipped behind another tree, but he couldn't let the VC Commander get away. Yet, at the moment, all he could do was watch the VC Commander put more distance between him.

The VC continued to fire on his position for a few minutes, and then the shooting stopped.

Steven checked his left shoulder and his right calf. Certainly his wounds weren't life threatening, but his calf was bleeding pretty good. He could feel his boot filling up. His shoulder bled some, but nothing like his calf. Steven peered around the tree. No one fired at him. He started running again after the VC Commander, who was now a good hundred yards ahead of him. Steven expected to get fired on again, as it seemed the entire town was under siege by the Viet Cong. Instead, he was gaining on the VC Commander again.

The two men had covered a number of city blocks. Steven had lost count, but the VC Commander ran through Nguyen Hue District toward the Saigon River. Steven was within fifty yards of catching the him.

A dull green Renault appeared at the next intersection at Ton Duc Trong and stopped in the middle of the street. The VC Commander ran toward the Renault. *Is he going to get in that car? Is he going to car jack that Renault? I can't let him get to that car.* Steven ran harder.

The VC Commander slowed as he approached the Renault. A Vietnamese woman got out of the car and frantically waved at him, encouraging him to get into the car. As he ran toward her car, the woman pulled out a small handgun. She tried to aim at Steven from around the commander, but he was in the line of fire. "*Get out of my way,*" she yelled. "I got a clear shot. *Get out of my way.*"

The VC Commander shouted back. "Just get in the car and get ready to drive."

Steven raised his M1911 up and fired off the four rounds at the commander. He hit him in the back, in the area of his kidneys. The VC reached the car, grabbed the door, swung it open and jumped in. In a flash, the female accelerated the green Renault away. Steven fired off a couple of shots at the windows and the tires, but to no avail. He was too far away with a handgun. He stopped running, moved out of the middle of the street, and sought cover.

He pressed his body up against the closest building, fearing more VC attackers. He was now far away from the Embassy, and he had only one shot left. As he continued to breathe hard from his run, his adrenaline wore off. He realized how much his left shoulder and right calf hurt. His foot now was almost sloshing in his boot. He sat and rested for a brief moment and tried to collect his thoughts. It occurred to him that he'd seen that dull green Renault and the Vietnamese woman before. She'd been with Pham Xuan An, arguing at Tan Son Nhut after the briefing. Clearly, this woman was connected to the Viet Cong. Was Lansdale and Tao's old friend tied up with the Viet Cong? This man had worked with the CIA for years. It just couldn't be. Could it?

Steven decided it was time to make his trek back toward the Embassy while it was still dark. The dark was his advantage now, as he moved from barrier to barrier as though he were being stalked by the enemy—which of course, he was.

Stopping at one tree, he pressed up against it and looked at his watch. His flight from Da Nang to Hawaii to meet General Krulak undoubtedly had been unable to land. *If I make it back to the Embassy alive, I can still go to Hawaii to meet Krulak.*

MIAMI

Santos Trafficante stared continuously across the desk at Gino DeLuca, who squirmed in his high back leather chair explaining why the heroin and opium coming out of Southeast Asia wasn't running as smoothly as it had in the past few years. The product wasn't keeping up with demand. Trafficante wasn't buying any of it. "I'm going to schedule a trip to Asia—as soon as I can set up a meeting with Shackley in Saigon."

DeLuca looked at the bodyguards in the back of the room. "Boss, the Feds aren't going to let you travel."

Trafficante jumped up from his chair and leaned over his desk. "The Feds got nuthin' on me. They keep bringing me before the grand jury. Squeezing me and my family, but I'm telling you, they got nuthin' on me." He reached in his breast pocket.

DeLuca jumped.

Trafficante pulled out his passport and waved it around. "If I got this, I can go anywhere I damn well please." He sat back down. "It's Marcello who continues to screw up. They're tightening the screws on him." Trafficante leaned forward in his chair. "I'm going to go see Furci in Hong Kong. It's business as usual for me. The Feds don't scare me. Hell, I'm still doing them favors."

DeLuca raised his eyebrows. "Are you going to whack him?"

Trafficante reached into a desk drawer, pulled out a cigar, and trimmed it slowly. "Furci has made amends." He cracked half a smile. "He went to Hong Kong and got us established there. No. Things are good with me and Furci."

DeLuca nodded.

Trafficante knew he had compartmentalized everyone well; one hand didn't know what the other hand was doing. *Perfect.*

"Okay, okay, boss," DeLuca said, still looking around the room. "What can I do?"

Trafficante worked at getting his cigar going, then took a couple of large drags. "I want you to go with me and Dominick Furci. We're gonna go get Shackley—bust some balls to keep the product flowing. We were able to keep the Corsicans in Saigon in our camp, somehow, and with Hong Kong working well, we need more product. With all these soldiers in Vietnam, demand has been good."

DeLuca smiled. "Dominick wanted to see his son?"

Trafficante pushed his glasses back up on his nose. "Dominick has been loyal to me for years. He deserves this. This is about family." He took another puff off his cigar then gestured with it as he continued. "When they see you traveling with me, after my trip, you're going to keep everybody in line. They'll know when they see you, it will be like they're talking to me." Trafficante got up from his chair so DeLuca would know the meeting was over.

DeLuca walked past his two bodyguards.

Trafficante pointed at him with the cigar. "It's going to be up to you to keep the supply line coming back into the States working well."

After DeLuca left, the bodyguards stepped through to the other side of his office door. By himself, Trafficante smiled as he took another puff off his cigar. "The CIA needs me to keep this network working for their black bag operations. The Feds ain't gonna touch me."

FEBRUARY 27, 1968

Lieutenant Colonel Steven Hebert was scheduled for a flight back to Da Nang to return to duty by March 1. The gunshot wounds in his shoulder and calf were now fully healed. He briefed Krulak on his portion of the research on MarCor 85 for Commandant Greene. The general's focus was on better ways for Marines to target the enemy, whether ground-based artillery or naval fire power and air strikes. While this pertained to Force Recon Marines, it also would apply to engaged Marines in battle, giving them the ability to call in fire power close to their position.

"I actually enjoyed riding swift boats, seeing how creative those sailors have been using flak jackets in front of their fifty caliber machine guns and flying with helicopter pilots dropping off operatives in black pajamas on assassination missions," Steven said.

This brought a smile to General Krulak's face. "Why did you enjoy it so much?"

Steven raised his right hand. "It gave me a first-hand view of their missions—and picking the brains of the soldiers." But deep down, it was a way to get as close to the action as he could—and he loved it.

Krulak jutted his chin. "That was how I managed when I was your age. What else did you report for General Greene?"

Steven leaned back on the metal chair. "I spent a lot of time at night in the jungles and the mountains with Lansdale in the fifties. I knew the fears of the night with the enemy stalking you. This time when I went out at night to process those thoughts, I did it thinking about how to construct a future battlefield. One of my first assumptions was that more battles will occur at night, and those future battlefields would have fewer soldier-to-soldier conflicts. Therefore, we need vision aid that would enhance the soldier's edge."

Krulak nodded. "Good. I've been studying ways to improve rapid deployment."

Steven bit his lip. "I contemplated ways to improve inserting Marines in position. Since the early part of the Conflict, the use of helicopters has improved moving and inserting soldiers faster than ever before. But I was troubled by the helicopter's limitations, particularly in the mountains of Vietnam where foggy conditions prevented insertion and extraction."

"Helicopters have to be made quieter and with better fire power," Krulak said. "Plus, we need to look at the use of swift boats to move troops, and where that could be used. We have to increase fire power and have more protection for the sailors and Marines."

Steven replied. "I did look at how the Navy Seals operated using rubber rafts. While that worked for the Seals, it would limit the number of Marines arriving at their designated landing without a sufficient number of rafts. *Boats must be made to run quieter and with a lower profile to avoid detection.* Armaments might even change to long-range fighting without much visual contact, much like naval battles evolved."

"What time is your flight back to Da Nang?" Krulak asked.

Steven looked down at his watch. "In about thirty minutes."

"I'll walk with you."

Steven slowly put weight on his right leg to stand up. "Thank you, General."

Krulak opened the door for him as they walked out.

Steven limped through the door, but then stopped. "General Krulak, there is one more thing, perhaps the most important thing. I've been studying the M16A1 rifle. You know, the brass tried to bill it as an upgrade of its predecessor M16, due to lower maintenance. In our final meeting with General Greene, he passed out a report that seventy-five percent of the rifles could misfire. Are we equipping frontline fighters with inferior armaments?"

Krulak raised his arm up and patted Steven shoulder. "I certainly hope not, Lieutenant Colonel Hebert."

As they walked through the operations center, one of the clerks stood. "General, I have two copies of General Westmoreland's report on the North Vietnamese Tet Operation. Everything is included with the exception of the still ongoing Battle of Hue. All the fighting seems to be over."

The two men stopped, each took a copy, and read over it. After a couple of minutes, General Krulak looked up at Steven. "So General Westmoreland's facts show that being on the defensive, protecting the cities around South Vietnam, has given the US an advantage to inflict heavy losses on the Viet Cong and the NVA. Westmoreland believes in a very real sense, when the Viet Cong moved out of the jungle camps, they became more vulnerable and gave us an opportunity to hurt them severely. That's why over forty thousand of the enemy have been killed in less than one month—which is over forty percent of all the enemy killed in 1967. So what do you say, Hebert?"

Steven chewed on his inner jaw. "I believe that's a fair assessment, General."

"Westmoreland, Army Intelligence, and the CIA's mistake was not being prepared for the size and ferocity of the attack Still, US Marines soundly defeated the enemy forces."

Steven smiled. "The Marines fought gallantly, General."

Krulak leaned over and spoke in a low voice. "Some military intelligence went so far as to say they had decimated the Viet Cong. Clearly, a blow had been struck at the communist effort. However, it was known in the halls of the Pentagon that Westmoreland requested more troops to finish off the enemy and Washington turned them down."

Steven nodded. He still was not able to rationalize who at MACV got Lucki Allen's report and tabled her findings regarding 50,000 Red Chinese involved in these attacks. The "official" report claimed 85,000 Viet Cong and NVA attacked in all of South Vietnam. That was just not possible by the numbers. Logic dictated there had to be more forces involved. Why was it repressed and not conveyed to the field commanders? Or, was this a political decision—the press couldn't be told that the Chinese were involved? It would be more political bad news for Johnson.

Steven followed Krulak through the door into the waiting area, a U.S. news feed blasted on the TV screen.

"I have returned from Vietnam, where I was reporting
live during the Viet Cong's Tet Offensive," a voice said.

However, no face appeared on the screen. Instead, still photographs taken in Vietnam slowly rolled across the screen. "The end result was neither a knockout by the Viet Cong nor a win for the US Marines."

From the pictures selected, Steven assumed the correspondent was giving his own version of the Tet Offensive.

"The American people have too often been misled by the optimism of our leaders in Vietnam and Washington, pointing at only the silver linings in dark clouds," the voice continued. "The military progress intensity of the US Marines over the past six months against Hanoi's offensive has forced the communists to realize they cannot win a war of attrition. Yet, our enemy has shown a propensity to match any additional US forces. As a result of the stand-off of the Tet Offensive, I can see either real negotiations or terrible escalation of the fighting. US powerbrokers must continue to seek on honest negotiations."

The montage paused, showing the somber face of the newscaster. "In my opinion, there can be no victory in Vietnam. The most we can hope for is a stalemate."

Steven and Krulak stood side by side, staring at the TV. Slowly, Steven moved his eyes to Krulak. "Wow."

Krulak shook his head slightly. "Did that SOB just called our military victory a draw? Where is the honor for our fighting men?"

Steven slowly rubbed his healing left shoulder. He glanced around the room. The officers exchanged frowns. Some threw their hands up in the air in total disgust, while others and shrugged their shoulders. Had this commentator really in Vietnam? Surely, he'd seen the US defeat the Viet Cong and the NVA. What was his goal of his commentary? He was clearly expressing his opinion—an opinion flashed into US homes—but would his opinion carry weight with the American people?

The American soldiers were capable and courageous. Given the tools and support they needed, they could easily win in Vietnam. The problem was politics. No one could win with one hand tied behind their backs.

As much as he didn't want to admit it, Steven had to agree with the reporter on one point. Politics and public opinion had pushed Vietnam into a stalemate.

THE END

www.ingramcontent.com/pod-product-compliance
Lightning Source LLC
Chambersburg PA
CBHW071633260626
47170CB00001B/76